The Titans

By
Benn K. Leavenworth

PublishAmerica
Baltimore

© 2010 by Benn K. Leavenworth.

All rights reserved. No part of this book may be reproduced, stored in a retrieval system or transmitted in any form or by any means without the prior written permission of the publishers, except by a reviewer who may quote brief passages in a review to be printed in a newspaper, magazine or journal.

First printing

All characters in this book are fictitious, and any resemblance to real persons, living or dead, is coincidental.

PublishAmerica has allowed this work to remain exactly as the author intended, verbatim, without editorial input.

Hardcover 978-1-4489-3484-3
Softcover 978-1-61582-980-4
PUBLISHED BY PUBLISHAMERICA, LLLP
www.publishamerica.com
Baltimore

Printed in the United States of America

To Joanna, for being a 'literary widow,' to Dominc, my son-in-law who helped me in my 'computer illiteracy,' to my children who comprise my biggest fan club, to Jim (may he rest in peace,) to Ev, to Rog, to Larry, and others in our writer's group, for their invaluable input and criticism, and finally to everyone who purchases and reads a copy of this book.

Preface

'—and there fell a great star from heaven…and the name of the star is called Wormwood; and the third part of the waters became wormwood; and many men died of the waters, because they were made bitter.'
Jochanin the Evangelist from Apocalypse.

'—How thou art fallen, O Light-Bearer, son of the morning! How thou art cut down to the ground, who didst weaken the nations!
'—They that see thee shall narrowly look upon thee, and consider thee, saying: "Is this the man who made the earth to tremble, who did shake kingdoms,
'—Who made the world like a wilderness—?"'
Prophetic sayings of Esaias

'—Lo, all the pomp of yesterday has become as Ninevah and Tyre.'
Rudyard Kipling: Recessional

'—Their throat is an open sepulcher; with their tongues they have used deceit; the poison of asps is under their lips; Whose mouth is full of cursing and bitterness. Their feet are swift to shed blood; destruction and misery are in their ways—'
Shaul of Tarshish: *Letter to the Messianic Community in Rome.* c. 60 A.D.

The Titans

Prologue

Footprint.
Human.
Had to be.
That's how it all began.
The compact, powerfully built man sat in a battered wooden chair up to a writing desk nicked and gouged with age.
At a far corner of the desk lay a section of the *Denver Post*. One article in particular caught his eye:

'Stillwell CO. Five indicted in 29 year old murder mystery.
'Persistent detective work and recent witnesses who, after 29 years of silence, came forward with information has led to a nationwide investigation, manhunt, arrest, and extradition of at least five suspects connected with the slaying of a pretty Stillwell co-ed, Virginia Wallace 29 years ago.
'More arrests may still be forthcoming.'

He could feel his heart pound as inner turbulence began to build.
Ginger Wallace had been one of his favorite students when he first came to the college.
He recalled the many times listening to a CD recording of her singing the 'Habanera' from Bizet's *Carmen*.
So bright, he thought. *So talented. So outgoing. So trusting.*

Also, so naïve.

She had been raised in a straight-laced, devout family, he recalled. Yet there was nothing abrasive or confrontational. Rather they had been the epitome of sincerity and grace. *Surely,* he thought further, *they deserved better than to have their daughter suffer such a fate.*

Just doesn't seem right.

Too bad her parents never lived to see this day, he reflected further. *Died of heartbreak, no doubt.*

His mood darkened as he looked across the desktop to a window framed with curtains of cheap looking fabric and garish floral design. Droplets of moisture beaded up on the cold glass pane. The dim outline of downtown Denver lay enshrouded in the November mist. Tiny lights sparkled in an early twilight that had settled like a pall over the skyline.

The smell of mildew and stale tobacco emanated from faded and stained wallpaper. Two feet beside his desk stood an iron frame bedstead. A threadbare, army surplus blanket of olive drab served as its coverlet. A frayed, patchwork quilt lay folded at its foot. The possibility of the early Colorado winter taking a sudden turn for the colder was all too real.

His tweed blazer, a Goodwill exclusive, fit in well with the décor of the ancient apartment. Appropriate too, he thought, for his position as director of St. Dunstan's new urban counseling center: dressy enough to command the respect of the street people, yet not too pretentious.

Sheets of crumpled white stationery lay scattered across the dingy green desk blotter. Immediately before him lay another sheet of stationery bearing words in masculine looking handwriting:

'Dearest Marie.'

Dearest Marie, he thought. *Well, that's a start.*

He felt an inner gratitude that Marie and the children finally were back in the family homestead in Stillwell. He hated the thought of the place standing empty for so long, an open invitation for vandalism.

The more he tried to focus on what to write next, the more his mind went in retrospect…

THE TITANS

...Footprint.
Human.
Had to be.

Those same words went through his mind five years before, as he stood dressed in khaki on a section of South Dakota basal bedrock. He had spent days exploring with a scientific expedition to a godforsaken section of the state. Thanks to a torrential flash flood of unprecedented swiftness that had washed away layers of rubble and silt, this stratum lay exposed to the withering Badlands sun for the first time in perhaps 65 thousand millennia.

The arid wind that blew across the bone dry creek bed and the unrelenting heat parched his lips.

His seared eyeballs spotted a footprint the size of a catcher's mitt. Could it have been some late Jurassic Era reptile? Exciting find, but no real problem here.

Certainly not when compared to what he would discover next. About half an hour later he had spotted another print in the rock that appeared—human?

Or nearly so.

What paleontologist wouldn't kill to come upon such a find?

Or an archeologist?

Or maybe a geologist?...

...He then recalled the translations of those cryptic messages recorded and translated from that highly radioactive, man-made artifact...

* * *

... *'The sun hung low in the western sky. Stillness pervaded the thick atmosphere as ripples ceased their heavy lapping among the grassy marshes. No breeze stirred the giant fern fronds that lined the primordial shore. The silence was broken by the sluggish flapping of scaly wings as a giant flying reptile ascended over the hardwood forest, sailing awkwardly toward a not-too-distant outcropping of a mesa-like rock formation. Spread across the horizon jutted a half dozen dormant volcanic peaks lazily emitting their* spumes of steam and smoke. Rays from the pale gold sky slanted in long angles through the dense foliage to penetrate the matted forest floor. A creature appearing to be half bird and half reptile darted across the mosses and rotting vegetation of a small clearing and disappeared into the dense underbrush.

'Off in the dark recesses of the forest, a coarse caw shattered the stillness that lay like a blanket. It stopped just as quickly as it had begun and quiet again descended on the thick jungle.

'Out from behind a palm tree stepped an upright, two-legged creature. From broad shoulders hung what should have been forelegs; however these appendages were obviously not intended for walking. They ended in flat, broad endings and bore six agile looking digits that appeared more appropriate for grasping. Future intelligent entities would likely call such a process a hand. Instead of fur covering his naked body, he seemed to be dressed from the shoulders to the thighs with an off-white foreign material. Flat leather padding strapped to the lower legs by a web of thongs protected the soles of the creature's pedal appendages. A broad band the color of the setting sun gathered about the waist. From that band hung an object generations eons later would call an hourglass. A dark, finely matted type of fur covering shielded the top of the head. A shimmering golden band of a kind of artifice encircled the high forehead. Instead of looking upward, the face looked forward, further accentuating the creature's uprightness.

'The body and face reflected faintly the color of the afternoon's golden twilight. The creature surveyed the extensive network of water and vegetation that stretched endlessly out to a distant horizon. Subtle, fleeting changes of expression rippled across finely formed facial features. An inner animation registered in the dark eyes an energy that subsequent species would label as intelligence.

'The creature bent over and picked up a rock that lay at his feet and hurled it in a high arc out over the broad waters. A splash disturbed the placid aqueous surface with ripples radiating outward to every distant shore.

'The water's stillness was further disturbed by the emergence of a melon-sized head, supported by a muscular looking scaly neck that rose ever higher into the air until it towered over the trees that lined the bank. Tiny eyes blinked with curiosity from the sides of the head. The neck and head rose yet higher until a massive mound of body also broke the surface. By now the waves washing the banks had approached billowy proportions, even occasionally breaking into whitecaps as the behemoth's body moved to an outcropping from a nearby peninsula. The neck stretched long toward the tender green growths that adorned the shoreline treetops.

THE TITANS

'Apparently forgetting the cause of the original disturbance that had rocked its placid depths, it began to feed on the tender leaves. After an indeterminate length of time it seemed to content itself with munching and eventually slid its bulky mass back into the marshy lake.

'As it disappeared into the still rippling waters a second upright creature stepped from out of the underbrush and stood beside the first. The second upright—whose skin color appeared a kind of blue sheen—held a long, thin shaft of metallic like substance in his right hand. The point separated into three tines.

'The new arrival's hands showed curious looking webbing between the fingers.

'The shaft bearer turned to his companion. Movements about the mouth-like orifice and lower jaw activated with animation. Sounds from deep within the throat filled the tepid atmosphere. Agile facial muscles shaped the sounds into syllabic nuances falling rhythmically across the aural sensory receptors of his companion, enabling him to interpret and translate the sounds into what future intelligence might call articulate meaning.

'"Magnificent beast," said the second upright. "You are right on schedule, K'hron-u."

'The first upright turned to his companion. "The habitat that you have provided him has been more than adequate, Oss'yahn-u."

'"Quite simple, actually," replied the spear-shaft bearing upright. "The burning of two lightest breaths (gases) was simplicity itself."'...

* * *

...The sun hung low in the western sky. An eerie stillness had settled over the arid landscape. Had the lower atmospheric dust shaped the setting sun into a large, dull-orange ball, or was it air moisture? Or was it both? The long afternoon rays cast multi-shaped shadows among crevices and crannies that cut between the endless panorama of Badlands buttes. The various strata of rock themselves changed color each passing moment with shades of beige to deeper oranges, reds, and purple. The broad sky deepened its blue in the east even as it shone a pale gold in the west.

Blending remarkably with the sandstone colored rock formations, the khaki-clad male figure emerged from the shadows cast by a low outcropping. He straightened briefly and pulled a shapeless felt hat from off a sweat-soaked head of iron gray hair. He withdrew a blue kerchief from his breeches pocket and wiped perspiration from a leathery, sun-darkened face. Blue eyes wearily surveyed the jumbled, moon-like terrain that stretched endlessly before him. A broad, dark mustache twitched slightly as a gnarled hand replaced the kerchief. He bent slightly backwards and pressed the small of his back in an attempt to massage out the weariness. Even when shifting from the strain of an unaccustomed stooped posture, his muscular build appeared to be of only average height.

A heavy canvas knapsack that lay at his feet emitted a clicking sound. He bent over, pulled out a Geiger counter, and aimed it in the direction of the clicking. He pulled a small alpenstock from his belt and followed the sound down a short slope.

Jagged faces of cliff formations showing multi-layered frescoes of igneous rock and sandstone that rose on all sides continued their kaleidoscopic change of color. As he descended into a shallow wash carpeted with loose, jagged stones, the clicking continued.

He faced a dilemma. A decision, if you will.

Should he follow the clicking or continue searching for fossils in the in bone dry creek bed?

Finding fossils had a greater urgency. Isolated though this area may be would it be but a matter of time before others would come rushing down here after these same treasures? The source of the clicking, on the other hand, was buried and would likely remain so until he could return and follow it up. What lay buried would remain safer than what lay on the surface.

For now he would seek for embedded fossils.

He paused to reflect. This particular arid expanse of valley had been of interest to no one; not even the copper colored people who had inhabited the area for untold generations. A decade prior, a desert drifter had set up camp. Of an early evening, he spotted a strange rock formation. Upon further examination, he thought it resembled a kind of bone. Returning to the nearest town a couple days later, he called a science station affiliated with the college where the man in khaki served on the faculty. A scientific team came and explored the area. They determined the stone to be a piece of fossilized femur from a (brontosaurus).

The rash of interest that followed turned up a treasure trove of giant skeletal remains from the late Jurassic era. The khaki-clad man recalled previous trips to the desolate valley.

He paused to readjust his knapsack and pushed on through the mummy-dry valley, nearly succumbing to the heat. In a terrain void of all shade, it permeated every minute space with the intensity of a brick kiln. Casting his gaze upward, he briefly caught the still brazen glare of the late afternoon sun. He looked longingly at the bluffs that surrounded the hollow. At least atop those bluffs breezes stirred. Even though they, too, may be as air from a blast furnace, at least there was movement.

Down here in the valley, he thought, the devil himself could not stand the withering stillness.

Slowly, he forced himself to resume his trek. As he pushed on, he observed the sparse, spiny vegetation that struggled to survive. None but the hardiest of thorn bushes had a chance in this hole.

Despite the dryness of the place, he again observed evidence of the recent flash flood. He knew that this valley could see torrents rush through it during a deluge and then be dry as dust mere hours later.

As he walked he spotted another phenomenon.

Off to his right and off to his left, he saw piles of dirt and gravel, streaking downward toward lower elevations between the crevices of bedrock. A few yards ahead of him he saw a stratum of rock that in no way resembled the rest of the dry surface. It appeared to be reddish brown sandstone, as yet unbleached by the sun. Evidently exposed to the sun and the air for the first time in eons, it also bore no resemblance to the layers that comprised the bluffs rising above him. Realizing that he may be looking at an earth surface possibly millions of years old, he spotted an imprint not thirty feet from him.

He saw a footprint that looked to have been made by an animal weighing at least two or three tons. The print could easily be the size of a large dinner plate. Projecting from it extended three sharp appendages, each the size of a modern hunting knife.

He stepped closer to the print and let his knapsack fall to the ground.

From it, he took out a roll of visqueen, a plastic mixing bowl, a cloth bag containing plaster-of-Paris, a quart thermos of water, and a small trowel. With his hunting knife, he cut a sheet of visqueen and covered the print. Then he mixed water and plaster-of-Paris in the bowl. He stirred the mixture until it was of the right consistency, poured it into the impression and smoothed it over with the trowel. When he finished, he again stood up and eyed his handiwork. In the hot, dry atmosphere, the mix should harden in minutes.

As he waited, he again looked out across the barren rock.

Just fifty feet away he spotted another footprint.

This footprint looked to have made by a human.

Further scrutiny, however, revealed marked differences. The maker of this print—if he wore shoes—would have had to have worn what we would now measure as at least size 20. In estimating what may have been the creature's height, he shook his head in stunned disbelief.

He recalled from reading the *Guinness Book of Records* of one Robert Wadlow of Alton, Illinois. That young man was quite a celebrity in his day. An oddity. He was forced to bend down at the entryway of nearly every doorway he entered. He was unable to stand erect in most living rooms. When he died at age 22 in 1940, his stature of 8 feet 9 inches remained a record to this day.

In continued amazement, the man counted the toes. Then he recounted them.

Something wasn't right.

He recalled lessons from his church's lectionary and from his catechism. The Genesis narrative mentioned the presence of giants roaming the earth during pre-Flood times. An ancient writing known as *The Book of the Wars of Joshua* also mentioned Canaanite foes that made Israel's soldiers look like grasshoppers. The Goliath that David confronted stood nine and a half feet tall,

Some of those ancient giants had hands and feet that bore six fingers and six toes.

He asked himself again, what kind of creature left this footprint? Maybe such creatures weren't really mythical after all?

Was he a freak? An aberration? A mutant? A throwback? Or was he typical of his species?

Was he even a 'he?'

The distant multicolored rock formations danced in the shimmering heat waves. Hot winds fanned his face as his brain surged with more questions than answers.

After having made plaster casts of both prints, he took out cloths from his knapsack, wrapped them, and carefully placed them back in his pack. He slung it on his back and trudged back to the top of the bluff to where he had parked his Jeep.

Two days later, back in his campus geology lab, he placed these two plaster casts in a remote cabinet where he kept them under lock and key,

* * *

A year later, back in the same Badlands area, the Geiger counter he carried again began ticking furiously.

He followed the clicking along the valley floor and stopped to chip into the face of a low-lying butte. The clicking intensified as he chopped a hollow into the soft sandstone. When he finally came to the source of the radioactivity, as he had anticipated, he found it was metal. However, it was not a vein of raw ore embedded in rock. He saw no specks, chips, or foil thin layers covering rough silicon or granite.

He chipped away more stone and saw a square handled object looking to be of cast iron.

The Geiger counter clicked louder, faster.

Further chipping revealed a long, thin shaft.

Why the radioactivity? Raw iron ore usually isn't this hot. Also, why so much energy still radiating outward after millions of years? What kind of radiation was it? Should he be exposing himself to something so potentially deadly?

Curiosity overcame caution and fear as he determined to see this investigation through.

Damn the danger.

He chipped further until he came to the end of the rod. He continued chipping until the entire shaft fell free of its igneous prison and rolled over into an adjacent hollow. He picked it up and examined it.

As he propped its butt next to his boot, he pulled it up beside him. It stood shoulder high. He marveled how heavy it was.

The point divided into three prongs forming a trident.

What was it? A spear? A javelin? A wand? Or a scepter?

Or was it all of the above…?

Chapter 1

... "Ah, such energy." The trident wielding upright pointed the shaft's tines toward the water. The narrow band of white gold encircling his forehead began to glow. The varied color of the gems set in the band sparkled.

He turned to his companion. "The very stuff of life, is it not, K'hronu?"

"Take care, Oss'yanhu, dear brother," said his companion. "It is easily overdone. One must be circumspect."

The sun dropped behind a distant plateau. Dull, orange rays extended across the still humid sky. Far to the east, purpling shadows fell upon the soft roseate glow above sharply rising summits. Ever darkening shadows enveloped the forest.

"Hyp'ryanhu has completed another cycle," said K'hronu. He pulled from his golden girdle the hourglass encased in a frame of ebony. White sands flowed through the neck until they emptied the upper bulb. "K'haos follows hard after him."

"They work well together," said Oss'yahnu, "as brothers should."

The darkness intensified, descending quickly over the primordial forest. The evening breeze carried the fragrance of wildflowers on the night air. Slowly at first, then gradually crescendoing, a cacophony of scraping and chirping rose from the grassy depths.

"The multi-jointed ones are serenading us again I see," commented K'hronu; "as they do every evening without fail."

"So small and delicate," sighed Oss'yahnu, "yet so hardy. They will outlive all of us, I fear. Certainly they will survive even the large beast you roused from the waters this afternoon."

"Paradox, is it not?" said K'hronu. "Small, weak things proving themselves mightier than the strong."

'Would that those among us—ourselves only a little less mighty than the Strong-Ones—understood this." said Oss'yahnu, *"A little humility would become us."*

'K'hronu raised his head. "I detect vibrations," he said. "We must hasten to Sh'yan-Grl'. Y'rranhu beckons."

'Standing motionless, they levitated barely a hand-breadth from the ground. Silently they slid over the terrain toward the distant light.

'Eventually, the light itself faded into the darkness…'

* * *

…In the waning rays of sunlight, the khaki-clad man continued picking rubble from around the metallic shaft.

After more thought, what with all his other equipment, he decided that trident would be too heavy and cumbersome to carry in the darkness.

He slid the weighty artifact back into the hole.

He would return for it tomorrow.

He piled loose gravel over the hole until he had it completely covered. He stood to his feet. With the aid of his flashlight, he stumbled his way over the rocky inclines until he reached the flat summit. Near the precipice, a two-tracked road bent close. Off to the side sat an aging dust-covered jeep.

As the last ray of orange faded from the western horizon, he pressed the ignition and turned on the lights. Soon he sped through the primeval darkness. The headlights picked the faint two-tracked trail. Shapeless mounds of rock loomed large and sudden on either side of the road. The breeze, no longer the blasting heat of a forge, felt cool to his face.

Half an hour later he spotted a cabin with a dim light in the window. He pulled up to the cabin threshold. Shafts of light cast long brilliance out across the short, coarse grasslands as unseen occupants swung open the door. The faint greasy smell of a Coleman lantern greeted the man's nostrils. He entered, letting the door behind him remain open. Voices from within rang out over the prairie in conversation and laughter.

"The old coyote himself!"

"We thought you got lost out there."

"Whose bones did you dig up this time?"

The man continued standing in the doorway. He took off his hat and slapped it against his worn sun tans to shake off the dust.

He looked around. "With ten thousand comedians out of work," he grunted. "I get stuck with you guys."

He tried to adjust his eyes to the lighted room. It appeared before him crudely furnished with old chairs and a table made of rough timber. A stone fireplace covered the far wall.

The men at the table sat engrossed in a poker game.

The newcomer in the doorway again paused and looked around. "Who's the guest?"

"Lt. Col. Ergil Filer," said a voice from beyond the doorway, "with the U.S. Army Signal Corps."

The man eyed the Lt. Col. with suspicion. For nearly a decade the scientific team from Stillwell College in Colorado, having been alerted by that desert drifter of the treasure trove of prehistoric relics embedded in the bare rock, had been wary of outsiders. Media people, treasure hunters, and feds had harassed the team over the rightful ownership of their finds.

"Been getting some disturbances on some of our Top Secret frequencies," said the colonel. "I'm checking to see if they might be originating in the area."

Another pause.

"By the way," the colonel continued, "is this the missing party? According to your roster this must be your Dr. Suess"

Yet another pause.

"Any relation to *the* Dr. Suess?"

"You're off on the wrong foot with me already," said the man in the doorway. He tried with only partial success, to cover his hostility and suspicion with levity. "You've mispronounced my name. His name rhymes with 'goose.' Mine rhymes with 'geese.'"

"You're just in time for a new hand," said one of the other men.

"I'm fussy who I play cards with," he said, still eyeing the colonel.

"Hey, c'mon," said the dealer. "Lighten up. It's okay."

Dr. Suess' facial features appeared to relax a little.

"Okay, deal me in," he said finally. "Get ready to donate to a worthy cause."

Overhead a myriad of stars, in timeless constellations, sparkled like diamonds.

* * *

The beginning of the fall term that following year had heightened the pace of activity on the Stillwell campus. Students rushed from department to department in frantic attempts to sign up for certain classes, to get schedules changed, to straighten out conflicts, or to settle accounts in the business office. Somewhere wedged in between enrollment week and opening day of classes, the science department head had called a quick meeting.

Twenty minutes prior to the meeting Dr. Suess, now clad in tweed blazer and rumpled striped shirt, leaned over the marbled countertop of the college physics lab. A tightly knotted tie hung uneven and wrinkled as he bent over.

A man with a narrow face and tousled white hair stood beside him. The wrinkled lab smock hung open over a cheap looking shirt and slacks.

They studied a wooden case on the countertop. Through a window built into the side they studied in further detail a sealed vacuum chamber. The ancient trident now lay atop a small pedestal. In the dim lavender glow, the metal showed its age; it looked as though it would easily disintegrate and crumble.

A maze of wires extended from the case to a battery of metal boxes fronting dials with crazily daring needles.

"I see you're monitoring everything very closely," said Dr. Suess.

The man in the laboratory smock checked his clipboard. "I've never seen anything like it," he said, knitting dark, bushy eyebrows. "Ever since finding it last year, this thing has been kicking out bands of radioactivity never known to science before."

He paused and looked askance at his colleague. "By the way," he said, "from the smell of your breath, you must have just had a Philly cheese and steak sandwich."

"It's to cover up the Scotch," said Dr. Suess

"What's the matter? Can't even do lunch without the stuff?"

THE TITANS

"Don't start on me, Mike, I'm trying to get psyched for that meeting." The smock clad companion plucked a ballpoint from his pocket and started marking on the clipboard. "The department will want a comprehensive progress report by next week. We'll have our work cut out for us getting everything ready."...

* * *

... The two linen-clad figures paused beside a mountain path and glanced upward into the night sky. The path followed the face of the precipice. Overhead, shafts of light beamed upward into the darkness.

They continued ascending the steep trail; the cliff wall to their left, and sheer drop to their right. Beyond their narrow ledge stars sparkled against the slate colored void that stretched below them.

'Oss'yanhu stopped and sniffed the atmosphere. "Not nearly so thick as the lower levels," he commented. "One can now really notice a difference."

"Come, my brother, we mustn't dawdle."

"Energized sandals are a god-send. But dare we risk depletion of their power?"

'K'hronu gave him a brief nod. The soles of their feet cleared the rocky footpath by a head-breadth. Silently, as shadows, they floated further up the winding trail and vanished into the night.

'As fleeting apparitions, faint as the rustling wind, they flew with the speed of thought until they resumed corporeal form atop a plateau.

"Sh'yan-Grl' dead ahead," said K'hronu.

Before them loomed an edifice of block granite. A broad expanse of steps led upward to a porch. Chiseled columns thicker than the most ancient of forest hardwoods stretched upward to support a roof ornate with frieze and mural. Light emanating from an unknown source seemed to diffuse and surround the giant structure, further accentuating the night's darkness.

The two companions mounted broad steps and entered a great hall. Here others of their kind milled about over the highly polished floor of pink marble. Like the two, their hands had six digits. Their hair and skin colors bore subtle and varied hues of the rainbow. Some, like the two, looked male. Others looked definitely female. Tunics of white or pastel linen or brightly colored silk appeared the popular attire. The males wore their hem length to just above the knee while the females wore theirs ankle length. All guests heavily adorned themselves with rings, necklaces, armlets, and bracelets about the wrists and ankles.

'As the two new arrivals worked their way through the revelers, they found staying together increasingly difficult. The laughing, conversing, and music precluded all serious verbal communication.

'A statuesque female in a scarlet silken gown seized K'hronu by the arm. She pulled him toward a fountain featuring a jade-colored triton.

"We erected this in honor of you," she said.

'K'hronu looked admiringly at the display. "Kh'llistro, dear sister," he said finally. "I'm impressed."

'Out of the triton's mouth gushed a stream of wine spilling into a surrounding pool. The lady took a ruby-studded silver goblet from a table of black mahogany. She held it briefly under the fountain until the maroon liquid spilled over and then handed it to K'hronu.

"I won't take no for an answer," she said.

"'Scheming enchantress," he said, reaching for the goblet. "You know I could never say 'no' to you,"

'He took the goblet from her. "Won't you join me?"

'She smiled demurely. "Maybe later."

'K'hronu took a sip and searched vainly for Oss'yanhu.

"'Now where did that lecherous rascal run off to?"

'The female took his arm. "He is a big boy," she said. "He can take care of himself. Come let us find some interesting people. Perhaps we can pick up a juicy morsel of gossip."...

... 'Oss'yanhu, for his part, saw a female in white silk approach him. The gown left her shoulders bare with the exception of a single strap. A rope of gold chord gathered her gown at the waist. With the exception of a slit up her left thigh, the hem gathered to just above the ankles. Gilt sandals with elevated soles and ankle straps shod her feet. Her golden hair piled high atop her head, interspersed with a network of beaded pearls. Diamond teardrop shaped earrings sparkled from her ear lobes. Around her neck she wore a gold necklace with a trident medallion.

'She stepped close. "Darling brother," she said, kissing his cheek, "how long has it been?"

"'Too long,' he said, returning her kiss. 'As K'hronu, to whom is given the stewardship of time, could readily attest to that.'

'He embraced her as together they forced their way among the partygoers.

"'I will say this,' he said. 'The old boy certainly knows how to put on a soiree.'

"'Shame on you,' she chided in mock seriousness, 'speaking so flippantly of our father.'

'Chandeliers suspended from an arched ceiling illuminated the hall with light from a hundred torches. The ceiling design swirled in brightly colored murals depicting the amorous adventures of satyrs and forest nymphs.

'Alabaster powdered the walls in subtle pastel colors.

'While Oss'yanhu and his female companion moved to the far end of the hall, the other guests exchanged knowing glances.

"'Aha, Oss'yanhu and R'ya "said one. 'What is this?'

"'Oss'yanhu, lord of the waters; R'ya, lady of memory. One shouldn't wonder,' replied another.

'The couple worked their way past the celebrants to reach an arched entrance. Beyond stretched a brightly illuminated corridor.

'Shortly after stepping through the colonnaded portals, R'ya hesitated. 'Where are we going, by the way?'

"'Ah, dear sister, I perceive that being pressed about by many guests is a weariness to you.'

"'But leaving the main hall like this? After all, this is more than just a social event. Father Light-Bearer had summoned us all up here for a reason.'

'He gave his head a reckless toss. 'We will not be missed.'

'His arm pressed her waist in the direction of the empty corridor. They stopped beside one of the arched doorways that lined the sides. Oss'yanhu guided R'ya in a turn through the doorway. Pushing aside heavily embroidered drapes they entered a small suite of rooms. Beyond the doorway a small balcony enabled them to step out into the night and observe the all-enveloping darkness. Stars sparkled in hard brilliance against the void. Oss'yanhu pulled her close and she slipped her arm around his. Their attention fixed on a particularly large star just above the horizon.

"'K'haos is ruler of all this,' he said, pointing to it. 'He's a lucky fellow.'

'R'ya stared pensively at the nocturnal skies. 'One should not desire what is not theirs, I suppose; however, the night does weave its own magic.'

'From below the summit, from the forest that stretched darker than the night *heavens across a limitless expanse of nether terrain, little nocturnal creatures, unseen,—tiny little winged things with many legs—began their serenade of night sounds. A cool breeze bearing the fragrance of woodland flowers fanned their faces.*

He drew her back toward the doorway.

"Leaving all this so soon?" she asked.

"Ah yes," he replied. "It is a temptation to linger, but come, other pleasant moments await us."

She searched his face with wordless questionings.

"I've arranged for a bit of refreshments to be brought up," he said finally. "Perhaps we can conduct our own little banquet."

She eyed him. "Aren't you a crafty rogue, though?"

Stepping through the curtain, they strolled further down the empty corridor, further away from the sounds of the talk, the laughter, and the music in the main hall.

She has cultivated coquetry to a polished art, he thought as they turned a corner and started up a broad circular staircase.

They followed the staircase up a flight and came to another network of corridors. They followed one until they reached another doorway. Again, a heavy drape of gold fabric stretched across it. Oss'yanhu pulled it aside. A flickering wall torch revealed a small chamber. An ornately carved hardwood table with matching stools occupied the center of the room. A tasseled and embroidered cloth stretched over the tabletop. On it set a tray laden with bowls of fruit and a flagon of wine.

R'ya studied the tray of delicacies. "You planned this, you knave," she said, "and quite thoroughly, I might add."

He pulled out one of stools for her and sat down on the one opposite. From delicately colored walls, flaming torches sent their lighted shadows dancing merrily across the room. "My ministering spirits do their work well," he said.

He offered her the fruit bowl and she took a gold colored pear. She took a bite. The hard, crisp fruit had a subtly sweet-tart flavor. The pleasing aftertaste left its sensation for some moments before leaving her with a desire for more. After taking another bite, her mood turned serious. "I have a sense of unease about all this."

He poured wine into her goblet. "How so?"

After pouring into a second goblet, he noticed her casting a worried look down into her cup.

Oss'yanhu fidgeted. Long a devotee for merriment, he did not like serious conversation.

"'I don't think Father Light-Bearer is telling us everything,'" she said.

Oss'yanhyu reached for a pear. "About what?"

"The plan."

He began eating his pear and then stopped. He too, fell into an unaccustomedly thoughtful mood. He put the half-eaten pear back onto the tray and leaned against the wall tapestry.

"Whatever are you talking about?" he said, after realizing the silence would not be broken unless he pushed the conversation into untried and uncomfortable territory. "There is only one plan and we're all privy to it."

She stopped her eating and likewise placed her fruit back on the table. "I'm not talking about the plan," she said, choosing her words carefully. "I'm talking about his plan."

"I don't understand."

"I don't understand either."

She continued staring down into her lap. "One hears rumors."

"Rumors," he repeated with a smirk. He reached for his goblet. "Let us have done with gravity," he said with a shrug of impatience. "A draught for the good times."

As she raised her goblet in his direction, he stopped her.

He stood up.

"Like this," he said, drawing her to her feet. He held out his goblet and curled his arm around hers. As they held their cups to their lips, their heads bent close. Their eyes met. They placed their wine cups back on the table and sought one another's lips.

When they finally broke contact, Oss'yanhu pressed his face against her perfumed cheek. "My darling," he whispered. "My sister, my spouse, my cherry; how I love you."

"Should we be doing this?" she asked softly. "If you want me, wouldn't it be better to seek Father Light-Bearer's permission?"

Her perfumed essence made him giddy with desire. For himself, he knew that his emotions would cause his body to emit a slight musk-like scent indicating sensual desire. He unclasped the golden peg that held her one shoulder strap. "Does he seek permission from All-That-Is-Good for the things he does?"

As Oss'yanhu pulled her toward him, he seemed unaware that their love scene reflected in the fiery glow of a brazier that cast flickering shadows against the cobwebbed, crumbling stone walls of a secret chamber in a low, remote part of the palace…

* * *

… *The flames leapt up from the small brazier pot and changed color as a mortal like male figure with a swarthy complexion held a small vial. He continued sprinkling a gray, powdery dust into the coals. The dancing flames took on transparency revealing yet more vividly the amorous pastime playing out before him.*

The figure then sat down on a tree stump that served as a stool. He hunched over the brazier, observing the two lovers in their clandestine encounter. Dark and light danced against the worn-looking stone walls standing unhewn and irregular, showing clearly the ravages of time. The room seemed bereft of furnishings save some shelving fashioned with logs flattened on the upper side. On this shelving sat several clay jars containing powdery substances. At either end set an animal skull with a candle jammed into the top. Opposite the brazier, in the limits of the fire's glow a crude oaken door was wedged into a carved recess in the rock.

'A dozen musty smells in an unholy scent permeated the cavern's stale air.

The figure's dark features continued staring into the vision, hands folded in his lap. Eyes, reduced to evil looking slits reflecting the glow of the fire, glared at the image of the lovers frolicking in the small veranda pool. A short, curly beard framed a broad mouth. Thin lips turned downward. Dark, curly locks cascaded over velvet clad shoulders.

The figure did not move.

He continued watching the lovers' lolling in the pool.

Tension in the chamber grew intense.

'As they reached for wine cups perched on the pool's edge he stood up. "You two have betrayed me," *he said in a low, portentous voice…*

* * *

… *The light shafts from the apartment chamber brought the veranda into view. The lovers—unaware that they had been observed—waded toward the deeper end of the pool. They held their goblets aloft, brushed aside rose petals and slid down into the tepid water.*

R'ya cast a languid gaze toward Oss'yanhu. "You don't know how long I've waited for this moment," *she sighed.*

"My darling," *he whispered.* "You will be mine."

THE TITANS

'He reached and drew her delicate shoulders in a tender embrace. "And I will be yours," he added. "Always."…

* * *

…Nervous rustling of papers and scraping of furniture characterized the atmosphere as the group of science faculty members assembled. The summer showers brought the smell of wet pavement through an open window. The damp air amplified the already live acoustics of the hard plaster ceiling. The white haired bespectacled men in rumpled tweeds or wrinkled dress shirts and women in stark hairdos and flat shoes sat in battered wooden chairs. An ancient oaken table bore initials clandestinely etched by students of generations past.

Again, the door to the conference room opened.

Dr. Sirotka entered breathlessly.

Dr. Suess glanced at his watch.

"Hey come on," said Dr. Sirotka. "I'm on time. What the hell you looking at your watch for?"

"To see if it's still running," came the retort.

Dr. Ian Ferguson, professor of mining engineering pulled out his deeply scratched chair. He cleared his throat nervously and lowered his massive head of unkempt gray hair. His wire frame bifocals rested low on his bulbous nose. He tilted his head to catch the right focus on the typed sheet.

"The Stillwell College Science Department will now come to order." His thick, Scottish brogue carried a tone of tired resignation. The meeting in the third floor conference room of an edifice of ancient Victorian yellow brick—plodded through old business. Outside a nearby window the small campus lay veiled in an autumnal mist.

Stillwell College had long been a private liberal arts school originally devoted to turning out mining engineers. While on scientific expeditions to the South Dakota Badlands six years previous, however, members of the faculty team had unearthed some startling finds that piqued nationwide interest. Both the school and the small town nestled comfortably in a remote section of the Colorado Rockies now had cause to feel uneasy about the new-found attention.

"We will hear the minutes of the last meeting." Dr. Ferguson's voice boomed off dull yellow walls of hard plaster. As the endless minutiae of reports and more old business ate up the afternoon, Dr. Suess held a sheaf of papers as he awaited the new business.

At last the welcome words: "And now, we entertain new business. I believe we have a report from Dr. Suess and Dr. Sirotka."

"The two men exchanged nods. Dr. Suess finally stood to his feet. "Mr. Chairman," he said, "members of the committee."

He began with an account of lonely trips to those same Badlands. He told of digging around the deserted, rocky wilderness, miles away from any other mortal. He told of descending into the shallow wash of loose rubble. He mentioned finding the two mysterious footprints and of chipping away at a butte wall until he found the trident.

"A what?" Dr. Zelda Hezron, a bespectacled stick of a woman in her fifties who chaired the zoology department looked inquisitively.

"A what?" snapped Dr. Suess. "What part of 'trident' don't you understand?"

"Just don't breathe on a Bunsen burner," said Dr. Hezron. "You'll cause an explosion."

"Just don't breathe in the conservancy," retorted Dr. Suess. "You'll kill the flowers." *That was almost too easy,* he thought.

Dr. Hezron glared but said nothing.

Dr. Ferguson made a feeble gesture to restore control.

"A trident, if you can grasp the idea," said Dr. Suess. "We have it on display in the physics lab. Several people from the Museum of Natural History have seen it."

"I've seen it," said Dr. Ferguson. "You say you found it embedded in a Jurassic Era stratum? Yet it's definitely not natural."

"Something obviously fashioned by an intelligence," said Dr. Suess.

"Of which this department seems to be in short supply," muttered Dr. Hezron. "Good thing for you you're on tenure."

"Good thing for you you're on life support," said Dr. Suess.

"Can we get on with it?" pleaded Dr. Ferguson.

Silence descended on the conference room. Outside the rain had stopped but the day had turned hot and muggy.

THE TITANS

Dr. Suess paused. It had been a whole year since his last summer expedition. During those same previous six years their findings had been confined to a reserve owned by the college. Their petrified skeletal remains had piqued nationwide interest, not only among the scientific community, but the general news media and the federal government as well.

The significance of the bones themselves turned out to be controversial. Scientists and self-appointed paleontologists debated their dating and authenticity. The school also found itself having to protect their property from vandalism and thievery by illicit tourist stand vendors, and amateur archeologists. They also found themselves involved in a bureaucratic snarl with Washington as to the relics' rightful ownership.

Dr. Suess and Dr. Sirotka determined at the outset that they were going to protect their latest unearthing from outsider's interference at all costs.

Dr. Leila Fuchs, a heavy, dark-haired woman from the Botany Department eyed Dr. Suess. "Just exactly how do you account for this?"

Her question snapped his thoughts back to the business at hand.

"Why must we always account for every damned thing we run across," he said tersely. "Truth is I can't."

His answer elicited another silence.

Finally Dr. Ferguson again spoke. "What we have, ladies and gentlemen, is something that could be the cosmological time bomb of the millennium. Do you have anything else to tell us?"

Dr. Suess could feel the perspiration under his shirt trickle down his back. The previous school year had been a busy one for Dr. Sirotka and him. The trident had presented thorny problems demanding scientific explanation.

Dr. Suess shuffled more papers of his report. He then gave them a brief summary of the past years' research.

First of all there was the intense signal of radioactivity picked up by their Geiger counter out in the field when they first unearthed the trident.

When they hooked it up in a cabinet that they had devised in the physics lab, they tried to find instruments to measure the strength, nature and source of the radioactivity.

Dr. Suess sat down and let Dr. Sirotka take the floor. "As Dr. Suess has said, the object is extremely radioactive,"

He glanced down at his papers a moment. "Our familiarity with the phenomenon of radioactivity, I'm afraid, sometimes causes us to forget how recent it really is. Its discovery occurred only a little over a century ago. Despite great advances in such fields as physics, chemistry, and medicine, it's becoming clear to me what we now know is minuscule compared to what may still be out there waiting to be discovered."

Dr. Ferguson eyed him. "Just what are you referring to?"

Dr. Sirotka took a deep breath before going on. "We have hooked the object to every measuring device, every instrument not only from our own campus, but also from Fort Lewis, Western State and every other campus in the region plus every lab and think tank with which we had even a modicum of good will."

"I'll bet that took some doing," said Dr. Hezron.

"Our preliminary findings are nothing short of staggering," continued Dr. Sirotka, ignoring her remark. "You are, of course, familiar with the X-Ray. We also have such things as Alpha, Beta, and Gamma rays. We have now detected hitherto other forms of radiation that may very well utilize the entire Greek alphabet.

"We have found some of these forms of radioactive signals to be so weak that they can be detected only by our most sensitive instruments. This we attribute to two factors: one, that many of them may have had their origin from extremely remote sources in outer space, and two, that they may be also of very ancient origin. Thus they could well be in an extremely advanced stage of decay."

He paused to let his words sink in.

"Just like certain on our faculty," muttered Dr. Fuchs to Dr. Hezron in an aside.

The others continued studying him in an attitude of suspense.

He tried to ignore the extemporaneous remarks. "There is one final interesting side discovery," he said finally. "Some signals seem to emit a series of regular pulsation, as if sent by some intelligent source."

A pause.

"It was almost as if some one were communicating with us"

A restless shuffling of chairs punctuated the silence. "You people are no doubt familiar with time travel as portrayed, for example, in such science fiction as H.G.Well's *The Time Machine?*"

"Don't ask Dr. Suess to read anything heavier than *Sports Illustrated*," whispered Dr. Hezron to Dr. Fuchs.

More silence.

Dr. Sirtoka took a breath. "Ladies and gentlemen," he said, "we may well be on the threshold of an era wherein this stuff is no longer fiction."

Again he let his audience grasp the import of his remarks.

"Human speech," he continued, "is, of course, like all sound in that it can be transmitted only through atmosphere containing moisture. In space, all we have is dead silence. However, ether waves radiate toward us from all corners of the universe.

"Now then, when we first suspected that this radiation possibly contained intelligent communication we knew we faced some profound challenges. Not the least of which was how to translate these signals into anything resembling an intelligible message.

"This was when we contacted a cryptologist lab with the U.S. Army Signal Corps. They have some very brilliant minds there who immediately became fascinated with our project. Getting their help and expertise was no problem.

"They came at our dilemma of recapturing human speech from a very interesting angle. While acknowledging that recreating sound outside terrestrial atmosphere is impossible, they realized the light waves travel through space faster than anything in our cosmos.

"To show how much they 'think outside the box' as it were, they began working on reconstructing visual images of extreme antiquity that could still be borne on radiation light years out into space."

Dr. Sirotka gave a shrug of incredulity. "I still don't know how they did it," he said, "but these physicists put together technology that somehow was able to reproduce images too faint for the naked eye. They then detected intelligences engaging in conversation. Even though they could not recapture the sounds, they were able pick up radiological impressions of lips moving. From these they were able to lip sync them into a form of conversation.

"Needless to say whatever sound patterns they were able to reproduce would make absolutely no sense whatsoever to anyone versed in any language—no matter how remote—in existence today.

"All they had at this juncture was the *reality* of *a* linguistic pattern. How to break it down into some form of vocabulary and syntax that could be translated would still presented a most daunting task.

"Here they also involved the masterminds of some of the most advanced computer engineers in the industry. Again they 'thought outside the box.' by going beyond the current computer technology of reducing all electronic impulses to a series of number '1's' and '0's.'

"They utilized the numbers '2' through '9' as well!

"They secretly devised a system so far beyond what is generally known in the industry that it still is kept highly classified.

"Even I don't know the details. This system, however, finally enabled the linguists to have enough material to work with. They could now begin to take audio signals and break them down into a language system they could analyze.

"They were then able to hire philologists to translate this raw linguistic data into our modern vernacular."

Again he paused. The others continued studying him while trying to grasp the full import of what they were hearing.

"There is another interesting side discovery," he said finally. "Some signals seem to emit a series of regular pulsation, as if from an intelligent source not only from the trident, but also directed *at* it from outer space."

He chuckled in disbelief. "Our findings almost resemble the translation of an ancient epic from some prehistoric troubadour or bard," he said. "Sort of like Homer's *Iliad* and *Odyssey*."

He sat down to a conference room enveloped in silence.

Chapter 2

"I have been summoned to appear before Father Light-Bearer."

K'hronu slapped his right fist across his chest as he faced the shining being before him. The creature stood at parade rest as a sentry before a gilded threshold. A silken purple curtain covered the doorway. The white marble floor with thin black streaks running through it glistened in the flickering torch light. An ornate frieze lined the walls near the ceiling.

Towering over K'hronu by a head, the sentry wore curled locks of gold. His face and well muscled body sparkled with an aureate sheen. Gold likewise colored his short battle tunic. Metal epaulets adorned the shoulders that held a similarly hued cape. A massive buckle fastened a belt that supported a laser-like sword.

The sentry snapped to attention. He then slapped his chest in another salute. "Cross the floor," he said as he stepped aside.

K'hronu started past him toward the high-arched entrance. The sentry eyed him with a furtive glance. "Be careful," he said.

K'hronu walked slowly down a carpeted streamer to a distant mahogany table. Beyond it a male figure sat in a broad chair with his back toward him. A head crowned with raven-colored locks protruded above the high, wing shaped back. The occupant seemed to be looking out a wide expanse of window at the starlit sky.

K'hronu stopped a short space from the table and planted the butt of his scepter into the carpeting. "You summoned me, sir?"

The figure in the chair didn't move.

K'hronu waited. Moisture began forming in the hand that held the hourglass.

The figure whirled the chair around on stone casters. K'hronu found himself facing the occupant still seated in a reclining position. The occupant pressed bejeweled fingertips. Curled locks cascaded past shoulders draped in a velvet shawl. Rubies the size of olive pits were set in a crown of white gold. A high forehead featured thinly arched eyebrows. Heavy eyelashes gave a brooding expression to eyes that constantly changed color. A patrician nose centered a pale, narrow face. A pencil-line mustache and goatee framed a wide, thin-lipped mouth. Under the velvet cape he arrayed himself in a rainbow-colored robe. Gems of every description were cunningly embossed into the garment. Puffed sleeves gathered in gold bracelets at the wrists.

"Who rules here?" He snarled.

'K'hronu took a deep breath. "You do sire."

The brilliantly arrayed occupant sat forward in his chair.

"Then why are my decrees so flagrantly disregarded?"

"K'hronu stared at him blankly. "I can't answer, sire."

The seated one turned slightly sideways while continuing to stare at K'hronu, letting silence fall on the chamber.

Finally he again spoke.

"Your brother is seducing your sister even while I sit here."…

* * *

… 'Kh'ronu left his father's apartment with emotions a seething cauldron. Minutes later he walked down a distant corridor. The pastel alabaster that colored its walls contrasted with his darkened mood. When he came to a wide portal, he parted the richly embroidered curtain and entered the sitting room of his own quarters. At the far end sprawled in a semi-reclining position lay a statuesque brunette on a settee of darkened hardwood.

Upon his entering she sat upright. A look of alarm crossed her fair features.

"Kh'ronu, my darling," she said. "What is the matter?"

"I've just come from father's chambers."

"And—?"

"Not good."

'Silence fell on the room.

'Kh'ronu sat down beside his beloved. "He is becoming exceedingly difficult."

'She waited for him to continue.

"He harbors all manner of suspicions of everyone," he said at last. "He is becoming *insanely jealous He sees the worst of motives in every little coquetry no matter how innocent."*

'A pause.

'He leaned forward with arms folded. "This in addition to his own unbridled passions, not only for fleshly pleasure but for power as well."

'He stood and walked to a small table in the center of the room. He reached for a tall, narrow pitcher. From it he poured golden colored wine into a silver goblet.

"I can see us headed for disaster," he said after taking a sip. He put goblet back and looked thoughtfully at the mural on a far wall. "I can see us headed toward a situation going out of control"

'The fair lady rose and stood beside her husband. She laid a hand on his shoulder in attempt to reassure him. "But are you not the god of time?"

'He clasped her hand. "Sometimes I can control events," he said somberly. "Other times I can only watch them happen."...

* * *

…Dr. Suess walked the ancient corridor of the Stillwell College Darwin Memorial Science Building. The third floor, pressed against the roof with an array of nooks, cupolas, and garrets provided cozy hideaways for faculty offices. As his shoes struck the polished, wooden floors, the echo of his footsteps bounced off the hard, plaster walls. He stopped by a dark, oaken door bearing '312' on a brass plate. The name 'Michael Sirotka, Ph.d.' spread across a frozen glass window. The heavy door rattled to Dr. Suess' knocking.

"Come in."

As Dr. Suess entered, Dr. Sirotka looked up from paper work spread across his desk. "So, how's your ugliness this morning?"

"Shut up."

"Got something interesting," he said as he stood to his feet.

Dr. Suess looked at the low, slanted ceiling, conforming as it did to the contour of the roof. Cramped, low bookshelves lined the two walls of the narrow office. Dr. Sirotka bent low to open a window extending from the floor to waist high. When he returned to his desk, he picked up a paper.

Dr. Suess eyed the paper. "A paternity suit?"

Dr. Sirotka ignored the remark. "As Abe Lincoln once said, 'nobody likes a smart ass.' Here," he said, handing it to Dr. Suess.

The paper bore the letterhead of U.S. Department of Defense, Cryptographic Division.

"Look at their response to our lab report," he said.

They had sent one of the readings of the radioactivity. A frequency they called the 'Omega Ray' had sent pulsating signals in regular patterns. Suspecting that it might possibly indicate an intelligent source, they sent graph charts of the signal to the government lab. There, some of the world's most expert cryptographers analyzed the code.

In the preface of the report, Dr. Suess read a pronunciation guide to some of the proper names in the translations. Many of the names used the apostrophe (') as part of the spelling. That, the report continued, represented a short 'eh' sound.

The report continued: 'One may find variances in the spelling of proper names. This may be attributed to the difficulty of the decoding of radiation impulses of extreme antiquity and/or from outer space.'

Perspiration from Dr. Suess' hands soaked the page as he read the report.

'Our specialists, after careful analysis, believe the following text to be a fairly authentic breakdown and translation of the content of your charts:

R'ya tossed restlessly on her couch trying to find a comfortable position for her distended body. The sudden appearance of another female in her bedchamber startled her. The new arrival's complexion bore a subtle suggestion of an olive-colored hue. Yet the cheeks remained colored a delicate rose. Brown eyes looked at R'ya with concern.

"'Sister,' said R'ya when she recovered from her surprise, 'thank All-That-Is-Good you're here.'"

"'Your time draws near, I see.' The new arrival was Thya, ruler of Thought and Justice.

R'ya leaned back against a cushion. "Oss'yanhu made me thus." She motioned toward her body. "And now he practically ignores me."

Thya pulled a low stool beside the couch and seated herself. Gently she took R'ya's hand. "Dear sister," she sighed, "I'm afraid you don't know the half of it."

R'ya eyed her with curiosity as her sister stood up. She took deliberate strides to the far side of the bedchamber to a wall bracket and took from it a crystal ball and placed it on the night stand adjacent the couch and stepped back.

"It grieves me to be the bearer of evil tidings," she said. "But Mother G'ya insisted on it."

R'ya's curiosity heightened. "Whatever are you talking about?"

Thya didn't answer immediately. She stood erect and held her hands motionless above the crystal. She closed her eyes and appeared to fall into a trance with her lips moving. As the sands from a nearby hourglass filtered through the neck,

R'ya waited.

The sands continued to filter, still nothing happened.

Then slowly, almost imperceptibly at first, R'ya thought she saw the ball's interior cloud over. As the mist took on a milky whiteness, Thya continued to stand rigid, eyes closed. The crystal began to clear again. This time it appeared green, as in a forest glade. Lush vegetation formed a backdrop to a clear water pool a short distance through the underbrush. At first R'ya saw no sign of intelligent life. Then a bush moved in a way that no breeze could have caused. She saw between the branches a glimpse of flesh.

She gasped as she saw Oss'yanhu's naked body kneeling in the thick grass making spastic like movements with a rapturous look on his face. She also saw the unclad figure of a driad, or wood nymph, kneeling submissively beneath him.

The scene faded and the crystal became clear once more.

Thya came out of her trance and sank to her stool weak and perspiring.

"I'm sorry to have to be the one to tell you this," she panted. "However we thought you should know."

For long moments R'ya lay back too stunned to speak. Finally hard lines formed around her mouth as she sat forward.

"Shameless, wanton lizard," she fumed, "flitting about and sporting with every attractive wood and water nymph he can lay his hands on. Shame on them all: copulating like dragon flies while I languish here, belly bloated like a melon and about to deliver his child."

She struggled to her feet. "Bring them back," she demanded.

Thya hesitated, then stood to her feet and lapsed into another trance. This time the crystal showed a blissfully nude Oss'yanhu immersed in a woodland pool, embracing a naiad, or water nymph on each arm.

R'ya thrust a forefinger at the crystal.

"I curse you, my husband," she shouted. "May none of your issue of whoredom be whole. May your offspring of bastardy be forever halt, disfigured, blind, deformed, diseased, or criminally mad.

"'May your desire for new conquests ever increase. May the satisfaction you extract from your harlotries ever diminish until at the last you are mad with despair and until you cry out to Father-Light-Bearer for deliverance from your all-consuming but unfulfilled desires.

"'May all those wretched and deformed mutants you spawn eventually turn on you and seek your miserable life."

'She placed both hands on her swollen belly.

"'May he who issues forth from my womb rise up against you until, in the end, he is your destruction."

From the pores of her skin emanated the telltale sign of grief: the smell of death.

'She turned to Thya. "And now, dear sister, leave me to grieve alone in my sorrow."

'Thya bowed and exited the bedchamber.

'With a shriek, R'ya seized shoulder strap of her tunic and tore it from her body. Anguished cries reverberated through the palace as she threw herself, face down, on the couch.'...

* * *

...Dr. Suess laid the report aside.

"What do you think?" he asked his colleague.

"Amazing," said Dr. Suess as he flipped more pages. The following page consisted of footnotes and comments on the previous pages.

"Are we into fantasy here?" he added.

Dr. Sirotka leaned forward against his desktop. "I think we're into something off the charts that's for sure."

Dr. Suess looked up from the page. "Like what?'

Dr. Sirotka leaned back in his chair and reached for a nearby bookcase. From it he pulled a volume of H.G. Well's *The Time Machine*.

Dr. Suess looked puzzled. "What's the connection?'

Dr. Sirotka leaned over his desk again. "You dumb shit," he said. "Don't you see? We may have in some of this radioactivity the ultimate time machine."

He related a favorite object lesson he used in his younger days as a high school physics teacher. He would place an Alka-Seltzer tablet in each of two tumblers of water that he kept hidden from his students. However, he would drop in one tablet some thirty seconds ahead of the other. He would let seconds lapse before holding up both water glasses before the class. In one glass the tablet on the bottom would be nearly gone, while on the bottom of the second glass, the tablet would be virtually intact. They would have little trouble guessing which tablet had been submerged in the water the longest.

This would illustrate the nature of matter, the nature of radiation, the nature of radioactive decay, and the methods of time and age measurement.

Thus would he teach them the following properties of matter: All matter had a beginning. Not all matter emerged in its present state at the same time. All matter is in a stage of decay, or disintegration. In this way he also taught them some important physical laws. According to the Law of the Preservation of Matter and Energy, neither matter nor energy can be created nor destroyed; however, matter can be transferred into energy and vice verse. Also, according the Second Law of Thermodynamics, heat flows from a hot or active object to a cold or inert object until both achieve a state of equilibrium.

"All radiation is a message from outer space or distant time, or both." he concluded. "We ourselves are continually bombarded with these messages. We are also sending out messages of our own in return. When we speak, for example, our verbal messages are carried across the medium of atmosphere. Gradually, because of resistance factors of distance and time, our verbal messages become too faint to any longer be detected by the human aural mechanism until the audio signal that we have sent out gradually dissipates. There is no reason to assume however that these signals disappear altogether nor should we assume that these signals cannot be retrieved given that we have receiving mechanism sensitive enough to detect them. Could it not be possible to retrieve some of these signals and convert them back into intelligible words spoken, for example, years, centuries, or even millennia ago?

"Isn't it possible, then, to likewise pick up radio signals borne on ether? To bring them back, and again, with finely sensitive recording equipment, reproduce them on our instruments and maybe also convert them into audio and even verbal messages? Given sufficiently sophisticated equipment, could not this be done with impulses incredibly ancient and thus reproduce recordings of events in epochs we arbitrarily label as prehistoric?"

For the moment Dr. Suess said nothing. *This is totally far fetched*, he thought.

For the time being, at least, he saw great wisdom in keeping the matter confidential.

Dr. Suess added. "That means come Friday's poker game, if any of the guys get inquisitive, we got nothing to say, right?."

"If we keep taking their money," said Dr. Sirotka, "they may have neither the time nor the inclination to get inquisitive about our research."

* * *

The sun's rays cast long shadows as it poised to disappear over the jagged peaks of the Colorado Rockies. Dr. Suess walked slowly down the quiet, darkening streets. Both sides fronted rows of rambling Victorian houses once by owned silver mining barons. He did not consider the sign of inactivity anything unusual. Residential streets of Stillwell, Colorado boasted little night life.

He cast an apprehensive glance at an enclosure a block away.

After more than two and a half decades this stretch of the walk still filled him with a sense of dread.

The enclosure extended in all its directions to about the size of two football stadiums. A cyclone fence half again the size of the average man bordered the entire area. At its top rolled stands of razor wire. Behind this cyclone fence arose a grass covered mound the height of a one story house. Naked branches of tree tops like skeletal claws extended above the plateau-like top.

Stillwell's own Mount Olympus, he thought; *a monument to our craven, gutless city hall.*

Every fifty feet hung signs bearing the message.

'No trespassing.
Enclosed property condemned as toxic waste dump.
Trespassers will be prosecuted.
By order of the Environmental Protection Agency."

He recalled what happened shortly after he came to Stillwell. People's Park, he recalled; another noble experiment in human relations by our city fathers gone sour.

An experiment that cost the life of one his students.

* * *

He slowly mounted the broad, wooden steps that led to his front porch and savored the night sounds already serenading from the spirea bushes. He checked the wrought iron mail box that hung from a delicately carved pillar.

Mostly junk mail, he thought, as he sorted out the envelopes.

He looked through the screen door. The only from the far side of an otherwise darkened front hallway could he see a weak light. It came from underneath a door that led to the library.

After dropping the mail on a nearby antique table, he moved cautiously through the murky twilight, avoiding silhouettes of a hall tree and an umbrella stand. The faint aroma of cooking wafted from the distant kitchen.

When he found the library archway, he pushed aside the heavy oaken door. He stood near the ornate ancient lintels. In the dim light he could barely see their layers of darkened varnish cracking with age. The baseboards and ceiling woodwork also showed the same signs of aging. The soles his shoes sunk into the thick oriental carpeting. Off to one corner he saw his worn and favorite recliner. Beside it he kept a tousled, art déco floor lamp.

At the opposite end of the room, beyond a battery of bookcases, a slight, fortyish-looking woman sat at a desk grading papers. Beneath the soft glow of a tiffany lamp spread a sheaf of student literary efforts. The wallpaper seemed to be impregnated with the musty smell characteristic of so many older houses.

The woman pored over her work with intensity as she perused the papers, occasionally scrawling remarks over them with a red pencil

"Marie?"

The bespectacled woman with plain looking features glanced up from the desk. Before she could get up, he moved behind her and laid his hands on her shoulders.

"Still at it, I see," he said, kissing her forehead.

He waited for her to tilt her head to enable him to kiss her cheek. She didn't move.

"I'm almost done," she did say however.

Resigned, he moved to his recliner and sat in an upright position. "So," he said, switching on the nearby floor lamp, "how did it go today?"

She finally turned her swivel chair in his direction. "Good of you to inquire," she said. "I suppose I should ask you the same thing."

He sat back and kicked out the foot rest. "Interesting."

His first wife had died a decade earlier, leaving him with two now grown children. Marie—herself a divorcee with two pre-adolescent children—came into his life five years later under rather unusual circumstances...

...The fall of that year ushered in the deer hunting season typically cold and with just the right powdering of snow. He and Dr. Sirotka had just driven their Jeep to a favorite hunting site about an hour's drive from town and, with assembled rifles, readied themselves for their foray across the prairie into the cold dusk of morning. The frigid air carried the smell of frozen grassland.

Across the road they saw a half dozen people carrying signs.

He could only guess how they knew he and his partner would be at this particular spot on this particular morning.

"Don't you realize what you're doing?" a slight, bespectacled young woman in light brown hair had shouted at them.

Dr. Suess and Dr. Sirotka had originally planned to separate and let one of the activists follow each of them into the open prairie until they were out of sight and out of earshot from the road. Once they were alone, they would give their adversaries two choices: either go back to the road or, with no witness around, face an armed hunter who is mad as hell.

The woman who shouted at them was the one who followed Dr. Suess.

"Please," she shouted. "Can't we talk about this?"

Dr. Suess shot her a hard look. "If you're out to stop people from killing animals, you're about a half million years too late."

As the sun rose higher in the icy mist and cast a pink hue over the low, frosted white hills, he again turned to his antagonist.

She stood shorter than he by half a head. She wasn't really all that pretty. Struggling to stay angry, he puzzled within himself as to why. Maybe it was because she didn't seem to be the stereotypical militant activist. No countenance twisted in anger here. He detected no stridency in her voice. He sensed docility in the pale eyes behind the round, wire glasses. Perhaps it was the soft looking, oval face with the receding chin. Her slim body contoured in soft curves: from the shoulders, to the breasts, to the hip line holding up the low hanging jeans.

It's the eyes, he concluded as his scrutiny returned to her face. They had reminded him of a doe antelope, not unlike some of the game he was now hunting. *Give her face maybe a five*, he concluded, *but I'd give her body an easy ten*.

He let his rifle drop to his side. *Oh hell*, he thought, *I can go hunting some other day*. The idea of shooting someone was crazy anyway. He knew he would never do it.

Instead, he stepped over to her and fingered the fringes of her jacket lapel.

"Nice jacket," he commented. "Looks like buckskin."

"It's synthetic," she said. Apparently she thought she had him.

He suspected she wasn't sure whether it was or not. It did in fact smell of genuine leather. "Don't you know," he retorted, "that synthetic fabric is petroleum based, and that the manufacturers are some of the worst polluters of the environment?"

She glared at him moment, and then seemed to soften. "Okay," she sighed. "Score one for you."

Silence fell across the frozen prairie.

Again he spoke. "You wanted to talk this over," he said, "how about in town over a cup of coffee?"

He studied her features, looking for clues as to her reaction.

At first she remained non-committal.
However, her answer finally came in a flat tone of voice.
"Okay."

* * *

Mid-morning they sat in a remote booth at the Last Chance Café back in Stillwell. Sounds of ringing registers and cheery conversation filled the room. The smell of hot cooking floated into the dining area from the kitchen.

He broke into the conversation of small talk. "Tell me, what do you do when you're not doing this?"

She looked slightly irritated. "What do you mean 'what do you do when you're not doing this?'"

He shrugged. How easy did he think it would be playing the field at this time of life? Neither of them were kids any more. He hadn't played the dating game in decades. Did people even date like they used to?

"After all, there has got to more to life than just politics," he finally managed to say.

"Could we order?"

He picked up his menu. "Oh yeah, of course," he hated the flustered feeling.

A young woman in a pink and white uniform with order pad in hand finally came to his rescue

He glanced at his guest then again back at the waitress. "Two sourdough glazes and two coffees."

He knew that she taught English and drama in the local high school. Although he already knew that and although he had seen her briefly a few times around town, he had never talked to her until today.

He also knew that she had been divorced three years before.

"So," he said. "How's it going down there in the trenches?"

"I imagine you already know."

Silence.

"Guess it's the same all over," he laughed with embarrassment.

He studied the front window a moment. Vapor formed on the glass, heightening the contrast between the warm, moist interior of the restaurant and the frozen autumn morning outside. The brief lapse in his attention caught him off guard with her next remark. "We were going to talk about the hunting of animals, remember?"

"All right, let's talk about the hunting of animals."

She paused. Again, the sound of laughing voices and ringing of the cash register filled the air.

"Okay, smart guy," she said. "Here's how it is. Recent research in animal behavior indicates that animals have far more sensibilities then we have previously given them credit for. Take Diane Fossey and her study of the mountain gorillas in Africa. Why they are so like humans it's scary. Other studies have been made of chimpanzees and the Orangutan. They not only show a whole vocabulary of communication, but also show a wide range of emotion

"They show care for and nurture the young in ways that approach human behavior. They grieve when they lose a loved one. They sometimes have very highly sophisticated social organization. They show fear, anger, even humor in ways that we weren't even aware of until just recently. Many of their species even teach their young survival techniques. We could have as much a 'nurture versus nature' debate about them as we do with ourselves. They have just as much right on this planet we do. After all, they too, are God's creatures."

"So you do believe in God then?"

"That's beside the point." Her voice took on an edge. "Right now the point is that if we don't speak up for those who can't speak for themselves, if we don't protect those who can't protect themselves, then who?"

Dr. Suess sat silent a moment

"Okay you won this round," he said with resignation. "You perhaps saved an antelope's life. How does that make you feel?"

"It does make me feel good," she acknowledged. "As a Chinese proverb has it: 'Better to light one candle than to curse the darkness.'"

Dr. Suess looked off at old timey photographs that formed the coffee shop's décor. "Yeah, I know," he said, still with resignation. "There is an antelope still out there on the frozen prairie. I could have shot it this morning, but instead it's still running wild and free."

Suddenly his mood changed. "You know," he said in a loud voice, "what we need is for the working class to overthrow the corporations and take over and run the factories directly!"

She gave him a puzzled look. He lowered his gaze and gestured to the couple in the booth next to them.

"Don't look now," he said, this time softly, "but I think those two old farts in the booth next to us were eavesdropping. Just wanted to rattle their cage a little bit."

Again he paused. "Thing is," he continued, "by tonight, that same little antelope, instead of hanging skinned and dressed in my garage, could very well be supper for some hungry mountain lion."

The approach of a third party bringing their orders broke momentarily their conversation.

He took a sip of his coffee.

"So what would you do then?" he asked, "start picketing the mountain lion?"

"Don't be ridiculous."

Dr. Suess unwrapped the wax paper around his pastry. "All right," he said testily, "so where does that leave us in for the hunting of wild animals?"

"Do you think that it's right?"

"Do I think what's right?"

"The hunting of animals?"

"I'm talking about *wild* animals."

"Wild is a label we give them. Why call them that just because they're in their natural state and haven't been rounded up and held captive by us instead of letting them run in freedom?"

"Freedom?" Dr. Suess looked at her with incredulity. "You think they have any concept of freedom? It's strictly a human aspiration that we've projected onto whatever mentality they may have. This 'freedom' you so fondly talk about is a razor-edged struggle for survival. When that antelope wakes up in the morning, he knows that in order to see the sunset, he has to outrun the fastest mountain lion. Conversely, the mountain lion woke this morning with sharp hunger pangs in her stomach and knows that if she doesn't catch the slowest or the weakest antelope, she will go to sleep tonight hungrier than she was this morning."

"Did it ever occur to you," she countered, "that that tension occurs when humans and urbanization encroach on their habitat?"

So what do you suggest; that we commit mass suicide?

No, he reflected. *I won't even go there. I'll stay on message.*

"Now, suppose we capture a wild animal," he continued, "keep it penned, but feed it regularly. Do you think it misses its freedom? No way. Freedom is a notion lost on animals. Hunger isn't."

Unnoticed by him, her expression darkened. "I still think there's something beautiful; something noble about an animal running wild and free. Don't you think that animals have sensibilities and feelings too?"

He shrugged. "Who knows?"

A pause.

"Regardless," he continued. "You ask 'do I think it's right?' Hell, yes, I think it's right. If our original hunter-gather ancestor of fifty to a hundred millennia ago hadn't killed them for food, clothing, and shelter, our species never would have survived."

"But now that we have become more advanced and civilized, don't you think we're capable of better than that?"

Dr. Suess paused and gave a disgusted sigh. For a moment he looked out the front window. The steam and vapor that clouded the view to the street outside had gotten thicker. Outside the sun had risen high enough into the sky to shed its golden light over the entire main street. However, vapor from nearby chimneys still hung in layers indicating the day to be cold.

Very cold.

He turned again to the spectacled young woman in the booth opposite him. "Regarding our being more advanced and civilized than our ancestors of fifty to a hundred thousand years ago, first of all—I debate that. Secondly, if it was morally okay for them to do it to survive, why is it not okay today? What the hell's changed?"

His booth companion shook her head. "But don't you feel the least bit of remorse, stalking and shooting those poor, innocent little fawns? How can you just simply walk up to one those sweet little creatures, look into those big, brown eyes, and pull the trigger?"

Dr. Suess wadded a napkin and flung it down on the table. "We don't stalk and kill baby fawns, dammit," he hissed between his teeth. "We go after the bucks—those big, dangerous adult males."

He took another sip of coffee. "You know," he said, eyeing her sharply. "Males? Adult sexist, chauvinist males? Only this time they're of a non-human species? Aren't they still the enemy?"

The lines around her mouth grew tense. "You know what I mean. Stop being a smart ass."

"I'm serious," protested Dr. Suess. "First of all, there's only one alpha male to mate with an entire herd of females. If he can outfight his rivals, they're shit out of luck. They become roving bachelors; beta males, if you will. If we hunters don't get them the mountain lions will."

He laid down his coffee cup and leaned back. A smile of complacency crossed his features. "In those cases what do your people plan on doing? As I suggested before, talk things over with the mountain lions?"

He did not notice the narrowing of her eyes. "Look," he said, "suppose there were no carnivores; only herbivores. We'd soon have an overabundance of animal life and our planet would be denuded of plant life. We need carnivores to keep the balance of nature."

Tense lines formed around her mouth

"After all," he said, "did you ever hear of the food chain?"

She heaved a sigh of disgust. "Yes I've heard of the food chain."

Dr. Suess shrugged. "Well then, how do we deal with carnivores devouring herbivores?"

"We don't interfere with nature."

"Aren't we nature?"

"We're different."

"Oh? In what way?"

She wadded her napkin tightly. "I can't believe this conversation," she said. "We are rational creatures. We are moral beings. We're supposed to know better."

"Are you saying that we're acting against our moral principles?"

"Whatever."

"Sounds suspiciously like you believe in Original Sin."

She threw down her doughnut. "That does it," she said, standing up. "I've had about all I want of this conversation."

Stunned, he looked up. In desperation he reached across the table and grabbed her wrist.

"Wait," he said.

She tugged against his grip. "Let me go," she demanded.

"Hey, come on," he begged. "I'm sorry. Please don't go."

She tried to pull away from him but his hold on her stayed firm.

"I—I have something else I want to talk over with you," he said, "I think it's pretty important."

She found herself strangely bothered by the contrast between his muscular grip and the pleading look in his eyes.

Her own eyes took on the look of a trapped animal. Her mouth quivered, but she sat down. She continued rubbing her wrist.

"Okay," she finally said in a husky voice. "Now what?"

He continued studying her.

"When I saw you this morning, I'll confess I hated your guts," he said. "However, I don't think myself as a vindictive person. It's hard for me stay mad for very long."

He again paused, and then went on.

"I'm going to level with you," he said, searching her face for any reaction. "Since my wife died, I've been a lonely man."

A lonely man? She realized that she hadn't been thinking much about his feelings.

Alpha male? *Yes,* she realized. *He's the alpha male.*

She reflected on the beta males in her life; the pallid, effete males in her field of education; the foppish dandies in her social circle.

She thought of the one that she married and divorced years ago when he no longer had use for her. Again she looked at Dr. Suess.

Him lonely? She thought. *Good god, what does he know of lonely?*

And yet? What was this strange animal magnetism emanating from him that had sent her pulse racing? How *many alpha males are there*, she thought. *How many chances do I have for one in my life? How many times does the likes of me get to know one?*

"I'm really sticking my neck out," she heard him say.

Again he stopped.

He shook his head thoughtfully. "Like I said, I'm really not angry any more. In fact I am frankly more than casually interested in you."

Her pulse quickened. His words were obviously not coming easy.

"More coffee?"

The waitress in a pink dress and white apron again appeared with two pots of coffee; one regular, one decaf.

Damn. He felt the momentum of the conversation broken.

He held his hand over his cup. "None for me thanks."

His eyes followed the female figure walking away. With a sigh his attention again reverted to his booth mate. Back to square one. How could he psych himself up to getting the back on track?

They heard ringing from the register up by the front door, followed by a tinkling as another customer left.

He took a breath.

"If you feel I'm out of line here, please forgive," he said. "I also realize there may be some big differences between us. Still, I can't help wondering that somehow, if we give ourselves a chance, that maybe we can find that we could be pretty darned compatible.

"All I'm suggesting initially is the privilege of seeing you occasionally. Nothing special: say, going to a restaurant, a theater, a concert, or sporting event. After all, Denver's not all that far away. We could reserve the right for either one of us if we see that it isn't working, to just break it off. If you're the one to decide this, for instance, I'd be disappointed of course but hey, I'm a big boy. I think I could handle it.

"In the meantime, I would just like us to explore the possibilities of where it would all go. If it leads to something more substantial, fine. If not, what the heck; chalk it up to experience?"

He paused. She continued to say nothing.

Quiet seemed to spread throughout the diner. He looked around at the other booths. Was everybody out there eavesdropping?

He took a breath. "I realize," he said, again picking up the thread of conversation, "that I've been doing all the talking. I'm sure you must have some thoughts on the matter."

For a long time she continued to say nothing.

Feeling perspiration under his shirt, he tried to appear calm. *Keep your mouth shut,* he chided himself. *The ball's in her court. As they in sales, after the big question, the first person that talks loses.*

Apparently the eavesdroppers had lost interest. They resumed their chatter and laughter. Lively repartee surrounded the front register.

At last she too, took a deep breath.

"Okay."

Chapter 3

...Marie still continued studying him as he stretched out in his recliner. "Was it something in the physics lab?"

She didn't know quite what to make of his answer: "That too."

She searched his face for clues. *He's so damned clever at covering up*, she thought.

"It *is* something," she said finally.

He sighed and moved his recliner into upright position. "You might as well know," he said, "I was in to see the dean today."

"And?"

Dr. Suess reached for a nearby stand. He picked a pipe from a rack and scooped into a humidor. He tamped the tobacco down into the bowl and scratched a wooden safety match.

"I was in just long enough to make an appointment," he said, puffing vigorously. "It confirms what I've known all along."

Marie eyed him quizzically.

He looked off into space. "Put it this way," he said. "When you first meet him, you don't like him; once you get to know him, you hate guts." Marie glanced at her pile of papers. *I should finish correcting these*, she thought. *But I'm not going to.* She pushed the chair back and stood up.

"I defy anybody," he continued, "to hold a conversation with him for five minutes without getting into an argument."

"I'm going to bed," she announced. She picked sheaf of papers and threw them back down. "I say the hell with all these."

He studied her briefly. What heavy emotional baggage lay behind that remark? This he had little trouble guessing. If he was getting increasingly frequent garbage from unmotivated college students, what must it be like on the high school level?

Dr. Suess stood to his feet and caught her in the doorway. "Night, love," he said, kissing her briefly. "I'll be up shortly."

He heard the steps under the carpet runner creak under the weight of her feet as she mounted the stairs. He listened to her heading for the back bedroom, then again settled back into his recliner. He continued taking long, slow puffs on his pipe.

Time for reminiscing, he thought…

…Time was when Sheila was still living.

His own children were still at home. *Seems like a whole other life now*, he thought; *a whole other world.* Two children, grown and away from home: one on the west coast and the other on the east.

About as far away as they can get.

There was no serious quarrel or estrangement. Their lives just got too busy with their own things; things like careers, spouses, a circle of friends that were total strangers to him, and children of their own. And he, the world's most neglectful of letter writers also had another life of his own. He had his classes. He had his research. He had his faculty friends. He had those Friday night poker games every payday.

There was also his increased drinking.

And then there was Marie and her children.

He recalled when his first family—Sheila and his natural born children—were still with him. He recalled how his son got expelled from school during his junior year.

He had been expelled for fighting.

Something about protecting a fellow student from bullying jocks.

The youth was delicate and aloof. Almost to the point of being invisible. His dark hair always seemed immaculately barbered with never a hair out of place. His pale gray eyes had dreamy look as if he saw a world no one else saw and was oblivious to the real world of the rest of the race. His silhouette stood slim and willowy to the point of near transparency.

Gilbert Wilkins walked with a tentative and deliberate stride and with a grace that would make most girls envious. His pale, slender hands seemed unsuited for any kind of hard manual labor, incapable of only the most delicate of tasks.

Like practicing surgery.

Or dentistry.

Or playing a musical instrument.

He was, in fact an excellent musician. In addition to being principal cellist in the high school orchestra all of his four years, he also played in the college and community orchestra.

Academically, he established a record of unprecedented brilliance with a straight 'A' average.

Being extremely shy and introverted, he seldom spoke. When he did his voice sounded soft and high pitched.

He tried to fit in with his peers by his clothing, but his jeans, instead of worn and frayed, were always new looking and neatly pressed.

Certain cliques among the male student body did their best to make life miserable for him. There were the 'greasers' with well slicked hair and black studded leather who were perpetually within an ace of either dropping out of or being expelled from school. There were the 'frats'—sons of prominent business and professional families and who held office in most of the student organizations and were considered generally the 'big men on campus.' Finally there were the jocks—varsity lettermen.

With their combined efforts, they saw to it that his merely walking the halls between classes was like walking a gauntlet with their cat calls, obscene remarks, and their pushing and tripping.

They devised dozens of ways of making life for him, at school, a veritable purgatory.

One day as Dr. Suess' son approached the youth from behind, the starting quarterback passed him and slammed the youth against the locker as he threw a clipping block into the back of the youth's legs, knocking him to the floor.

As the youth remained, dazed and bleeding, on his hands and knees the assailant quickly moved around to the front and unzipped his pants.

"Give you five if you do it right here," he shouted above the laughter of the gathering crowd of students.

"I'll give you five," said Dr. Suess' son.

So saying, he drove his fist into the assailant's mouth.

With two students now dazed and bleeding and on the floor, a male teacher grabbed Dr. Suess' son by the collar and hustled him off to the principal's office. The next seventy-two hours were characterized by a series of conferences: principal-student conferences; principal, teacher—student conferences; principal, teacher, counselor—and student conferences; and finally principal—student and parent conferences.

The story of what really happened was finally sifted through all the versions—each antagonist, victim, student witness and teacher had their own story. The upshot was that Dr. Suess' son was given indefinite suspension.

"Don't worry about it, son," said Dr. Suess. "I'm proud of you."

His son shrugged. "I know, dad, but what's going to happen when I go back? Now the guys are all accusing me of being a fag too."

"Don't worry about it," said Dr. Suess again. "I'll enroll you into St. Swithin's Academy over in Gunnison."...

...By the time he had finished smoking his last pipe bowl down to the ash, the hour had gotten quite late. He would steal off to bed and try not to awaken Marie. He himself could use a good night's sleep in preparation for tomorrow's meeting with the dean.

* * *

As Dr. Suess entered the dean's office, he surveyed a large, paneled room. Heavy velvet curtains framed the windows. His feet sank deep into the luxurious carpeting before stepping onto the plastic runner that led to an oversized mahogany desk. He continued to stand as he studied a male figure seated across from him. As the occupant sat with his back toward him, he appeared to be reading a periodical.

Atop the glass desk top sat a brass plate bearing the name: 'J. Negley Jone, Ph.D.'

J., of course, stood for the first name, 'Jaked.' From the day the dean first arrived at Stillwell, Dr. Suess thought the name odd. 'Jaked' he had reflected; rhymes with 'naked.' In conversations with those who knew the man from his youth, Dr. Suess wondered why he didn't go by such nicknames as 'Jake' or even 'Jack.' Must have been a family name, they concluded. He evidently considered it to have had enough snob appeal that he was willing bear the taunts of his peers.

In any event, the name was commonly known among the current student body. It also had become the source of dozens of obscene jokes around campus.

Dr. Suess waited. He studiously avoided calling his superior by name because the very sound bothered him, rather like the tenacity of an irritating little ditty.

On the wall facing the seated occupant hung an oil painting the size of a sidewalk slab. The figure was of a man assuming a Brahmin like pose. He held his head in a self consciously lofty expression. His right arm leaned against the back of a richly upholstered chair that was pulled up to a glass topped conference table.

After long moments, the occupant whirled around. Dr. Suess faced a large man in a double-breasted pinstripe. A pink carnation graced one of the lapels. The figure appeared broader in the middle than at the shoulders. Auburn, wavy locks lay carefully draped in a comb-over. He parted his hair a mere inch above his right ear. Large, languid eyes looked out at him from beneath bushy eyebrows that arched on a high forehead. A patrician nose balanced the small lenses of rimless spectacles. Heavy, sensuous lips broke into a benign smile. A dimpled, pock marked chin accentuated massive jowls that bore a perpetual five o'clock shadow.

"Yes?" The voice resonated deep, but disarmingly gentle.

"I have an appointment," said Dr. Suess.

The dean stood up, towering over the scientist even more. Without giving answer, he stepped to a nearby liquor cabinet and opened a glass door.

"Scotch is your favorite as I recall," he said without turning his head. He reached for a heavily ornate decanter half full with an amber colored liquid. He poured the liquid into two tumblers and returned to the desk. He handed one to the scientist and he again settled back into his swivel chair.

So much for the no liquor rule on campus, thought Dr. Suess.

The dean held out his glass. "To the erudite life."

He took a sip, apparently unconcerned whether or not Dr. Suess joined him in the toast.

"So," he said, setting the tumbler on his desk, "how's the family?"

"Fine, thank you."

Dr. Suess finally took a sip from his drink.

The dean laid folded hands on his desk. For a moment he seemed content to say nothing. "Marie is happy in her new assignment?" he said at last.

"Yes, she is thank you."

A lie. She hates it. However he was not about to volunteer this to the dean.

Another pause.

"And the children; are they doing well at school?"

"Quite well, thank you."

The dean turned sideways in his chair and looked thoughtfully off into space. "Good." His mellifluous voice stretched the word out deliciously.

He swung the chair around, again facing Dr. Suess. "Adjustment to a new family situation is critical where children are involved; especially when they're adolescents."

"I agree."

The silence lengthened. *Doesn't look like we're going to get to the point unless I bring it up*, thought Dr. Suess. "Yesterday I was in the student records office."

"And?"

"I found several transcripts where my student's grades had been altered."

Again, silence hung in the office.

Dr. Suess eyed the dean. "What's going on?" *Isn't grade tampering a felony*, he asked himself?

The dean leaned back in his chair and steepled his fingertips. Again he paused and looked off into the far recesses of his office thoughtfully.

"Isolated incidents, I assure you," he said, staring at the ceiling.

Dr. Suess could feel the back of his neck getting red. "Why even isolated incidents?"

The dean continued sitting back. "Well," he said, laughing briefly. "It was deemed the prudent thing to do."

He leaned forward, whirled around, and leaned his arms across his desktop. "Actually," he said, leveling a gaze at Dr. Suess, "as I see it, once you have entered your grades into the students' master files, that's as far as you need legitimately concern yourself."

Dr. Suess struggled with an inner turmoil. *What the hell kind of professionalism is this*, he thought. "What about intellectual honesty? What about academic integrity?"

The dean again leaned back in his chair. "Good points, actually. Don't think I haven't thought of that."

He once again shifted to a forward position. He again rested his elbows on a large desktop blotter and folded his hands. "Not to be construed as policy, I assure you," he said. "Consider them—shall we say—as anecdotal?"

Dr. Suess said nothing. *I'm not going to give you any peg to hang your hat on*, he thought.

The silence lengthened.

"Is there anything else?" the dean said finally.

Dr. Suess rose from his chair. "I think not," he said, backing away. "I think we've covered it. Thank you for your time."

"Quite all right," Dr. Suess had exited the office, the dean had again whirled around in his chair. Reaching toward a bookshelf, he picked up the academic journal and again began turning pages.

As Dr. Suess neared the door dark thoughts assailed his mind. *Should I or shouldn't I? It would be so easy. Just make a couple of phone calls, see a couple of people and the shit would really hit the fan.*

Nah, he thought with self loathing at the idea.

With a shrug, he left the ad building, his mind a seething cauldron and headed for the science building.

Maybe I'll be with people with a semblance of sanity, he thought.

Five minutes later, he entered the physics lab to join Dr. Sirotka viewing the encrusted trident behind the thick glass. The purple light of the florescent bulbs lining the small chamber shed an unearthly glow. Needles on monitoring instruments darted crazily.

On the marble table top Dr. Sirotka had spread a long sheet of graph paper covered with wiggly markings.

"Those people at the cryptology lab are something else," he remarked as Dr. Suess entered. "I don't know how they do it."

He pulled a printout from an attaché case that lay beside the graph.

Waves of the Devonian Sea rolled gently against mounds of white sand and rustling blades of razor-sharp beach grass. The sea itself appeared less like a mighty ocean than that of a giant, saline lake lying shallow and listless. Tideland marshes that bordered its shore extended far enough into the distance to where they almost reached the horizon. Although the Devonian tide moved a great distant inland, it did so only because of the flatness of the terrain. Were a (human) present to measure the tide's depths, they would find high tide to be only centimeters deep.

Wisps of smoke rose sluggishly above peaks of active volcanoes that dotted the horizon.

'Out across the waters, a great distance from shore, the head of an upright species broke the surface. Shortly, broad shoulders and upper body broke the surface as well. Oss'yanhu used his trident to steady himself as he continued wading landward. The soaked linen of his tunic clung to his body, accentuating the muscular contours as the water dripped in rivulets. During the long trek inland, the gentle sea breeze and warmth of the sunshine rippled the hem of his robe. By the time he reached the forested shoreline, however, the garment had completely dried.

'As if by instinct, he walked among the hardwoods until he reached ferns and giant prickly palms. The forest seemed to open its impenetrable undergrowth before him

Just as quickly it seemed to swallow up the trail behind him. Sounds of bird, insect, and animal life that engulf a modern tropical rain forest in a deafening chorus here were noticeably absent. Mesozoic life forms tended to be large and sluggish and not given to as much noise making as were their distant counterparts. An (apteryx—early ancestor of the modern bird)—flapped an ungainly flight through the leafy treetops.

'A (stegosaurus) lumbered through the dense undergrowth, browsing from the tender shoots as it went. It paused from eating just long enough to eye with such curiosity as its tiny brain could register at Oss'yanhu walking by. As soon as the broad leaves of the

undergrowth closed in behind him, the behemoth seemed to have quite forgotten about the foreign intruder and resumed its eating.

By the time the sun had risen to a high noon, Oss'yanhu had trudged deep enough into the forest to where its character changed. The ground seemed drier and of higher elevation. Ferns and palm trees yielded to a predominance of coniferous saplings and towering hardwoods. Pine seedlings replaced rotting broadleaf mulch and mosses as carpeting for the forest floor. He stopped before a brush arbor that arched between two giant cypress trunks. An adolescent female upright whose nut brown locks were wreathed in a laurel branch greeted him. Her filmy silken gown flowed away from white thighs in the mild breeze as she clasped her hands in a gesture of obeisance.

He glanced down at her. "Is my mother in?"

She stepped aside to usher him through the arbor. "She awaits your arrival."

He followed the direction to which she pointed. He saw a footpath leading off in the distance between two tall stands of ferns. Oss'yanhu followed the driad, or wood nymph, for an indeterminate length of time. At last they reached a clearing. In the middle arose a low mound bearing a gigantic throne made from a naturally formed tree trunk. Upon it sat a tall female of regal bearing.

She extended her arm. A forefinger bore a ring signet the size of an olive. With it she beckoned him to draw near.

As he approached, she rose to meet him.

Her ebony hair was parted in the middle. Two wavy strands, banded in gold at the shoulders, fell to her waist. A bejeweled crown of white gold set atop a high forehead. Thin, well-shaped eyebrows framed eyes of deepest indigo. Lips red as rubies smiled as he approached. Despite a marked maturity in her mien and demeanor, her face showed no sign of aging. A silken stole of gold sheen draped across the shoulders nearly to her feet. A wide golden belt held her deep green robe at the waist. Emerald and gold colored sandals shod her feet. Her right hand held a carved hardwood scepter with a fist-sized pearl at its tip.

He stepped toward the throne and reached out to the scepter. "You sent for me?"

She placed the scepter on the ground beside the throne and walked down the small knoll toward him. When a mere pace away she stopped.

"Let us not stand on ceremony," she said taking his hands in hers.

She turned her cheek to receive his kiss.

They embraced briefly. "It has been entirely too long," she said.

He stepped back a pace. "It's good to see you, mother."

She started walking away and gestured for him to join her. He fell in stride beside her until they reached a kind of park or arboretum. Plants blooming with orchids, rhododendrons, and other exotic looking blossoms flourished in abundance.

"Collecting quite a variety, I see," said Oss'yanhu.

"I mean to eventually have every species of plant that grows on the planet represented here."

Oss'yanhu surveyed the garden area. "It's really quite impressive," he said. "How long have you been at it?"

"How long indeed?" She shook her head. "Eons if a day. Preserving the planet and all the species of fauna and flora has been my mission from the first. I, for one, take my mission seriously."

He detected an edge of resentment in her last statement. Misgivings rose mutely within him as he sought to let the matter drop.

He pointed to a large, purple blossom that hung nearby. "What a beautiful specimen," he said, changing the subject.

"It's doing nicely. We've been working a long time on that one."

They stopped beside an oblong granite slab suspended between two rocks forming a kind of bench. She gestured for them to sit. As they settled on the bench, she seemed content for the moment to sit in silence.

Finally she spoke. "We need to talk."

He looked curious.

Not without a little apprehension, he waited.

"Things are not well here," she continued. "Nor have they been for some time."

He knew that. After all, his mother had long since ceased living with his father. For millennia now she had insisted on staying in her tropical garden home and had steadfastly refused to join the others in Sh'yan-Grl', Y'rannhu's palace atop the summit of the mountain on the side of the North.

He searched his thoughts for something to report to her. "Father accuses K'hronhu of dalliance."

"And well he might," she said with disgust. "He probably taught him all he knew."

Oss'yanhu said nothing. Disturbing thoughts assailed his mind. Had his own frolicking also been discovered?

That his father was far from the ideal husband was nothing new to him.

"'As beings that are supposed to be god-like,'" his mother continued, "'we leave much to be desired.'"

'The conversation fell to another silence. She turned to him. "When was the last time your father offered up any sacrifice of worship to the Strong-Ones?"

'Oss'yanhu couldn't remember.

'She went on to give him a history of their race. Generations past both she and Y'rranhu were as one of the myriad of blessed spirits of the celestial realms. Silent, unseen, they flew on flights the speed of thought to the far reaches of a universe of untold dimensions at the Peerless One's slightest behest. They had different names then: Y'rranhu was known as Lord Light-Bearer and G'ya was known as Yd'th.

"'We were not as yet husband and wife,'" she told him. "We were as the other blessed spirits. Biological differences as male and female was a concept as yet unknown and became a factor in terrestrial life only. The erotic intensity in a moment of orgasmic passion while mating was merely a fleeting physical counterpart to the intensity of bliss the blessed spirits experience permanently in a non-physical way while in the presence of the great Am. Lord Light-Bearer, already holder of many special honors and recognitions was bestowed yet another.

"'He had been appointed court director of the celestial choirs. He proved himself to be gifted and talented beyond measure. As reward for outstanding efforts in this capacity, he was awarded yet further honor.

"'To him was given the responsibility of overseeing the development of the new planet of marbled blue and white. This orb had been designated as it were to be the cosmic conservatory. He now had been given the responsibility of overseeing the development of plant and animal life.

"'Of course, he wasn't expected to have to do this alone. Strong-Ones appointed me, Yd'th, to be his helper.'"

'As they occupied their terrestrial home, Strong-Ones granted them the ability to assume terrestrial bodies that would be more compatible with their new abode. Among the new powers he granted them was the power to reproduce others of their kind as he did other species of animal life. However, they were creatures much more complex and the relationships would be much more finely tuned and delicate than the lower orders. As new entities, also, they had assumed divisions similar to lower orders into male and female. Light-Bearer as Lord Y'rranhu, ruler of the firmament, had become male. Yd'th became G'ya possessor of god-like power over the earth and all things growing became female.

THE TITANS

'They were given charge to love, mate, and be fruitful and to multiply. Their offspring were given to them as helpers in the overwhelming task of managing this entire world and its firmament.

'They also were bonded in a pledge of fidelity to one another. Thus was the origin of Oss'yanhu and all his siblings.

'To Oss'yanhu was given charge of waters that covered the earth. K'hronhu, his twin brother, was given charge of time: its passage, and all the changes that it brings. Hy'perion and Kh'aos, another set of twin brothers kept the sun and earth in proper relationship with one another, and the moon and stars respectively and all the nocturnal forms of plant and animal life. The fleeting elusiveness of thought became the ledger main of K'hronhu's sister, R'ya. These and many other children—all equally gifted, equally empowered—endowed with beauty, grace, and other god-like qualities were also born to Father Y'rranhu and Mother G'ya. All seemed to fit delightfully in every perfect detail as part of a divinely ordained plan for the development of this planet except for one little problem.

'Y'rranhu, once having assumed the body of terrestrial flesh and having tasted the delights of biological mating showed not the slightest interest in honoring his marriage vows of fidelity. He began sporting with his own daughters as soon as they reached any semblance of physical maturity. They then became heavy with child and then he, in turn, also became profligate with his granddaughters as well. In all these, he showed the faithfulness of a cuttlefish. Thus began the introduction of much confusion and troubled times in a hitherto world of peace and harmony.

'Oss'yanhu further complicated things with his fling with the wood nymph that idyllic afternoon when their frolic was seen in the crystal ball by R'ya and Thya. In due time the poor damsel gave birth to the first of R'ya's misbegotten.

'The nymph's child came forth an undersized specimen of monstrosity with one leg.

'G-ya, out of pity for this little one grotesquely unique among a previously splendid race of beautiful demigods, took special pains to endow this cursed little freak with untold intelligence and cunning outstanding even among the T'tanyu

'She dubbed the little one Eikendom.

'Succeeding generations then produced all manner of mutants who owed neither love nor fealty to any intelligences or beings celestial or terrestrial. In defiance, they engineered and monitored the development of all manner of species of plant and animal life that were deviant to the original plan and were under the control of neither Y'rranhu nor G'ya, nor yet to the celestial Designer of all things. Worse, their behavior and activities threatened the very existence of the rightful and legitimate orders.

'For all his position and wise ways, Y'rranhu seemed to labor under the delusion that he could keep all this from the eyes of the All-Seeing-One.

"He of all beings," sighed G'ya, "should know that from Am nothing is hidden."

'Oss'yanhu looked puzzled. "But how could he so delude himself."

'G'ya shrugged. "Pride," she said. "It makes fools of all who fall under its spell."

'G'ya replied that originally Y'rranhu, as Light-Bearer, was to have reported back to the celestial realms regularly to give an accounting of his terrestrial works and to receive additional instructions from the All-Wise-One. However, for untold millennia he has been delinquently negligent of this. One result of this dereliction to duty is that he himself had forgotten the Peerless One's awful power and attributes.

'G'ya stood up and began walking along the path further past a grove of giant bamboo.

"'I have purposely stayed away from your father's palace," she said, fondling one of the bamboo's needle-like leaves.

'Again Oss'yanhu followed alongside. "But why? Might you not have exerted a moral influence on him? Could you not have been his conscience as it were?"

'G'ya paused and faced her son. She placed both her hands on his broad shoulders. The sun's rays filtered long and golden through the trees and foliage. Giant butterflies made their last foray into the floral underbrush for nectar before roosting for the night. Perfume of a hundred varieties of flowers spiced the evening air.

"'Ages past, I tried that." She looked sadly into her son's eyes. "But now, I'm afraid he has since become downright incorrigible."'...

...Dr. Sirotka pulled out another sheaf of printout. "Here's something else," he said. "It contains footnotes from the editors and cryptologists themselves. It's very interesting."...

... 'Could we be running into a situation with this ancient race of super beings?

'Take for example young children from birth to 5 years. We never learn as much, as fast, or master such basic abilities as speech, walking, word and color recognition, toilet training, motor skills, and conceptual and cognitive skills as we do during this short but most formative period of our lives.

'Were we able to continue to learn as much and as fast; were we able to absorb as much for the rest of our lives we would all become geniuses of such proportion so as to make our current meaning of that word obsolete.

'Are we here observing a history of a people that learned at just exactly that kind of pace? Did they perpetually maintain an attitude of inquisitiveness as that of a modern three year old? And how long did they live? Perhaps millennia? Are we at last observing the history of a genuinely superhuman race?...'

* * *

...Autumn coloration had already tinged the leaves that provided a shady arbor to Stillwell's campus. Dr. Suess, finishing his last morning class, headed for the administration building that also housed the campus post office. He mounted stone steps rounded with age and noticed an autumnal nip in the air. Fall comes early to the Colorado Rockies.

Reaching into his mailbox, he pulled out an envelope bearing the letterhead of the Campus Human Relations Committee. Alarmed, he tore open the envelope. As he walked back across the campus, he looked to see if he walked alone. Then he tore open the letter.

The committee had cited him for a breach of the new Campus Code of Human Relations.

He knew the incident they had referred to. He recalled during the second day of Geology Lab.

He had long been an aficionado of the comic strip 'Li'l Abner.' He often would spice up interest in his class discussions with allusions to the strip's characters such as Mammy and Pappy Yocum, Daisy May, and, of course, such characters as Hairless Joe, Lonesome Polecat, Earthquake McGoon, and Evil Eye Fleegle.

Although the strip had long become defunct before the current class of students had ever reached the age of reading readiness, he introduced them to Al Capp's world of Dogpatch, U.S.A. by pinning well-preserved prints of the strip's laminated copies on his bulletin board. He recalled putting one panel showing Hairless Joe and another showing Li'l Abner and Daisy Mae.

According to the letter, a student had complained that the caricatures were insensitive. Lonesome Polecat demeaned Native Americans, Hairless Joe demeaned the homeless, and, of course, Daisy May demeaned women

This despite the fact that Dr. Suess had always explained to his students that that was the whole object of the strip. Al Capp was a master satirist. Dogpatch, U.S.A. was not just an impoverished community in southern Appalachia. It was Anytown, U.S.A. The family name 'Yocum' was actually 'McCoy' spelled backwards phonetically. Li'l Abner himself was not just an incredibly stupid lout in his late teens—a product of an extremely benighted milieu. His family and friends (and even his enemies) were not merely members of a parochial sub-group of retards. Li'l Abner was everyman. The other characters were from anywhere, U.S.A.

Al Capp did not discriminate. He demeaned everybody equally.

In the letter, the Human Relations Committee had enjoined Dr. Suess from mounting any more comic strip panels on his bulletin board.

He quickly stuffed the letter inside his blazer and headed for the dean's office.

He knocked.

"Entres," sang out a voice from the other side of the door. Dr. Suess entered and found the dean sitting in his customary manner: with the wing back of the chair facing him and the dean leaning back, facing the wall bookshelf and reading a journal.

Dr. Suess seated himself in the chair across from the desk and waited. Again, the patrician face of the dean's portrait gazed down at him with the same expression of benign hauteur.

As seconds ticked by, his sense of irritation mounted.

He tactfully cleared his throat.

Still no change in the dean's position. At length, the dean slowly turned around, faced Dr. Suess and smiled.

"Henry." His words had a low, drawn-out tone. "How long have you been with us?"

"Thirty years." He felt his forehead start to break out in prickly heat. "Why do you ask?"

The dean steepled his hands and glanced toward the ceiling. "A most impressive tenure, I must say."

Dr. Suess waited.

"Tell me," the dean went on, "have you been happy here?"

Dr. Suess sighed briefly. "Well," he said, "one would be foolish to stay that long and not be, wouldn't you agree?"

The dean didn't answer. Dr. Suess clenched his fists as they rested in his lap. "Do you mind if we get to the point?" he said. "I have a class."

The dean sighed and reached into a side drawer. He held up a magazine published by an organization known as the YOUNG EARTH SOCIETY. "Did you know that you have been quoted in this publication?" he asked.

"No, not really."

The dean placed before Dr. Suess a page open to an article alleging that the age of dinosaurs coincided with the age of man. To substantiate their contention they quoted a report written by Dr. Suess when he discovered the footprint of a Triceratops in the rock sedimentary bank of a primordial stream. Not fifty feet away from it in the same stratum was imprinted a human looking footprint.

The dean eyed Dr. Suess. "Henry, don't tell me you are going to side in with these people?"

"Does that article also point out," Dr. Suess said with a sigh of boredom, "that the footprint had six toes and was evidently made by someone over nine feet tall?"

Chapter 4

Three days after his last visit to the dean's office, Dr. Suess stood in the doorway of the science hall. He looked at the letter in his hand and then out across the campus. He shook his head. After a brief pause he started toward the ad building.

Two minutes later he again found himself seated in the dean's office.

Without saying anything, he placed the letter on the desk in front of the dean. The portrait from the wall behind him loomed larger than life as he bent over the letter. It was hard to determine which look was the most overbearing; the subject in the picture or the man himself seated on the other side of the desk.

The dean studied the letter a moment. Then he laid it down again and looked at Dr. Suess.

This time, he wasn't smiling.

"Apparently you've offended some student's sensibilities."

"What does that supposed to mean?"

Dr. Suess, while fighting inner turmoil, fixed a steady gaze at the dean. In all his dealings with the man, he tried to avoid addressing him by name. He long knew that the dean had the 's' dropped from his name. 'Jones' just simply sounded too plebian.

"Oh, come, come, monseur," he heard the dean saying. "We both know what this is all about."

"But I've been posting those comic strips on my bulletin boards for years, even decades."

The dean leaned back and steepled his fingertips. "I know."

"You've always wanted your teachers to be innovative," Dr. Suess added. "You yourself have consistently wanted us to try novel approaches in presenting our subject matter to heighten student interest."

"I know."

With the laminated strips in question, Dr. Suess had done just that. Over the years he had devised ways of incorporating the antics of Dogpatch citizens into the presentation of his geology lectures. The lighter touch paid off. Despite the perceived dryness of the subject to many a young college student, his freshman geology class remained a perennial favorite for those fulfilling their science requirement.

The dean leaned back in his chair, smiling a tight smile. "I realize that your little innovative teaching techniques have helped to amuse many of your students," he said.

Dr. Suess continued to eye him. He recalled a commencement a few years back…

…The senior class that year had wanted to initiate an annual teacher of the year award. Since the dean had neither approved nor disapproved of the idea, the class officers went ahead and took donations from their classmates and had a plaque made.

Dr. Suess was the intended recipient of the award.

They gave it to the dean to present during the commencement ceremonies. When he made no such presentation, the class officers questioned him about it afterward. He then assured them that it was purely an oversight.

Later that day he called Dr. Suess into his office. There, in the privacy of his office he made the presentation…

… "Tell you what," said the dean after a pause. "I'm sure all this will blow over. In the interim, why don't you just sort of—well—go along with it?"

Again, Dr. Suess cast him a hard glance. *It would so easy*, he thought. *Just blow the whistle; if 'Babs' were to find out, this guy is in a world of doo-doo.* "What do you mean?"

The dean leaned forward in his chair. Again the smile vanished. "Take down those comic strips, Henry."

* * *

"Do you know why I summoned you?"

Y'rranhu, seated in his chair, fixed a hard gaze at Oss'yanhu. The eyes changed color from a languid brown to an agitated green. Their pupils narrowed.

'Oss'yanhu avoided his father's withering stare. He surveyed the alabaster walls of the apartment. Torches fastened to brackets in the wall, banished the night's darkness.

'He studied the ornate hardwood furniture: the backless chairs, the settee, the table with the marble top, and—over in one corner—the bed covered with colored linen sheets, bordered with tall ebony posts and topped with a frilly canopy.

'I haven't seen you in many days, my son," said Y'rranhu in a voice disarmingly gentle. "I've missed you."

"'I have just come from an extended visit with mother," said Oss'yanhu in a subdued tone.

"Really?" said Y'rranhu with a portentous edge to his voice.

"'Surely you don't object to my visiting mother?"

"'Of course not," said Y'rranhu in a half-hearted attempt to sound reassuring. His eye sockets clouded to a milky white to conceal his emotional state.

"'However," his voice again took on a hard edge. "You weren't at the last banquet in Sh'yan-Grl's hall. Your failure to show was a disappointment."

'Oss'yanhu fumbled for words. "It won't happen again, father. I assure you."

Y'rranhu leaned back and steepled his fingertips. "I know it won't," he said, forcing a laugh. "It was a just little social get together. Nothing of importance was discussed."

'He studied his son's continued discomfiture.

'He finally gave Oss'yanhu a wave of dismissal. "Give my regards to your mother," he said with a hint of sarcasm.

'After Y'rranhu had dismissed Oss'yanhu from his private chambers, he arose from his chair and sat down on the small, ornate settee across the room. He rested his chin on folded hands and looked darkly off into space. The night sky, framed by marbled pillars in an expanse beyond the floor-to-ceiling window spread endlessly black. Gradually it turned from the color of slate to gray then a pale blue, to a pink, to a peach, and finally into the broad light of a new day. Even with the further passing of time during which the sun rose further in the heavens, he still did not move. Again, at nightfall, still he sat. Day followed night which in turn was followed by yet another day.

'In all this time, Y'rranhu took neither nourishment nor drink, nor yet even left his chair. His eyes evolved to a relaxed brown. His pupils widened in a relaxed state. Head resting on folded hands, he continued to stare it his marbled floor and brood.

'A fleeting breeze caused the embroidered drapes that bordered the opened windows to flutter briefly. At the far end of the chamber behind him suddenly appeared an adolescent female. A laurel wreath encircled the thick ebony locks of her head. More laurel adorned her wrists and ankles. A chain of purple blossoms gathered a gown of filmiest gossamer about the waist. Small, finely shaped hands held a tray laden with fruit, pastries and a flagon of wine.

"My lord," she said with a look of concern, "I beseech you, take your breakfast. You worry me."

'As he turned toward her, his face brightened. "Io," he sighed. "Bless you, dearest child. You are indeed a comfort."

'He gestured for her to approach him. The faint musk smell of lust that permeated the room frightened her. As she stood alongside him with the tray, he fondled her briefly. She quickly placed the tray on a low, nearby table and tried to distance herself. However he grabbed her and he pulled her onto his lap.

'She noticed his pupils widen. His eyes turned from a relaxed brown to an aroused hazel color.

"Would you like to make sport with me?" she whispered as he kissed her.

'He pushed her aside and stood up. "Not today," he said, shaking his head. "I want you to summon Tyra, my wise woman."

'She darted off with the speed of a humming bird. In a trice, she stood again in the chamber doorway, this time with an older looking female. The curly black locks cascaded down to the older female's waist, framing a face that looked beautiful despite the age lines creasing the forehead and the crow's feet about the eyes. A silver band with a crescent shaped mounting set on her forehead. She wore a light sleeveless gown of silken lavender. A finely stitched purse hung from a thin, silvery belt. In her right hand she held a silver wand.

"You summoned me," she said. "Why?"

'Y'rranhu rose to his feet. "Ah, Tyra," he said, beckoning her. "You look more beautiful than ever."

Ignoring his beckoning, she didn't move. "What's the matter?" she said with an edge to her voice. "Do you weary of taking liberties with children?"

Y'rranhu gave her a patronizing smile and folded his arms. Then he turned from facing her and glanced out the window. "You flatter yourself," he said. "It is not your body I crave. It is your wisdom."

"So you admit it?"

"Of course I admit it."

She stepped to the center of the room. "What is it you want to know?"

He turned to her again, this time looking serious. "I want to find out what is going on. It's as simple as that."

She moved to the small table. Pushing his breakfast tray aside, she produced from her purse a fine, gray powder and poured it into a small, porcelain dish. She stepped back and pressed the tip of her wand into the powder. Gray smoke began billowing up toward the ceiling.

Y'rranhu again sat down and watched with interest. "Can you tell me what's happening with G'ya, my dear wife?"

Why don't you try to visit her and find out for yourself? She thought. An attempt at reconciliation wouldn't hurt you a bit.

Tyra continued holding the wand to the powder without answering. Silhouetted forms began appearing in the smoke. Soon the smoke seemed to clear and the silhouettes formed a vision, a kind of holograph flashback as it were, above the table.

G'ya had just risen from her massive tree-stump throne. Oss'yanhu was coming up the path as she stepped down from her earthen dais to greet him. Their lips moved in an obvious exchange of words. G'ya turned her head and Oss'yanhu kissed her cheek. Then they embraced briefly. The vision faded as Oss'yanhu stepped away from his mother and grasped her shoulders.

Tyra withdrew her wand.

As the last wisps of smoke rolled ceilingward and disappeared, Tyra turned to Y'rranhu. "Did you see enough?"

He stood to his feet and slammed a fist into his other hand and he again turned to the wide doorway. He stepped through to stand on the small balcony beyond. His gaze swept the yawning expanse below.

His eyes turned red. His pupils shrunk to near nothingness. "I knew it," he fumed. "That treacherous, ungrateful stripling."

He turned back into the chamber and looked directly at the two females. The anger that boiled up within him elicited the smell of garlic.

"Oss'yanhu harbors incestuous lust toward his own mother."

The nymph and the wise woman stepped away from him. "I wouldn't be too hasty with that conclusion, my lord," said the wise woman with a tremor in her voice. "After all, the vision showed only normal, filial love between mother and son, nothing more. It showed nothing untoward."

So the old lecher is becoming insanely jealous, she thought. He sees his children's lives through his own lascivious prism.

Y'rranhu's eyes narrowed as he turned away. "I know their ways," he growled. "I understand them only too well."

Again he began pacing the floor. His eye sockets covered over with a red glow. "Oss'yanhu will pay," he added. "I'll see to it that he pays."

* * *

Tyra stood beside an oaken table in her dank, subterranean chamber.

Beside her stood a diminutive one legged figure dressed in a single ragged brontosaurus skin. He supported himself with a crudely improvised crutch.

"I detect grave mischief afoot on the upper world," he said in a hoarse voice.

Stalactites and stalagmites formed a labyrinth extending far into the yawning darkness. Through the cold, damp atmosphere a dripping sound of water droplets echoed through the hollow caverns as tiny streams ran off the nearby giant limestone formations and fell into a naturally formed pool. The little man watched as she held a clay mortar while simultaneously grinding a mysterious powder. A long narrow passageway up a rocky incline led to a crude, wooden door.

From behind it, Tyra heard a timid knock.

She waved him off. "Be off," she demanded. "I have company."

He gave her a pleading look and then turned reluctantly back into the deeper recesses of a dark passage.

Tyra turned toward the door. "Come in."

She looked up from her worktable as the massive door slowly swung open. Her mouth fell agape as she studied the figure in the doorway. Like a ribbon of death a putrid smell of sadness filtered through the cave's wet atmosphere. Io stood trembling, her midnight dark locks hung in disheveled strands across a smudged and tear-stained face. She held the torn strands that still remained of her gown across her bruised and naked body.

Tyra dropped her pestle, seized a robe of coarsely spun cotton, and ran to the girl. "My dear child," she gasped, flinging the robe around her. "Who did this?"

Io sobbed out the name: "Y'rranhu."

Tyra ushered the young girl down the rugged incline into her chamber. She led her over to a small couch and laid her in a semi reclining position. Here she covered the quivering nymph with another soft cotton robe. She took a handful of leaves and dipped them into a limestone pool. Tenderly she pressed them to the girl's bruised face while smoothing back her hair.

"You are safe now," she said. "Try to relax."

She took a clay pot from a rocky ledge near her table and filled it with water. From another clay jar she measured out powdered spices and teas. Aromatic smells permeated the cavern as she stirred the mixture. She placed the pot on a rock overhanging a small cooking fire. The exotic aroma of the tea became heavier as the water started bubbling. She took a long-handled ladle and poured tea into a clay mug. This she carried to the girl on the couch. Tyra stood beside the nymph while she drank the contents. When Io had emptied the mug, she handed it back to her benefactress.

"Try to get some sleep, my dear," said Tyra as she turned and headed for the table.

* * *

Y'rranhu tossed about on his milkweed-stuffed mattress and pushed the colored linen sheet away from his shoulder. He looked beyond his canopy-covered bed. Trying to fight the lingering night drowsiness, he blinked at the dawn's slanted rays that filtered into his chamber. As he thrashed his hands in a struggle to gain an upright position, he struck something soft, yet solid. He slid his hands over a mound of cotton fabric as he felt body contours.

During the night someone had crept into bed with him.

Indignant at this intrusion, he jumped to the floor and pulled back the sheet. Facing away from him lay a hooded figure in gray homespun. The pupils of his eyes widened. The eyes themselves flashed green in surprise.

"Io," he shouted. "What's the meaning of this?"

She blinked her eyes and looked at him with sadness. "Please don't send me away," she pleaded. "I have nowhere to go."

THE TITANS

"That is your problem."
"But you have humbled me."
"And what of that?" he snorted. "Give me one good reason why I should let you stay."
She eyed him fiercely. "Because I am with child—your child."
Y'rranhu stood to the center of the bedchamber a moment as if stunned. Then he walked slowly to the floor-to-ceiling windoway and sat in a low-backed chair. For a long time he continued to sit, head pensively resting against his fist as he studied her.
"Having my child, eh?" he said finally.
He stood up and began again pacing the floor, hands locked behind him.
He looked up. His eyes again flashed green with anticipation.
"This is beginning to present possibilities," he said. He stopped and walked over to her. He clasped her hands and gently pulled her to her feet.
"You are quite right," he said softly. "It would be wrong of me to send you away."
He paused, released her, and began for the third time to pace the floor. With one hand stroking his chin, he appeared in deep thought.
"Yes," he continued. "You will stay with me—always. I will set you up in your own apartment—adjacent to mine. You will neither go out from here nor leave this palace. You will be forever cloistered here. You will take knowledge of no other male. Whoever touches you, or so much as looks upon you with lust will plead to death for mercy."
He looked again out through the curtained doorway that led to the veranda and outdoors. His eyes turned brown and he appeared more relaxed.
"Through you, my precious, and through the fruit of your womb," he said, still gazing toward the expanse outside, "I will exact my revenge on the treacherous Oss'yanhu."

* * *

Dr. Sirotka scrutinized the graph chart of one of the transcripts.

Encased in glass, bathed in the purple glow, the trident lay as always. Yet the popping and ticking and squiggling of pens against the moving graph paper continued.

As he spread out the report, he turned to Dr. Suess who was just then approaching.

"Where have you been?"

"Picking up my check. You know—payday?"

"No, I mean besides that?"

"Getting it cashed. Tonight's poker night, remember?"

A pause.

"I also have been in the company with some very good friends of mine," Dr. Suess added. "Probably some of the most intelligent minds on this campus."

Dr. Sirotka eyed him with surprise. "Really?" he said. "Anyone I know?"

Dr. Suess smiled wryly. "I think so: Hairless Joe and Earthquake McGoon."

Dr. Sirotka didn't answer. He turned again to the report spread out across the tabletop.

* * *

The atmosphere grew thick and humid as the long, golden rays of the afternoon sun filtered at an obtuse angle through the green broadleaves and muggy haze. Sensing the oppressiveness of the rotting jungle, the reptile and insect life sought refuge from the rising temperature by crawling under the more remote, shadowy recesses. The aquatic creatures kept themselves well submerged in the still and often stagnant pools and lakes. Even the giant butterflies did not flutter about. Smoke from smoldering volcanoes on the horizon lay low and diffused as atmospheric pressure prevented it from rising.

'Suddenly a hulk came crashing through the broad-leafed, prickly palm and giant ferns. Heavy footsteps striking the earth resounded dully through the hot, dank air. The bushes parted and a bulky form appeared through the vegetation, reaching almost to the hardwoods' lower branches. It kept its small, pointed head close to the ground. Its beak-like mouth kept up an almost non-stop snip-snipping among the youngest, tenderest of shoots and saplings. From the base of its skull, continuing up along its high arched back and out to the tip of its long, tapering tail, it armed itself with two rows—spreading in a 'V' shape—of a series of triangular bone-like armor. Three spike-like projections, the length of an upright's javelin or sword, jutted from the tip of its tail, completing its arsenal.

THE TITANS

'While the rest of life languished in the afternoon heat, the behemoth seemed content to be lord over all its environs.

'As G'ya had explained to Oss'yanhu on a previous walk through this particular section of the jungle, she and her helpers had finally seemed to have succeeded in engineering a species with bodily defenses so formidable that it had practically no natural enemies.

'At last, through genetic manipulation, she had optimistically explained, we have developed a creature that is invulnerable.

'The creature continued snipping with contentment. After an interminable length of time it stopped and looked up.

'Did it really sense another trembling of the earth beneath it?

'The trembling increased.

'It sensed a regular, rhythmic pounding as though footsteps of another monster approached. Darkness blocked out the steep-angled rays as a giant shadow fell across the sparkling green foliage. The startled creature sniffed the air and listened with tiny ear-like recesses in the side of its head. Its long, pointed neck and head swiveled and thrashed in every direction as it tried to discover what it now detected to be a strange, fishy smell and a hollow, deep-throated hissing sound. As the crushing of underbrush accompanied the heavy footsteps, the creature now saw the source of the disturbance.

'It saw, hovering above it, a tower of muscular scale flesh that glistened wet with a metallic sheen. A mound of mass seemed supported by a pair of giant hind legs and broad, three-toed hooves with toenails the size of an upright's hands. High above, it brandished forelegs the length of an intelligent upright's arms with grasping claws sharper than any thorn. The massive body reached almost to the branches of the hardwoods. Eyes that glistened like fire stared out from a boulder-sized head.

'The fecal smell of fear combined with that of vomit began radiating from the creature's ponderous form. It looked up into a pink, yawning void ringed by teeth the size of an upright's dagger.

'The intruder's cavernous jaws widened. A pointed tongue slithered and salivated over the rows of the glistening teeth. A forearm grasped after the creature. A low, guttural sound from deep within the assailant's throat accompanied the thrust.

'With a burst of adrenal energy, the creature recoiled into a defensive position.

'The monster radiated its own aggressive smell of garlic. A hoarse growl reverberated through the oppressive stillness as the intruder's forelegs took another swipe at the creature. With lightning speed, the creature spun sideward and whipped its spiny tail up at the scaly mass.

'Another roar echoed through the jungle as the surprised intruder jumped back; its huge hind legs showing surprising alacrity. Its chest began oozing blood.

'For a moment neither antagonist moved. The garlic smell became oppressive. The creature kept its head low; its lethal tail high. The intruder maintained its distance, still towering over its potential prey. It continued the guttural hissing as it eyed fiercely the tiny head that now moved slowly from side to side across the ground. The intruder tried taking surreptitious strides sideward to gain advantage of a strategic angle. With each maneuver, the spiny tail would follow, move for move. The intruder lowered its head slightly, warily eyeing the large, triangular-shaped spines that ridged up the creature's back.

'Somehow, the intruder's tiny brain registered the reality that the only hope of overcoming its prey lay in some sort of distraction. Surely, its dull-witted quarry would not be so thoroughly obsessed with its own survival, that it could not lose focus by some insignificant diversion. That's all it would need: any distraction, however small.

'Suddenly, from about an upright's spear-throw off through the jungle, the creature heard a raucous caw. Out of curiosity, it glanced away briefly to see a winged reptile lumbering its way from the treetops upward toward a distant mountain crag.

'The intruder was on its victim in a trice. Gigantic jaws clamped long, rows of rapier-like teeth on the creature's neck with a crunching sound. The fecal odor of fear surged with renewed power as it found itself locked in a life-or-death struggle. In its last death-throes, the creature's tail made two final thrusts at the intruder's body, inflicting deeper wounds against its chest.

'After feeble, spasm-like twitches, the creature finally stiffened out and lay still.

Ignoring its own deep, flowing wounds, the intruder spent the remaining moments of daylight devouring the carcass. In the fading rays of twilight, it lumbered off deeper into the jungle.

'Once the sun had sank behind the western mountains, a swift curtain of darkness descended on the forest. With it came a coolness that dissipated the thick humidity. Chirping of a thousand night creatures swelled to a deafening crescendo. Stars by the hundreds shone overhead in a rock-like brilliance.

'Out of the leafy shadows stepped a female upright.

'For a moment G'ya stood over the remains of the spiny, armored creature; the rib cage of a freshly killed carcass. What little light that filtered down from the stars

THE TITANS

reflected the sad lines of her drawn face. She bent low to the hem of her garment and tore off a swatch. With it she reached down between the creature's still wet bones and soaked up some of the blood.

Then she stood, turned away, and vanished into the night.

* * *

High above the lush vegetation of the hardwood treetops jutted a craggy summit that formed part of the range of the distant mountains. In the night's darkness, trees of the timberline formed a black, bushy silhouette against the slate gray rock. The upper black surface of the precipitous mountain rock outlined its ridge against the starlit sky.

Something besides the cool mountain breeze stirred.

A small, dark outline moved along the top of the cliff toward the precipice. Just short of the edge, the shadowy form of G'ya stopped and gazed skyward. A gust of cool, moist breeze flipped her flowing robe and unfurled it upward and outward like a banner waving at the stars. The breeze stiffened, now catching her hair as well. One lock whipped across her face; the other billowed luxuriantly into the inky void beyond her head.

Her right had still gripped the blood-soaked cloth. She held it aloft and let the breezes raise it also toward the sky. Her eyes fixed on the stars overhead. It's been so long, she thought.

She reached into the dim recesses of her memory back to a time before there was a time. What is time, anyway? She thought. Is time merely measured eternity? Is time movement; movement of electrons, atoms, and molecules? Does eternity, then, mean cessation of all movement of these particles of matter? If this is the case, where is the gravity? What holds matter together? Did matter really exist back in eternity, or was eternity back in an era wherein energy was the only reality?

Time also means transfer of energy, as does the movement of heat from a hot object to a cold, thus cooling the hot object and warming the cold until both objects reach an equilibrium of temperature. Was eternity back when the universe uniformly registered the now considered theoretical absolute zero?

She tried to recall what it was like back then, but in the intervening epochs of T'tanyu's terrestrial existence, it all became so hazy; only the dimmest of distant dream now; yet she could not shake an acute awareness of eternity and presence of Strong-Ones as if he continually tugged at her elbow. Dimly but definitely could she discern being in the courts of *Strong-Ones*. The courts with their splendor encompassed worlds upon worlds; worlds within worlds; universes superimposed upon universes and universes within universes. Was the universe to which her world belonged a mere speck of stellar dust and itself really a particle of a gigantic atom or a molecule? Is each atom, each molecule, respectively, an entire solar system, a galaxy, or a universe in its own right?

Will intelligent beings someday, for example, discover the properties of light energy and use it to reproduce images on a simple flat plain, and perhaps call it light pictures, or perhaps, photography, with a similar but opposite image and call it a negative? Would they, in fact, utilize this newly discovered technology and guess that this is merely an example of how whole universes can be mirror images to one another?

Would future intelligences while possibly insisting that nature abhors a vacuum, forget that before nature ever was, vacuum was the only reality? Would they, while insisting that two things cannot occupy the same space at the same time do so without realizing that even with the densest of matter, there is a universe of space between each atom, each molecule? Or that it is possible for matter, anti-matter, pre-matter, quasi-matter, half-matter all to occupy the same space without colliding because their molecules or whatever their equivalent particles move through the same space all in different orbits, or different frequencies? Or traveling different tracks, so to speak?

Did time really begin before creation? When first did the myriad of countless disembodied intelligent entities, such as were both she and Lord Light-Bearer, become aware of self-conscious existence? Was theirs a non-corporeal birth as it were? "Begotten, not conceived" was the way *Ultimate-Source* had explained it to them during a primordial orientation. How could any intelligent being possibly measure how far back in time that lecture had taken place? After all, only recently—relatively speaking—had it even been possible to reckon time arbitrarily by measuring the orbit of a single tiny planet around a medium-sized star, one of millions in its own galaxy? And how long is that orbit? 364.25 spins on its own axis? What a quaint way to reckon time when one stops to think about it, she thought.

Especially when one moves out beyond the immediate confines of terrestrial experience and its environs and moves outward past even the remotest outreaches of its solar system to solar and stellar systems beyond; when one moves out past even the farthest limits of its galaxy to the billions of other galaxies, on out to places where time and distance meld together and possible future intelligences may very well talk of them in terms of light years? Interesting concept, she conjectured: measuring the speed of light in terms of how long it takes her tiny orb to circle the sun. Light, she thought, the only *thing faster in all of the entire everything is God himself who can out speed light only by being omnipresent: everywhere at once. We ourselves, she thought, in our disembodied state can travel only at light speed and even that can take us millions of light years to complete any mission that Strong-Ones may send us.*

'But what of that?

'When we dwelt in eternity did it really matter? Was it not only when Strong-Ones set in motion the whole of creation process of the material universe did any concept of time really matter?

'And yet, was not the uniformity of the created universe a marvel to behold? An atom, electron, or proton was held together the same way whether from her own planet Earth, or whether it came from a stellar body millions of light years distant. The elements and compounds and all the properties of matter followed the same patterns no matter where in the entire universe. Hydrogen behaved as hydrogen. Everywhere it exists it is the same unstable and volatile element as earth inhabitants know it. No matter where in the universe it may come in contact with oxygen, a chemical reaction that future intelligence very likely will call combustion with a resultant ash that eventually will be called water. This, also, whether here on earth, or whether among the primordial gases being churned out from the remotest constellation. Whatever gradualism with the development of terrestrial organic matter, there was no such evolutionary development of basic building blocks—again, such as electrons, protons, and atoms—of the entire non-organic universe stayed as they were formed from the Big Bang on.

The nature of energy remained uniform as well. Light behaves as light, whether from earth's sun, or its more closely neighboring stars, or again whether from bodies so distant they can barely be seen from her home planet. Light diffused through a spectrum, such as water, can be bent and/or diffused into a spread of colors such as red, orange, yellow, green, blue indigo, and violet.

Time and space changed none of this.

'And through how many billions of these time units did she have to reach back in her memory to re-create the day when Strong-Ones spoke?

'Spoke?

'Yes spoke.

'He whose very essence was Ultimate Power had only to order into existence whole universes and they were. And how long did the original cataclysm some would later call the 'Big Bang' take place? Three earth minutes? And during those three earth minutes were there, in their own right, mini-eternities wherein energy converted to countless forms

of primeval stuff such as half-energy, non-energy, quasi-energy, anti-matter, half-matter, quasi-matter, and particled phenomena that were none of these before there formed that first hydrogen atom of matter as we know it today? How many of these, lasting only milliseconds of our time reckoning, contained self-conscious intelligences that looked upon their worlds and reckoned them as eternity?

'Once the cataclysm had occurred, however, the rest was history, she reflected, or at least T'tanyu history.

'She recalled the awe as she witnessed gigantic clouds of pre-stellar gases boiling outward in all directions into the ether void. She recalled seeing softly glowing clouds of every color of the rainbow spectrum spinning away from the explosion epicenter at the speed of light, spinning, spiraling, and finally setting their own gravity centers as they did so.

'Future intelligences might call them a cosmic fireworks, as in celebration of their various holidays such as New Year's or Independence Days.

'She recalled how Strong-Ones had her and her compatriots to pay close attention to one galaxy in particular: one of billions spinning out in ever widening radii. As the whorls of millions of stars began spiraling in ever tightening circles, he called their attention a particular star. He bade them watch as particles broke off and began spinning in whatever forces of thrust, inertia, and gravity counterbalanced one another into a permanent orbit. They watched one particular fiery orb spin third place out away from its star and, as two of its gasses—hydrogen and oxygen uniting in combustion and forming a water vapor ash—began to cool and liquefy. At first the orb's surface consisted merely of liquid water with dense boiling; clouds of vapor forming a permanent system overhead.

'She recalled the many volcanic upheavals form solidified lava crusts that formed the primeval ocean floor. Some of these upheavals and lava spills broke the water surface permanently and, combining with the collision of gigantic tectonic plates of bedrock, formed landmasses and continents.

'At this juncture, Strong-Ones, using later mortal's equivalent of a cassette recorder, fast-forwarded his biological processes, and gave Y'dith and Lord Light-Bearer bodily residences with a degree of protoplasmic complexity that the planet would not see again for eons.

'At first it was just the two of them: Y'rranhu and G'ya. For countless epochs they would be the only ones to witness development of single-celled protoplasmic jellies in a warm, saline sea. They also saw the development of a single-celled cellulose spores that

washed up on sand. As the waves washed back and left them to dry, however, they germinated and spread. Soon the rocks of the shore became covered with green, single-celled mosses. More complex plant forms, such as other mosses, small ferns, and lichens followed until eventually the entire land mass became covered with green plant life that flourished, died, and in turn, provided nutrients for subsequent plant forms that increased in abundance and further complexity and formed tender shoots until some developed their cellulose stems into a woody like substance, forming trees.

'Meanwhile, in the seas, simple unicellular protoplasmic and cellulose species multiplying in kind and variety formed in the ocean depths. In addition to the single-celled creatures other cells began to divide, multiply, and reproduce—initially asexually and then later—much later—began the complex sexual reproduction, forming into hydra, roundworms, flatworms, and later a primitive form of ichthyosaurus. Eventually some of the more adventurous of these crawled out of the depths and onto the shore for short periods. Still others stayed and made land their permanent abode.

'As the plant and animal life grew, multiplied, and became more complex, and as catastrophes, cataclysms, and upheavals caused great and drastic changes in life forms, they were interspersed with long periods of tranquility that allowed new life forms to grow and flourish.

'In the hundreds of millions of intervening years G'ya found it increasingly harder to recall that early life of celestial bliss she enjoyed with countless other spirit beings as they basked in innocence in the glory of uncreated heavenly courts that dwarfed even the material universe itself.

'How long, she reflected, were the uncounted eons past wherein she as well as Lord Light-Bearer took as a matter of course the splendor of eternal celestial courts that now were becoming only a vague memory?

'Again she recalled how that once Lord Light-Bearer had become Y'rranhu and had possessed a terrestrial body and enjoyed fleshly pleasures of earthly reproduction and love, he made no attempt to confine his amorous adventures within the bonds of marriage but rather began a career of profligacy.

'He even lied to the myriad of young nymphs and naiads under his care, telling them that carnal union with him guaranteed them immortality. He then had sons like Oss'yanhu follow his sordid example.

'Now that her partner in this grand experiment had betrayed his own vows of fidelity to her, betrayed his own race, was his mission or even her mission still valid?

Was her own oath of fidelity, the holiness of her calling, and her particular mission just as binding?

"Now it had happened. The thing that she had dreaded, the warning she gave to Oss'yanhu during their walk in the garden, had come to pass. Mutant, aberrant beings have now become reality. They now walk the earth, stalking prey to satisfy their insatiable appetites. Against them, none, in all God's creation could form a defense. All creatures, great and small, lie helpless within the range of the King of Tyrants.

The chilling night breezes blew cool in the marked contrast to the stifling lowland atmosphere of the day. Still G'ya held the gore-drenched rag aloft.

"'Hear me, oh Strength-Above-All-Strengths," she shouted into the stiffening winds. "I uphold before you mute testimony of things undreamed of."

"'This, this is the state of your creation; your garden.

"'This, this is how we now rule.

"'Hear, hear, O Wise One and be aware.

"'Behold, behold, O Strong Ones, and take note.'"

* * *

When Dr. Suess finished reading the report, he turned to Dr. Sirotka. "There's one thing that intrigues me about all this."

Dr; Sirotka looked at him questioningly. "What's that?"

Dr. Suess hesitated a moment. "Put it this way," he said finally. "We know very little about how others of the animal kingdom actually communicate with one another."

"I don't follow."

"Smell," replied Dr. Suess. "We of all God's creatures probably have the dullest sense of smell of all the higher life forms."

"So?"

Dr.Suess again pointed to the text. "Don't you get it?" he said with a look of incredulity. "During rutting season for instance, a buck can tell by the scent a doe gives off whether or not she's ready to mate."

"Okay?"

"And when a dog, wolf, or other canine has cornered a quarry—whether to fight, kill, or eat—they smell its fear."

A pause.

In the ensuing seconds only the faint ticking of the ancient Seth Thomas wall clock broke the silence.

Dr. Suess studied the transcript.

"Here we have," he said at last, "is the description of an epoch wherein life forms both humanoid and animal, could tell another creature's emotions by a heightened sense of smell; a thing I don't think possible today."

Dr. Sirotka shook his head. "This thing is beginning to get surreal," he said in a subdued tone of voice.

Dr. Suess again turned to him. "By the way, has the dean seen this yet?"

"No."

"Good. Let's don't tell him; at least not for now."

As Dr. Sirotka returned the papers to the attaché case, Dr. Suess started for the door. His partner's voice arrested his footsteps. "What are you going to do now?"

"Thought I'd grade some papers."

Dr. Sirotka pulled the attaché case from the tabletop and let it fall to his side. "I've got papers to grade, too. Why don't we say the hell with it and kill an hour or two at Deadman's Gulch?"

Deadman's Gulch set on a side alleyway immediately around the corner from Stillwell's main street. The coziness and obscurity of its location made it a favorite faculty watering hole.

Twenty minutes later Dr. Suess had wedged himself into a corner booth with a scotch on the rocks. Dr. Sirotka sat opposite him nursing a martini.

"To heavy mischief," said Dr. Suess, hoisting his glass.

Dr. Suess then told him about the letter from the human relations committee.

"You're in good company," said Dr. Sirotka. He explained. As Dr. Suess had used allusions to the comic strip 'Li'l Abner' to spice up interest in his classes, Dr. Sirotka had a gimmick as well.

Whenever Dr. Sirotka's classes did poorly on a test or exam, he expressed his displeasure by wearing Groucho Marx glasses while handing back the test papers.

The week before, Dr. Sirotka received a similar letter of complaint from the Human Relations Committee. It seemed that a student deemed the Groucho glasses to be anti-Semitic.

Dr. Suess reflected on the time of the dean's arrival five years previous. The retiring dean had been an institution at the college. He had the love and respect of student and teacher alike. Little was known about the current one other than he came from a small college in the northwest that prided itself in being progressive and experimental. Dr. Suess' relations with him had been dicey from the start. Over the years they had only grown worse.

So much for not promoting from within one's ranks, he thought.

"That get-up was Groucho Marx's shtick for decades," shrugged Dr. Sirotka, "and nobody ever minded it. In fact, everybody thought it was a hoot. When I mentioned this to the Human Relations Committee, they said that it was not that the mask was anti-Semitic. It was just that times have changed and that now, with the new sensitivity and consciousness-raising, it is *perceived* as anti-Semitic."

Dr. Suess reflected on a conversation from a Dr. Eric Scholtz of the engineering department.

Dr. Scholtz had long kept a laminated print of a Don Martin cartoon from *Mad* magazine. The cartoon showed a middle-aged mother allowing her son to go alone into a men's public rest room for the first time. The son was an overgrown galoot of a fellow clad in a sailor suit with shorts.

He also sported a bearded five o'clock shadow.

While in the restroom he washed his hands at the bathroom sink. When he stood before the towel dispenser, he read the instructions above it with a puzzled expression.

The sign said 'Pull down and tear up.'

The last panel showed him walking away from a dispenser torn out of the wall and lying on the floor in a heap of crumpled metal.

The STUGO complained the picture demeaned the mentally retarded, or as they put it: 'the developmentally challenged.'

Know what? Dr. Scholtz had said. Their phrase 'developmentally challenged' is itself now a no-no.

The latest buzz word is 'differently abled.'

"The inmates have taken over the asylum," sighed Dr. Suess.

Dr. Sirotka reached in his trousers pocket and pulled out a wad of bills. "Time to take our minds off all this," he said. "I'm really staked for the game tonight. How about you?"

Dr. Suess stared off into space. "Now something?" he said disgustedly. "I haven't had time to think about tonight. Right now I'm not much in the mood for poker."

They studied their drinks in silence.

Finally Dr. Sirotka again spoke. "Know what the kicker in all this is?" he said with a wry smile. "I myself am Jewish."

Chapter 5

By the time Dr. Suess had left Deadman's Gulch, darkness had settled over town and campus. He stepped to the curb still several blocks from his house and paused. The streetlamp overhead filtered its light down through broad leaves now well colored with autumnal orange. He felt a definite nip in the late September air.

He hadn't originally intended to stay this long. One drink and go was his original intent, but whenever he got together with Dr. Sirotka, it never seemed to work out that way. The drinks kept coming as did the conversation. He must have spent a good chunk of his paycheck tonight. He also must have spent the last hour swilling down a gallon or more of black coffee. He succeeded only in starting home with a fuzzy brain and full bladder.

For long moments he stood at the curb and tried to focus his thoughts.

Finally forcing himself to concentrate on his way home, he stepped to the street. About a block away, he saw the barbwire enclosed mound of earth with the 'trespassing forbidden' signs. Like a gigantic mass grave, its presence loomed large and ominous, making it impossible for even the casual stroller of Stillwell's wide, sylvan streets to ignore.

Whenever Dr. Suess passed this site—after an evening with friends at Deadman's Gulch—the next couple blocks had a sobering effect on his alcohol-befogged brain.

It had once been the city park…This dark mound of earth once echoed with happy voices of locals in summer and voices of skaters gliding gracefully over the frozen rink under the welcoming glare of floodlights in winter.

Decades prior to Dr. Suess' coming to Stillwell, the park had been used by families as a favorite picnic and recreation area. It was also an idyllic place to just relax. The city recreation department had maintained immaculate pavilion and rest room facilities as well as a well laid-out softball diamond; all maintained by the city recreational department and funded by the good tax-paying citizens.

That was before it became the 'people's park.'

Or as certain local wags coined it: 'Needle Park..'

Now it stood dark and silent…

…After continued careful walking, his eyes zeroed in on the half block of sidewalk that remained between him and his house. *Walk in a straight line,* he told himself. *Just a lousy half block. What's so hard about that? Take it slow. You can do it.*

With this determination, he began putting one foot in front of another in the direction of the rambling Victorian mansion in the shadowy distance. The darkened, deserted neighborhood took on a surrealism as the extended, grayish white porch emerged ever closer. The wide front steps swayed in rhythm to his unsteady stride.

Good thing no neighbors were out, he reflected as he crossed the porch threshold.

Another reality occurred to him. *They could be watching behind their living room curtains.*

Nosy bastards, anyway, he thought, *the hell with them.*

He fumbled for his house key. The key finally found its way into the lock. He heard the bolt slide with a thud that echoed in the hallway immediately inside. He pressed the heavy oaken door and its hinges squeaked in protest. He pushed it aside and peered into the darkness. From a doorway in a far wall that led to the library, he saw light streaming through the crack under the door.

Was Marie waiting up for him, or was she correcting papers?

He entered the library, trying as best he could to avoid the staggering. She turned in her swivel chair and stared at him. "Are you all right?"

He felt gratitude for her tolerance of his bouts with John Barleycorn. Had this been his first wife, he could now be looking forward to a good twenty-four hours in the dog house, as it were.

He shuffled to his recliner without kissing her. This was out of neither slight nor yet out of neglect. He did this out of her aversion to the smell of alcohol.

"Sorry about my coming home late," he said as he settled into his recliner. "It's been quite a day."

He told her about the letter. He told her about Dr. Sirotka's experience with the Groucho glasses.

She heaved a sigh and turned again in her chair. She held up a paper that she had just corrected. More red was written on it than black.

"You wouldn't believe what I'm getting these days," she said as she continued holding up the paper. "I have incoming freshmen that don't even know how to properly form their letters, much less spell or construct a sentence."

As he compared his classroom situation with hers, he feared for her safety. *Those Neanderthals would just as soon beat up on a female teacher as a male*, he concluded.

Dr. Suess shook his head.

Marie studied her alcohol saturated husband. *This saddens me*, she thought. *He's such a good man; good to me, good to the children.*

He's also a fantastic lover; so macho, so passionate.

At first she had a hard time getting used to it. It seemed that she was experiencing more pleasure than she deserved. She hadn't known that sex was supposed to be like that for a woman.

She marveled at the contrast between him and her first husband…

…Even while they were married, she sensed that number one's lovemaking was strangely mechanical—even obligatory. At what was supposed to be the climax of passion, she sensed that his mind was somehow somewhere else.

She harbored misgivings; that something was wrong.

Was it she? Was it her fault? Was she somehow not giving him the right kind of pleasure to arouse the male animal that she thought raged within every man?

As their relationship degenerated, she began to hold vague suspicions as to what was really wrong…

…She threw the paper down in disgust.

"Not only am I getting handed this garbage," she said, reverting to the original subject, "but I am getting static as well. I have students who actually insist on their right to be wrong."

Again, he reflected on conditions at her high school. *Everyday she walks into that blackboard jungle,* he thought, *she has to contend with overage, overgrown, overbearing, oversexed, and underachieving losers.*

Dr. Suess rose from the recliner and went over to her. *Damn the alcohol fumes,* he thought.

He pulled her to her feet and kissed her. She did not remonstrate with him for his breath but instead removed her glasses and he kissed her again, pulling her close until he could feel her breasts press against him. In the lingering moments, as he felt the moist longing, he saw her eyelids flutter. As he embraced her, he slid his hand down the small of her back. He hand moved beneath her jeans waist until he touched her rear cleavage.

"I'm going upstairs," she whispered. "The children are with their father this week-end."

Immediately this triggered within him a reaction, despite the visitation stipulation that her ex's lover was not to be in the house when the children were there.

Marie also related as to how it took quite a legal battle to have even that in the contract.

He tugged gently at her waist. *God,* he thought, *second marriages can get complicated.*

* * *

Christmas holiday, thought Dr. Suess as he sat in the lounge area of the Silver Lode Lodge, what a godsend. Been a good three months since that wildly passionate September week-end, he reflected, when the children were with their biological father.

He leaned against the cushion of the oaken couch. He propped a slippered foot against the low, rough-hewn coffee table. He savored the warmth of the blaze that roared in the massive stone fireplace and the warmth of the toddy he held in his hand. He took a puff of his briarwood and admired the antlers that crowned the bust of a giant bull elk mounted on the fireplace wall. The wall itself, consisting of dark cedar logs, stretched up to a cathedral ceiling. The lobby and lounge remained deserted. Early afternoon typically saw most of the guests out on the slopes. The lodge proprietors had done their work well in seeing to it that the skiing surface lay ideally hard-based with an additional four inches of fresh power.

Through the broad picture window he could watch a parade of skiers latching onto tow ropes for a swift ride up to the high white crags in the distance. Angry looking clouds swirled about the highest summits and dark silhouette of pine forest that bordered the mountain's base.

Marie and the two children had left for the slope over an hour ago, leaving him alone and that felt good. He took a sip of his toddy and recalled Marie's getting into one of her rare snits over his drinking. *You mean we're paying for an expensive week-end up here just so you can sit around and drink?*

He admired his bulky knit sweater of Scandinavian design. Marie had given it to him at Christmas, just a few days before. *She's a great gal,* he acknowledged to himself as the toddy mellowed his thoughts. *Maybe I should get off my butt and get out there on the slope.*

They had made the Silver Lode Ski Lodge their favorite ski resort for a number of reasons.

Number one, it was handy, situated only an hour's drive from home. They could go and come back the same day, go for an overnight and bed and breakfast. Or—when they had a little more time—it proved handy for a weekend or Christmas holiday.

Reason number two, it was inexpensive. Unlike the trendy popular places like Vail or Aspen, it provided a suitable getaway for folks of more modest means, such as college professors and their families.

Reason number three, many of their friends came here.

"There's the old lounge lizard now."

One of those friends had just now cast a shadow across the coffee table.

Dr. Sirotka, similarly attired as Dr. Suess, moved to sit beside him.

"Full as an egg, too, I'll bet," he added.

"Oh, Mike," said Dr. Suess, gesturing to the couch. "Set your old bod down here."

Dr. Sirotka settled back on the cushion. "You seem preoccupied."

Dr. Suess folded his arms stared straight ahead. "I am."

He reflected on a recent incident at the high school involving Marie's daughter and her counselor…

…Traci, now a junior had been called into her counselor's office ostensibly to discuss her plans for college.

Your grades seem to be pretty good, the counselor had said. I don't think you'll have any trouble getting in.

However, the counselor went on, there is just one little factor that I am concerned about.

Traci didn't understand.

For a moment the counselor hesitated. "As you may know," he then continued, "there is more to college than just grades."

She wondered what he was driving at.

"What I'm trying to say," said the counselor, "is that the social aspect of campus life is also very vital one's well-being and success."

The girl still wondered where this conversation was headed.

"Put it this way," he continued. "Life at college these days moves pretty fast. It's not like living at home."

And?

"For the naïve and artless, the culture shock can be pretty devastating."

She looked at her watch. "I have to get to class."

The counselor waved off her remark. "No problem," he said. "This is something I think we need to discuss."

"What do we need to discuss?" said Marie's daughter with a slight tone of impatience in her voice.

Again the counselor hesitated. "Well," he said at last. "As I said before, campus life moves pretty fast. An incoming student needs to be prepared for that."

Prepared for what?

"I just want you to know what to expect," he said, leaning back in his chair.

"Mr. Grimley," she said, again looking at her watch. "I really must go. We're having a quiz."

The counselor leaned forward over his desk. "As I said 'don't worry about it.' I can fix it."

Another pause.

"Tell me," he said finally. "Have you ever had sex?"

"Have I *what?*"

The counselor smiled a tentative smile. "To put it in the vernacular: have you ever been laid?"

A prickly heat rash broke out on Marie's daughter's forehead. She stood up. "I think I'd better go," she said, eyes beginning to water.

The counselor also stood up. "No," he insisted. "We need to discuss this."

As he reached out in a futile gesture to detain her, she fled the office…

…I wish Marie would have just let me go up to that high school, thought Dr. Suess, *and punch that pervert's lights out.*

But Marie had insisted in handling the situation herself.

The recollection had also somehow brought to his mind an incident during his early years at the college. Ginger Wallace, a student secretary of his had elicited in him a concern with her attraction toward the counterculture denizens of the 'People's Park.'

Those people are bad news, he had warned, I wouldn't associate with them if I were you.

At times he had difficulty understanding the girl. Parallel to her predilection for those euphemistically called Bohemians, she continued to be active in her parents' church with youth fellowship, choir, and doing solos before entire congregation.

Yet she hobnobbed with trash, he recalled.

Just didn't compute.

THE TITANS

But I find them interesting, she had said…

…Dr. Sirotka's voice again snapped Dr. Suess' reverie.

"Hope you'll forgive my mixing business with pleasure," he said as he hoisted an attaché case he was carrying onto the coffee table, "but I thought I'd better show you this up here."

He laid the attaché case atop the coffee table, lifted the lid, and handed Dr. Suess the latest cryptology report.

"'You have a visitor, my lady." A slight breeze blew the filmy skirt tight against the nymph's body contour in the arbor doorway.

'G'ya had been sitting almost hidden between the labyrinth of roots that formed the wings of her uprooted tree stump throne. She looked up from the petals of giant white orchid that she had been examining.

"'Oh, thank you, Kh'llisto. Show the visitor in."

'R'ya, heavy with child, waddled awkwardly as she followed Kh'llisto through the entrance. G'ya rose from her throne and descended the earthen dais toward the newcomer.

"'Greetings, my dear," she said, kissing R'ya's cheek. She stepped back and studied R'ya's protruding belly.

"'Your time draws near I see. How do you feel?"

"'Quite well, considering."

'G'ya eyed her with concern. R'ya's voice did not have a convincing ring to it. "I know of your betrayal," she said.

'R'ya cast a wistful eye to the ground. "Must every T'tanyu male have the faithfulness of a mollosk?"

'G'ya started down the path that led to a distant exit. She motioned R'ya to join her. The path led out of the clearing into an area of dense undergrowth on either side.

'For the space of an earth hour or better, she called to her attention an endless number of table slabs. Upon them stood jars containing cultures of newly spawning life forms.

'Other paths led off to garden plots growing experimental botanical life.

'She pointed to a sapling. "Here we have started a whole new concept with flora. It's a new variety of tree. It is predicated on the assumption that Gaia's climate will not always be as mild a globe world wide as it now is. We know that there will come an era

wherein some latitudes will see days that will grow extremely cold intermingled with others as mild as today. These trees will draw their nurture from the soil during warm days. This nutrition will be in the form of a liquid that rises in the trunk, out the branches, and into the leaves. Here the leaves will draw on the sun's energy and will thus form the sap into a sugar type nutrient at the same time it will breathe the gases of life just the reverse of that of animal life."

R'ya shook her head. "Amazing."

"When future conditions grow cold," she continued, "these trees will shut down their leave's feeding process and the leaves will fall to the ground. There these dead leaves will decay and form fresh fertilizer to the soil, enriching it further.

"These experiments will prove far more advanced than our current conifers and ferns."

They followed more extensions of the labyrinth of corridors between the walls of greenery.

For a moment R'ya stood in a wooded archway that served as another entrance. She knew that before her lay an area that few even among the T'tanyu had ever seen.

R'ya surveyed the area furnished with more tables of upturned rock. Beyond them, pressed against a wall of hedgerow and thicket lay a series of low, earthen mounds. The mounds served as shelving for an array of clay pots and jars. Several of the table tops also bore globes of transparent silicon. Others bore small, glazed flasks jammed at their tops with cork and housed gelatinous cultures of gray and pale yellow.

G'ya gestured for R'ya to sit with her at a table in a remote corner of the clearing.

"I'm experimenting with a new life form," she said.

R'ya eyed her with curiosity as she watched G'ya thrust the point of her wand into an open rectangular aquarium of clear silicon. Several centimeters of sand lined the bottom. When G'ya stirred the sand lined bottom with her wand, some of the grains fell away, exposing three leathery looking eggs.

"Lizard?" said R'ya, guessing the obvious.

"Our best in this species is doomed," said G'ya.

She related to R'ya the incident involving the armored lizard's fatal encounter with King Tyrant.

"That monster represents the ultimate aberration in that whole order," she concluded. "We have to start over."

She pointed to another aquarium. Here again, she stirred the sandy bottom. Again, R'ya watched the operation with curiosity. At first she saw nothing. Then she saw the sand begin to move. Even after G'ya withdrew her wand the sand continued to rustle and stir. Something broke the surface and R'ya saw a tiny, oval shaped head. Then she saw eyes unlike the rounded eyes of many other reptiles. Intelligent looking, oval shaped eyes looked out as if they possessed powers of an upright.

"But it's so small," said R'ya. "What possible chance would it have against an enemy; say, for instance, against King Tyrant?"

"These are just newly hatched babies," said G'ya. "Some of the adults, when full grown, will have reached a length three or four times the height of one of us. They will be without propellant appendages like arms or legs. Instead, they will possess muscular ability to glide along the ground with the swiftness to out-speed any predator. They will also be adept at climbing trees to escape the clumsy flesh-eating giants. They will be agile swimmers—equally at home in the water as on land.

"For their food, they can lie in wait in the trees or under the water. With speed of lightning they will seize their prey and crush it in their powerful coils. Or they can drag it down into the water and drown it and then devour it at their leisure.

"Without awkward appendages they can gracefully propel themselves along on any surface. Their movements are actually more efficient that way."

R'ya admired the intricate design of its scales as it glided over the sand. "It is beautiful," she said. "What will you call it?"

"I dub it Herpetia."

* * *

"You will soon receive visitors,"

The misshapen little creature stared with evil triumph out of his one eye. Tyra glanced askance at the cripple supporting himself on his one leg his with a crude crutch.

"I know you know many things," said Tyra as she continued to eye him with obvious distaste. "Since you know this, perhaps you can tell me who these visitors are and the nature of their visit."

The mouth of the filth encrusted creature broke into a toothless grin. "I prefer to leave it as a surprise."

Tyra broke off busying the mixing of potions. "Your visits as always prove interesting," she said sardonically. "If I am to receive visitors, I see no need for you to hang around."

Eikendom looked her in feigned hurt. "Why must I always be shunted off so unceremoniously?"

She shook a wooden spoon at him at him threateningly. "No more words," she stormed. "Begone!"

He shrugged and turned reluctantly toward a remote narrow passageway.

"'Holy men,'" she fumed to herself, "why must they be called that when in truth they are anything but?"

She continued busying herself with the pounding of mortar and pestle, when she heard a knock on the crude, oaken door that served as entrance to her subterranean chamber.

"Come in."

She saw Y'rranhu stand in the doorway. Io, in a cotton robe with cowling up over her head and swollen of body, stood with him.

"Good of you to knock," she said, glaring at Y'rranhu.

Y'rranhu raised his head in an attitude of hauteur. "I may be a rogue," he admitted, smiling. "But never let it be said that I'm a boorish rogue."

Tyra continued grinding with her mortar and pestle. "Are you going to just stand there all day?"

Y'rranhu turned to Io. "Come, my dear. She is in a one of her moods. Let us leave and come at a more propitious time."

Tyra stopped her stirring. "It is obvious that you're not here on a social visit. I'm always in one of my moods when I have to deal with you," she growled. "Just state your business, please."

The smile vanished from Y'rranhu's face. His eyes changed from brown to an agitated hazel. "You are quite right," he said with an edge in his voice. "I need to know what is going on with that dear wife of mine."

Tyra put aside the pestle and strode to another table. "As if she were the one who bears watching," she said as she took a jar of gray powder from a nearby shelf. She poured some of the contents into a small dish. She pressed the tip of her wand into the powdery mound, causing the billowing up of dense, yellow smoke. As it billowed to the ceiling, it became transparent and a holograph depicted G'ya and R'ya bending over a glazed aquarium. They stood with eyes fixed at the tiny creature that glided over the container's sandy bottom.

"'Amazing experiment,'" said Y'rranhu with unaccustomed sincerity.

He turned to Io. "Your mother is an amazing woman," he said in a low voice. "I always knew that one belittled her powers and talent at one's peril."

THE TITANS

Io wrapped her gray cotton robe about her. She pulled back the cowling that covered her head and studied the creatures more intently as if trying to piece together what it all meant.

Y'rranhu took a step back and continued to eye the holograph. "Yes, this is most amazing," he said, stroking his goatee.

"Have you seen enough?" said Tyra. "My arm is getting tired."

Y'rranhu glanced at her. His eyes again changed from a languid brown to a hazel color that began radiating a sparkle. "Keep the vision going," he ordered.

With a sigh she continued holding her wand to the powder.

Y'rranhu stared, transfixed. The pupils of his eyes widened. The eyes themselves changed to a deep blue. "I have never seen anything like it," he said in a subdued tone of voice.

In the vision, G'ya and R'ya left the clearing. At Y'rranhu's direction, Tyra kept the holograph focused on the aquarium instead of following the two women.

Y'rranhu's eyes narrowed to mere slits. "You will now see an example of my powers," he said, turning to Io. "You will realize how fortunate you are to be amorously linked with me. You will quite forget the way I have treated you."

He turned again to Tyra. "Keep it going," he said again.

He turned his attention back to the aquarium. His eyes turned green with an intensive inner fire. He stared at it with a burning concentration that frightened the two women. Hours went by and still he stared. Tyra became numb with fatigue, but still the vision persisted. Far into the night and into the dawn of the next day, Y'rranhu still stood, fists clenched and hanging to his side, before the holograph without moving. Another day and still the women dared not move. As days stretched into weeks, the two women desperately fought a sense of foreboding.

Still Y'rranhu did not move from the spot.

The legless creatures from aquarium grew. They writhed and struggled as they fought among themselves for room in the increasingly crowded enclosure.

Finally the inevitable.

The head of one of the creatures slid over the top of the aquarium and out onto the table. Another followed, and another. Soon, scaly, intricately designed creatures covered the table top. In a matter of time, they slid down the stones that served as table legs and began crawling about the clearing.

Y'rranhu raised his arms. "Now I will bring about my changes," he said.

He addressed the writhing creatures. "You will no longer be large, powerful, but relatively harmless creatures," he said. "You will not longer depend on your powerful coils to crush your prey. You will not have to lie in wait in the treetops or in the river's shallows.

 "'I will endow you with teeth not rows of sharpened incisors for holding you prey and chewing. I will endow with only two. They will be long and sharp. You will be able to thrust them forward or withdraw them at will. I will insert large sacs of venom inside your head and your fangs will be hollow conduits with which you can inject the venom into your victim, thus paralyzing and killing him.

 "'You will be terror of all other living creatures."

 'Shortly the beasts glided across the grass and disappeared into the bordering thicket.

 "Done," said Y'rranhu. With eyes gleaming, he turned to Tyra.

 'He appeared to relax. His eyes reverted again to a languid brown. "You may conclude the vision."...

 ... 'In far recesses of the cave, unmeasured distances below the abode of the wise woman, Tyra, sat the misshapen man on a pile of guano. High in the darkness above him untold multitudes of Fledermauser hung precariously upside down from the jagged ceiling.

 'A dank, musty smell hung heavy in the stale atmosphere. The diminutive denizen sat and pondered the murky, evil surroundings. From fissures in the floor beneath his one sandaled foot spumed columns of blue flame. They flickered spectral shadows off the cave walls and emitted the sweet, sickening odor of sulphurous gases.

 'The undersized caricature of an upright seemed to relish his forbidding abode. Here he had his meager needs met. These gaseous jets furnished him with fire for the roasting of the bats he captured for his meat.

 'At his side set an earthen jar. He reached down took out a pinch of grey powder He sprinkled the mysterious looking stuff into bluish jet of flame just before him. Smoke billowed up over his head and then cleared to transparency. As ghostly shadows from the other flaming jets danced overhead, he studied holograph immediately above him.

 'The holograph divided into a split vision. One scene showed Tyra in her subterranean apartment with Y'rranhu and Io. The other revealed the sylvan glade of G'ya's arboretum.

THE TITANS

'He rubbed his hands with obvious glee.
"'Splendid," he chuckled."Utterly splendid."

* * *

Dr. Suess handed back the report to Dr. Sirotka. "We need to keep this under wraps," he said. "If word of this gets out, we'll be the laughing stock of academia."

Dr. Sirotka put the paper back into his attaché case.

"The dean's getting antsy," he said. "He wants us to have something to show for all this."

"I think we can concoct some sort of snow job," said Dr. Suess looking down into his nearly finished toddy. "By the way, I have an appointment with him first thing after the holidays. Can't say as I'm looking forward to it."

He tipped the glass to his lips and finished the draught. "In fact, just thinking about it makes me feel like another one of these."

Dr. Sirotka eyes him apprehensively. "Shouldn't we be going kind of easy? What's Marie going to say?"

Dr. Suess stood up.

"Actually Marie has been a pretty good scout about it," he said as he started for the taproom. "However, as it is, I'm afraid she's going to shit when she sees my bar tab."

* * *

The following fortnight saw the beginning of the winter term. Again, Dr. Suess found himself standing before the door bearing the appellation, 'J. Negley Jone, Ph.D. Dean of Students.'

"Entres." A resonant baritone responded to the knock.

Dr. Suess entered. Again, the dean leaned in his overstuffed swivel chair facing the wall bookcase. "Sit down, Harry," he said, still facing away from him.

Dr. Suess sat in an armchair across from the desk of highly polished mahogany.

Harry?

He sighed. *I guess if I had a name like 'Jaked Negley Jone' I'd have an attitude too*, he reflected.

While he waited, his thoughts whirled in a maelstrom of disturbing thoughts of his Marie. She *was* upset over his bar tab at the ski resort. He asked himself: what about the usual bi-weekly poker game? Last Friday it was to have been held at Dr. Sirotka's house. Every payday since Dr. Suess taught at Stillwell he and a small group of faculty males customarily got together for a few hands of poker.

In an attempt to mollify her he passed on the opportunity to join in last Friday's game.

Finally the dean whirled around and faced him.

"I've another grievance from STUGO," he said. "Does the name T. Bolton Wentworth sound familiar?"

Dr. Suess cast him a hard look. "Don't play grand inquisitor with me. You know damn' well I had him in freshman geology last term."

After failing his mid-term, Mr. Wentworth's hold on a passing grade remained tenuous at best. He simply had not handed in several very important long-term projects.

"It wasn't as though he hadn't ample notice as to the deadline either," Dr. Suess added.

As he continued to relate the incident, he didn't mention that he was struggling with a headache and a hangover from end-of-the-term faculty bash of the evening before at Deadman's Gulch.

Fighting a throbbing head and bloodshot eyes, he paced the aisles between the desks of the exam hall. He had instructed the students to sit at alternate desks. For an added precaution, Dr. Suess also gave two separate sets of exam sheets.

The dean found himself taking several moments to recover from this sudden outburst from Dr. Suess. He fidgeted briefly with a nearby paperweight.

"You always were a stickler for honesty," he said at last, trying to regain his composure.

He finally leaned back and pressed his hands in a steepled position. He waited for Dr. Suess to continue.

Dr. Suess had spotted the student in question seated at his desk with an opened textbook in his lap. Dr. Suess bent over the student's shoulder.

"Your textbook, please," he whispered, "and your blue book as well."

Dr. Suess took the items and dismissed Mr. Wentworth from the examination hall. After the student had left, Dr. Suess looked around at the curious onlookers. "Never mind," he admonished. "Just keep writing."

He then took Mr. Wentworth's exam materials and strode up to his desk. He drew a line under Mr. Wentworth's last sentence and with a red pencil wrote the following footnote:

'Test not valid. Student was using his textbook as an aid, contrary to prior instructions. This was *not* an open-book test. Students were instructed to clear all textbooks, notebooks, and personal belongings before being handed an exam paper.'

'Signed H.I.S.'

He had been very careful not make any outright accusation of cheating either verbally to the student, nor yet anything in writing to go in the student's anecdotal record despite catching Mr. Wentworth red-handed.

"Another concern the STUGO has expressed," he heard the dean then saying, "is about the possible inequity in your dual test system."

Dr. Suess' momentary inattention snapped to an abrupt halt.

"What inequity?" he asked with indignation and incredulity.

The dean cleared his throat.

"It seems," he said studying the STUGO memo. "That they are concerned that one set of questions may be more difficult than the other. They are concerned that there may be an element of favoritism hidden within the composition of these tests."

Dr. Suess' mouth twisted in disgust. "Okay, let me tell you how I make up my tests," he said.

He went on to explain. First, he wrote out fifty questions singly on 3"x5" filing cards. Then he shuffled the cards face down and dealt them out in two piles of twenty-five, as in a card game. After turning the piles face up, he made up the two tests. Only then did he know which questions would go on which test.

"I've made every effort to cover myself," he said.

The dean nodded. "Very prudent on your part."

A long pause.

Again, the dean sat forward, leaning over his desk. "STUGO is very concerned that Mr. Wentworth, as a consequence, is failing the course."

"If Mr. Wentworth had shown sufficient concern at the outset," said Dr. Suess, "he wouldn't be in the situation he is in."

The dean leaned back in his chair. "You are quite right," he said finally, "but there are other factors into play now."

Dr. Suess eyed him. "Such as?"

The dean cleared his throat. "As you may well be aware," he said. "There are new cross-currents in educational philosophy in our schools today."

"I haven't been aware of any."

The dean tilted his head further back. "Ah, therein may lie the problem."

"Problem?" Dr. Suess looked askance at him.

"We have been re-thinking the traditionalist, elitist, and competitive system of evaluating the students' progress for some time now. We now feel that students have often been hurt by this."

"Hurt?"

"Failure is always damaging to one's self-esteem," continued the dean. "In fact, it can be downright traumatic."

"Or devastating," said Dr. Suess.

The dean nodded. "Yes—or devastating," he said, apparently missing Dr. Suess' note of sarcasm.

Typical, Dr. Suess reflected. *He's so full of himself he's too dense to notice the subtle, little insults from his subordinates.*

"What happened to the educational truism that we can learn from our failures?" he asked.

The dean didn't answer.

Dr. Suess continued his stare. Over the bookshelf behind the dean hung a framed parchment denoting the college's Phi Beta Kappa chapter. Dr. Suess thought he could sense where the conversation was headed.

"But he was caught cheating," he reminded the dean. "He was caught red-handed. What about integrity? What about individual responsibility? What about intellectual honesty?"

"The student government grievance committee alleges that you put the student in question under too much pressure," said the dean, ignoring Dr. Suess' questions. "They allege that the student in question was under such stress he felt that he had no other alternative but to cheat."

"By 'student in question,'" said Dr. Suess, "we're still talking about Mr. Wentworth, I take it?"

So that's the gimmick, he thought. He sat silent for an additional minute.

"And what do you allege?" he said finally.

Again the dean leaned forward. "What I allege is not important," he said, looking down at Dr, Suess through his narrow glasses. "As an administrator, I see my calling as one of seeing to it that the ongoing contact between classroom teacher and student functions as smoothly as possible."

He paused. "Dr. Suess," he said lowering his voice. "I try to be true to that calling."

When were you ever that, thought Dr. Suess.

The dean's attention again reverted to the paper in front of him.

"The STUGO grievance committee has met with the Faculty Senate," he said with continued magisterial gravity. "They have made the following determination: You are to give the student another chance by giving him a make-up exam within fifteen days."

"And if he fails again?"

The dean sighed. "Mon Deux, you do make things difficult, don't you? I believe that were it I, I would see to it, come fifteen days from now, that that student's record reflects a passing grade."

Again, the Dr. Suess sat silent. Was it his imagination, or did it suddenly feel hot in there. *One word,* he thought; *just let 'Babs' get word and this guy would be toast.* But why didn't he? Was it cowardice, or was stooping to blackmail just too distasteful?

The dean again leaned back in his chair and again wore his benign smile. Dr. Suess' eyes wandered about the office. On a far wall a plaque shaped like a shield bore the college's coat of arms and the following motto: 'Primo Veritas.'

'*Truth first,*' Dr. Suess reflected.

He thought of something. "What about open hearings?" he said, leaning forward. "What about due process? Aren't I entitled to have my chance to present my case before the grievance committee?"

Again, the dean steepled his fingertips. "Technically yes," he said softly. "You do have a point. However, just as a pragmatic matter, I believe it would not be politic on your part to make waves at this juncture. You do, however, have fifteen days should you decide to push it."

Not politic on my part? He almost said these words. *According to whom?*

Silence.

He condemned himself for his reticence.

Dr. Suess looked out the window just beyond the dean's head. Clouds had darkened the afternoon prematurely. A fine spray of sleet began tapping a tattoo against the window pane. The wet, sloppy precipitation made ideal skiing conditions of just a few days ago seem like a distant memory.

The dean stood to his feet.

"Just between you and me," he said, sliding his chair under his desk, "even though you are right, I wouldn't advise it."

Taking the hint, Dr. Suess also rose to his feet.

The dean strode across the office carpeting to open the massive door.

"By the way," he said as he stood beside it, "how did that little old poker game go the other night?"

Dr. Suess passed into the corridor. "I wouldn't know," he said, looking back briefly. "I wasn't at that little old poker game."

Chapter 6

Dr. Suess leaned his elbows against the darkly polished oak lip that ran the length of the bar. He had been at the Deadman's Gulch since the late afternoon happy hour. Dinner time came and went and by early evening the place had pretty well thinned out. As the evening wore on, however, it began to fill up again. How easily time slipped away from him on such occasions.

Marie had been more than patient, he acknowledged.

Slowly, he nursed his rum-on-the-rocks. He let it burn its way down into his throat and warm his inwards. He concentrated on the sensation of the alcohol's relaxing effect radiating out through his arm and leg muscles. He savored the mellowing glow it produced in his brain. It sometime bothered him when he noticed that it was beginning to take more and more drinks for him to get this feeling. He had heard stories from drinkers even more seasoned than he how that after awhile, all the stuff begins to taste like water.

You know you have a problem when that happens, they had told him.

Thank God, I'm not like that, he thought.—*yet*.

If you think you've got a drinking problem you have, he reflected further, coining a support group's cliché.

He barely noticed the arrival of someone climbing up on the stool next to him. He cast a casual glance in the newcomer's direction. Maybe we'll see if misery loves company, he thought.

"Who you lookin' at?" a voice demanded.

Oh, oh, one of those, thought Dr. Suess as he tried to keep his head straight forward. From out the corner of his eyes he saw a stranger, small and sinuous looking. His chiseled features had the intensity of a pugilist. His short, sandy colored hair lay unkempt across the top of his head. He held a cigarette in hands that fidgeted with a Scotch on the rocks. The backs of his hands bore the tattooed slogan: 'born to' and 'raise hell.' Underneath his worn leather jacket a dirty T-shirt bore the words: 'I killed for this T-shirt.'

"I don't like guys who wear neckties," Dr. Suess heard the voice saying.

Dr. Suess turned to the voice's origin. "And I don't like guys who don't like guys who wear neckties," he shot back.

Eyes couched in the leathery face increased their hostility. "What are you, a smart ass?"

Dr. Suess barely gave him a glance. "Don't you like it?"

"No."

"So why don't you take your mouth off from it then?" said Dr. Suess as he turned to leave.

"Hey, I'm not done talkin' to you."

Dr. Suess faced him. "You're too mouthy to be so little," he said.

He pointed to the man's collar bone. "What's that on your shirt?"

Without thinking, the man looked down. Dr. Suess flicked his forefinger up across the man's face. As he again turned to leave, he felt a hand grasp his left shoulder. With the speed of a striking rattler, he whirled around and slammed a right into his antagonist's mouth. With a muffled groan the man rolled off his stool and fell dazed and bleeding to the floor.

As he picked himself up and headed for the men's john, the taproom fell to a stunned silence.

Dr. Suess looked around at the wide-eyed and now thoroughly sobered crowd. With a smile he backed his way toward the exit.

"Just a little disagreement," he said, trying to sound reassuring. "Just go back to your drinking."

Out on the wintry streets again, his mood darkened. Packed snow underfoot creaked and crunched with every step. Large, wet snowflakes began falling across the glare of the intersection streetlamp.

The sense of foreboding came over him again. The darkened wall of dusk enshrouded evergreens suddenly elicited a sense of menace. It seemed alive, malevolent; as though something unworldly and evil blocked his path with threatening, predatory force.

Like a giant white ghost looming out of the wintry shadows the landfill that was 'people's park' soon came into view from the feeble glow of a distant street lamp. Cold and stark it now rose behind its tight cyclone fence and razor wire barrier, a mute reminder of what once was. There was a time when the area would have been well illuminated with lighting to guide an ice rink full of nocturnal skaters…

…The pavilion provided a warming and shoe-changing shelter. The winter use of the park equaled or even exceeded its use by the summer patrons.

In the pavilion the city also maintained a concession stand that dispensed hot cocoa, cookies, and hot dogs to nourish the tired and hungry college students and townspeople.

That was before out-of-town fringe types laid claim to the area.

That was before the park became the scene of a disaster from which Stillwell was still reeling…

…Half a block further, he set himself to inching his way up the slippery porch steps.

Once inside the dark, cavernous vestibule, he instinctively found the hall tree and hung up his coat. The only light came from beneath the library door.

Marie was still up.

When she looked at him from her desk, her expression changed to one of dismay.

"Where have you been?" she demanded.

This was not like her, he thought.

"Have you been fighting?"

He looked at his right hand. He hadn't noticed the swelling and the bleeding.

"The guy deliberately tried to pick a fight with me," he said weakly. "I couldn't get him to leave me alone."

She stood to her feet. "That does it."

He looked at her with a hurt look on his face. "Come on, be reasonable," he pleaded. "Like I said, he started it."

"My husband fighting in a bar?" she said, eyes glaring. 'What's the matter with you, anyway?

"When some one wants a piece of me," he insisted. "I don't back down."

"You fool" she said, raising her voice. "What you did was a recipe for disaster. He could have buddies in the bar—or out on the parking lot. They could have been armed. You could have gotten killed. If you were being harassed, why didn't you complain to the proprietor?"

"And have everyone think I'm a wuss?"

She shook her head in disbelief. "Who cares what a bunch of drunken rabble think? I can't believe this."

She cased a quick, angry look of into space. "My husband," she repeated, "a college professor? A Ph.D.? Acting like a common hoodlum?"

She started for the door. "Good night, Henry."

He reached out to block her exit. "Hey, don't be that way," he said, trying to muster a little chutzpah. "C'mon, smile."

She stood close with arms folded. "If I smile now," she replied. "What you'll get is a forced smile. Is that what you want?"

Again, she started for the door. "Good night, Henry," she said with a stiff formality in her voice.

He let her pass. As she disappeared into the dark corridor, he headed for his recliner and collapsed into the soft, leathery upholstery. The library fell to a deathly silence. How long he laid stretched back in his chair, he wasn't sure. As the nocturnal hours dragged by, he continued in a semi-stupor.

* * *

With the first rays of dawn filtering though the curtained windows, he sat up with a start. The blinding sunlight hurt his eyes. A sudden realization came to him.

Today he had an eight o'clock.

He glanced at his watch. Eight-thirty.

He rose slowly, painfully out of his chair. He pulled his coat from the library hall tree and started for the front door.

The streets of Stillwell muffled with the silence of a wintry morning. When he reached campus, instead of going to the science hall, he headed for the administration building.

An hour later, he emerged from an office bearing the words 'personnel' on its door, and stepped into the ancient hallway. *Dr. Sirotka should be through with his morning classes by now*, he thought.

He found Dr. Sirotka sitting in his garret office. Dr. Sirotka looked up at him his battered wooden desk.

"Hey there, you pleasant old fart, where the hell have you been?" he asked with an bemused smile.

"Don't start with me Mike," sighed Dr. Suess as he settled in a chair opposite the desk. "I've had a bad twenty-four hours."

Apparently concluding it prudent to change the subject, Dr. Sirotka reached across the desk for his attache case.

"Got some new reports."

* * *

To withed in agony on the narrow cot; her swollen body rolling from side to side. Another spasm. Her scream reverberated throughout Tyra's grotto. Tyra clasped her hands to her head as she ran from one cooking fire to another, trying to decide which curative potion to administer next.

To thrashed about, alternating between arching her back and howling as pains continued to wrack her body. The linen sheets that wrapped her were drenched with sweat. She threw her head back on her pillow as strands of wet hair clung to her twisted face.

"Tyra!" she sobbed. "Help me! Please help me!"

Tyra ran to her bedside and held her head up from the pillow. "Drink this," she whispered, "and try to relax."

Tyra, in her panic and bewilderment, faced a situation hitherto unknown to the super race of T'tanyu, namely difficulty in childbirth. One of the blessings of such a hardy race had been that childbirth had been a heady, ecstatic experience; akin to a prolonged orgasm.

That it should be painful and difficult had caught Tyra quite by surprise. She laid one hand in Io's belly. With the other she embraced her. She placed a gentle kiss on Io's sweaty cheek.

"It's going to be all right, dear," she said without conviction.

Suddenly a scream so piercing that it caused Tyra to lose control of her bladder shot through the cave. The cave's close air waxed thick with the foul smell of fear. Io's lips curled back exposing clenched teeth as again, she arched herself. The scream gave way to hoarse animal grunts coming from deep within her throat. She gave one excruciating roar that rose with an unprecedented crescendo. Tyra reached under the sheet between Io's legs.

"It's coming," said the wise woman breathlessly. "I can see its head."

She didn't know whether Io heard or not. Amid deep moaning, Io didn't seem to respond.

With a worried look, Tyra carried the bundle to a nearby cistern. Soon she had the newborn stretched across a linen sheet atop a flat stone to finish the cleaning. Shortly Tyra paced the floor with the tiny infant tightly wrapped in a linen swaddling wrap. The first cries indicated a healthy set of lungs and vocal chords.

She brought the young babe over to the cot.

"It's a boy," she said, smiling.

Io lay still.

"Io, dearest," she whispered in mounting panic. "Here's your child. He's a male."

Io still didn't move.

Slowly Tyra straightened up and turned back. She quickly strode over to a wicker cradle and placed the baby in it. Though wide-eyed and with limbs thrashing about, the child remained strangely quiet.

Tyra returned to the cot. With a look of profound anguish, she covered Io's still form. Then she turned and hurried toward the cave's entrance in search of her handmaidens.

She felt herself struggling with another situation that the T'tanyu, as a super race, had little occasion to cope with, namely death.

The next day a procession of white clad women slowly wended their way single file through a grove of low hanging willows. On their shoulders they bore a linen enshrouded figure on a stretcher. As they marched, their voices rose and fell in rhythmic accents in chanted lament. At a clearing they finally placed the bier on a cord of wood stacked on a flat granite slab.

'The acrid fumes of smoke mingled with grief's dead odor.

"Light the pyre," ordered Tyra.

'One of the mourners carried a clay fire pot suspended from a lanyard. She poured coals around the linen wrapped body. A smoldering of gray smoke began curling up into the humid atmosphere. Shortly roaring flames rose skyward. As dense black smoke rolled above the tops of the hardwoods and as the sweet, pungent smell of burning flesh filled the air, they chanted the following dirge:

"'Our lords ask us a song.
What shall we sing?
All flesh is as grass.
Like a flower, it flourished.
Today it flourishes in wild beauty,
Tomorrow it is gone.

"'O, Mother G'ya,
Where are your children
In whom you vested fond hope,
And now have died a-borning?
Yesterday she grew as a tender beauty
And today, she is not.

"'Willows don't weep for me,
For I am at rest
In the land of the happy spirits.
Weep rather
For the sisters
Who must remain.'

"'Flames, burn brighter,
Smoke, rise higher
Above the firmament.
Fire, fire, burn and purge

Until the earth
Is clean one more.'"

* * *

'Three weeks later, after the child had been put through the rites of water purification, Tyra finally entered Y'rranhu's private apartment bearing the infant in her arms.

"'Lord Y'rranhu," she announced, bowing low in the doorway. "I present you with your son."

'Y'rranhu looked up in mild surprise from a breakfast of figs and berry juice. He rose from his settee and started toward her. He took the child from her and cradled it in his arms. He eyed the bundle with obvious satisfaction.

"'Splendid looking child," he said. "He looks like a true son of royalty."

'He abruptly stopped his pacing the floor as if struck by a thought. "By the way, where is the child's mother?"

"'By the way, she's dead, my lord," was the answer.

'He continued holding the child and again glanced thoughtfully down at the tiny face. Then he turned to Tyra.

"'No matter," he said, handing her the baby. "Here, take the child. Nurse him. Wean him. Raise him. When he is of age, bring him to me.'"

* * *

... 'Deep within the bowels of the unending expanse of cave the runty little mongrel hunkered in the dark, portentous grotto he called home. He sat on a boulder and held in his hand a scabbard containing a double-edged sword. As he polished the gold surface to a finish of dazzling brightness, he smiled.

"'Soon we shall see how this plays out," he chortled. "I who was cruelly misshapen at birth and then cast out to die by the beautiful folk had a few surprises of my own. From the first, it was not my fate to perish as their abandonment had intended. Secondly they underestimated my toughness and cunning even as an infant. Thirdly, thanks to my mother R'ya's curse, I am just the first born of a whole generation of freaks from which the whole T'tanyu race will shrink from horror."

THE TITANS

Shadows from the blue jets of volcanic flame danced against the irregularly shaped cavern walls.

The rumpled dwarf savored the gaseous odors that the flame jets emitted as he finished the polishing of the oversized weapon.

He stood up.

"And now," he said with obvious relish, "to deliver this work of art to its intended recipient."...

... "Mother?"

The young male voice prompted Tyra to straighten up from the cauldron she had been stirring. She turned to see a tall youth standing at the entrance of the cave. His complexion and body shone a subtle bluish-green. His hair tumbled about his ears and temple in tightly curled locks of forest green. He took two steps into the cave and stopped. In his hand he held a broad-sword sheathed in an ornate, gilt-edged scabbard.

"I found this beside my bed," he said.

"There is something that I must tell you," she said, walking slowly toward him. "I am not your mother."

She gave that statement a moment to sink in.

"I am your guardian," she said finally, "your guardian, your nurse-maid, your mentor, if you will. Your real mother died in bearing you."

The youth still looked bewilderedly at the sword.

"And who is my father?"

She turned away from him again and reached for clay dishes from the cupboard. "Today I will take you to him. Have some breakfast."

He laid the sword atop a slab of granite and pulled up to a heavy mahogany table. "What is his name?" he asked.

Tyra placed before him a bowl of fruit, a platter of bread and a mug of steaming tea.

"You will learn his name in due time," she replied.

A realization came to her with which she had tried to avoid coming to grips. P'sudohn in appearance bore a striking resemblance to Oss'yanhu. Would Y'rranhu suspect that Oss'yanhu, not he was the youth's real father? Would he in his jealous rage rail against the poor, innocent Io for playing the harlot, long since dead though she may be? Would he take his rage out on the living? Would he in a fit of anger strike the youth dead? Would he in his wrath want to strike her dead as well?

Unscrupulous miscreant though he may be, he still holds awesome power in the universe and when crossed he can be vary dangerous.

Fear that could not be expressed in words gripped her inner being.

Yet she could not avoid this meeting. For all the years that she cared for the boy she knew this day was coming.

The moment of truth; a day of reckoning.

She braced her self, but kept her fears to her own counsel, and prepared for the inevitable meeting.

With face set as flint she led the youth to the cave's entrance.

'An hour later she stood in the doorway of Y'rranhu's apartment. The youth towered over her as he stood alongside.

"You servant announced us, I take it?" she said, concealing her feelings. Fear and loathing alike screamed within her to show expression.

However, her countenance remained as stone.

Y'rranhu sat at a small, dark-wood table peeling off a pomegranate. He turned to face the two arrivals still standing in the doorway.

"Ah," he said, rising from his settee, "it's good to see you."

"I'm here on business," she said, forcing calmness in her voice.

She gestured to the young giant beside her. "Just fulfilling my obligation."

Y'rranhu took two more paces toward the couple. "You're looking well."

He's toying with us, she thought.

He paused then gestured to the youth. "And who might this be?"

"Interesting you should ask," she said with an edge to her voice. "This is your son." *You know full well who it is, you evil scum.*

Y'rranhu's eyes widened slightly. His eyes metamorphosed a deep blue as he looked first at the youth and then at Tyra.

He broke into a slow smile.

"Well, don't just stand there" he said, gesturing grandly to the opposite dining table. "Come in."

'As they settled onto the couch, Tyra thought: he's setting us up.

Y'rranhu returned to the settee. "And what is the young man's name?" he said, still smiling.

Don't even know the name of your own son, thought Tyra. *Good for you.* "The young man can speak for himself," she said with a nod.

"My name is P'sudohn."

THE TITANS

Y'rranhu sat silent for a moment while he studied the youth.

"A splendid young man," he said at last. "You did your work well, Tyra."

Tyra eyed him with disbelief. She waited for him to explain.

"You probably are wondering about his appearance," Y'rranhu had rightly guessed. "Have no fear my dear Tyra. You see, both he and Oss'yanhu are the fruit of my loins. If I so chose, I can genetically prepare any of my offspring for their destined work. In this case, I have chosen the both of them for mastery of the sea and all waters."

The pupils of his eyes disappeared as they clouded over with a pale yellow

A wave of relief swept over Trya.

"I believe he will do very nicely," continued Y'rranhu.

The youth eyed him. Do what very nicely? He wondered.

Tyra gestured toward the sword that P'sudohn still held in his hand.

"P'sudohn is curious about this sword," she said. "He found it this morning under his bed."

Y'rranhu paused from his eating and again rose to his feet. "Show me your hands," he ordered, ignoring her words.

The youth held out his hands.

Y'rranhu admired the webbing between the fingers.

"This is turning out better than I had hoped," he said. He moved briskly to a wall bracket that hung in a far corner. A cloth of woven tapestry covered its shelves.

He turned again and took deliberate stride toward the couch.

"Stand up," he said, glancing toward the youth. "I have something to give you."

With a questioning look, P'sudohn stood to his feet.

Y'rranhu held up a gold chain necklace. At its base hung a medallion in shape of a trident, tines pointed downward. He reached up to place the necklace around the young man's neck. He then pulled at the neckline of the youth's tunic and dropped the medallion down inside his garment.

"Wear this necklace at all times," Y'rranhu admonished. "The day will come when you can wear it openly."

P'sudohn continued looking puzzled.

"Young man," said Y'rranhu, gesturing toward the expanse of water shimmering in the distance outside the apartment window. "Today I give you your inheritance."

With a more relaxed stride, he returned to his settee. His eyes turned a languid brown. His pupils dilated in obvious satisfaction.

"There is one problem," he said with a subtle smile. "To actually take possession, you're going to have to fight for it."

He got up and stepped to the chamber doorway. Drawing aside the heavy door curtain, his eyes turned back toward the chamber and then glanced out at the corridor.

Taking the hint, Tyra and P'sudohn started for the exit.

"I have every confidence that the young man is more than equal to the task," said Y'rranhu with a nod.

Just like you, she thought. *Never a gift without some catch to it. The man is poison.*

As they passed him, he briefly caressed Tyra's arm. "For what it's worth," he said, lowering his voice, "I am grateful."

Tyra turned to P'sudohn. "It's time we left."

Y'rranhu looked admiringly at the youth as the couple marched away down the corridor.

"I do wish you god-speed on your mission, young man."

Young man, thought Tyra. *Never once did he call him 'son.'*

When they disappeared around a distant corner, Y'rranhu returned to his pomegranate.'

* * *

Tyra and P'sudohn worked their way down a long staircase toward the palace outside exit. Out on the grounds they walked a broad expanse of formal gardens, sparkling fountains and stone statuary.

They continued walking a good hour until they came to an outcropping of rock. A small entrance to a cave set at its base. Here they entered and worked their way to Tyra's subterranean apartments.

When they reached the bottom level, P'sudohn paused. "What mission was my father talking about?"

Without answering, Tyra strode over to an herb cupboard and withdrew a small vial. She pulled the stopper and poured purplish-gray powder out on a granite table top. She recapped the vial and returned it to the cupboard. She then stepped to a cooking fire and pulled out a smoldering rush weed. She pressed the glowing tip into the powder. Immediately a cloud of dense lavender smoke billowed toward the cavern ceiling. P'sudhon stared transfixed as the smoke cleared to a transparency. Peering into the hologram like cloud, he saw another image of Tyra appear. However, in the vision she *looked to be in a kind of forest clearing or leafy bower. As she began walking along a garden path, he saw R'ya walking beside her. Tyra was engaged in an attempt to placate an obviously angry R'ya.*

"'How could he do that?' Psudohn heard R'ya say.

"'Do what?' the holographic vision of Tyra answered.

"'Betray me.'

"'Oss'yanhu is as treacherous as quicksand,' R'ya hissed.

'Vision Tyra studied the flame of jealousy that burned in R'ya's eyes. "'How so?'

"'R'ya continued walking with deliberate stride and tightly clenched fists.

"'A fortnight ago I held an oracle,' she said. 'I saw Oss'yanhu wallowing in a stream: his natural haunt for pastime.'

'She paused, and then went on. 'That in and of itself means nothing. However, in this instance I saw him embracing a naiad. They were sporting together.'

'She paused in her discourse of indignation as the two women continued walking.

"'I have monitored the lecherous eel's comings and goings,' she said, picking up the thread of conversation. 'He shamelessly frolics about and takes knowledge of every comely young naiad he can get hold of; in every stream, every pool, and sea cove.'

'After another prolonged silence, R'ya stopped walking. Again she turned to her companion. 'For once I am in complete agreement with Father Y'rranhu. He has decreed that Oss'yanhu must die and his dominion be given to another.'

Tyra pulled the reed out of the pile of powder and returned it to the cooking fire. The last remains of the transparent vision smoke rolled upward toward the ceiling and dissipated into the cave's murky interior.

P'sudohn looked questioningly at Tyra. "What does this mean, little mother?"

Tyra turned toward the cave entrance. "I want you to meet someone."

She gestured to another youth who had just entered the cavern. The newcomer's face and tunic glowed like burnished gold

"I am D'heus," he said with a nod.

Tyra gestured to the two youths. "You two have much to discuss that I mustn't hear," she said, turning to go further back into the distant recess of the cave.

'She stopped and again looked back at P'sudohn.

"Go with him," she said.

Puzzled, P'sudohn fell in stride alongside D'heus as they emerged into the sunlight.

"I'll make this brief," D'heus said.

He pointed to one outcropping of rock that rose over the forest treetops not far distant.

"Meet me there tonight at midnight," he said. "Discuss this with no one; not even Trya. There will be others meeting with us."

D'heus disappeared and P'sudohn headed back to Tyra's cave in thoughtful silence.'

Chapter 7

'A cool breeze stirred as slivery clouds chased one another in front of a full moon. The roiling billows nevertheless permitted enough moonlight to reflect off the bare rock. The form of D'heus appeared ghostly atop the rock's summit. The clouds dispersed as he lifted his face to the night sky. From below his feet, from out of the forest shadows, he heard a voice softly calling his name. "Are you there?"

"P'sudohn," he whispered, "of course I'm here. Come on up."

'A silhouette emerged from the leafy darkness and mounted the rock until the light of the moon revealed the figure of P'sudohn standing beside him.

'D'heus clasped P'sudohn by the right wrist. "Welcome, brother."

'P'sudohn glanced about the bare rock. "What is it we must discuss only in this godforsaken place?"

'D'heus pressed his finger to his lips. "Soft."

'He pointed to the arboreal void below the rock's precipice.

'From a steep slope, P'sudohn now descried other shadowy figures emerging. From among them, P'sudohn noticed a giant figure standing a good head and shoulders taller than the other shadows moving against the darkened foliage. The taller figure moved apart from the rest and stood alone. D'heus pulled him over to P'sudohn. Despite P'sudohn's own stature, he still had to look up to the new arrival. He could tell, even in the moonlight, that the black skin stretched over the taut, muscular body shone a bluish sheen. High cheek bones were etched prominently over the broad, square face. A silvery ring hung from the center of widened nostrils. Small rings pierced the earlobes. A tight-fitting helmet of shining metal crowned the shaven head.

The stranger stood naked to the waist and wore a loin cloth of slivery white. Similarly colored sandals adorned the feet and thongs wound around the sinewy calves.

A large hand with silver armlet about the wrist reached toward him.

"I am called K'haos," said the giant in a deep voice, "lord of the night."

Curiosity welled up inside P'sudohn. He eyed the dark, sinister figure standing before him. "Are you not T'tanyu?" he asked in puzzlement. "Does not your presence here jeopardize our secrecy?"

He detected a sardonic grin on the broad face. "I rule the darkness," he said. "From me nothing said or done in the dark is hidden. I know all that occurs in the absence of light."

P'sudohn turned to D'heus with a worried look. "Will he not betray us?"

D'heus chuckled briefly. "Tell him, K'haos."

"I was always here," replied the giant. "Before even light was called into being, I was there. I will always exist. Y'rranhu has no claim over me. I am the absence if everything there is."

The night wind began stirring among the trees below them. It emitted a low moan about the bare rocks that surrounded them.

"Whether the T'tanyu rule or the Ullympu," continued K'haos, "it matters not to me."

P'sudohn noticed that by now others had assembled close. D'heus turned and stepped away a short distance to where he could the more easily address the group. His eyes searched the farthest recess of the crowd of warriors who stood out under the cover of the night foliage.

In the far distance rose a mountain that topped off in a plateau. From it thrust upward into the night loomed the palace, known as Sh'yin-Grl'. Soft light—diffused in a dim halo-like glow—surrounded its imposing exterior. From its windows and doorways glowed the light of torches and candles.

Also from it the sound of music and merriment radiated out into the night sky.

D'heus realized the celebrants to be too preoccupied with their revelry to hear anything beyond the palace's confines.

He now made bold to raise his voice.

"My brothers," he shouted, trying to project his voice to the most distant of the rear ranks. "I stand before you as one who is also motherless. My mother R'ya died desolate and alone, forsaken by the very one who made her with child.

"Dare I mention it? Yes, I will! You, my brothers, are all progeny of the hated and

treacherous Oss'yanhu. I call upon you this very night. Purge yourselves. Purge your very souls of the evil and treachery that has spawned you.

"Let us covenant among ourselves from this moment on to rid our world of this filth and corruption.

"Hail Victory!"

"Hail Victory!" the crowd out in the darkness roared like a hoarse, giant beast in response.

"The T'tanyu have failed—utterly," shouted D'heus. "Sh'yan-Grl' must be overthrown."

* * *

'A chorus of adolescent female laughter lifted over the sylvan setting. Oss'yanhu tilted his head back in blissful excitement as nubile young bodies snuggled close.

"'I cannot believe my good fortune," said a girlish voice, "being set upon by the very lord of all the waters."

'Oss'yanhu spread his arms across a mossy bank as he lay chest deep in a shady pool. Behind him in the grass lay his tunic and trident.

"G'ya, dear mother, help!" he shouted in mock distress. "I am being attacked from all sides."

'Giggles filled the air as naked young ladies swan dived beneath the surface. Oss'yanhu's laughter gave way to heavy panting as he felt himself pulled deeper into the water.

'A head of wavy brown locks broke the surface, clinging tight against a rosebud like face as the youngster moved close to kiss Oss'yanhu on his mouth.

"'Oh, dearest delight," she sighed. "Make me happy today."

'Suddenly her expression changed to one of alarm. "Oh no," she gasped, pointing behind him.

'Oss'yanhu stood up full height in the shallow pool and gave a quick look behind him.

'He caught a fleeting glimpse of P'sudohn running back into the forest carrying the trident with him.

'Without bothering to put on his tunic, Oss'yanhu climbed out of the pool and began running in hot pursuit.

'For the better part of the day, P'sudohn continued to run through the humid forest,

still carrying the disputed trident. Behind him, he heard the frantic crashing of underbrush.

'*As the day dragged on into the afternoon, perspiration and fatigue began to show on P'sudohn. His breathing reduced to sucking wind into a painfully heaving chest. His legs felt rubbery as they responded to his mental commands with increasing difficulty.*

'*Relentless footsteps continued crashing behind him in the underbrush.*

'*Eyes wide with panic, he searched for a place to hide. Everywhere he looked he saw nothing but broad green leaves. Still, the heavy footsteps of his pursuer came, hitting the ground ever closer.*

'*Unable to run further, P'sudohn dropped to the ground behind a tree. He closed his eyes and leaned a weary, sweat-soaked head against its trunk. waiting for the inevitable.*

'*As he was sinking to the verge of despair, an idea occurred to him.*

'*He pressed the butt of the trident shaft down firmly into the soft soil and pointed the tines in the direction of the ever nearing footsteps. Suddenly, through the greenery appeared the powerful figure of Oss'yanhu covered with sweat and grime and with eyes ablaze. With Oss'yanhu almost upon him, P'sudohn raised the trident and pointed it to Oss'yanhu's mid-section.*

'*Oss'yanhu threw his hands in the air. His eyes widened and his mouth flew open as he doubled over, almost falling on P'sudohn.*

'*P'sudohn stared in fascinated horror at the mortally wounded Oss'yanhu rolling over to one side and slumping to the ground. Still on his hands and knees, P'sudohn studied the widening pool of blood soaking into the grass. A sense of alarm shot through him as he heard crashing in the bushes from another direction.*

'*D'heus suddenly stood before him. He reached down and helped P'sudohn to his feet. He waited for P'sudohn to recover sufficiently to stand on his own.*

'"*Well done, dear brother,*" *he said, helping him brush off dirt and dead leaves.* "*You have dispatched the scoundrel rather neatly.*"

'*He registered disappointment that P'sudohn did not seem to share in his satisfaction.*

'*In the meantime, P'sudohn had discovered something that in the excitement of combat he had quite forgotten. The sword that mysteriously appeared at his bedside still hung from his belt.*

'*It had never been unsheathed from its scabbard.*

THE TITANS

'An expression of remorse set in his face as he studied the body that lay at his feet. "It is an ignoble victory, I fear," he said. "I killed a naked and unarmed man."

* * *

'Y'rranhu spread in a reclining position across a satin covered couch. He smiled to Tyra who had just entered his apartment. His eyes shone a bright blue with pleasure.
'"You have something to show me?"
'She stepped to his mahogany table. "I assume that this will be of interest to you."
'She produced a small, porcelain dish and laid it on the table. Then she withdrew from her sleeve a narrow vial. She pulled the stopper from the vial and poured powder into the dish. Eyeing the small pile of the white granular substance, she then pulled a wand of rush weed that she had kept tucked in her sash. As she pressed the tip of the rush weed into the powder, smoke began billowing upward. When the smoke gathered as a cloud against the ceiling, it began to clear.
'In the cleared smoke a vision appeared.
'Y'rranhu and Tyra observed a haggard P'sudohn stagger through the jungle. The sight of Oss'yanhu's body receded further into the background. P'sudohn approached the bank of clear, placid pool and paused. A death-like stillness descended on the humid atmosphere. P'sudohn slipped down into the cool water and closed his eyes, letting the refreshing liquid soothe his weary body. He leaned back against the bank.
'"Where are those delightful little creatures hiding?" he sighed.
'He felt the exhaustion within his body become more profound as he slowly slid beneath the pool's surface.
'His eyes took a moment getting accustomed to the underwater world. He swirled around and settled on the sandy bottom. Long strands of seaweed gently swayed with the current where a small stream flowed into it. Fish eyed him with curiosity and darted fitfully away. He studied with fascination the pale green light fading away in bubbles to the darker green shadows in the distance. This new world lay all about him in silence.
'Welcome to your realm, he thought with mounting elation.
'In the distant gloom he thought he saw something darting among the shadows. The figure loomed larger than an ordinary fish. He saw it again. This time he noticed that it looked like a T'tanyu.
'A short distance away two young female faces broke the wall of seaweed and stared at him with curiosity. As they continued to observe him, they kept their distance.

'He gestured to the surface.

'When his face broke the waters he looked up at the luxuriant foliage and gasped for air. Out in the middle of the pool, the two young female heads surfaced, spouting water from small, delicately formed mouths. Two others followed. Soon four heads bobbed about the middle of the pool still eyeing him with curiosity.

'Again, he gestured to them.

"Don't be afraid," he said, trying to reassure them.

'Still they kept their distance.

"I am your new lord," he continued. "Oss'yanhu is dead."

"Dead?" Dismay darkened the pretty faces. "Oh dear!"

The four naiads looked questioningly at each other.

"How did it happen?" asked one in a distressed tone of voice.

P'sudohn hesitated. "It seems," he said with diffidence, "that I killed him. I'm sorry."

'Still they came no closer. Their heads continued to bob in the water.

"But why?" said one as she started to weep.

'Again P'sudohn hesistated. "It is complicated," he said at last. "Suffice it to say that Y'rranhu willed it. I think it better that I not worry your pretty young heads with all the details as to why."

'Another pause.

'Finally one summoned enough courage to once more speak. "Are you cruel?"

'P'sudohn eyed her wistfully. "There has been enough cruelty," he sighed. "I have no intention of treating you with any but the utmost of kindness. Please come to me."

'Gingerly, they paddled their way toward the bank.

'The smoke dissipated and Y'rranhu studied the fading scene with obvious satisfaction. "P'sudohn is doing splendidly," he said. The blueness of his eyes intensified. "He is already demonstrating masterful skill at winning over his subjects."

'Tyra slipped the vial back into the folds of her skirt. "Will there be anything else?"

'He looked at her startled, as if he had quite forgotten that she was still in the room. "No," he said. "You may go now."

'As she exited into the corridor, she paused and glanced back toward the doorway,

'This is just the beginning, she thought. Some day you too will be replaced, you poisonous jellyfish, and D'heus will be your successor.'

THE TITANS

* * *

"Good morning Henry," the dean's voice sang out as Dr. Suess entered his office,

Dr. Suess stared straight ahead as he pulled up close to the desk. He tried to avoid looking at the nameplate: 'J. Negley Jone, Ph.D.' Off to the side he saw a similar nameplate but with the addition: 'Dean of Students.'

For a long moment the dean leaned back in his overstuffed wing-back, fingertips in a steepled position. He pushed the chair as far back it would go without his falling over, stared at the ceiling and began singing:

"'Jesus loves me, this I know,
For the Bible tells me so—"

Dr. Suess suppressed an impulse to laugh. *Nothing this guy does is ever funny*, he thought. He recognized this seemingly ridiculous eccentricity as another of the dean's psychological mind games; a sort of softening up process in preparation for a major confrontation.

Look up horse's petoot in the Dictionary, he thought, *and you'll see a print of his portrait.*

The dean abruptly ended his singing and leaned forward again. "So," he said, looking directly at Dr. Suess, "how are things with the true church?"

Dr. Suess looked puzzled. "Excuse me?"

"Are you not Catholic?"

"Episcopalian."

Dr. Suess chided himself for volunteering even this bit of information. Another pause.

"Oh, really?" The dean pursed his lips and turned to look out the window at the gray February snow. About a block from campus stood a large stone church with a high, thin spire. Darkly narrow indentations framed stained glass windows that sparkled between the surrounding evergreen. The morning sun struggled to bring occasional shafts of light through the heavy clouds.

"I have never seen you at St. Sebastian's," he said, nodding in the church's direction.

"I attend the chapel at St. Dunstan's Priory." Again, he hated volunteering the information.

The dean continued looking out the window. "But monsieur that's forty miles down the canyon," he said, still pursing his lips. "Why there?"

Dr. Suess did not answer right away.

"Because they still use the old prayer book," he said finally. *Not that it's any of your business,* he thought.

"But monseur," he heard the dean continue. "Some of the community's most prominent families attend St. Sebastian's."

Dr. Suess eyed him. "What about the Holy Family?" he said with a wry smile.

The dean didn't answer. Again he appeared lost in his own thoughts.

"And therein may lie her problem," Dr. Suess added.

Still no answer. *Either he's not listening to me,* thought Dr. Suess, *or he's too dense to realize that I've just shot him a zinger.*

He decided against giving his real reason for his bi-monthly trips all the way to St. Dunstan's…

…When he first came to Stillwell he had, in fact, attended St. Sebastian's a few times. The first thing that confronted him upon entering the vestry was a life-sized porcelain statue of the church's patron saint covered with gold leaf. The gilt edged likeness of the naked martyr bothered him. He could not look directly at the pained, yet ecstatic expression of the figure's face as it was tied to a post and taking arrows to its body. He found it incongruous that an ancient Christian saint seemed to actually take delight in suffering for a faith to which some of the wealthiest Stillwell families of modern times gave the barest of lip service…

…His reverie was cut short by the dean's next remarks.

"So, you're a communicant," he said. "How interesting. I'd have thought you're loyalty was to Rome, but it's not. You pay allegiance to Canterbury."

Dr. Suess' face hardened. "I pay allegiance to heaven."

"Ah, yes," said the dean, ignoring Dr. Suess' last remark. "She's a gracious lady, the Church of England; all the pageantry of Rome with none of the guilt."

Again the dean smiled grandly as he added: "If I may say so, ours is a marvelous faith."

Dr. Suess reflected on his church experience. Yes, he did appreciate the dignity, the show of reverence that characterized outward expression of corporate worship. He loved the traditions, the stained glass windows, the symbols, and the trappings. He loved soothing cadence of the ancient liturgy. He loved the sturdy chord progression of the old hymns. He loved the colorful processions, the musical excellence of the choir and the organ.

However, it sometimes bothered him that he sensed his contemporaries, rather than doing it for the glory of God, were doing it just for show.

When he expressed this reservation to the dean, the dean sat back and glanced at him with a cavalier expression. "Ah yes," he said, "but we're so good at it."

Another pause.

Dr. Suess finally broke the silence. "Are we here to discuss religion?"

The dean leaned forward in his chair.

"You are quite right," he said. "I have a communication from the police department regarding an assault and battery charge against you," he said, picking up a piece of paper. "Apparently you struck another patron in a local tavern the other night."

"Apparently I did and apparently he asked for it. My attorney is working on a defense even as we speak."

The dean seemed to relax a little. He carefully laid the piece of paper back into an attaché case that lay on the corner of the desk. "Good," he said, drawing out the word. "Then we can put that little matter to rest."

He picked up another paper from the same attaché case and looked at it a moment. "However, I do need to share another concern with you."

He studied the paper a moment. "Dear, dear, dear," he sighed. "Henry, whatever are we going to do with you?"

Dr. Suess leaned back in his chair and looked askance at the dean. "And what is it this time?"

The dean continued studying the paper. "I have another complaint from the Human Relations Committee."

Dr. Suess shrugged. "At risk of being repetitive," he said, "what is it this time?"

The dean still studied the paper. "It seems that now the complaint is sexual harassment."

Dr. Suess knew immediately the incident in question…

…That particular morning he was again late for his eight o'clock. He could sense the students' undercurrent of resentment at his recent violations of his own rigid standards of punctuality.

He fumbled for the key to unlock the classroom door and, as the students filed past, a girl stopped and said: "Dr. Suess, are you gay?"

He cast a jaundiced eye toward the student who had fired this little gem. *Insufferable twit,* he thought. He remembered that she had the reputation of sleeping around with every jock and athletic coach on campus.

He was certain that he knew what was behind that little salvo.

Marie's first husband.

"No," he retorted in a mock sinister voice, "what you would say if I were to tell you I'm a dirty old man?"

He had subsequently received letters of complaint from the Student Government Office and from the Faculty Senate. The dean now held copies of these letters. Dr. Suess was to submit in writing letters of apology to the student in question, the STUGO, and the Faculty Senate respectively. He was also to apologize verbally to his entire eight o'clock class…

… "Of course, Henry," he heard the dean saying, "I will insist upon seeing copies of those letters before you submit them to the parties in question."

In the ensuing silence, Dr. Suess reflected on matter of Student Wentworth's make-up exam…

...Dr. Suess had dutifully written the make-up as per the dean's request. Dr. Suess thought it such a dummied-down, simplified version of the original that he was actually ashamed to give it. He then took the trouble to phone Mr. Wentworth's dorm and speak with the student personally to set up a mutually acceptable time and place.

Dr. Suess arrived at the empty classroom well in advance to get the room ready and to prepare himself mentally to perform what was a patently distasteful duty.

As it happened, Mr. Wentworth never showed up...

... "I don't think so," said Dr. Suess at last.

The dean arched his eyebrows. "I beg your pardon?"

Dr. Suess continued looking at the paper in question and then handed it back. "Screw it."

The dean sat a little higher in his chair. "I beg your pardon?" he said again.

Dr. Suess eyed the dean with an expressionless look. "Like I said," he replied, "screw it."

The dean became visibly agitated. "I say," he demanded, "what is the meaning of this impertinence?"

Dr. Suess sat back in a more relaxed position. *This stupid shmuck doesn't realize I'm holding more high cards than ever*, he thought. *He married into money and he could lose it. One word from me and 'Babs' would cut him off without a cent.*

Nah, what the hell; I'll get him with this one instead. I can always lower the heavy boom later. "I have just been to Personnel," he said finally. "I have applied for early retirement; effective at the end of the school year."

* * *

Dr. Suess sat at a rickety chair in front of his ancient, worn desk. He surveyed the cramped, somber walls of his office. The smell of mildew and stale moisture hung heavy in the air. Outside the small, floor level window he saw gray, rotting snow lying everywhere about the campus.

He reached down to a small door opening to a side compartment. Back in the recesses of his desk he saw a bottle labeled 'Bacardi Rum.' He reached for a tumbler beside the bottle and poured himself a tot. After taking a sip, he replaced the bottle and closed the door.

The springs of his chair creaked in protest as he leaned back and propped his battered ankle length boots on the desk top. He ritually unzipped his tobacco pouch and scraped his pipe bowl. He felt the tensions of the morning fade as he tilted his head back and puffed clouds of fragrant smoke into the air.

You're a bad boy, he thought. *You're polluting.*

His mind went in retrospect to the early days of his relationship with Marie...

...He had inferred from her answer at the Last Chance Café that he at least had his foot in the door, as it were. He then called her later that week and announced that he had two tickets to the Denver Opera that coming weekend.

He would count it a privilege were she to accompany him.

They were to drive up to Denver the following Friday afternoon for dinner and the theater.

He recalled stopping by her condo. His first surprise was her appearance at the door.

Where was the prim, severe school teacher-activist he had known?

Gone were the wire rim glasses. Contact lenses, he gathered. And what had she done with that honey blond hair? He asked himself. No more the plain, indifferent hairdo. Tonight she had taken those long straight tresses and swept them up in a swirl around the back of her head so tastefully done it beggared his description. And the face? He always had been impressed by her clear peach-colored complexion, but what did she do to it tonight? What skin treatment did she spend time with for this event? Was it skin cream? Was it some exotic Israeli import from the potash deposits from the Dead Sea area? Or was it merely a cucumber? She now looked downright radiant—like one of the T'tanyu goddesses described in the trident messages from the past.

She wore a formal, slack suit combination of black velvet with gold trim. She invited him in. As he stood in the vestibule, he surveyed the simple but elegant surroundings furnished in an Early American motif.

"Pardon me while I get my wrap," she said as she disappeared into a front closet.

She emerged shortly and allowed him to help her on with a jacket, also of black velvet. "The children are with their father this week-end," she said as she buttoned up the front.

As he helped her into the car, he recalled the weather forecast had predicted some pretty heavy snowstorms.

During the afternoon drive from Stillwell to Denver, they enjoyed clear, dry weather over a hard bare terrain. The skies shone deep blue and gold in the sunset with no hint of anything but clear weather.

As they entered the lobby of the theater, Dr. Suess took one last look at the still clear skies of early evening.

He had purchased seats front row box in the first balcony.

Overhead chandeliers illuminated the auditorium's gilt-edged interior. When the heavy, crimson curtain rose, the music swelled in accompaniment to the chorister's opening of a performance of Lehar's *Merry Widow*.

At intermission, he escorted her to the outer lobby.

"Touch of the bubbly?" he suggested nodding toward a cash bar.

"Why yes," she said. "How thoughtful."

He fought the crowds and then shortly returned with two drinks: champagne for her, Scotch-on-the-rocks for him.

While still taking her first sip, she noticed that he had already downed his drink.

"That went fast," she commented.

He didn't answer. He let her finish and then gestured toward the doorway that led to the auditorium.

"Time to get back," he said, still ignoring her remark.

After the performance they re-entered the lobby. They knew immediately that they were in trouble. The light from the incandescent bulbs on the marquee that hung over the sidewalk outside reflected a swirling maelstrom of snow flakes the size of corn starch. When they pushed their way through the exit, they immediately found themselves sinking ankle deep in downy white stuff. It covered a sidewalk and street that had lain hard and bare when they first entered the hall. Already, the curbing contour had been obliterated, making the street all but indiscernible. Even rapidly walking pedestrians resembled Lot's wife of Genesis, looking as they did like pillars of white powder.

The couple took two steps out into the blinding whiteness then stopped. Dr. Suess pressed Marie's arm a little tighter under his.

"Looks like it's going to get messy," he commented.

He had previously congratulated himself for saving the expense of a parking pavilion by finding non-metered street parking two blocks away. That self-congratulation now dissolved into dismay as they trudged through ever deepening snow drifts. In the gray-white swirling distance he saw a snowy mound that indicated where his car lay buried.

When they arrived at the curbside pile, they hesitated.

Standing calf deep in the accumulation, Dr. Suess braced himself and began brushing snow from the passenger side.

"No sense in both of us standing out in this," he sighed.

He finally cleared enough metal to enable him to open the door. The smell of wet wool greeted his nostrils as he reached under the seat for a window brush. He then helped Marie into the passenger side.

After sweeping away more fluffy white stuff from the windshield, he eyed the crust of ice underneath.

Damn, he thought as he felt frigid moisture seep through his dress gloves, *forgot the scraper.*

With the help of a plastic credit card, he eventually cleared enough to give the driver's side a modicum of visibility. Soaked from precipitation and sweat, he wearily crawled in behind the wheel.

Would it even start?

He heaved a sigh and a brief prayer as he turned the ignition. A sense of relief followed as the engine jumped to life. After pumping the accelerator, he glanced over at Marie.

Now what? He could almost sense the both of them thinking the same thing.

Turning the steering wheel leftward, he could feel the front wheels crunch against the drifts. Shifting into drive, he tensed as he felt the car creep away from the curb. Once underway, they seemed to gain momentum as they flew past a wake of blinding white. The sight of half buried silhouettes on either side of the road did little to reassure them. They could feel the crunching resistance to their front wheels increasing by the second.

Upon reaching an expressway interchange, driving chunks of snow flew horizontally at their windshield. Their headlights could pick up only a swirling mass of white immediately beyond their front bumper. Dr. Suess rolled down his side window and tried getting better visibility by leaning out.

He saw only blowing drifts rising up past his hubcaps.

Driving back to Stillwell tonight clearly was out of the question.

Soft lights of a neon sign blinked weakly through the swirling snow. Upon closer approach, Dr. Suess made out the words 'Wayside Motel.' As they pulled into the entrance of the motel driveway, he felt the car start to fish-tail. Only with the most adroit of driving skill did he get the headlights to point toward the motel porte-cochere. He finally crunched to a halt, shut off the engine, and sat back trembling from tension and fatigue.

He looked at her. "Do we really have a choice?"

Taking silence to imply consent, he pushed open his door.

Fighting swirling blindness, he helped her out her side. Just outside the office door, they hesitated. How is this going to look?

Are we really ready for this yet?

Once inside, they stepped to the main desk. "You're in luck," said the clerk, eyeing her computer. "We're filling up fast."

Dr. Suess hesitated. He had noticed another motel not fifty yards away. "Uh—how about the one next door?"

The clerk punched a computer. "Again, you're in luck. They've got just a single left."

Dr. Suess gave a sigh of relief. "We'll register the lady here. Reserve the single next door for me."

He and Marie exchanged glances of further relief as the clerk made a quick call. "All set," she said, hanging up the phone.

Marie looked anxiously out the window. "Are you sure you want to go over there?"

Dr. Suess started for the door. "Hey, it's only a hundred feet or so. I could do that blind-folded."

Long moments after having checked in, Marie surveyed her room. Bone-weary, she eyed the shower stall and began stripping off her clothes. She felt waves of relief roll over her as her bra fell from her shoulders. She slipped out of her panties and gingerly stepped under the cascade of warm water. *Always have to adjust to the temperature of strange shower,* she thought as she fine-tuned the hot and cold knobs.

Above the sound of the rushing water, she heard a knock at her outside door.

"It's open," she shouted.

An alarming thought shot through her: What if it wasn't Henry? Would the storm reduce the chance of unwelcome strangers?

She stepped out from behind the curtain and peered through crack of the bathroom door. She felt welcome relief at the sight of the compact, muscular figure now covered with a powdered white. As she rubbed her body with a large, coarse towel, she realized another problem.

All her clothes lay atop her bed in the room.

He also saw her clothing strewn across her bed and sensed her dilemma. Stomping the snow off his feet, he walked to the other bed that was closest to the front door and sat on a corner, facing the curtained picture window.

"I'll just sit here," he said, his back to her, "until you're decent."

She stepped to where her clothes lay, dropped her towel, and began dressing herself. She was about to think it noble of him to turn away like this when she saw herself in the dresser mirror. She noticed that her reflection was clearly visible to him out of the corner of his eye despite his turned back.

He felt a pillow slam his head from behind.

"Jerk!" she shouted.

He stood and turned around in time to face her rushing toward him, fists clenched. As she swung, he caught her wrist and held on.

Suddenly she realized she was still clad only in panties and bra.

With the hand that still held her, he pulled her gently toward him.

"Please," she whispered edging for her other clothes. "Not now."

He sighed and turned again to the picture window.

"And keep your eyes away from the mirror," she said as she finished dressing. "I have children to think about."

"There's a restaurant here," he said. "I was only going to suggest we get something to eat."

* * *

The doorway to the bar and restaurant arched a darkened chaos of laughter, clinking glasses of a capacity crowd and of the ringing cash registers. From out of the murky void they heard a voice: "How many?"

"Two. Non-smoking, please."

The hostess led them into the interior twilight. She stopped at a small table and lit a candle jar that began to glow softly red. The hostess laid two menus on the table. "Anything from the bar?"

Dr. Suess helped Marie into her chair.

After he looked at the cocktail and wine list he said: "I'll have a martini."

Marie ordered a glass of burgundy.

"Place seems unusually busy," she commented as he settled into the chair opposite. "Must be others marooned like us."

After the waitress brought their drinks Marie took a sip of her wine.

Glancing at him, she noticed that he was already handing his glass back to the waitress who had just reappeared with an order pad.

"I'll have your 'Late Night Special,'" he told her, "and another martini, please."

"I'll just have a Caesar Salad," said Marie.

When the waitress returned with his drink, he took a sip and studied her face as it reflected in the soft glow of the table lamp. "What are you thinking?"

"You mean right now?"

"Yes."

She hesitated. "For two people who hardly know each other, I think we've been quite intimate."

His gaze took on an impish expression. "I don't think we've been intimate at all."

"Oh, shut up," she said in mock severity.

He felt a sharp kick under the table.

A thought occurred to him. They could run into Dean Jone here. He would probably have some sweet young thing hanging on his arm. *Oh, well*, he thought, *were that to happen, he would have more explaining than we.*

In any case, he concluded, he would very likely pretend to not recognize us.

A sizzling sound broke the momentary lull in the conversation. Just within range of the lamp's glow two hands held plates exuding the aroma of freshly cooked cuisine.

"Anything else?" The voice came from the darkness above the glow.

Dr. Suess handed the waitress his glass. "I'll have another."

When the waitress returned with his drink, he studied it a moment. "I know," he sighed. "You think I drink too much."

Her silence was pregnant with eloquence.

"All right," he shrugged. "I admit it. Actually I didn't always drink like this, but since my wife died—"

He didn't finish. Silence settled over the table as they began eating. He observed her eating a section of hard-boiled egg from her Caesar Salad.

"Did it ever occur to you," he said as he paused between bites, "that eggs are animal life?"

She laid aside her knife and fork. "You're not going to start that again, are you?"

He resumed eating. "Just teasing," he said.

Then it happened. "Ohmigod, look!" he whispered, pointing to a murkily lit dance floor.

Her gaze followed his pointing. "What?"

Amongst the crowd milling about in front of a small bandstand, they spotted Dean Jone dancing with a young woman.

"It could be his wife," said Marie without much conviction.

"Not a chance," laughed Dr. Suess. "I know his wife. Adele Smithson Jones—'Babs' as he calls her—is a somewhat older woman."

Marie's eyes widened with anxiety. "What if he sees us?"

Dr. Suess went on to explain. For him to try use blackmail would bring more problems back on him than he wanted to contend with at this juncture. *I'll just keep it my little secret,* he thought *unless he tries to make waves with me.*

He then explained to Marie further the relationship between the dean and his wife. Adele Smithson was a woman of means.

She's loaded, was the way Dr. Suess had explained it to her. Her family's ancestral estate in England is the campus of Kaxton College.

"She is on their Board of Regents and is out of the country a good bit of the time," he added. "Theirs is a marriage of convenience."

Another silence punctuated by background laughter and ringing registers. At length he again attempted conversation. "How long have you been at the high school?"

"Seven years."

"From the area originally?"

"Actually from California."

"Where did you go to school?"

"Brigham Young University."

"You're Mormon then?"

"Was."

The conversation lapsed briefly.

Marie again spoke. "How about you, are you a 'was,' too?"

Dr. Suess sighed. "I'm a lot of 'wases.'"

She looked at him questioningly but said nothing. She had apparently left it to him to explain.

His family had come from Prague originally. He had come from a long line of government civil servants in the old Austro-Hungarian government. Although originally Jewish, his great grandfather had to convert to Catholicism to qualify for the position. After the Great War, as they called it back then, his grandfather took a post with the new Czechoslovak republic. In the thirties, his father also entered civil service. He rose rapidly until, in 1938, he became assistant minister of Education under the soon-to-end Eduard Benes regime. Just before the Czech president capitulated to Hitler and the Nazis in March of '39, his family fled to England.

They spent the World War II years there, finally immigrating to the US in 1953.

In the interim, they had also converted from Catholicism to the Church of England.

He wanted to ask what she was now, if anything, but thought better of it. "I notice that you—don't make mention of your husband."

"We're divorced; four years ago."

"I see," he said. "Sorry."

Not really, he thought.

She sighed. "He wasn't the easiest person to live with," she said after a brief pause. "He seemed deathly afraid of dirt or germs. He showered at least two or three times a day. He covered his hand with a handkerchief when grasping the doorknob of a public building. I suppose in common slang one would call him a neat freak."

Some marriage, though Dr. Suess. *A vegetarian and activist matched up with a compulsive Mr. Clean. It's a wonder the kids don't wind up being emotional basket cases.*

"It eventually had to happen," she said, picking up the conversation.

"What eventually had to happen?"

"He found somebody else."

"Sorry," he said again. He looked at her. He acknowledged that despite being a little on the plain side, he began to feel an increased attraction for her. He began to think realistically of some sort of long term commitment.

Wonder how it would work out, he thought.

He waited for her to continue.

"I helped him through dental school," she sighed. "Then he found someone he said that was intellectually more his equal; a classmate of his."

His hand reached across the reached across the table for hers.

"Maybe it was all for the best," he found himself daring to say. "That sonofabitch showed that he didn't deserve you."

Her eyes locked in with his. "Thanks," she said; then added stoically: "Nice of you to say that."

"After all," he continued, "What kind of low life would use one woman and then leave her for another woman."

The silence that followed seemed to crackle with electricity.

"Who said it was a woman?" she said finally. Immediately upon hearing herself say those very words, shards of painful memories came flooding back into her consciousness. Like Elsa Lancaster, wife of the actor Charles Laughton she lost her speech. Not only was she stuck dumb, she had to be hospitalized for short time.

Could she even now cope any better?

We'll soon find out, she concluded.

He didn't know what to say.

Maybe he should have pursued the subject of religion instead. *This conversation is getting sticky*, he thought.

He searched deep into his memory.

Yes, he realized. *It all fits.*

He had met Marie's ex-husband once at a cocktail party. He knew him to have had a successful dental practice in the area.

He originally did not make the connection with Marie.

He recalled a fairly tall, well-built man. He recalled disappointment at the soft looking face. Dark brown hair was swept back in loosely gentle waves. Pale blue eyes accentuated a look more pretty than handsome. His broad face sported the thinnest of beards. A pencil moustache framed a rosebud mouth.

Dr. Suess allowed as to how the small, delicate hands were perhaps just the right for practicing dentistry.

When the man walked he bounced on the balls of his feet and held his head high with a sway backed posture.

Dr. Suess recalled being irritated at the way the man did not laugh a real, masculine guffaw at broad, earthy humor. He never seemed to dig guy jokes. He, rather, giggled constantly at what Dr. Suess considered the most frivolous and insipid of situations.

He nevertheless recalled the man's being the life of any party. His reputation for wit and repartee were legendary. Any macho male with a testosterone overload and foolish enough to make snide remarks about his effete speech and manner did so at his own peril. Marie's ex would invoke on the poor schlep's head a barrage of rapier ripostes for the rest of the evening.

With such poor slobs he was ruthless.

He would leave them with no recourse but to wander off with their tail between their legs as it were.

More silence.

He leaned toward her. He felt the soft contact of her lips as they pressed close.

"I think you're a nice person," he said softly.

Her whispered response penetrated deeply. "I think you are too."

Another pause.

"In a way," he said finally, "I'm glad things turned out like they did."

She looked thoughtfully into table lamp. "I am, too," she said.

She added: "In a way."

She leaned back in her chair but left her hand lying under his. She took another sip of wine and watched anxiously as he emptied his martini: his fourth for the evening.

"I'm ready to go," she said, glancing down at her half finished salad.

After paying the cashier, they discovered an inside corridor connecting the wing where her room was located. When they reached the room, they looked out the picture window and found that the snowing had slacked off considerably; however, the blowing and drifting continued. As they opened the door, Marie felt the biting sting of the wind against her face. Looking with misgiving out across the waves of deep, rippled snow, she turned again to Dr. Suess.

He could stumble and fall into a snowdrift before he's halfway across the lot, she realized. He could freeze to death without anyone knowing.

"You don't have to go over there," she said.

He caressed her face and again he felt the moist tenderness of her lips.

Been celibate since Sheila died, he thought. *I don't want this to be just a one night stand*, he told himself. *The heavy stuff can wait.*

He kissed her again. "Let me try," he whispered.

* * *

He opened his eyes to a blinding shaft of sunlight. He felt his head throb in rhythm to his heart beat. His tongue felt thick and fuzzy. He struggled to extricate himself from the tangle of bed sheets that seemed to bind him like a mummy. They felt intertwined with his clothes and he felt a cold draft on his stocking feet which protruded beyond the edge of the coverlet. He turned his head and eyed the still form in the bed across from the night stand. When he tried to address the blond head half buried in the pillow, his vocal chords responded only after some effort.

"Marie?" he said hoarsely.

She turned her head toward the ceiling. "What time is it?"

He struggled to bring his watch hand out from under the covers. He spent more moments trying to focus on the dial.

Eight forty-two

I've got a nine o'clock, he thought. His mind raced in panic. Then, realizing it was Saturday he looked at Marie with a sheepish smile.

After struggling to his feet, he looked himself in the mirror. He studied the bloodshot eyes and bewhiskered face under a head of unkempt hair. He blinked in disbelief as the face stared back. He noticed his topcoat, blazer, and tie hanging in the closet. He felt certain that no one could count the wrinkles in his shirt and trousers. *If she still cares for me after seeing me like this,* he concluded, *there must be something to it.*

He heard shuffling. He turned to see her grab items of clothing from the foot of her bed and pull them under the covers.

"Hope you've got a good memory," she said as she struggled to dress herself, "because you're not going to get an encore."

From the direction of the motel office, they heard the roar of an engine and a scraping sound.

"They're plowing out the driveway," he said, feeling in his blazer pocket for his room key. "Bye the way," he said, fumbling with the room marker, "what happened last night?"

Once in her slacks, she slipped out of the bed and buttoned her blouse. She pulled the drape away from the window, letting in additional sunlight. When his eyes could stand the brilliance, he saw foot tracks just outside the window leading away from her doorway. He saw the imprint of a prone figure in the snow about twenty feet away from the building. The other motel loomed a good hundred feet away.

"You could have spent the night out there," she said.

Though he fell a short distance from her door, she had to almost carry him back to her room. She then struggled to get him into the other bed.

Dr. Suess shrugged in embarrassment. "Let's go check out."

An hour later, their car sped along a freshly plowed canyon road.

As the road wound down into the valley toward Stillwell, Marie finally spoke. "It's pretty likely people are going to talk."

"But this is the 21st Century," said Dr. Suess, casting a quick glance. "Do you really think so?"

The town gossips are like a bunch of vipers, she thought. "Yes."

He drove on in thoughtful silence. A huge ball of wet snow had fallen from an overhang. Chunks of snow flew up and hit the windshield. For a moment, he had difficulty seeing the road. He pressed the wiper button.

"We have receipts from separate motels," he said. "Won't that convince those who need convincing?"

She slid down into her seat. "Let them believe what they will," she said with resignation. "With those who believe us, receipts won't be necessary…"

Chapter 8

... "Henry, you sly devil, you did it!"

"Did what?" Dr.Suess eyed Dr. Sirotka with puzzlement. The two scientists were sharing a booth at Lena's, a working man's watering hole at the edge of town. Ever since Dr. Suess' altercation with the belligerent stranger, Deadman's Gulch was off limits to him.

"You blind-sided the dean."

Dr. Suess had just finished telling of the conversation with him the day before and of his previous visit to personnel to fill out retirement papers.

Dr. Sirotka sat nursing a draft Killian's while Dr. Suess quaffed a martini.

"I had better quit while I'm ahead," he said, eyeing his empty glass. He placed his hand over the top of the glass as a bar maid approached.

"I'm due at the middle school," he continued. "Got a conference with the counselor."...

...Tim, one of Marie's children, had been expelled from school day before yesterday. Before Marie could arrange a substitute to enable her to go, Dr. Suess volunteered to go for her. Dr. Suess seemed to actually proud of the boy.

The incident involved Tim's social studies teacher who was going to give a pop quiz. To minimize the possibility of cheating, she divided the class into two sections to be given separate tests. The determining factor in deciding who got which test was the shape of one's navel.

The teacher walked down the aisles of the classroom. When she passed each student, she gave a copy of the 'A' test to the student who was an 'outie' and a 'B' exam to the student who was an 'innie.' When she approached Tim's desk, he said nothing.

The teacher stared at him in bewilderment.

Well? She had demanded.

Well what?

Are you an 'innie' or an 'outie?'

Neither was the reply.

She didn't understand.

I'm a 'none-of-your-businessie,' he then had said. So I guess I don't have to take the test…

…As Dr. Sirotka smiled in approval, Dr. Suess shook his head.

"I figure a kid with that kind of chutzpa needs some heavy duty back up," he said as he made as though he was about to leave.

Dr. Sirotka held out his hand. "Wait," he said.

He opened an attaché case that lay on the seat beside him. "I've got another report from the Cryptology Office."

* * *

Y'rranhu sat in a slouched position on his open-backed couch and studied the delicately embroidered curtains fluttering in the breeze.

He contemplated the archway they framed, leading as it did to the balcony beyond. A silken clad nymph stood in the main doorway.

"'A visitor to see you, my lord," she said.

"'Show the visitor in."

He saw a powerfully built male standing behind her in the doorway. The male radiated a shimmering golden hue. He held in his hand a scepter that ended in a sunburst.

Y'rranhu turned in his settee and sat up. His eyes took on a bright blue. His pupils widened. "Ah, Hypp'ryon," he said. "It is good to see you."

"'You sent for me."

Y'rranhu gestured to a nearby stool. "Please sit down."

'After Hypp'ryon seated himself, Y'rranhu studied him at length. His eyes changed from deep blue to the pale gray of despondency.

'Finally he said: "Do you love me?"

'Hypp'ryon shot an anxious glance. "My father," he said with anguish in his voice, "what a question! Of course I love you."

'Y'rranhu stood to his feet and began pacing the floor. "It seems," he said, "that a thing like filial love is something that I can no longer take for granted."

'Hypp'ryon waited for his father to continue.

'Y'rranhu stepped to the front of the doorway that led to the outside balcony.

'He sighed.

'"Once there was a time," he began, "so far back that even I can scarce remember it now. But there was a time I recall being borne with all tenderness in the Everlasting Father's all-encompassing bosom.

'"Loved as an only begotten son was I, when no other Light Beings were as yet created. So became I then most-favored eldest brother: chief among many equals, as it were.

'"Bathed in celestial light, arrayed in apparel gorgeous beyond words, plaited with every jewel and precious stone conceived and created by divine mind and power. Bracelets, necklaces, amulets, and rings on my fingers and bands of purest precious metals counted I as common attire. Crown of many crowns with their attendant authority rested lightly on my brow.

'"Father-of-Lights spared not himself any honor to bestow upon me. So exalted he me above all other sons of light.

'"As if that were not enough, he also endowed me with every possible grace, ability, and power. So governed I vast universes with unbridled power and dominion. Answerable was I to none save Father-of-Lights himself.

'"He made me curator of vast innumerable galaxies. He made me director of the court musicians of the heaven-of-heavens itself. There celebrated celestial choirs made music indescribably beautiful for his ears alone.

'"As the final zenith of privilege, he made me to preside over his marvelous conservatory of life's laboratory: this small exquisite orb of marbled blue.

'"Did Everlasting Father himself thus err and become the original doting parent in creating the original prodigal son? Why does he then hold me more culpable for his overindulgence? As creatures of terrestrial flesh lust for carnal pleasures, so do not creatures of the spirit lust for pleasures of the spirit, namely power?

His eyes turned green with agitation.

"I see myself now doomed to play a role from which there is no turning back. For having overreached myself, I see the descent and fall once begun, never reversed. So be it then. Let us play this thing out. I will seek even greater power and glory till we see with eternal finality which of us is master.

"I will ascend unto the sides of the North."

Hypp'ryon stared at him in disbelief. What was he saying?

'Ascend to the sides of the North?

"'Ascend to the sides of the North? Surely, father, you don't mean this?"

Fear's thick smell began filling the room. Hypp'ryon stepped back in horror at the change he saw in his father's countenance. The eyes narrowed to mere slits in his head. The pupils likewise became as slits, like those of a lizard or other reptile.

Was it Hypp'ryon's imagination or did his father's face really assume a scaly texture?

"'Yes! Ascend to the sides of the North." Y'rranhu's voice took on a growl. "I will exalt myself above the stars of the Almighty. I will be like the Most High.

"Better I should be cast down. Better to reign in the land of the dead than to serve in the celestial realms."

His face appeared normal again. He began pacing the room. His eyes reverted to their normal brown.

"'As I ponder, I find it amusing that I have been given by the Almighty yet another honor: I and I alone am prince. A sovereign if you will, of a whole new universe.

"'A universe of the damned."

Hypp'ryohn sat stunned.

"'My father," he whispered. "Never have I heard you talk like this."

"My son," said Y'rranhu, still looking at the balcony, "you will see and hear things still more shocking than this."

Hypp'ryhon rose to his feet and likewise began pacing the floor. "This universe of the damned," he said. "How can you speak of such a thing with such relish?"

Y'rranhu turned from his gaze outside and cast a sidelong glance toward his son. "Because I have no intention of suffering such a fate. Because I have no intention of failing in my mission."

Hypp'ryhon continued to stand with his back to his father. "Gracious sire," he said, wringing his hands, "you know me well enough to know that I do not frighten easily, but I must tell you, this kind of talk terrifies me. Do you really intend to wrest power from the Originator himself?"

"Precisely."

'Hypp'ryhon stood as stone. Was he really hearing what he thought he was hearing? Did his father's words that he heard just now denote a seismographic change not seen since the very beginning of creation itself? Were we being called upon to challenge all the heavens of heavens?

'Again the eyes turned green.

'Hypp'ryhon's head dropped. "I have never even seen him," he said.

"'Nor have I, actually," said Y'rranhu with a laugh.

'He turned to his son. "But there are those who claim to have seen him. They refuse to describe him to the rest of us, however. I only know that to most of the intelligences in the universe, he is only a brilliant light in the most holy of sanctuaries. Personally, the more I think about it, the more I am convinced that he is only a mechanical device created by some Trickster of extreme antiquity to foist upon the rest of the universe an elaborate fraud. I mean to enter that sanctuary, expose this fraud once and for all, and seize power over all that is for me to inherit. It will be a great opportunity for all of us,

"'Think of it, my son. For you it will mean not only controlling the sun in this solar system, but you will control all the suns in all solar systems; all from here, our beloved Sh'yan-Grl'"

'He turned briefly away from his son and looked pensively off into space.

"'Yes," he said to himself, "I will return to the courts of the Everlasting One where at one time I had been wont to direct the celestial choirs to sing for his exclusive pleasure. I'm sure I will have little trouble appearing again as a guest conductor, as it were. However, this time—instead of leading the choir in praise of Am, I will order them to sing praises to me. This will signal the beginning of the revolt."

"But if your plan fails, father, and you become as you say, Lord of the Damned, is there not already an underworld ruled by my brother, D'is?"

'Again, Y'rranhu replied with animation. The green in his eyes brightened. "If I fail," he said. "I will be lord over a domain of the damned far more frightening than any underworld now ruled by D'is."

'Hypp'ryhon picked up his solar scepter and held it thoughtfully in his hand. He studied the delicately fashioned marble walls of his father's apartment. Theirs had been a good life—the T'tanyu. For eons they had been privileged to be party to perhaps the grandest experiment in the universe: the development of the phenomenon known as

biological life on this tiny, but beautifully marbled planet. Their objective had been to help construct a unique, garden like paradise. They, in turn, would be the beneficiaries of this lush fiefdom.

Why can we not be content?

"'You seem deep in thought.' His father's voice arrested his reverie.

He turned and gestured to the outdoors. "The sun rises higher," he said. "I must attend to my duties."

Y'rranhu's gaze followed his son's exit. His eyes turned dark as though a light was being extinguished.

* * *

D'heus stood atop the summit of the counsel rock. He eyed the host of intelligence being warriors that stood on the broader surface at his feet. Immediately beside him stood the pale green form of P'sudohn with trident at the ready. The others stood a slight distance away as they faced D'heus' platform.

"We call this meeting in daylight," he announced, "because we have good news: we are now powerful enough to no longer have to act clandestinely. I call on Yp'llu to come forth and give his report."

A well-muscled young male whose skin and tunic shone with an aureate sheen stepped out of the crowd and neared D'heus' rocky platform. He turned to the crowd.

"My name is Yp'llu, I had been commissioned to seize Hypp'ryion's world, the world of the sun and the heavens," he said. He held up the sunburst scepter. "I did not have to kill to get this. I found Hypp'ryon earlier today lying in his chariot. He had just taken his own life with his dagger. The chariot and skies are now mine."

D'heus nodded in approval.

"We now control the waters," he said. "We control the day. We control the night. Our power grows hourly."

P'sudohn approached D'heus with diffidence. "A word with you, my lord," he said. "In private, if you please."

D'heus looked at him inquisitively. "What is it, my brother?"

P'sudohn gestured toward a thicket of trees. "If you please, my lord," he repeated. "This is for your ears only."

D'heus sighed and followed P'sudohn to the grove of trees in question. "All right," he sighed with a note of impatience. "What is it?"

THE TITANS

P'sudohn cast a furtive glance about before speaking his mind. "Last night after you left," he said finally. "K'haos continued to address the troops."

"And?"

"I heard him issue the following orders: 'We will leave the T'tanyu and their offspring with nothing but their tears to weep with. We will leave no bower or dwelling standing.

"'No blade of grass will again grow in the ground that bears the imprint of our soldier's footsteps.

"Is that your intention, my lord?"

D'heus looked thoughtful. "Of course not," he said. "This orb is ours to conquer, not to destroy. We must leave as much of it intact as possible. After all, when the T'tanyu are eliminated, this will be our home."

Again he paused. "I am sure K'haos means well but he misunderstood. We must alert him and put him straight immediately."

P'sudohn looked worried. "That may not be easy, my lord," he sighed. "He is currently in orbit and will not be available again until darkness falls."

D'heus took a determined stance. He planted his fists against his sides. "We can at least countermand his directive," he said, "and then explain things to him this evening. It is absolutely essential that we in the high command present a unity and common cause before our troops."

He started to leave when P'sudon took his arm.

"Now what is it?"

"I fear there's more," he said with a heavy countenance. "There are those in our ranks that covet our positions of leadership."

D'heus sat dejectedly on a fallen log. For long moments he assumed a pensive pose, leaning his chin against a closed fist.

"A fine thing," he sighed. "Our rebellion threatens to die a-borning because of nascent insurgency in our own ranks. Very well then, tell me the worst."

P'sudohn sat down beside him. "We have our own race of naiads," he said, "called the Khorkhornu. Their leader, M'Theus' even now is plotting our overthrow. They aver that male leadership has prevailed far too long on this orb."

D'heus stood to his feet. "I will nip this little rebellion in the bud before the day is out," he said. "I will summon Kherm' to bring M'theus' to me. I will turn her beauty into ugliness. I will turn her lovely, flowing locks of hair into a den of writhing, poisonous serpents. Any male who desires her will be turned to stone the minute he gazes lustfully upon her. I will in like manner also curse those of her race. I will then banish them in exile to a remote island in the most dismal section of our planet."

He started for the edge of the small grove. "Come, brother, we must go forth and review our troops. We must take precautions necessary to prevent any other rebellion from breaking out in our ranks."

As they stepped out from their sylvan hideout, D'heus continued. "I fear that we may have labored under the delusion that our contingent is of the same noble character as the great and mighty T'tanyu once were. I fear that's Rya's curse has proven altogether too powerful, too all-pervasive. Yes; according to her curse we hold command over an exceedingly sorry lot of misbegotten miscreants. They cannot be trusted. Their loyalty even for a moment cannot be taken for granted. We must be constantly on our guard. We must rule with an iron hand. We must rule with intrigue and meet treachery with treachery. We will plant informers in their ranks. We must pit each warrior against his brother. We must divide and conquer in our own forces or perish."

D'heus glanced up at the waning afternoon sun as it lowered itself behind the smoldering mountain peaks on the horizon. "We must act quickly," he said. "I perceive that Yp'llu has a son, Phay'tu, who even now plots to usurp his father's domain by flying across the heavens in a pair of jerry-built wings in order to intercept his father's chariot."

"He must be stopped."

They mounted up the rocky trail to the summit of the counsel rock. In the distance they saw a blurred whirling. It looked like a whirlwind that appeared to be coming closer.

"Not to worry," said D'heus. "This is Kherm' my messenger. Let us see what tidings he brings. Perhaps we can finally hear some good news. The Strong-Ones knows that it is long overdue."

The whirling hovered briefly above them and then landed beside them on the rocky surface. The whirling stopped and took bodily form. Immediately before them P'sudohn saw a a male youth, exceedingly handsome. He wore a tunic radiantly golden. He wore a strange looking helmet from which protruded the wings of an eagle. The sandals that covered his feet extended another pair of wings.

"I bear good tidings, my lord," he said. "I have just learned Y'rranhu has summoned all the T'tanyu to meet with him tonight in the great hall at Sh'yan-Grl'.

"That is good news," said D'heus. "Bless you, my son, you bring me just the message I was waiting for. Tonight we will band our army together and accomplish our mission.

"We will then deal with all traitors and rebels."

* * *

Night's velvety star-studded blanket stretched like a ceiling across the firmament above the outcropping used by D'heus as his counsel rock. The flat surface stretched out below for the space of what intelligences into the future might someday consider to be the size of their football field. He held in his hand a scepter, the shaft of which measured the full height of his stature. It was topped with a miniature golden model of our solar system.

He planted the shaft of the scepter beside him as he began to address the legions of intelligences assembled on the plain at his feet.

"You may wonder why I again summoned you under the cover of darkness," he said. "Tonight is going to be different from all other nights. Never in all the history of our race has there been one like it; neither will there ever be."

He eyed his troops assembled, rank upon rank, with misgiving. In no way did they equal in nobility, beauty, and stature of the T'tanyu. Before him gathered the offspring, the seed, of men foretold by his mother R'ya as she denounced his father, Oss'yanhu.

With the exception of himself, P'sudohn, Kh'aos, and Yp'llu, to a man they stood before him hunchbacked, clubfooted, dwarfed, or otherwise cruelly deformed and disfigured of face and body in countless grotesque ways. Many wrapped in bandage, issue of running sores totally defying remedy.

These wretches bear in their bodies the curse of sins not of their doing, he thought. They are to be pitied.

Nevertheless he purposed not to pity them, but rather he would weld them into a wonderfully fierce fighting unit.

My school will be hard, he resolved. I will show no mercy as I turn these wretches into a phalanx of splendid, predatory animals from which the decadent T'tanyu will shrink in terror. We will attack as one.

'One race.

'One kingdom.

'One leader.

Tonight they will climb the mountain trail to the great summit palace, Sh'yan-

Grl', seize it, and destroy the race once known as T'tanyu. They will then re-dub the palace itself with the name U-lympu. From it they will then be the ones to reign where the T'tanyu for eons once ruled.

'A voice from out the crowd called to him.

"Brother P'sudohn," he said in response. "Come forward and be recognized."

'P'sudohn approached D'heus and bowed. "My lord," he said, "what of the wise woman, Tyra. Is she to be destroyed with the others?"

"'You bring up a good question, my brother," replied D'heus. "I hereby decree that the wise woman, Tyra, will be given opportunity to swear allegiance to our cause. If she so swears, she will be spared. If she refuses, she will be destroyed with the rest.

"Tonight the T'tanyu, as is their custom, are assembled in the great hall, Sh'yan-Grl'," he continued. "They will be involved with much revelry and will not be expecting us. Opportunity to fall upon them and destroy them may not come like this again."

'He then raised his scepter and gestured toward the high plateau silhouetted in the distance against the night sky. Sh'yan-Grl's roofs, parapets, and massive columns reflected the lights that emanated from within the great hall.

'Still pointing with his scepter, he turned and stepped in the great hall's direction. "Onward, bothers," he ordered. "Destroy them utterly."

* * *

'An hour later D'heus' warriors raced through Sh'yan-Grl's great hall, its apartments and its ante-chambers, smashing, shredding, and otherwise despoiling every piece of tapestry, cloth, earthenware, and furniture that fell under their rampage.

'Much to their surprise, however, they found the great palace deserted.

'Even Y'rranhu was not.

'Well into night, then, their fury somewhat abated, they reassembled into the great hall. D'heus mounted a staircase, the better to maintain visual command of his troops, and began to address them.

"'My bothers," he began, "I am sorry that I cannot afford you the privilege of personally destroying the T'tanyu. However, I now officially take possession of this palace and rename it U'lympu."

'He pointed with his scepter toward a stairway that led to the wine cellar.

"'To the wine casks," he shouted. "U'lympu reigns!"

'The warriors burst as a flood, surging toward the winery.

THE TITANS

"*Wee-hee-hee-hee!*" shouted one,. "*Wa-bee wa-bant wa-bine!*"

"*Wa-bee wa-bant wa-binerooney!!*" shouted another.

'Soon the great army degenerated into a milling, riotous crowd breaking into the newly brought-up wine casks and proceeded to all manner of excess of revelry and debauchery. From the nearby forests, many warriors had sought out and seized the terrified nymphs and naiads and dragged them terrified and screaming into the banqueting hall for their wanton pleasure.

'Shrieks of triumph filled the air."*Wa-binka, wa-booki! Off the T'tan-yu!*"

'Others of the sorry band fanned further out into the larger expanse of rain forest, grassland and mountain range, seeking fresh victims upon whom they can satisfy their lusts and their appetites.

"*Boshi-bazhinka!*" they shouted. "*wa-be wa-bant fa-bee-males!*"

'P'sudohn ran to his brother's side. "My lord," he pleaded. "We must do something, quick!"

"*Ya-ya-ya-ya-yee-hee-hee-hee!*" they screamed.

'D'heus eyed the surrealism playing out before him. "You're quite right," he said, his voice taut with alarm.

'He mounted a dais at one end of the hall.

"'My brothers," he shouted. "Stop! This is your world you're wrecking."

'The screaming and the revelry only got louder.

'D'heus thrust out his scepter to halt a grinning little hunchback who was just then rushing past him.

"'You there," he ordered. "Help me put a stop to this."

'The little hunchback stopped and sought to brush away drops of wine spilled on his soiled tunic. His head twisted toward D'heus.

'He gave D'heus and evil grin. "We have to stand up for what we believe in," He said, breaking from the unintelligible gibberish.

"'And what do you believe in?" demanded D'heus.

"'Oh—hoo—hoo—hah!*" laughed the hunchback as he rushed off to rejoin the destruction.

'D'heus and P'sudohn stood as stone on their respective spots on the dais. Among all the misshapen and malformed creatures that now ravaged the palace, they alone stood erect, noble of face, and body prefect in every way.

'Yet they stood by helpless as they watched the dissembling of the once splendid T'tanyu dynasty.

Tears began rolling down D'heus' chiseled features. "My brother," he pleaded, "we've got to stop them."

P'sudohn shrugged. "We had control of them once," he said with a note of despair. "But I'm afraid we've lost it. Control: once it is lost, can never be regained."

D'heus moved to a stairway leading to the top of the dais. "We must try," he said in desperation.

He ran to a beggar with one eye. "You there," he shouted as the fellow was tearing down an expensive looking tapestry. "Stop that!"

Scabrous lips opened exposing sparse and rotting teeth. An obscenity exploded from the creature's mouth as he resumed shredding the tapestry.

D'heus ran helplessly through the great hall, arms outstretched in a futile gesture to restrain the ill begotten bodies that milled about him.

P'sudohn also stepped down from the dais just in time to avoid being crushed by a falling statue.

With great exertion he pushed his way through the petulant mob to reach his brother.

"My lord," he shouted, taking D'heus' arm. "I fear for your safety. Let us get out of here."

D'heus resisted his brother's arm. "What," he shouted in incredulity, "leave U'lympu? This is my domain now. Abandon it? Never!"

"Ee-bee-bee-ba-boo! We the greatest!"

Overhead, crooked legged wretches laughed with glee as they swung from the massive chandeliers of priceless crystal.

P'sudohn pulled harder on his brother's arm. "Don't be a fool, my lord," he pleaded. "Let us leave before the roof falls on us."

Still D'heus hesitated.

High above his head, chunks of plaster began falling from the ceiling.

"Come on," P'sudohn pulled at him with increased sense of urgency.

More chunks of plaster began showering them like hailstones. P'sudohn had barely moved his brother the length of an upright's height when they saw the massive chandelier finally giving way.

A thunderous crash shook the entire hall as a boulder-sized weight of crystal smashed to the floor, sending dagger like shards flying as missiles in all directions.

The mighty fixture missed D'heus by a mere arm's length.

P'sudohn grasped his wrist and pulled him to his feet.

"*Fast, brother!*" he shouted amid the crashing crystal and falling furniture. "*Let us leave this place of destruction.*"

"*No!*" said D'heus. "*This is my domain. I mean to restore order.*"

He strode off across the hall waving his arms and shouting at the rampaging little troglodytes.

"*Stop, stop,*" he pleaded to a small band of revelers who were busy shredding a heavily embroidered drape. "*This is your home. This beautiful mansion is now ours! Preserve, not destroy what is ours.*"

Amid the surrounding cacophony they stopped and stared at him with a vacant stare that belied any semblance of understanding.

One crooked legged dwarf broke into a grin exposing a mouth vile as any cesspool. Round, runny eyes narrowly set beneath a protruding forehead slanted into a look of evil glee.

He grabbed a bejeweled wine goblet and threw it at D'heus. "*Hee-hee-hee!*" he screamed in mindless merriment.

With an obscene epithet he hurled another vessel at D'heus barely missing him by a handbreadth.

Other small objects followed.

P'sudohn seized D'heus by his tunic and edged him toward an exit. More knick-knacks flew in their direction. Peals of insane laughter accompanied each volley.

"*To the veranda!*" urged P'sudohn.

In their attempt to reach the exit, they were shoved against the wall by runty little creatures bolting through the open doorway.

When they finally reached the veranda, they looked upon a sunrise characterized by further widespread trashing of the formal gardens below. Mobs of horrid little creatures spread in an ever widening swath of destruction of shrubbery, lawns, fountains, and statuary.

Wretches with both arms protruding from the same shoulder pulled up orchids by the roots and waved them overhead. Mutants that crawled like spiders stripped ferns of their carefully groomed fronds. Two-headed creatures crawled to places out into the forest seeking to further expand their mayhem and pandemonium. Animals as well as nymphs and fauns fled before their onslaught.

"*Once we had an army,*" said D'heus with heaviness. "*Lose control and it's just a mob.*"

He gave a gesture of futility. "*Once mastery escapes our grasp,*" he said, repeating himself in helpless despair, "*never mind trying to get it back.*"

'A look of sudden realization crossed P'sudohn's features. "Tyra the wise woman," he said in alarm. "We must reach her and warn her before the wild things find her."

'D'heus and P'sudohn pushed their power sandals off the ground and sped down the mountain trail with the speed of thought, past hordes of raging wild things still stripping and despoiling the erstwhile luxuriant foliage.

'After an indeterminate length of time, they slowed down to a normal run. They continued for more days until they had reached a quiet part of the forest.

They stopped and listened.

'All about lay a silence heavy with portent.

They heard not an animal sound.

No caw from a bird or flying reptile.

Even the insects withheld their chirping and scraping sounds.

Breathless and bathed in sweat, the two demigods looked at each other. "Over there." P'sudohn pointed to a thicket that lay at the foot of a mountain.

They pushed aside dense thorn bushes until they laid bare a giant boulder resting against the mountain's base. The two of them exerted great effort in pushing aside the boulder that made the cave opening wide enough for them to squeeze through. As they shouldered their way through, the dense thorn bushes whipped back to their original position completely covering the entrance. They worked their way to what had previously been her subterranean apartments.

'She was not there.

'As they stood in complete darkness, the damp smell of mildew struck the nostrils.

"'Tyra!"

P'sudohn's voice reverberated and bounced off cave walls until it disappeared into the cave's depths.

'Silence.

'It was evident that she had fled further back into the labyrinth. They lost all sense of time as they began searching for her.

From deep within the cavern's bowels they discerned the faint flickering of a torch.

With hobbling movements the sputtering light moved gradually closer.

'After lengthy moments they finally saw the flame of the burning torch. The flickering light bounced off jagged rocky wall formations.

They saw the bearer of the torch not to be Tyra.

Before them stood a male creature no higher than their knees. Beneath matted hair that lay unkempt and incredibly filthy reflected a face besmirched with earth and dust.

One bloodshot eye stared hostilely at them. A single brontosaurus skin garment worn and ragged hung over a bony, misshapen body. A beard, equally matted and unkempt hung to his waist. The hand that did not hold the torch grasped a crudely fashioned crutch which served to support him on his one leg.

P'sudohn eyed him with obvious disdain. "Where is Tyra?" he demanded, "and who are you?"

"I am Eikendom; a shaman," He answered in a gravelly voice. The words came from a sepulchral mouth. "Tyra sent me to see what you wanted."

"Do you know what is going on outside?" asked D'heus.

The little man's expression waxed grave. "Yes," he replied. "Tyra and I know all about it."

"Are you not afraid?" asked P'sudohn. With a look of continued contempt he added. "After all from your appearance you could pass for one of them."

Eikendom returned his look of contempt. "Hah! I was born to the beautiful T'tanyu. Because my appearance even as a new babe was so shocking to them, they tried to deny my very existence by casting me off into the forest to die abandoned. But I fooled them. Even as a newborn I was tougher and more resilient than they gave me credit for. So I survived. However, I predated the rest of the Ulympu. Were I to encounter any of them, they would neither know me nor acknowledge me as one of them."

"I would be to them as the hated T'tanyu."

"Then you know your lives are in danger. Are you not afraid?"

The grotesque little man continued fixing his one-eyed stare.

"Not in the slightest," he said. "They'll never reach us. Even if they were to find the entrance, they would quickly become disorientated and lost forever in these unending underground chambers."

D'heus continued looking troubled. "When they say 'death to the T'tanyu,' they mean it."

The little man laughed a wicked laugh. "Even if we were of a mind to flee, where would we go?"

A winged creature, a bat-like reptile perhaps, fluttered out of the darkness.

"We are just as safe here as anywhere," he added.

D'heus cast a sudden anxious glance at P'sudohn. "G'ya," he whispered, "and K'hronhu. What of them?"

P'sudohn nodded. "They were never part of the corruption that went on at the palace," he said. "Yet they are T'tyanu. With the wild things that's all that matters."

D'heus turned in the direction he thought to be the exit. "We must warn them," he said, pulse racing. "There is no time to lose."

Eikendom raised his torch. "I'll show you out," he said. "You'll never find your way otherwise. Follow me."

He began taking little hobbling steps. D'heus and P'sudohn followed slowly behind. The little man's hopping and halting made the pace maddening.

Eventually they saw a gray shaft of light and caught a breath of fresh earth air.

"On your way then," said the little cripple, "and good luck."

As D'heus and P'sudohn squeezed their way through the opening and as they forced their way through the thorn bushes, they glanced anxiously in all directions.

No sign of life.

"A relief," said D'heus.

"Quickly," said P'sudohn. "No time to waste."

For days the erstwhile commanders of a once-powerful army slinked through the jungle by night, hiding form from the misshapen wretches by day. At last they came to an arboreal archway.

"It looks different," observed D'heus.

What had previously been well-trimmed and landscaped with meticulous care now appeared choked over with undergrowth.

They marveled how quickly the well-groomed park-like reserve had reverted to jungle wilderness.

"We'll have to hack our way through the entanglement," said P'sudohn.

D'heus drew his sword and began chopping away at the stout vines and bushes that blocked the entrance. As they passed under the archway they found that the previously wide clearing area was no more. Everywhere weeds and bushes had grown to shoulder height.

"We'll have to keep cutting," shrugged D'heus.

When nightfall came, they crawled under the shelter of a grove of ferns.

"We'll continue our search in the morning," was the last thing D'heus said before fatigue overtook their consciousness.

When slanted rays of a new dawn hit their bower, their eyes opened to a once carefully groomed arboretum as choked with undergrowth as were the arched pathways the day before. They stood to their feet and with sinking spirits viewed the thicket that was the conservatory for the entire planet.

Through the tangled brush they spotted the top of G'ya's dais and her massive tree trunk throne. They continued for half a day hacking their way across erstwhile open clearing, through long narrow passageways that once led to other clearings. Occasionally they would encounter upturned stone benches and still standing table tops.

'Some of the tables contained a piece or two of pottery. Others were covered with shards of broken clay. Dry, hardened residue of once gelatinous cultures stained many of the slabs.

'On they searched through the once well-cared for maze. Was it hours? Days? Weeks?

'One mid afternoon, the two stopped amid the entanglement of weeds. The heat of the afternoon sun made their faces and hands wet with perspiration.

"No sign of life anywhere," sighed D'heus as they returned to the dais.

"'Apparently G'ya and K'hronhu perished with the others," said P'sudohn, shaking his head.

'D'heus pointed to an object that lay on the ground near the dais, almost hidden under the wild growth.

"Look," he said, "an hourglass."

"'It's K'hronhu's," said P'sudohn, picking it up. The hourglass had not been broken and the sand was still intact.

'Consternation crossed P'sudohn features. "Does K'hronhu yet live? Of all the sons of Y'rranhu, he alone fell not into the temptation of profligacy.

"Would this be sufficient spare him the fate of the others?"

"'Shortly before she took her own life," said D'heus, "my mother related to me Y'rranhu's jealous rage over a proper mother and son greeting, but in Y'arranhu's warped, perverse mind, he inferred an incestuous relationship."

'His countenance darkened. "Would he hold the same grudge against K'hronu absent any proof? Was our illustrious father so insane in seeing all manner of evil in others simply because he himself has become the embodiment of evil?

"'Incestuous relationship indeed!"

'He spat out the words with contempt. "He expresses indignation over what he himself has practiced constantly.

"'The hypocrite!"

'D'heus paused. Thick, humid silence that pervaded the atmosphere pressed in on them.

"He vowed that they would both pay and pay dearly."

'Again D'heus paused. With eyes heavy with sadness, he again surveyed the tangled

jungle that the conservatory had become. "Wicked and powerful. Alas, I fear that they make for a dreadful adversary."

P'sudohn set the hourglass on one of the remaining table tops. Sands started filtering through the narrow neck. "Look!" he said. "K'hronhu lives. He will live as long as time will last."

In silence they searched the dense arboreal growth that surrounded them.

"Look," D'heus said again. With a startled look he pointed to a nearby tree. Although neither had noticed it before, the trunk size indicated great age. Its gnarled branches extended overhead in all directions as did its equally gnarled root system.

Immediately in front of them, about head high in the bark appeared a rough likeness of a female upright's face.

"G'ya lives as well," D'heus exclaimed. "She is not dead either. She has simply morphed herself into another form."

"Time and earth shall live," said P'sudohn. "While they yet live, there is still hope."

There is still hope.

The words echoed through D'heus' mind. Yes, he reflected, there is still hope.

"They will yet live," he said, "long after the wild things themselves are dead and gone."

P'sudohn sat wearily down on a rock. He struck a pensive pose, resting his head on his hand. "One thing I am sure of," he said. "I am bounden to descend the lower regions for another visit to Tyra the wise woman."

He paused.

"I need further answers."

He paused and contemplated the surreal orgy that played out in their world. "Perhaps you are right," D'heus said sadly. "How quickly we have let things get out of control."

He turned to P'sudohn with a wry smile.

"Welcome to U'lympu.'"

Chapter 9

'P'sudohn slowly made his way through the labyrinthine caverns that led to the subterranean apartments of the wise woman, Tyra.

'I must reach her, he thought. I must reach her before these scurvy, misbegotten scoundrels, the Ulympii, find her. The planet now crawls with them. They squirm their way through the underbrush. They infest the tall, majestic forests. Their miserable bodies cover the lush, verdant grasslands.

'Everywhere they tread their sorry feet, they reduce our beautiful world to a wasteland; a cesspool.

'Alas, the T'tanyu are not. Where have they fled? Back to the distant celestial realms? Will we ever see an end to R'ya's curse?

'Is our world doomed to be forever left to the mercy of these wretched troglodytes?

'At last he crossed the entrance to her central chamber and saw her bending over a low slab of marble that served as a table or work counter. She turned to him at first foot fall of the threshold.

"Mother, we need to talk," he said.

'She stopped her work of pounding crystals in a mortar with a stone pestle and eyed him quizzically.

'He stepped further into the cavernous interior and sat wearily on a stone stool. "Things are not well up on the surface."

'A pause.

"Why am I not surprised?" she snorted.

"In fact, the situation has deteriorated," he sighed. "To put it bluntly, I'm afraid all is lost."

He then explained to her the entire story of the U-lympu coup against the T'tanyu and the resultant anarchy.

Tyra studied P'sudohn's depressed state with a sense of alarm. "What do you want of me?"

"I need your help."

She looked at him. So, it had come to this, she thought. She recalled untold eons past. Shortly after Lord Light-Brearer the spirit being was begotten a creature of mortal flesh, she, then also a spirit being, was incarnated into becoming Y'rranhu's younger sister. The estrangement came early when the incarnate Y'rranhu's appetites for fleshly delights led to his endless peccadillos.

Their relationship became as an uneasy truce since.

She sighed. "How can I help?"

He turned to her but hesitated before speaking. "I need to see my real mother," he said finally. "I need counsel that only she can give. I also need to make amends with the man I slew when he was naked and unarmed."

Tyra put the pestle on the marble table top and straightened up with a look of dismay. "Your mother is dead," she said. "You know that."

P'sudohn shrugged. "I was hoping you could help me make contact," he sighed.

"Making contact with those in the land of the spirits is something I have never done," she admitted.

"You're saying that I'm asking an impossibility?"

Tyra moved to the bench and sat beside him. "Not entirely, I don't think," she replied. "But what you ask is at best, very difficult, and also extremely dangerous. You could very well find yourself in the underworld and unable to return."

He turned to her and clasped his hands in a suppliant gesture. "Please," he said. "If you can arrange it, I will gladly take the chance."

Tyra stood to her feet. "Meet me at the riverbank at dusk," she said. "I will have you again meet Eikendom the shaman. For safety reasons, he has kept knowledge of his existence from Y'rranhu and the other T'tanyu. If I can persuade him to help us, he will lead you on this mysterious journey to the underworld."

She turned toward the most remote section of her cave. She picked from a rocky shelf a large conch shell and blew on it. The low-pitched blast reverberated against the distant walls of limestone. The echo seemed to amplify as it bounced and slithered its way like a creeping thing against the jagged walls, rolling down into the farthest reaches of the blackest of corridors that snaked and twisted their way into the most sinister of oblivion.

THE TITANS

'She and P'sudohn waited.

'Long moments they waited.

'Apprehension within P'sudohn mounted as the mysterious silence prolonged itself. After what seemed an eternity, P'sudohn heard footsteps. Or perhaps a single footstep, hopping on one foot. The hopping sound got closer and the sense of foreboding became more intense.

'Again there appeared before P'sudohn the creature whose image made the hair rise on the back of his neck. In the murky cavernous gloom, he saw again the creature that stood only to his knees. One large, bloodshot eye stared evilly at him from a head and face nearly covered with matted unruly hair. At the end of a long and scrawny arm, a gnarled hand held a twisted walking stick. He still dressed himself in the mottled, moth-eaten garment of brontosaurus hide. He supported himself on one leg shod in a worn sandal.

'He pointed a bony finger toward P'sudohn.

"I know what you want," he said in a voice that sounded like rumbling gravel.

'The filthy little creature stirred within P'sudohn feelings of revulsion. "And just what might that be?"

'The visitor's eye glowered fiercely. "Don't trifle with me, young man," he warned. "I know you. I know your people. I know your leader. I know all about the doings of both the T'tanyu and your newly-emerging U-lympii.

"'I know the course on which you are headed and I know your ultimate destiny."

'P'sudohn tried to appear unmoved. "And what might that be?" he said again.

"'Think hard, boy," said the shaman. "Think hard on your worst fears, your most dreaded nightmares. You face a fate that would beggar any of these."

'P'sudohn continued trying to appear non-committal, he nevertheless took a step back away from this strange, little man.

"'I need help," he confessed in a somewhat subdued tone of voice. "As I told Tyra, I have done ill. I have killed a man while he was naked and unarmed; all for the sake of usurping his kingdom. I have committed wanton debauchery with young female subjects entrusted to my care, namely the naiads that inhabit my lakes and streams. I can cleanse away from my body the filth and mud of the riverbank merely by bathing in the water, but I am at a loss as to how I can cleanse my soul. Were O'ssyanhu still living, I would beg his forgiveness and thus be shriven, but now that he is in the land of the departed I am at a loss to contact him unless I go into that forbidden land and *seek him out. I also would like to seek counsel from the mother I have never known because she died giving me birth."*

The shaman lowered his voice slightly. "What you ask is difficult—and dangerous. I cannot guarantee your safe return. However, if you are insistent, I will arrange it."

He turned again to the cavern's interior. He stopped and addressed P'sudohn yet one more time. "Meet me at the riverbank at dusk."

* * *

"The dean is getting antsy."

Dr. Sirotka unrolled the latest printout from the U.S, Defense Department Cryptology Division.

"He has been asking some rather pointed questions about our extra-curricular projects. I think he suspects that we're up to something."

Dr. Suess sat back in his seat.

"We are," he said. "Let's don't kid ourselves about what we've been up to. He's probably chomping at the bit to find out."

He paused. Then added: "We've got to see to it that he doesn't."

Dr. Sirotka stood to his feet. "Meet me here tomorrow at four. If any cryptology printouts come in the morning's mail, I'll bring them with me. One thing we should start working on soon is a fake report that will satisfy the old fart."

He turned to leave. Dr. Suess stayed and finished his martini. He felt a presence beside the booth. He looked up in surprise to see stocky, middle-aged woman standing beside their table with a bill in her hand.

"Did you want to pay your bar tab now?"

Damn Dr. Sirotka, anyway, he thought. "How much is it?"

"One Killian's draft and two martinis."

He pulled some bills from his pocket, mumbled something about keeping the change, and shuffled toward the exit. *I will be good customer. I will be a good customer*, he kept repeating to himself. After being barred from Deadman's Gulch, he didn't want to jeopardize his welcome in the one remaining bar in town.

THE TITANS

* * *

Dr. Suess continued the shuffling gait down the familiar streets. Blossoms on the budding trees braced his dampened spirits as he savored the spring evening.

Fragrance from lilac bushes floated out to him from a corner of the fenced off landfill area. As the sight of the large grass-covered mass moved into view, blocking out all other scenery, the perfumed breezes took on the heavy, cloying air of a funeral parlor.

He recalled that in the spring of his third year it happened…

…Shortly after the city had set out the outdoor eating benches for the picnic season to begin, families began getting an early start on barbecuing in the grills and with the softball games.

Color plashed vans began appearing in the parking lot alongside family cars. Unconventionally dressed young people with long hair also began using the facilities.

At first every one let well enough alone. All seemed to content to live and let live; to just have a good time.

Then some of the young people showed up at the families' picnic tables begging for food. As the numbers of counterculture types increased, fumes of marijuana smoke began floating across the greensward.

Townspeople wanted the police do something about it, but the police replied that they had been given orders not to intervene as long as no one got rowdy.

After all, the then mayor had said, use of marijuana per se, though technically illegal, was a victimless crime

As long as it remained so, he knew that the good people of Stillwell would understand.

However crime in the park would not long remain victimless…

…Finally he reached his corner and soon was mounting the broad, creaky steps of his front porch.

As he made his first uncertain steps across the porch floor boards his alcohol befogged mind went again in retrospect to that third summer; the summer of 'the peoples' park.'...

...The weather had turned out to be unusually hot and humid. The revelers in the park created an additional nuisance for the residential blocks in the immediate proximity. The muggy atmosphere became thick with the stench of marijuana smoke and human waste.

Despite the heat, the neighbors were forced to stay indoors with windows closed.

They complained to city hall.

The city fathers did nothing...

...Out of the darkness, like a large, black void, the screen door suddenly loomed in front of him.

He was grateful at finding it unlocked and that the massive front door hung open.

With increased infusion of undesirables now infesting the community, how long could this unsecured bliss continue, he wondered.

He continued shuffling through the darkened front hall, past the softly lighted library. He crossed an also darkened living room and followed a dim light that illuminated the dining room.

White embroidered linen covered an antique dining table. At the far end toward the small pantry, he found a place setting for one. A metal dome covered the main dish.

Late for supper, he thought. *She's good about keeping it hot for me. I owe her.*

Beside the place setting, he found a note which read: 'Am in the library grading papers. Please clean up after yourself.'

He sat down to the table and began eating.

While he ate, he spread out the cryptology report off to one side and began reading.

He noticed that the point of view had changed.

THE TITANS

* * *

'When I reached the appointed place at dusk, I waited. I was sure that I had the place that the mysterious shaman had indicated. I had feverishly worked my way through the forest thicket, fighting against the gathering twilight to reach this spot on a steep bank beside the broad, slow-moving stream. On the far shore lay more forest thicket that appeared all but impenetrable. As evening shadows lengthened, I noticed something strange. Night birds who usually fluttered about and sang their tunes of evening were not. Their absence sent the forest into an unaccustomed silence.

'Convinced that this was omen of profound foreboding, I waited. And as I waited, I became drowsy. I lay down on a moss hummock futilely resisting numbness and waning consciousness.

'Suddenly I woke with a start.

'I still don't know whether I actually fell asleep or just nodded off. It seemed not more than a moment, but I realized how deceptive the sense of time loss when one falls into a deep sleep. Still feeling groggy, I pulled myself to my feet and looked around. The time of day still seemed to be dusk—that hovering split second between the last faint rays of waning daylight and darkness. At first glance all looked the same.

'The familiar landmarks were all still there. Then I noticed something strange and unsettling.

'I saw that all had changed.

'The riverbank beneath no longer lay thick with moss and grass; rather, it appeared a slimy mud mass, covered with dead leaves and old straw worked into a thick, watery clay and sloping down into heavy, brackish waters lapping sluggishly at its edge. The stream no longer appeared sweet and fresh, but rather it slithered murky and foul smelling. The broad, slow-moving waters stank of an open sluice conduit.

'Trees off in the forest had dropped their foliage and stood with twisted, naked branches against a slate colored but starless sky. The fresh, woodsy air that caressed my face during daytime now burned my nostrils with a pungent, acrid smell.

'I looked out across the stream and saw a gray mist mingled with sulfurous smoke rolling in toward me.

'Out of the mist I heard a splashing of oars. I then descried the gray prow of a skiff slicing through the waters toward me. As it neared, it broke free of the mist and I saw a long boat oared by a tall, gaunt boatman standing astern. Though I surmised the figure to be my appointment, this did nothing to quiet the unease that gripped my soul.

As the prow sliced up onto the muddy bank and slid to a scraping halt, the oarsman planted his oar into the ooze of the river bottom and gestured to me.

Resisting the desire to turn and run, I tentatively stepped aboard. Fighting to keep balance the boatman back-paddled until we slid again into midstream.

'A sense of apprehension settled over me like a thick blanket as we continued moving further out through the fog toward some unknown shore. The gnarled, moss laden trees that hugged the shore receded further into the distance as the stream seemed to broaden. The silence continued to be punctuated only by muffled splashing of my boatman's oar.

'Overhead in the night sky, I now saw roiling masses of clouds tumbling as if embroiled in a noiseless storm.

'I noticed the terrain start to change from forest to bare plain.

'I noticed debris of broken logs, intelligence-made articles such as wagons, fence rails, and gate posts. I saw carcasses of animals and uprights floating past or lying in the muddy shallows.

'I noticed flashes of lightning flickering behind the massive clouds overhead. The random flashes of sheet lightning seemed to come no closer, but rather continued indistinct in some far off storm that raged on all points of the horizon.

'I also noticed that we now were sailing past wooden hulks of derelict vessels wedged at crazy angles in the mud. Tattered strands of canvas hung limp from the broken rigging. The water now also became more congested with piles of rotting bones of every species of beasts and men. The stench of death all but pressed out the ability to draw breath into my lungs.

'Where are you taking me? I was about to ask as I felt our keel slide into the slick mud. Our forward motion gradually came to a halt with a sucking sound in the marl beneath us. The boatman motioned me to get out.

'With trepidation, I studied the watery slough that lapped at the gunwales of our craft. Blackened ripples smelling of decaying plant life bubbled up through ooze into which my feet now sank into the mire. As I studied nearby broken tree branches, I saw shards of broken pottery and sharp rocks jutting out from the shallow surface. I feared stepping down onto something hard and sharp gashing my foot

'Gingerly we pulled our feet out of the mix of mud, marl, and water. We slowly struggled with a tow rope to pull our craft toward deeper waters again. Each step being followed by a hollow, gurgling sound. The shallow water rolled out toward a shore that sloped upward so gradually that we near despaired of ever reaching dry ground.

THE TITANS

'We seemed to be in a terrain of unending tidal mud flats.

'As we struggled awkwardly through the ankle deep filth, I perceived an increase in the number of skeletal shipwrecks. I also began to notice numbers of building ruins. The mud beneath my feet appeared to be impregnated with garbage, decayed vegetation, and human waste. The lightning that had continued to flicker behind the cloud banks now began flashing a pale red.

'I now also noticed wraith like figures—some clad in long, ragged robes of homespun and others stumbling about naked in the mist. As the mist continued to lift and as the spectral figures became more numerous, I noticed something further unsettling.

'The figures moved about me without a sound. Rather, they looked upon me with mouths agape, exposing rows of sparse, rotting teeth, or no teeth at all. Bloodshot eyes that pierced the darkness were embedded in cadaverous faces. I now saw bared arms, legs, and bodies covered with ulcers and putrefying sores. The naked bodies stood either as skeletons or as green, bloated blobs of once human flesh. Men with hair and beards hopelessly snarled and women with hair hung long and matted glared at me with accusing eyes that burned like fiery orbs of despair.

'As we pulled our boat further and as I sought to climb back on board, the diseased and noisome throng pressed in on us, I summoned up enough courage to address one who seemed extraordinarily mendicant: "How big is this place?"

"'As big as big itself," came the reply in a hollow voice that reverberated across the wasted terrain.

'Soon others began to crowd around our craft. I felt fleshless hands grasping for my tunic.

"'Take us with you," moaned a spectral voice as I felt myself being pulled away from the boat.

'More apparitions crowded in. Despite my attempt to jump back into the skiff, I felt myself being pulled away into the limitless expanse of marsh. I felt claw-like hands pulling my hair. Their foul breath nearly suffocated me. As mightily as I tried to fight them off, the more I felt myself being dragged out into the slough. In desperation, I fought to prevent myself from being dragged away from the gunwales.

'I finally managed to find voice to call to my pilot for help.

'From out the corner of my eye, I saw my boatman flailing at the miserable forms with his oar. I heard the dull thud of wood smashing against cadaverous skulls.

'Thankfully, I finally found myself able to crawl back into the boat.

"Lie low between the seats and look neither to the right nor to the left," growled my boatman in his multi-voiced words.

Before I could answer, my boatman motioned to me. He had found water deep enough to again float our punt free. As he struggled to steady his boat against the current, I gingerly squeezed between the gunwales and settled amidships. He began pushing with his oar past the slime and rotting seaweed out into the deeper water. Thus I continued to be ferried over the dark, murky waters that broadened again to a wide, shallow swamp. The same naked, gnarled trees slipped by in either side. Musty smelling mosses again hung from twisted, leafless branches.

'An occasional giant blackbird would take off from its arboreal perch and lift sluggishly into the dirty sky, emitting an ominous cry. It would then quickly disappear into the gray, swirling shroud. As the trees grew thicker, I perceived the water beside the skiff to begin taking on a swifter current.

'Soon the current picked up yet more speed and my boatmen no longer needed to paddle. I no longer saw the shadow forms nor did I any longer hear voices or moaning. Near as I could discern, the boatman and I had entered country where we were quite alone. The black, twisted tree forms grew so thick that they appeared impenetrable. To both our starboard and larboard the shores formed high, muddy banks, now narrowing the waters into a swiftly flowing stream.

'I noticed walls of a canyon beginning to rise from either bank. As the walls rose higher the shores from both sides of the stream grew ever narrower.

'The reality dawned on me. I saw that the broad expanse of water from the brackish tidal flats now narrowed into a canyon with the powerful, rushing torrent now a scant few meters wide.

'I feared that were we to continue, the current would become too swift for my pilot to control his craft and we would be quickly swept under the seething froth. I also feared that ever shrinking banks would soon preclude our even landing.

'My boatman thrust his oar into the river bottom and, with a mighty heave, edged our craft to a stony bank. I heard ground scraping against the planks and saw my pilot step into the water, wade to the bow and pull us onto the dry ground. He reached for my hand and drew me out of the boat.

'He pointed to the small strip of gravel that comprised our bank. "This is as far as I can take you." his voice resonated in a deep sepulchral tone that carried quite well above the roar. "You must step out now and continue in that direction on foot."

'He pointed to a distant blackness that blotted out the horizon. I could see nothing *but an ever narrowing shore line on either side of the swollen waters; a shore line hemmed in by sheer faces of gray-black granite rock. Towering far overhead, roiling masses of black clouds all but blanketed a slate gray sky that glowed faintly with an unearthly sheen.*

I noticed the black barrier to loom larger than the entire landscape itself. Out of the darkness rose a mountain that seemed deceptively close because of its immense size. Again I perceived a thin band of light bluish gray stretching over the towering summit.

"Follow the shore line," he continued, still pointing toward the distant mountain. "You will eventually come to a place where the stream disappears into an underground cave."

He paused. His next words bore a frightening unreality.

"When you get there, dive into the water."

His voice, still resonating deep and funereal, carried quite well above the roar. "You will be carried into the stream as it goes under the mountain. Once inside the mountain, you will find yourself in a cavern. There will be a walkway along the bank of the stream. Follow the path until you eventually come out the other side of the mountain. You will come onto a bright, open meadow. You will be entering the Elysian Fields, the Land of the Blessed Spirits. There you will meet your mother, Io."

He turned and stepped back into his skiff. Then, almost miraculously, he back watered against the powerful current until he disappeared into the distant forested shore line.

Terrified and bewildered, I stood alone in the dark and evil mist. Pressing in on either side rose lofty slate colored cliffs. Jagged contours of granite formed a rugged and broken façade that plunged downward into the turbulent waters. Ahead of me loomed the black, sheer rock that formed the base of the mountain. My every thought was drowned out by the all-pervading roar.

A sense of urgency seized me to push on in my journey even if it meant walking the narrow treacherous path of loose gravel and moraine and risking a plunge into the dark, unknown waters.

Yet overwhelming dread kept me riveted to the spot.

I finally forced myself to set one foot in front of another.

The course of the stream did not run straight forward. Twists and turns in the canyon walls followed the tortuous winding. Each bend of the stream revealed new and dangerous obstacles. Occasionally the gravel bank gave way to gigantic boulders, slick with moss over which I was forced to climb. Each footfall felt slippery and treacherous underfoot. One misstep could send me helpless down into the turbulent froth.

Meanwhile the dark, forbidding walls on either side continued to press in on me. I noticed that the rugged, angular lines of the cliff walls suggested profiles of giant faces. Was it my imagination or were they really faces of evil spirits glaring down in me?

The entire scene seemed to have a life, a personality—malevolent and threatening—of its own.

Did it portend an appointment I had with Fate? With Destiny? With my own Damnation?

The long trek to the distant mountain gave me time to further ponder my situation. The darkened slate colored canyon walls, the roaring torrent at my feet, the dirty gray sky above me, and the churning storm clouds overhead reinforced upon me afresh a frightening reality: I was alone, a sole mortal in an alien world to which I did not belong.

Was D'is, the grim lord of this vast dominion, aware of my presence? Was he even now seeking me? Did he know of my whereabouts? With his magic helmet that made him invisible whenever he wore it, he could be anywhere; even at my elbow without my knowing it. As I stumbled over the slippery gravel, could he be biding his time, toying with me, waiting to permanently imprison me in this hellish durance vile?

I looked about in mounting terror and felt a strong wind roaring down between the canyon walls. With it came a lowering temperature. The frigid air numbed and discolored my flesh. My light linen tunic had always constituted appropriate clothing for the mild and humid climate of my world of the living. It now proved inadequate for the unforgiving cold of this awful place. My limbs moved with increasing difficulty. My teeth began an unaccustomed chattering.

I looked at the clouds above and now saw jagged forks of lightning, flashing cold and white against the billowing black and precipitation descending toward me. It appeared as small pieces of cloud or frozen vapor. Perhaps future intelligences acquainted with more temperate climes would call it snow, sleet, or perhaps hail. Chunks of the stuff began flying at me in greater fury, stinging my already frozen face. As though that were not enough, I noticed further evil.

The chunks came not a pristine white as one would suppose to be the case with snow, frozen vapor, or ice. The chunks that assailed me seemed impregnated with a dirty brown mixture of dust, decayed matter and dung. My tunic and my body soon became smeared with the pestilential slop. Its stench became nearly overpowering despite its accompanying chill.

THE TITANS

'I pushed on further along the slender bank of loose gravel, trying mightily to maintain my footing on the slippery, treacherous terrain. I looked to the direction of the deafening roar and watched the churning flood smash and foam up over gigantic rocks. Eddies and whirlpools spumed and spun out in dizzying array, sending deep whorls between the boulders. Surely waters of such force could suck me under and smash every bone in my body against an unforgiving rock in seconds.

'I continued pressing on for an indeterminate length of time. How long is this canyon? How big is this place? (As big as big itself.) How long have I been here? Is it still the duration of the mortal world's night? Or have I entered a region where earthly time means nothing? (You mustn't stay overlong,) so said the admonition (lest you find yourself unable to leave.)

'What has become of our splendid race? We who were little less than The Strong-Ones himself are now through our own greed, lust, petty jealousies and ambitions have brought our people to near annihilation? And what of our attempt to remake our world through a new race of morally superior beings only to see them spawned forth as a legion of damned souls, ugly of body and of spirit?

'Another thought entered my already ominous reflections. What of these wretched Ulympii? Even if we were to demolish their miserable bodies, do they not also possess indestructible spirits? Do their spirits continue to infest our planet? Will they at some distant time again manifest their ugly selves with some future mischief?

'Enough of such ponderings. I must not give counsel to my fears in so dire a moment as this. I must take courage and continue on to whatever dark destiny leads me.

'What sort of madness pushed me into entering this forbidden realm in the first place? Why was I so foolish and naïve to believe that in so doing I could be shriven and redeemed from my own lust driven and violent past?

'Suddenly—amid my dark musings—I saw it. My gravelly bank had dwindled to nothingness and I found myself precariously maintaining my balance above the dirty gray froth that roared just a handbreadth from my feet. Immediately ahead I saw that the flood seemed to disappear into a sheer face of rock.

'I had reached the mountain.

'Still fighting to keep my footing on my slippery perch, and amid much shivering and trembling, I struggled with conflicting notions. Should I turn back? (Could I even do this, given the forbidding terrain?) Should I dive into the torrent as per my pilot's instructions?

'Or should I just give up and await whatever fate lies in store for me?

"Somewhere deep within me, I found resolve to break free of this stalemate of wills and I plunged into the seething current.

"In a trice, I felt myself sucked violently forward in the watery abyss so cold it took my breath away and nearly made my heart stop beating. I feared the icy waters would so chill me that I would lose control of all my bodily functions. I felt myself bumping and crashing into innumerable submerged rocks and boulders. Amid the freezing depths I lost all ability to swim or to steer myself in any direction. I felt myself spinning head over heels completely out of control.

"Just as I thought my lungs would burst, I felt myself popping to the surface. Almost as if by an unseen hand, I was thrown onto a dry, gravelly bank.

"Here I lay for a long period of time regaining my breath and recovering from my bruising. I finally staggered to my feet. I found myself, soaked and trembling, standing on a flat, stony surface. I appeared to be astride a narrow path with a broad cave wall rising on the other side. Behind me the current continued to roar in my ears. I noticed that I stood not in total darkness. I was able to discern the gray shapes of boulders, stalactites, and stalagmites that formed the yawning chamber

"Dimly in the distance, appeared the source of the light.

"I now saw a cave opening to an outside world; however it appeared but a pinprick. I had truly expected to reach it in but a short while. I found, however, to my dismay that the apparent shortness of the distance thoroughly deceptive. I trudged onward for an indeterminate length of time and seemed nowhere nearer the cave's opening.

"The distance was far greater than I had originally guessed.

"I felt a balmy breeze fanning my face and found the opening of light beginning to increase in size.

"I finally seemed to get nearer. The breeze now carried a subtle scent of apple blossoms. I sensed within me, a lifting of my spirits. The despondency which lay upon my soul like a thick blanket began to roll off my shoulders as the losing of a heavy burden. Eventually I stood at the cave's entrance to a strange, new world.

"Only as I stood at the cave's entrance did I appreciate its immense size. The roof towered overhead like canopy higher than any temple I had seen. To my left the stream, now a torrent, bubbled and frothed as it spilled over into a mighty cataract. Tumultuous waters frothed and tumbled over the precipice until they cracked thunderously onto a pile of boulders a far distance below. The water at the bottom of the falls, now pristine as crystal, fell away and broadened into a glittering stream of a gently flowing river. As water spray soaked my garments, I looked to the right to a path winding down my side of the mountain into a broad valley. A luxuriantly verdant landscape stretched off to the horizon that led first to a wide stand of forest and then to a distant purplish mountain range.

The air carried an invigorating freshness that prompted me to step down the path toward the meadow below with an alacrity not felt since I was a child.

'I viewed a world unlike I had ever known. Arched overhead stretched a sky unprecedented in its richness of blue. On searching the landscape, however, I was unable to discern the source of light. I could see no sun. I detected a subtle rosy glow—perhaps more felt than seen—that permeated the entire world. As zephyrs continued to fan my face, I picked up additional scents: lilacs, wild roses, and larkspur.

'I started down the path and noticed the blades of grass waved in the breeze as if to beckon me down further into the meadow. Now I saw among the grasses that waved toward me, flowers of every imaginable color and variety. Further beyond the rolling lea, trees—conifers, deciduous, and palms—stretched out toward the mountain range on the horizon. Among the trees grew ferns of every size with fronds waving delicately in the soft breezes.

'A sense of ecstasy welled up within me as I progressed further down the path, deeper into the rolling meadow. I felt my head clearing and my body becoming lighter. I found myself skipping and leaping down the path. A sense of serenity and happiness built up within me with such power that tears began filling my eyes.

'In all this scene of beauty and placidity, I had yet to see a sign of intelligent life,

'Suddenly from a nearby bush I saw a small, four legged creature, the like of which I had never seen before. It was covered with short brown hair, had long protuberances jutting up from its head that I assumed to be a kind of ears. From its rear grew a fluffy ball I took to be a tail.

'Behind it leapt a larger creature that I also could not recognize. The second creature appeared larger and more powerful, especially about the shoulders. Around its neck grew a luxuriantly mass of dark brown hair. The rest of its body looked to be colored a tawny light tan. Its long thin tail twitched nervously and was tipped with another tuft of dark hair.

'It followed the first creature out into the open and then stopped. It yawned, revealing sharp, pointed teeth indicating it to be a flesh eating creature, yet it made no attempt to devour the smaller, weaker creature. Rather, they seemed to take delight in playing and frolicking together.

'Calls from a varied species of songbirds greeted my ears. Trills, warbling, and whole strains of melody surrounded me with soothing music.

'I now noticed birds of many exotic colors and of brilliant plumage flitting among the tree branches. They seemed covered with a feather like material instead of scales.

'From the corner of my eye I caught a brief impression, rather like a spot or floater in my eye. I saw it for the fleetest of moments, and then it was gone. Then there appeared another—then another. Now I became aware of multitudes of the fleeting phenomena darting to and fro around me. They flit about like shadows; more like thought images or impressions. Now they seemed almost visible; now more felt than seen. Soon the entire valley seemed filled with these shadowy impressions. They swirled about me in a myriad of shadows, moving faster than the speed of thought. I fixed my gaze almost to the point of eye strain to get a more accurate fix on what they actually were.

'They seemed to assume intelligence and were in some way seeking to communicate with me.

'They continued to dart about; now close, now flying off to the forest, and then back again, now whisking themselves away to a distant vanishing point. I strangely sensed in them a benign nature that made me loathe seeing them dart away.

'I perceived one of them holding a stationary position directly in front of me. The faint sound of voices singing as in chorus now also came wafting over the air ever stronger. The beauty of it was so overwhelming me that I could scarce contain myself.

'The presence directly in front of me began to take on a visible substance. I saw a female figure of incredible youth and beauty. Her raven locks flowed behind her. Her milk white complexion contrasted with the rose of her cheeks. Dark eyes fixed a loving gaze on me that melted me within. Her graceful form pressed against a lavender gown that also billowed out in the breeze.

'With a flash of insight I recognized her.

"'Io," cried I with tears streaming down my face, "my mother! My real mother! Is it really you?"

'A wistful expression crossed her features as she held out her hand. "Please," she said with gentle pleading, "you mustn't touch me. You and I are of two different worlds. Personal contact could jeopardize your return to the land of the living."

"Where am I?" I asked.

'Still holding out her hand she answered. "We are in the land of the Elysian Fields, the abode of the blessed spirits. You have also passed through Hades, the abode of the despairing shades."

THE TITANS

"Then it works," I said. *"Mother, Tyra's magic works. Bless her. She has granted my request to see my real mother."*

"You have disturbed my rest," replied Io, *"but no matter. I am glad to see you nevertheless."*

"Oh Mother," I pleaded, falling to my knees, *"don't leave me yet. Let me stay with you awhile."*

Still holding out her hand, she shook her head. *"You have disturbed the peace of all of us,"* she said. *"You are not one of us and you must leave before your presence contaminates this place."*

"But why can't I stay?"

"You have killed," she replied. *"You have killed one of your own who was naked and unarmed to satisfy your own ambitions."*

"Please," I sobbed with outstretched arms. *"Don't send me away."*

"I have no choice," she said with wistfulness in her voice.

"But is there no hope for me?" cried I.

"You must go back," she warned. *"Your only hope is to seek out the one you have wronged and obtain his forgiveness. If you fail, you cannot end up here and you will never see my face again."*

Again, I stood to my feet.

"But must I go through that awful place again," said I, gesturing toward the mountain cave and waterfall.

"You must return to the upper world before their night is spent or you will not return at all."

"But I have been a long time away from my world," said I. *"Is it not already too late?"*

"We do not reckon time the same as you," she said. *"Here terrestrial time is meaningless; it is frozen into eternity. Perhaps not as many earth hours have passed as you might think. But you must hurry."*

To my dismay, I saw her begin to take on opaqueness, a transparency. *"But how am I to swim upstream against such a strong current?"* said I in mounting panic.

"You are a god," she replied sternly. *"You are P'sudohn, lord of the sea."*

"But this is not my world," I cried as her image began growing faint. *"What good are my powers here?"*

"You must try," she said as her voice grew fainter. *"It is your only chance,"* were her last words as she vanished into the daylight.

'Other spirit beings seemed to have vanished as well. Never have I sensed such warmth, such acceptance, and such love as I felt from these amorphous apparitions. That scarcely discerned I their essence only heightened my desire to know them more intimately

"Don't go," I pled amid my anguish of soul. "Please don't leave me."

'I stood alone in a yet unbelievably beautiful landscape. As I looked about, however, I discovered something new that I found alarming.

'I noticed the flowers nearest me starting to wilt. The grasses under my feet took on a trampled, dead look. In panic, I started back up the path from which I had come. The grass had already turned brown. The urgency that thrust me toward the cave filled me with sadness over my necessity to leave.

'Despondency and dread again descended upon me as I turned down the dark path into the cave and further away from the light. After a seemingly unending period of walking along the darkening path, I finally reached the spot where the blackened waters gushed up from the underground river.

'I paused.

'I would now be swimming underwater against an unbelievably powerful current. Could I, even as a demigod, survive such an ordeal?

Summoning up all my courage, I plunged into the roaring spray.

'Once submerged, I gripped rocky hand holds on the ceiling of the underground cavern to hold myself from being swept away by the force of the raging flow. Slowly and with great exertion, I pulled myself along, finding rocks that I could grasp to draw in my struggle toward the other side. I felt my lungs start to burst and I felt my strength all but spent.

'As I reached overhead for stony handholds, I discovered something of a godsend. Occasionally I felt my hands reach rocky handholds that appeared not to be submerged. My bursting chest welled in gratitude as I pushed my face up against the tunnel ceiling and into a small pocket of air. With the desperate gasp of a dying man I gulped the sweet invigorating oxygen into my weary lungs. With renewed strength, I would then plunge back into the torrent and worked my way further until I again found a small air pocket against the cavern's roof.

'Numbly and against the paralyzing cold, I pushed on. After much further struggle I felt my hand again break the surface. This time I felt no stony overhead. With both hands, I grasped rocks above the torrential froth, pulled myself upward and my head likewise burst into the air.

'Dark and rancid though it was, the air felt life-giving as I sucked it into my lungs. With a final burst of reserve, I dragged myself trembling onto the rocky shore. How long I lay on the dark and gloomy shoreline, I do not know.

'I felt a hand touch me.

'The robed figure of the boatman stood over me and gestured toward a distant landing where he had beached his skiff. Though weak with fatigue I joined him as he helped me toward the boat. This time we paddled against the current. The banks bore the same dreary landmarks which began taking on a familiarity to me now, but no less foreboding.

'Had I stayed too long?

'Would I survive the perilous journey?

'Would I actually be the only surface creature to enter the realms of the departed and return to the land of the living? A privilege never before afforded any other creature?

'My boatman continued through the shallow, dusky slough. We again rowed past scenes of shipwrecked hulks, of crumbling structures, of rotting carcasses.

'"We must get you back to your own shore before our leader, D'is, the god of the underworld, finds you," said the boatman. "If he finds you, he will claim you as one of his own. He knows you're here and is even now looking for you."

"But where is he now?" I asked amid rising anxiety.

'"He could be anywhere," replied my pilot. "As long as he wears his magic helmet, he is invisible."

'What my pilot said next only added to my dismay.

'"D'is has a special reason for finding you. He is the son of Oss'yanhu and Kh'illistro. He considers himself the rightful god of the sea. He looks upon you as a usurper, an interloper. He is consumed with the notion that you have stolen that which is rightfully his. His being assigned over the realm of the dead was given in consolation, poor substitute though he found it. He is bent on claiming what he considers his birthright."

'My pilot's words sank like lead in my inward parts.

'"Furthermore," he added. "He hates you with a passion for having killed his father."

'At this my sense of urgency that we leave this place knew no bounds.

'After continued paddling across vast stretches of the murky terrain, I finally saw emerging through the mist, the familiar bank. I felt the keel beneath my feet slide across the slimy mud. Not waiting my boatman's bidding, I stepped onto the treacherous edge and, lest I slip back into the water, scrambled up to more level ground. Without so much as a 'bye-your-leave' I heard the craft slide back into the muddy waves and saw it disappear into the swirling oblivion.

I felt my feet sink into the ooze as I surveyed a scene thick with naked gnarled undergrowth. Out of the enshrouded forest, then, I saw a hooded figure moving silently toward me. It stopped a short distance away and pulled back the hood.

Before me stood the gaunt, wasted Oss'yanhu.

I fell at his feet and sought to grasp him at the knees, but he backed away, holding out his hand. "If you value your well-being," he said in a voice resonating unearthly hollowness, "do not touch me."

"I killed you," said I weeping. "I killed you when you were naked and unarmed."

I raised my head and gazed into the cadaverous face.

"I forgive you," he said. He raised his hand in a gesture of benediction.

"But," he added, "beware of my son, D'is. He is god of this place. I may forgive you but he will never forgive you. Leave before he finds you."

In panic I fell on my face before him.

"Be shriven. Go in peace." With this pronouncement, the figure disappeared in the mist.

I stood to my feet, alone in the dark forest, uncertain. What prompted me to turn around and look toward the darkened waters, I do not know.

From the dank fog another shrouded figure came sweeping across the thickened waves toward me. Sudden terror seized me as the figure began to take form. It reached up at its head and plucked from it a leaden helmet and threw it to the ground. Immediately, there metamorphosed before me a dread, most frightening creature. The face was the fleshless face of a skull. Deep within the eyes burned a blue flame. The bony body seemed clad in a warrior's armor. The mouth appeared clenched with sparse, rotting teeth. It stood not on feet but rather the cloven hoofs of an animal. The mouth opened as if to speak and a forked tongue slithered out.

"I am D'is," it said in a voice that sounded like multiple voices. "You have killed my father. You have invaded my domain and now you must pay."

With horror I watched all before me—the ground, the trees, even the waters themselves, became enveloped on a wall of blue flame. I felt the mud from beneath my feet grow hot and smolder. Columns of sulfurous smoke began spewing up from newly formed holes in the very place where I stood.

"Strength of all strengths," cried I. "Deliver me!"

THE TITANS

'With hot gasses searing my lungs, I sought to escape by running I knew not where. As the burning swirled about me in my flight, I felt my foot catch an exposed tree root and I plunged headlong against a rock. The blow immediately sent my consciousness into oblivion.'

* * *

'I awoke delirious and confused, not knowing where I was nor in what state. I opened my eyes into dazzling sunlight. I felt a cool breeze against my face. I felt my body resting on a soft bed of lush grasses. I looked about on a scene of verdant woodland. I looked up into the tree branches overhead and saw a canopy of wide, green leaves. Trembling, I stood to my feet and saw, a short distance away, the clear, limpid pool of fresh water.'

'I staggered toward it and felt pain and swelling on my head. I felt soreness and blistering on my face and saw, a short distance away, my garment burnt and singed.

'Also in the lush grass I saw the imprint of a pair of cloven hoofs.

'I knew then that I had no dream.

'Drinking in the fresh sweet air, I felt renewed and invigorated as I had not felt since my dread otherworld journey.

'I was once again back in the land of the living.'

Chapter 10

... P'ssudohn knelt down to get a closer look at his reflection in the water. He waited for the rippled waves to level out and soon the surface became placid as a mirror.

The image that stared back shocked him.

He saw an ancient: a wizened, bony old man. His luxuriant seaweed hair had turned sparse and white. Bloodshot eyes stared dully up from the shimmering surface. The light green luster of his skin had turned a macabre, bilious color. Withered lips collapsed inward to a toothless cavity of a mouth. He reached about in the lush green grass for his trident. He finally found it all but hidden beneath a growth of weeds.

'As he held it up for inspection, he found pock-marked and deeply pitted rust spots.

With great effort, he pulled himself to his feet. He took feeble, faltering steps off into the forest in search of other intelligences. He continued following the river bank for an indeterminate period of time, but found no one. During his hike through riverbank and forest, he savored the sights, the sounds, and the perfumed breezes. Flowers and ferns flourished as he had always known them. Leafy foliage from the trees extending far overhead grew as luxuriant as ever.

Yesterday? Was it really only yesterday? Or had time played a trick on him? Everything seemed as before.

Yet he sensed that all had changed.

Where was everybody?

He continued his walking through the forest.

Far to the horizon rose mountain peeks of smoldering volcanoes, emitting their columns of sulfurous smoke. He entered a section of the forest where grew the giant hardwoods, arching high and lofty overhead. The leafy arbors all but blotted out the sun. Sturdy, dark branches extended above him suspending strands of parasitic grape vines.

Nightfall came and he dined on fruit hanging from nearby trees. Exhausted, he fell to the ground into the oblivion of slumber. Next morning he woke to a world that was as the one he had closed his eyes to the evening before. He breakfasted on more fruits and berries and set off on another leg of his journey. A fresh breeze stirred through the sparse, hoary locks of his head.

Late afternoon, he finally reached the broad, salty marshes of the Devon Sea. Am I still Lord of this domain? He asked himself.

He stepped into the reedy shallows and began wading. He trudged innumerable distances, following always a shore lined with marsh grass, underbrush, and trees. His footsteps sent ripples radiating out among the salt water algae, lily pads, and kelp. Across a bayou he spotted a myriad of small islands thick with trees and vegetation. Hulking bodies of two brontosauruses broke the waters. Tiny heads at the end of long necks reached up toward the higher and arboreal delicacies.

Behind him he heard a sluggish flapping of wings. He turned to see a giant pterodactyl forcing its way through the firmament toward a distant mountain crag. At the second setting of the sun, he headed for a place on dry land to spend the night. A sobering reality again occurred to him.

He had still seen no one.

Relentless fatigue suppressed his misgivings as he laid himself down on a bed of moss.

The third day he set out again to follow the shoreline. He came at last to terrain where the jagged shore line and the clusters of islands, bayous and inlets gave way to a broad, limitless expanse of beach and open sea. The horizon lay unbroken by any sighting of land. The sea stretched flat and calm, broken only by an occasional patch of beach grass waving in the breeze driven ripples. These patches stretched far to the horizon as the sea itself appeared only knee deep as far as the eye could see.

He knew the Devon Sea to be the one wide, shallow ocean that enveloped the planet of his day. These mildly saline waters were broken only by one great land mass known as Pangaiea which eons later would break up into continents as those in the historic era would know them.

He spent many days walking the vast, limitless shoreline; the wide, shallow sea to his right, the flat expanse of lush green land to his left. He came at last to a landscape where trees grew sparse and eventually receded further inland, leaving the landscape carpeted with scrub brush and tall, bent grasses. Earth beneath his feet became a white, sandy beach.

'A flash of recollection burst into his memory. He recalled learning from Tyra how Y'rranhu, the Father-Light-Bearer had plotted to re-enter the celestial realms, how he had planned to force his way back into the court of the Strong-Ones. He recalled being privy to Y'rranhu's intentions of once again directing the sanctuary choir.

'There is nothing, Y'rranhu had planned to say as he pointed to the hidden sanctum. Inside that sanctuary shines only a burst of light. It is really only a cleverly crafted mechanism designed by the Trickster untold eons past to bedazzle and delude the gullible. We owe it nothing. The voice you hear from time to time is nothing more than an artificial contrivance to simulate intelligent speech. You will all stop singing your praises to a non-existent being.

'Henceforth you will direct the singing of your praises to me.

'Worried lines crossed P'ssudohn's brow. He recalled also Y'rranhu relating that should he fail in this audacious plot, that he would be consigned to reign over his minions in a hellish abyss that would make even the present underworld of lost souls shrink with horror.

'He also recalled a vision that the wise woman Tyra had long ago shared with him regarding the relating of all this. Was her vision now coming to fruition?

'In the vision she had seen a small group in the angelic choir raise an objection. But we have seen him, they had said. We have seen him face to face…

'…Then what does he look like? Y'rranhu had then demanded. Those who claimed to have seen him either would not, or could not answer.

'There you have it, the Father-Light-Bearer had then replied. Enough delay. When I give a signal, instead of singing any more praises to the Strong-Ones, you will sing your praises to me.

'At his cue, about a third of the choir began tentatively to sing. Two-thirds, however, stood resolutely silent.

'Immediately, the ground beneath the sanctuary shook. Black clouds of smoke and stellar gasses billowed out into the spacious firmament above. Blue lightning played like threads of lace about the bodies of Y'rranhu and of those who had started to sing. Shortly, Y'rranhu and the singing rebels each disappeared in a column of smoke. The soil where the rebels stood showed only a patch of burnt ground.

'Far off to the distance of space, as screams filled the universe, a gigantic star began *shooting across the heavens followed by a fiery trail of debris whose glow lingered long after the whole doomed procession had disappeared to a pinpoint over the ultimate horizon...'*

* * *

"Ah, brother Seuss, a word with you."

The dean's greeting aborted Dr. Suess' hurried stride toward the science wing of the main hall. The dean's condescension in addressing him as 'brother' did nothing to mitigate misgivings. Dr. Suess shifted his attaché case from one hand to another and turned to face his superior.

"I trust you are quite well," the dean continued.

"Quite well, thank you."

The dean gestured to the entry of the faculty lounge. A row of windows bordered both sides of the doorway.

"We can go in here."

As Dr. Suess followed him into a lounge furnished with worn furniture, he noticed the dean seating himself at the battered couch against the far wall. This would give him visual control of the entire lounge and all the corridor traffic that passed by as well.

For himself, Dr. Suess found an easy chair a slight distance away and at an oblique angle from the couch.

This way I can either maintain or break off eye contact whichever I choose, he thought.

"So," said the dean after he had comfortably ensconced himself in the couch. "How have you been?"

"At risk of being repetitive," said Dr. Suess, "quite well."

The dean hesitated. At length he began speaking. "Henry, how long have you been with us?"

"Thirty years," he said. *Not like him to forget such data,* he thought.

"Tell me," the dean continued, "have you been happy here?"

"It would have been foolish of me to stay this long and not be," Dr. Suess said guardedly. *Seems like we had this conversation before,* he thought. *This is getting to be like a broken record.*

Another pause.

"Would you agree with me," said the dean as he again resumed speaking, "that staff morale and unity is vital to smooth workings of an institution such as ours?"

"I would say it helps to keep the troops happy."

The dean pulled an attaché case across his lap and opened it.

"I have something that might amuse you," he said.

Dr. Suess said nothing.

"It's from the campus human relations committee," the dean continued. "It seems that there is another complaint."

Again, Dr. Suess knew immediately what it was. A couple of weeks previous he had walked across the main quad in an unusually sanguine mood enjoying the balmy spring weather when he was approached by a somewhat younger man. He nevertheless seemed older than the typical student.

Probably a new instructor or grad assistant Dr. Suess had conjectured.

The tall slim gentleman walked in a foppish gait. "Excuse me, sir," he said in an effete tone. "Could you direct me to the nearest rest room?"

Dr. Suess eyed him momentarily. "Sure thing," he said finally, "which one?"

He fought to suppress expression of amusement. Apparently a member of the clandestine campus informants had overheard him. In view of his announced plans for retirement, discipline or forced apologies were out of the question.

The dean flipped the memo back into his attaché case. "I—just thought you'd like see it," he said with a simper as he closed the lid.

He then sat back deeper onto the couch, steepled his fingertips and stared thoughtfully at the ceiling. For a moment he seemed hesitant to speak.

"Henry," he said finally, "how well do you know Dr. Sirotka?"

He knows we're close, thought Dr. Suess. *What's he after anyway?* "Quite well," he replied after still another pause. "That should be fairly obvious to anyone who knows the both of us."

Another pause.

"For some time," began the dean, "I've been concerned about him."

"Oh?" Dr. Suess determined not to give him any more than that.

Again, the dean hesitated. "He—seems to be acting strange of late."

"How so?"

"Well," said the dean in a near whisper. "He—how can I put this?—seems rather secretive."

He heaved a thoughtful sigh. "It seems that he is carrying on a private project. A kind of research of some sort. I was wondering if just by any chance you would be privy to anything."

"Maybe," said Dr. Suess, "and then again, maybe not. I don't understand the sudden concern."

The dean tilted his head in a pensive position. "Perhaps you're right," he said in buttery voice. "Perhaps it's nobody's real concern. Perhaps it's just idle curiosity on my part. But I was just wondering if—"

"If what?"

Another pause.

"I was just wondering," said the dean, repeating himself, "if you would just, you know—just as a personal favor—"

Personal favor? Thought Dr. Suess. *Since when do I owe this sonofabitch a personal favor?*

"Can we get to the point?"

The dean pursed his lips. "Well, I was wondering if perhaps you could find out anything."

Dr. Suess eyed him. "You mean spy on Dr. Sirotka?"

Maybe now is the time 'Babs' found out, he thought. *He doesn't realize his cattin' around is no secret among the faculty. Trouble is, we got so many wimps on this campus, they're all afraid to say anything.*

Why hell, he continued, *to get on his good side, we have courageous giants who'd gladly scoop their salary out of a toilet bowl—in pennies—if he asked them to.*

Now that I've given my notice, what have I got to lose?

But, he concluded, *maybe spilling the beans would spoil half the fun.*

The dean's expression took on a pained look. "The word 'spy' is such a harsh, sinister word. What I meant was, I was merely wondering if—well, if you could notice anything—you know—just from casual observation. I just might be able to arrange a healthy retirement bonus."

"Is this a bribe?"

"Oh, but monsieur," said the dean. "I was hoping we wouldn't use such an accusative term. I prefer to think of it as—shall we say—a reciprocal exchange of emoluments."

Silence.

Dr. Suess glared at him in mock indignation. "As a devout churchman," he said, "where is your sense of Christian ethics?"

The dean cast him a sidelong glance. "Come, come, Henry," he said. "Let's be realistic here. You know as well as I that the average churchman does not take his religion all that seriously."

"As apparently neither do a great number of her clergy."

Dr. Suess stood up.

"I do know this," he said, turning to the dean who still remained seated, "that research concerns a report from a government agency and is classified; I couldn't disclose its content to you in any event."

Dr. Suess left the dean still sitting in the lounge. He resumed his course down the hall toward the science wing and turned aside to the door that led to his office.

Never in all my born days, he thought, *have I met a man so full of himself.*

He laid his attaché case atop his battered wooden desk.

So I lied to the dean about the classified report, he thought, *but I figure the nosy bastard is fair game.*

He opened the attaché case, took out the Cryptology Division's latest communiqué and began reading:

P'ssudohn resumed his trek along the shore. Suddenly, in the moist sand, he spotted a gigantic three-toed hoof print. He tried to recognize the animal that had left the print. He heard a rustling in the nearby underbrush. After moments of hearing only the sound of large, powerful jaws munching vegetation, he saw a massive creature emerge, the like of which he had never seen before. It plodded slow and ungainly through the beach grass in search of more tender young shoots. Legs thick as tree stumps supported a powerful looking body clothed with cartilage plates of gray, scaly armor. A spiked, spiny tail twitched nervously among the bent grasses as its tip marked a thin trail in the white sand. Tiny eyes set wide blinked at him in a vague curiosity and then stared dully. Its nostrils flared briefly and snorted moisture that sprayed the growth in front of it. At the base of the skull flared a broad process of armor plate. Three horns longer than P'ssudohn's arms thrust menacingly from its brow.

THE TITANS

He pointed to the creature with his trident. As the indifferent beast turned away toward more scrub brush, P'ssudohn called out to it: "I dub you as future generations will dub you: Triceratops."

Chapter 11

Days later Dr. Suess left Dr. Sirotka's office carrying his attaché case. He had just been given another cryptology report. As he descended the stair case that led to the Main Hall's front exit, he felt a twinge of disappointment that Dr. Sirotka was not going with him to Lena's. Too busy he had said. However, Dr. Suess suspected that the real reason was his increased drinking. Dr. Sirotka no longer cared to join him at the local watering holes.

He recalled going back to Deadman's Gulch the night after the altercation...

...The proprietor told him he didn't want him coming in there any more. Dr. Suess had pled with the proprietor to let him come back; to give him one more chance. After all, the other guy had started it. And besides it was only one time.

That was one time too many, the proprietor had said.

But I won't be any be any more trouble Dr. Suess had said. I'm not really a troublemaker.

Good, the proprietor had said, I'm sure the owner of wherever you're doing your drinking these days will be grateful...

...*Screw that place,* thought Dr. Suess as he entered Lena's.
Screw Dr. Sirotka.
Screw them all.

THE TITANS

He settled into a remote booth and ordered a Scotch on the rocks.
Then another.
Then another.

He slid the attaché case beside him and opened it. Before examining its contents, he reflected on his life with Marie and her children.

After that concert date in Denver, things began to move fast in their relationship. Soon they were having him over for breakfast.

Both Marie and he realized that sooner or later they would have to make a decision: move toward a permanent commitment or break it off. Sooner or later they would have to broach the subject to the children.

He recalled the leisurely Saturday morning around the breakfast table at her place…

…The children had joined them and the four seemed cozily ensconced in the small condo eating area shielded from the howling blizzard outside.

"It's good that you kids were able to join us this morning," he finally said to the children.

He fidgeted with his napkin a moment.

"You mother and I have wanted to discuss something with you for sometime now."

Silence. The children looked around at both their mother and him with puzzlement.

"Your mother and I love each other very much."

More silence. He could hear himself breathe. He threw down his napkin.

"Your and mother and I have felt it important to include you in on a very important decision."

He looked into the eyes of the two youngsters. He saw in them a worldly wisdom beyond their years.

He also saw hurt.

He also saw understanding.

"Your mother and I," he said again picking up the thread of conversation, "have for some time now been thinking that it was about time that—that we became a family."

The response was immediate.

"Cool," said the boy eyes wide with enthusiasm.

The daughter jumped up from her chair and threw her arms around him.

When he was finally able to pull her off, he turned to Marie.

"Looks like we got their vote," he said with a smile…

…Pulling a sheaf of printed material, he studied it a moment. *This doesn't look very recent*, he thought. *Looks like another change in point of view and of vantage point.*

In fact he observed that it looked like a different spectrum of rays altogether. *Dr. Sirotka has been sandbagging this one. Fine friend he is, holding out on a buddy.*

Fighting vision blurred from alcohol fumes, he began reading:

The dense silvery cloud finally parted revealing a multi-colored curtain of silk that extended about a hundred meters in both directions and was suspended with golden rings on horizontal poles of highly polished hardwood. Vertical ridge poles of similarly darkened wood interspersed themselves equidistant from one another. Gold thread tassels bordered the hem of a curtain embossed alternately by miniature golden grapes and pomegranates. At the center of the curtain hung a flap or overlay that appeared to serve as an entrance.

'At either side of the entryway stood two shining intelligent beings. They arrayed themselves in shimmering robes of linen type material. Wide, golden sashes held the garments at the waist

'The skin of their faces and hands radiated sheen like molten gold.

'Their eyes burned with an intensity that those of a much later epoch would describe as laser. They wore their golden wavy locks short and neatly trimmed.

'From behind the shoulders of each sentry projected processes that resembled the large wings of a gull or eagle. The glowing whiteness of their wings contained a geometric design pattern: hundreds of small, dark circles resembling spots on the wing of a peacock.

'Or they resembled perhaps the eyes of an intelligent being.

'The clouds parted further, revealing galaxies of stars in the pale gold firmament. However, instead of radiating a cold white sparkle as seen from Earth, they shone in multi-colored brilliance.

THE TITANS

'Faint sounds of singing permeated the atmosphere.

'Suddenly above this sound came the roar of a rushing wind.

'A warrior watcher appeared before the two sentries. He too glowed from head to foot. His attire, however, had the appearance of a battle tunic, shortened to just above the knees. From a wide, golden girdle hung a sword of blue, laser like light.

'As the warrior-watcher confronted the sentries, he slapped his right fist against his chest.

'"I am M'kh-ay'l reporting," he announced.

'"I recognize you," said one of the sentries. "The Sh'khynyu awaits you."

'The sentry stood to one side and slapped his chest in a return salute. "Enter."

'The warrior watcher disappeared behind the curtain. The sentry resumed his original spot adjacent the opening. His comrade glanced at him from the corner of his eye.

'"I trust that he will take care how he approaches the Peerless One," he said. "I fear ominous tidings afoot."

'"Do yourself no care, my brother," replied the first sentry. "Brother M'kh-ay'l has entered the Sanctuary many times before. He knows the procedure."

* * *

'As the folds of the multi-colored curtain closed behind him, M'kh-ay'l surveyed the expanse of courtyard. The ground beneath him appeared an alabaster white, finely grained sand like substance. Yet it compacted into a dense, solid soil. Mid court stood a large basin of polished bronze shining bright red.

'He walked to it, stripped off his tunic, climbed a short staircase that led up to its rim and immersed himself in its waters. He then reached for the horns that projected at one of its corners and climbed out.

'He stepped back down to the courtyard surface, still dripping wet. Another robed shining intelligence with a linen towel draped over one arm approached him.

'"Thank you, Iannhu," said M'kh-ay'l, taking the towel.

'"I trust you can exercise proper care in approaching the Oracle," said Iannhu as he assisted M'kh-ay'l.

'M'kh-ay'l began dressing himself. "Not to care," he said. "I am familiar with the ritual."

*Iannhu handed M'kh-ay'l a small vial and he started for the far wall of the curtained courtyard. He paused at another hanging curtain.

'On the other side lay the inner sanctuary.

'Slowly he approached the curtain and even more cautiously stepped into what appeared to be a kind of tent or pavilion. The inside appeared bare of all furnishings except for a small golden chest or box. A frieze of sharp, pointed ridges ringed the top. Two golden statues of winged intelligences perched atop the chest. Their heads bowed down and their hands clasped in an attitude of worship. A ball of light or fiery arc flashed between their wingtips*

The silence filled M'kh-ay'l with foreboding as he surveyed the stark interior.

'He withdrew his sandals and stepped closer to the altar. He uncorked the vial and poured powdered perfume onto the ball of light. Very quickly billows of purple smoke began rolling up toward the corners of the sanctuary. An aromatic odor filled the air. He could also hear a faint rumbling and feel a tremor beneath his feet. The ball of light increased in size.

'M'kh-ay'l jumped in terror as the perfumed smoke ignited the flame into an all-encompassing ball of fire burning with a blinding brilliance.

'M'kh-ay'l fell to the ground face down. Even with his eyes shut, his eyelids could not shield him from the brilliance that blotted all else from sight.

'He marveled that despite the cessation of his heart beat and breathing, he was still alive.

'He heard a voice.

"'Tell this to those without," roared words that sounded as though they came from a crowd of hundreds of thousands of shouting fans at an athletic stadium of a much later epoch, or perhaps at a similarly vintage political rally.

'M'kh-ay'l clapped hands over his ears to protect himself from the pain of the resonance.

"'Thus Am speaks," it continued. "This is the burden concerning Light-Bearer."

* * *

'As the sentries continued waiting beside the outer entrance, they became visibly anxious. Their faces expressed relief at the sight of the parting curtain and at the reappearance of M'kh-ay'l.

"How fared you," asked one sentry.

THE TITANS

'M'kh-ay'l did not answer.

'Shock and dismay registered on their faces as they studied him. With stunned expression, he stared out into the space. He staggered slightly, fighting to keep his balance. Thin blue streaks of lightning played over his body. He gestured to his mouth and shrugged.

'He motioned for the sentries to bring him writing material. One sentry disappeared and shortly returned with a scribe; a hoary ancient. The scribe bore a scroll, quill, and ink pot under one arm and a folding stool and writing stand under the other.

'Thus accommodated with stool and stand, M'kh-ay-l sat before the open area and began writing.

'When finished he handed the scroll to the scribe. He noticed that silvery cloud that surrounded the area receded revealing rows of shining intelligences tiered as in a massed choir. To their sides stood others holding harps, lutes, viols, timbrels, brass winds, flutes, and other instruments of music.

'The scribe mounted a podium, unrolled the scroll and began to read:

'"This is the burden regarding Lord Light-Bearer," he began.

'"I am not ignorant of your designs. Because I gave you sufferance does not mean that I do not know, nor does it mean that I condone them.

'"Do not confuse my sufferance of your mischief as weakness, indecision, or fear on my part.

'"I simply bode my time until you, in your hubris, made your final move to return to my sanctuary in your foolish attempt to topple me. In so doing, you have played into my hands.

'"Lord Light-Bearer, you shall yet be brought down to depth of Sh'ohl, the side of the abyss. All who know you shall look askance. They will ask: "Is this the one who made G'aia to tremble? Who shook fiefdoms? Who made the terrestrial garden a wilderness? Who destroyed the habitation of intelligent ones, and released not those held in captivity?"'

'As the scribe finished, the lightning that surrounded M'kh-ay'l dissipated.

'His eyes again became clear. His body posture appeared more relaxed.

'The scribe stepped down from the podium and M'kh-ay'l mounted it in his place. He faced the massed singers and musicians with arms outstretched.

'His speech had returned.

"'Am he praised through all eons," he intoned.
"'Am he praised through all eons," sang the choristers in response.
"His name has no equal." (His name has no equal.)
"Mighty are his works." (Mighty are his works.)
"His ways are unfathomable." (His ways are unfathomable.)

* * *

"We're closing."

Dr. Suess looked up from his drink with a start. He saw a tall woman with a face like chiseled granite standing beside his booth. Her lean, leathery arm bore a tattoo in the image of the Madonna. Her upper torso was covered with a wrinkled white T-shirt. An apron, also faded and wrinkled, covered a body and legs dressed in well worn jeans. Beside her he saw tables where chairs had already been stacked.

He looked at the clock on the wall behind the bar. One-fifty, bar time.

That meant real time was one forty.

The waitress stacked more chairs. "Come on, doctor," she said. "We all got homes to go to; even you."

He slipped out his booth. *Better do like she says,* he concluded. *This is about the last place in town where I'm welcome.*

Stepping to the sidewalk, he marveled how still the night lay in the balmy spring weather.

Again, despite the fragrant buds and blossoms that graced the trees surrounding the landfill, the mood took a dark turn. Soon when they would broaden into green leaves could they do much to hide stark reality that was the mound behind the high cyclone fence; a grim reminder of what happened that summer a quarter century ago?...

...Ginger Wallace had been his student secretary during his first three years. He liked her diligence and efficiency. He had a strong paternal interest in her, advising her on personal matters regularly. He admired her sweetness and effervescence.

He also harbored a concern over a certain rebellious streak she showed along with the flakiness of a free spirit.

He had subsequently learned that ever since her freshman year at her local community college, she was actually living a double life. She continued to be active in her parents' church with Bible studies, choir, and youth fellowship. At the same time she began running with a wild crowd at college plunging full tilt into booze, drugs, and promiscuous sex.

As the season progressed and the weather grew warmer, the crowds increased.

Including a large contingent of long-haired youth.

In addition a new element had now joined them.

Biker gangs appeared in platoon strength. They seemed to take great delight in tooling in around the picnic areas. This in violation of city ordnances requiring cars, vans, and other vehicles be kept in the parking lot.

Also contrary to city ordnances banning the use of alcoholic beverages, these groups consumed them openly and copiously.

In defiance of a law closing the park at 10:00 P.M. many of these people brought campers, trailers, and tents with intent of staying overnight.

Other things went on; things like using drugs and practicing open sex.

The problem soon extended to the town itself. Color-splashed vans and ancient jalopies were blocking street traffic, double parking and parking on peoples' lawns. Convenience store owners were complaining of drive-offs at the gas pumps. Restaurant owners complained of deadbeats leaving without paying their bill.

Townspeople stopped using the park altogether. Even most college students refused to use the park.

He remembered cautioning Ginger against getting in too thick with these people. He recalled the delicately oval face, the full lips with the ready smile, the brunette locks, and the open trusting look in the brown eyes.

But I find them interesting she had insisted in her little girl tone of voice. I'm a people person.

They're a seedy, unsavory bunch, he recalled admonishing her. You're better off not getting mixed up with them.

They have a wolf-pack mentality.

But she wouldn't listen.

At first the townspeople's complaints to city hall fell on deaf ears. After all, the city fathers had argued, as long as they aren't hurting anybody, why not live and let live?

However, citizens in the surrounding blocks complained of impromptu rock festivals that caused music to be blared over PA systems 24/7 depriving the townspeople of their sleep.

In addition what with their speakers, amps, and large spot lights they were running up some big electric bills.

All paid for by Stillwell taxpayers.

Sometime early summer, municipal authorities in acceding to the townspeople's' demands and decided to intervene.

But it was too late.

As the park, now filled to over capacity by strangers, resembled a garbage heap alive with maggots, the town found itself being sued by an out-of-town activist group known as People Inheriting the Earth (PIE.) The plaintiff insisted that the elitist townspeople had no right denying access to anyone. Every one had rights to the park; it belonged to the 'the people.'

"'*The people,*" he reflected. *Interesting. Any resemblance between 'the people' and ordinary folks like us is purely coincidental. In their lexicon 'the people' is just a philosophical abstraction.*

PIE declared the area a 'people's park.'

The earth belongs to all of us, the suit contended. To claim private property is theft.

A bunch of losers, he reflected, *who never had anything, never will have anything, yet they want everything. They were pandered to by the useful idiots that ran our city in those days....*

...He stopped at a corner and hesitated. He tried to figure out the direction of his house. *Must be the darkness of the night,* he tried convince himself.

I can't be that drunk.

"Need a ride, Dr. Suess?"

He turned in confusion to focus on a taxi from the local cab company that had just pulled up. Good idea he had mumbled as he struggled to get into the back seat.

His drowsy mind cleared with the fresh air rushing into the rear window. *Good man*, he thought. *He knows where I live.*

The large gray form of the rambling Victorian house loomed out the night shadows. He reached into his pocket and pulled out some bills. He had no idea of the charge or whether he had enough for the fare.

Would hate to bother Marie if I didn't, he thought.

Especially this late at night.

He handed the bills to the driver.

"Keep th' change," he mumbled as he staggered to the front sidewalk. With further effort, he finally mounted the broad steps that led to his front porch.

Upon entering the chasm that was the front vestibule, he found it dark and silent as death. Tiptoeing across the floor to avoid waking Marie and the children, he pulled off his blazer and threw it toward the hall tree. He heard the hall tree fall to the floor with a crash that rang through the house. As he stood beside the fallen object a realization came to him. He had forgotten to pull his left arm out of the sleeve.

This he did quickly and then left the blazer and the hall tree lying on the floor as he headed for the library.

He turned on a desk lamp from the wall switch. Across the desk blotter laid the following note:

'Henry dearest:

'By the time you read this, I very likely will have already taken the children and checked into a motel.

'I love you, darling. I am not leaving you—at least in the formal sense. I just need time to get away. I'll be back shortly.

'I also want you to get help.

'Please take this very seriously. It is no longer a trifling matter.

'People who matter to you very much are being affected profoundly by your choices.

'Your loving wife,

Marie.'

He made a sweeping gesture toward the empty, silent hallway. *Not leaving me?* He mused darkly. *What the hell does she call this?*

Marie, my sweet Marie, he thought. *How unbearable life would be without you. My two older children are so distant.*

And that a distance not just in miles.

He never realized his loneliness until he met Marie. In his alcohol befogged mind he saw himself at a crossroads. Either give up the comfort of John Barleycorn or give up Marie.

If you think you've got a drinking problem, you have.

The aphorism of a famous drinkers' support group pushed its way back into his mind.

Oh, God, he sighed as he took a couple of steps toward the door.

He took two more steps before falling headlong into his recliner.

* * *

He opened his eyes to the glare of sun rays filtering through the tiffany stained glass window. Again, without looking at his watch, he knew that he had missed another eight o'clock. For years he had been a stickler for punctuality, not only for himself but heaven help the student who came late. Now however—?

Screw it, he thought as he struggled to his feet. He staggered out into the vestibule where the hall tree still lay on its side with his blazer tangled on one of the hooks.

He picked up his blazer and stepped to the porch. He found skies overhead blue and cloudless. Ordinarily, he would have rejoiced at such a day. However, with aching eyeballs and pounding head, he greeted the day with less than unrestrained enthusiasm. He fumbled inside his blazer pocket for a pair of sunglasses.

Fifteen minutes later, he reached the campus and fell in behind a group of students who had just finished their mid-morning classes and were headed for the union building.

Half way across the quad, he veered off toward the science building in hopes of catching Dr. Sirotka before he left for lunch. He mounted the steps eyes downward to avoid having to greet anyone. When he stepped across the threshold into the vestibule, he removed his glasses.

Dr. Suess caught Dr. Sirotka in the hallway just as he was closing the door of his office.

"I was just going to the Old Heidelberg to grab a quick sandwich," he said. Dr. Suess fell in stride beside him as he headed the front door, Dr. Sirotka held up his attaché case.

"I've got something new to show you."

Chapter 12

Twenty minutes later they seated themselves in a narrow booth in the Old Heidelberg restaurant. They had both ordered the house luncheon specialty: Thuringer sausage on black rye with bean salad. When the waitress asked if they wanted anything from the bar, Dr. Sirotka shook his head.

"Coffee is fine for both of us," he said before Dr. Suess could respond. Dr. Sirotka placed his attaché case on the table beside him

"I have been reading Dr. Steven Hawking's writings," he said. "I've been fascinated in his work in cybernetics. Through the use of a computer he has just about traced time back to the actual Big Bang itself. As a professional atheist, he also made an interesting statement. He said of his latest discovery: 'We have either looked directly into the face of God, or we have found the ultimate proof that he doesn't exist.'

"Right now I'm not sure which. "'Dr. Suess shrugged. "What are you getting at?

"Dr. Sirotka opened his attaché case and handed Dr. Suess a sheaf of papers. "Forget everything else we've gotten back from the cryptology lab and take a look at this."

* * *

Lord Light-Bearer knew well the scene before him. A good runner's league (About 3.5 miles or 5 kilometers—ed.) behind him stretched the white sands of a broad

seashore. It did not resemble terrestrial seashore; certainly not the expansive but shallow Devonian Sea that covered much of what would later be called the Western Hemisphere. Future intelligence would also refer to these times as the Mesozoic Era.

The waters lay still as glass. No waves washed the shore nor did any undercurrents disturb the surface. Crystalline purity made the sandy bottom clearly visible even to the greatest depths that extended out to the horizon. The sky stretched overhead a pale gold. Distant stars sprinkled in the aureate firmament varied colors: orange, red, blue, and purple. From the shore inland stretched a meadow of emerald green richness. Trees with leaves of every medicinal quality grew abundantly in a well-manicured greensward. Before him lay an open area paved with stones of granite that fronted a colonnade shaped in a semi-circle and sheltered by tile roofing supported by stout buttresses of hewn granite-like blocks.

'Across the entire length of the dais spread a kind of bench or seat cushioned with velvet. Finely carved arms of hardwood divided the bench into sections of twenty-five seats. The center seat held a high back and appeared more elaborately furnished than the others as though it were a kind of throne or seat of judgment. To the twelve seats on either side sat elderly male intelligences dressed in white linen robes. In the center sat one whose hair and beard glistened a white sheen. He too arrayed himself in a long robe of white linen. A broad, golden sash encircled his midsection. The skin of his face, hands, and feet glowed like molten metal. On his head sat a high miter like crown sparkling with a multi-colored network of jewels. In his right hand he held a golden scepter that glistened with seven diamonds, each radiating faceted brilliance resembling stars.

'He extended the scepter toward Lord Light-Bearer.

"'Lord Light-Bearer,'" his voice reverberated like the sound of a waterfall, "come before me."

'Lord Light-Bearer stepped across the paved area to where the scepter pointed.

'The one holding the scepter continued. "Do you know why we have summoned you?"

'Lord Light-Bearer drew the lengthy train of his rainbow hued robe about him. He folded his arms in a casual stance. His eyes turned a dull, listless gray.

'A pained expression reflected in the eyes of the twenty-four elders as they read insolence in his body posture.

"'Stand to when you appear before me!" roared the one in the center. "Remove your shoes. You are on holy ground."

'With a slight groan of protest Lord Light-Bearer stooped to remove his sparkling gold sandals. He resumed his stance only slightly straighter than before, showing a begrudging gesture of respect.

"'As to why you summoned me,' he said with a hint of patronizing. 'I haven't the slightest idea.'"

The molten color of the scepter holder's countenance glowed with white heat. "'I haven't the slightest idea, Lord!' he boomed out over the landscape."

"'I haven't the slightest idea, Lord,' said Lord Light-Bearer in a more subdued tone."

'A brief silence.' "Give me an account of your activities."

"'I roam the earth,' said Lord Light-Bearer, trying to recover his shattered braggadocio. 'I go to and fro and up and down in it. Sometimes here; sometimes there.'"

'A pause.

He raised his head in an attitude of hauteur. "I monitor it," he said, "just as you monitor me."

"'And what were you doing here without our calling you up?' the one on the center throne asked. 'Just what were you doing when we summoned you?'"

"'I was preparing to direct the celestial choir,' Lord Light-Bearer answered, 'as you had once assigned me to do.'"

"'And did we call you back here to do that?'"

'Again silence.

The one on the throne eyed him a moment. "Tell me," he said finally. "Are you happy with the relationship between us?"

"Reasonably so, my lord."

"'Reasonably so?'"

Another silence.

"'Have I treated you fairly?'"

"'Quite fairly, my lord.'"

The one on the center throne looked to his right and then to his left. "Have any of you ever witnessed me belittle or slight him?"

Twenty-four heads shook in the negative. The one on the center throne again leveled a gaze at Lord Light-Bearer. "Is there any honor or recognition that I have unjustly withheld from you?"

"'There is none, my lord.'"

The one on the center throne sat for a brief moment. He leaned forward, resting his elbows on his knees as he continued to study the arrogant figure before him.

"'Then why,' he said finally, 'do we have this?'"

He extended his right fist forward. From a large signet ring on his index finger he flashed a ray of light that dissipated immediately in front of Light-Bearer. Full dimensional images that intelligent beings in the future would call a holograph formed in the light.

Before them, in the vision, Lord Light-Bearer leaned against a mahogany table top. Opposite him stood Hypp'ryon.

"'Hear my words,' they heard the holograph saying, 'and hear them well. I will ascend into heaven. I will exalt my throne above the stars of God. I will sit also upon the mount of the congregation of the sides of the North.'"

"'I will ascend above the heights of the clouds.'"

"'I will be like the Most High.'"

The holograph and light vanished into the ring

His eyes turned a nondescript hazel as he sought to avert the gaze of the center throne's occupant.

"My lord," said Lord Light-Bearer, now noticeably more subdued, "I meant nothing seditious by those remarks. I was merely seeking to boost the morale of Lord Hypp'ryon by reinforcing to him the exalted nature of our terrestrial mission, I think I might have maybe gotten a little carried away with my own rhetoric perhaps, but I assure you I did it in all innocence of any evil intent."

"Every idle word," the face of the one sitting on the center throne darkened, "will be called to account."

The faces of the twenty-four elders registered apprehension.

Again he extended out his ring hand. "How do you account for this?"

The scene widened to show an expanse of shining beings extending out to shimmering clouds of gold and silvery hue. Singing with the depth of resonance that could be felt as well as heard filled the colonnade area. High atop a giant podium of granite stood Lord Light-Bearer.

"'Stop!' they heard Lord Light-Bearer shout.

The vast choir fell to silence. "From now on," continued Lord Light-Bearer, "you will no longer sing praises to the Great Am. Hence forth you will sing praises to me."

Some choristers pled with him not to commit this sin.

"Enough!" he shouted to those who objected. He glared at choristers who sat in a state of shock. "Who of us have actually seen the great Am? To us is he not merely a ball of light in the inner sanctuary? Could he not merely be a mechanical device invented by some Trickster eons past? What homage do we owe him?"

'He raised his hand to give them their cue. As he gave the downbeat, about a third of the choir timidly and tentatively intoned the opening phrases.

The remaining choristers stood silent.

'Again, the holograph vanished into the ring. 'Lord Light-Bearer looked away. He did not want the One seated on the center throne to see his eye sockets darken.

"'As you yourself have put it," said the throne's occupant slowly in a low, sinister voice. "Enough."'

* * *

Dr. Suess' Thuringer sandwich lay in front of him untouched. He continued examining the report Dr. Sirotka brought with him.

He tried to analyze the narrative from the standpoint of a literary critic. From what point of view did this communication reflect? Was it still from an eyewitness on prehistoric earth? Or was it from a vantage point in outer space? If that were the case who or what is the intelligent being sending this message? And to whom? For what purpose? Who is the intended recipient here?

"This stuff is dynamite," he said as he re-read the page. He held it off to one side as he took a sip of the now cold coffee. He laid the sheet back on the table top. The faint aroma of cooking wafted in from the kitchen. The subtle smell of stale beer emanated from the bar. Far in the distance he heard the ratcheting sound of the barkeep inserting new tape into the cash register.

"One thing puzzles me," he said.

Dr. Sirotka looked at his watch. He then observed the thinning of the noon hour crowd. His eyes swept a dining room ornate with furnishings darkly quaint to resemble a Black Forest motif. He watched as two waitresses dressed in Bavarian dirndls spread fresh linen over nearby tables.

"I got a one o'clock," he said. Dr. Suess shifted his weight to a more upright position.

"Hey, don'tlet me keep you," he said. "I'll study this some more on my own and get back with you."

Dr. Sirotka settled back in his chair. "The hell with it," he said. "Let's stay on this. What was your question?"

THE TITANS

"It's the narrative," said Dr. Suess finally. "Who is the one giving the account here? It's not being told by these T'tanyu or whatever they called themselves. It's obvious that this stuff is being told by an objective outside observer, but whom?"

* * *

The forest lay even quieter than usual that first afternoon. As Ypp'llu directed his fiery orb to begin what was to be his final ascent, the moisture in the firmament enveloping the jungle and swamp seemed thicker than usual. The sun as a fiery yellow ball burned fiercely in the pale, gold sky. Steamy moisture reduced the brilliance and radiation. Even the broad palm leaves hung limp in the oppressive atmosphere.

Finally, almost imperceptibly at first, the spongy earth began to tremble; not a steady tremble, but rather interminable hammering of blows. The trembling grew louder, now accompanied by the crashing of young trees and saplings. A wall of vegetation bordering a small clearing was suddenly crushed asunder by the appearance of the terrible lizard.

'The King of Tyrants paused.

The head the size of an upright creature slowly surveyed the wall of splendid gold and green that bordered the glade before him. Eyes hard with a cold fierceness, yet with a faint glimmer of despair driven by a pang of hunger, blinked uncomprehendingly as he searched vainly for some prey to come stomping through the underbrush.

'A mouth large enough to swallow an upright hung agape. Two rows of teeth the shape and the size of an upright's dagger glistened white in the afternoon sun. His tiny forelegs reached out into the air. Rapier like claws flexed open and shut as if grasping for an imaginary victim. He straightened nearly upright on his massive hind legs and made a guttural sound. He continued searching in vain hope that an unsuspecting quarry would yet be heedlessly feeding in the thick underbrush. The yellow ball that was the sun hung even lower as the King Tyrant's powerful tail thrashed the surrounding bushes flat in his desperation.

'Suddenly he stopped.

'His walnut sized brain sensed foreboding. To his primitive understanding, it seemed as though a curtain was being drawn across the sun. Dark was descending on the jungle much too early; much too quickly. In the distant sky, a spheroid with a blackness void of all color moved toward the sun with a rapidity that could be seen.

'Soon it moved directly in the sun's path, changing the fiery orb into a crescent. In a brief space of time it drew a pall of darkness over the earth. Then it seemed to have stopped; as if fixed in the position.

'Any intelligence observing the phenomenon would know that, in reality, it had merely changed direction and now headed directly earthward. Its trajectory became apparent by its increasing size as earth's atmosphere became a black as midnight. Winds began to whip up, causing trees to thrash about wildly. The fierce mugginess of the afternoon now turned cold.

'For the first time King Tyrant knew fear.

'In dumb panic, he ran back into the jungle, unknowing as to where.

'For him, as for all creatures, there was no place to hide 'Contrary winds howled fiercely as a fine grain of gray ash flew at a sharp angle, tearing foliage, tree and bush. The winds mounted in fury, uprooting even the tall hardwoods. Any surviving species with a sense of hearing could now hear a roar above the winds as a wall of water rose from the Devonian Sea and bore down on the strewn remains of the forest. Frothing breakers, high as a brontosaurus, came rolling in from the distant horizon and crashed murderously, sweeping away all in their path. 'After an indeterminate length of time, they flattened into surf turbulent with destructive, salty currents. Fine volcanic ash descending from overhead, now bore pieces of rock the size of emus' eggs.

'The pelting of the waters continued. Huge boulders the size of King Tyrant's head now also descended from blackened skies. Minutes, hours, even days passed and still ash and rocks crashed into the waters

'After an interminable length of time the winds finally abated. The shower of ash and rocks continued pummeling an earth amid an atmosphere dark with clouds of moisture and volcanic rubble. The wind blew no longer violent, but steady and cold—very cold.

'It blew with a coldness that made all terrestrial life—hitherto unaccustomed to coldness—impossible.

'Rocks and rubble descended on the waters until they formed a kind of landfill. This landfill continued building up until the waters became isolated into brackish, saline pools.

'Gradually the clouds separated, revealing a bilious, yellow sky. A new sun—no longer Ypp'llu's domain—crossed the heavens. A lifeless quiet descended on the barren landscape.

'The thick, brackish waters receded. From deep within the earth's bowels now *bubbling up between the fissures, came rivulets of fresh water. Eons passed before new forms of mosses spread across the rocks. As more long ages passed, other plant forms appeared: lichens, grasses, saplings of evergreens, and finally deciduous, leaf-bearing shoots.*

New forms of insect life began buzzing through the savannah.

'Along the bank of a stream a new life form glided through the grass. Plate like scales in intricate design glistened in the primeval sunlight.

Just as silently as it appeared, the serpent slid out of sight.'

* * *

With the bustle of students hurrying to their nine o'clock classes echoing behind him, Dr. Suess stepped with deliberate stride down the ad building hallway toward the door the bore on its window the following sign:

'J. Negley Jone, Ph.D., Dean of Students'

He paused at the threshold before knocking. A sardonic grin crossed his face. Even now he faced the temptation to blow the whistle as it were. Either 'Babs' was hopelessly naïve or, as more likely, in a state of denial. In any event her being out of the country some six months of the year left her husband with ample opportunity for clandestine adventuring.

Her insistence that her 'Nigel' as she was wont to call him, remained trustworthy seemed impregnable. She would then hie off to the U.K. to supervise the trusteeship of Kaxton College, the institution of higher learning that maintained its campus on her family's historical estate. A muffled "entres" answered his knock. Dr. Suess opened the heavy dark wooden door and began walking over the thick carpeting toward a broad, mahogany desk at the far end. The large man in the double-breasted pinstriped smiled at him. Still in his chair, he leaned against the dark paneled wall.

"Good morning, Henry," he said as he steepled his fingertips. "It's good of you to stop by."

Dr. Suess held out a slip of paper. "Especially since you sent for me."

"Sit down, Henry."

Dr. Suess pulled up an armchair on his side of the desk and sat down.

The dean gestured to a small oaken cabinet behind him to his left. "Please don't think me rude if I not offer you a drink," he said, "but in view of your current struggle, I thought better of it."

"Thoughtful of you, but no matter," replied Dr. Suess. "I'm rather fussy about my drinking companions these days anyway.

"*Hypocritical bastard*, thought Dr. Suess. He reflected on school rules forbidding the use and possession of alcohol on campus during school hours. Though the dean had gotten away with maintaining a liquor cabinet for years, Dr. Suess knew that were he ever to have been caught with liquor in his own office, no contractual tenure provision could ever save his job.

The dean's voice snapped his reverie. "And how's Marie these days?"

"Well, thank you."

He condemned himself for his hypocrisy. In that so-called bastion of learning, he continued fearing for her safety. *To coin a cliché*, he concluded, *the inmates have taken over the asylum.*

"And the children?"

"They are well."

The dean leaned back in his chair and stared pensively toward the ceiling. "Beautiful spring day, is it not?"

Dr. Suess allowed as to how it was indeed a beautiful spring day.

With a sigh, the dean again sat forward. This time he pulled open his desk drawer. He pulled out a white sheet of paper and a pair of shears. With the shears he began cutting an inch off the right hand margin. He then replaced the sheet back in the drawer and took out a ruler. With a pen he drew a straight line down the middle of the strip.

Dr. Suess fought an impulse to laugh as he watched the dean turn over one end of the strip. *Nothing this guy ever does is funny*, he reminded himself.

Well manicured hands tore a strip of scotch tape from a nearby dispenser and taped the twisted end of the strip to the other, forming a sort of looped figure eight.

"You called me in here to watch you cut paper?" Dr. Suess couldn't resist saying.

"Observe, Henry," said the dean, ignoring Dr. Suess' remark. "I have just made a moebius. Do you know what that is?"

"Only since ninth grade. It's an unending plane surface."

The dean laid the paper construction aside. "It's a very interesting concept," he said, turning to Dr. Suess. "Have you ever thought of any philosophic implications in such an abstract design?"

"Not lately."

Again the dean sat back and stared at the ceiling. He continued staring at the ceiling as he resumed his conversation. "Henry," he said, still leaning back, "Have you been happy here?"

"Seems like we've had this discussion before."

This is getting monotonous, he thought.

"Of course." The dean gave a slight chuckle.

"How forgetful of me. Tell me, do you consider yourself to be fair-minded instructor?"

Dr. Suess sat motionless in his chair. "What I think is beside the point," he said as he kept his face void of emotion. "You have only to look in my files. Past evaluation reports from other administrators, colleagues, and former students have been unanimous in considering me one the fairest, most impartial teachers on this campus."

The dean nodded. "I have consulted those files," he acknowledged. "However impartiality is not at issue here."

"What is at issue here?"

"Fairness." "I thought impartiality and fairness were synonymous. I don't understand."

Here we go, he thought, *more of your damned semantics games again.*

Another pause. The dean again leaned forward. "I have had several of your students in to see me," he began. "They accuse you of being unfair."

Dr. Suess remained motionless. "What seems to be their problem?"

"Number one, they accuse you of giving too many tests. Number two, they maintain that your tests are too difficult. Number three, they say you grade too low."

"But I test and grade as I always have."

"That may very well be true," admitted the dean, "but, be that as it may, that has been the complaint."

Another pause.

"However," the dean continued, "my job is to take the students' concerns and relay them to the instructor. What you do about it, I leave pretty much up to you."

Dr. Suess for some time had listened to his wife tell about her high school students voicing the same complaint every time she gave them an assignment.

"I have noticed a recent immaturity in our students," he said. "My wife has run into this at the high school level for years."

A look of hardness crept into Dr. Suess' expression. *You sonofabitch*, he thought, *last year seventy percent of the seniors graduated with honor. You haven't helped the situation.*

The dean reached for an educational journal that lay on his desk. He opened it, again leaned back in his chair, and began reading. Suddenly he stopped, handed the opened periodical to Dr. Suess and pointed out to him an article.

"Henry," he said, "perhaps you're still not quite attuned to current changes in our educational philosophy. We now have a system of grading and student evaluation that measures not only objective accomplishment, but we also take into consideration certain intangibles such as self-esteem."

Dr. Suess sat back in his chair and crossed his legs. "And how do we enhance a student's self esteem," he said with a feigned smile, "when we send him out of here to work for, say, an oil company as an exploration geologist only to have the company fire him after just one month because the kid is incompetent?"

The dean again glanced toward the ceiling. "Ah yes," he smiled, "coming to the defense of the money-grubbing oil companies I see."

Dr. Suess felt color rise in his neck. "Money-grubbing or not," he said. "The fact remains that they have hired a lot of our graduates over the years."

A thought occurred to him. "Tell me," he said, still smiling, "did you drive to work today?"

"I drive to work every day."

"Thank the oil companies." Dr. Suess moved to an upright position.

"Or take the mining companies," he said with an edge to his voice. "Think of the liability and just plain hell to pay when a mining accident occurs just because one of our graduates was too dumb to notice dangerous working conditions? What happens to their self-esteem then?"

"You point is well taken," said the dean. "However, there is another concern that the students have shared with me." "Which is?" "It is in regard to a motto you post in the front of your room."

"Is it the one about excuses?"

"Yes, I believe it is."

"'Results not excuses,'" quoted Dr. Suess. "We can make excuses for just about anything, but when we do, that's all they are."

"Many of your students do not feel comfortable being confronted with that motto every day."

"Which is exactly my point," said Dr. Suess. "I don't want my students to feel comfortable; I want them to feel challenged."

The dean sat thoughtful a moment. "As I've already said," he sighed, "I am merely relaying to you your students' concerns regarding your teaching methods. I am in no way trying to tell you how to teach your class."

That's because you know I'm retiring at the end of this term, thought Dr. Suess. *You that know if you tried, I'd tell you to kiss off.*

And besides, he reflected further, *I've still got my ace in the hole.*

He couldn't believe that a woman as smart as Adele Smithson-Jones would not already be privy to the escapades of her playboy husband. *Her spending half her time in England hasn't helped matters*, he concluded.

In any event Dr. Suess suspected that the dean would again try to alter his grades over the summer. Grade tampering was something he knew better than to put past his superior.

Dr. Suess still writhed with inner turmoil as he stood at his classroom chalkboard. He feverishly wrote questions across the entire panel in anticipation for his next class. Spring weather had only recently opened the leaves just outside his window, sending sunrays of a delicate green into the room, carrying with them the fragrance of lilac and apple blossoms.

He recalled that spring over two decades ago…

...Ginger Wallace had just brought in files that she worked on in her apartment. Her dress and appearance brought him up short. Her hair looked heavily sprayed and stuck out in spikes. Her face looked pale. Heavy mascara darkened her eyes. Dark maroon lipstick adorned her lips and dark nail lacquer covered her nails. Black slacks and blouse and a vest of black, wet leather adorned her petite, shapely body.

He stared at her in disbelief. What is this? He demanded. Hallowe'en is six months away.

It's the new me, she said airily.

Has this something to do with that crowd in that so-called 'People's Park?' he then had asked her.

She simply replied with a giggle as she walked away.

That was the last he saw of Ginger Wallace...

...He glanced anxiously at his watch and resumed writing. He knew that the soft, balmy weather would reinforce the torpor or 'spring fever' already afflicting most students. When he finished, he began pulling charts that were suspended on rollers

"Dr. Suess?"

He turned to see a fortyish looking man about to enter the room. Apart from wrinkles on the forehead and crow's feet around the eyes, the face looked vaguely familiar. The once brown hair now had streaks of gray and had thinned out on the top of his head. The visitor had also grown a moustache that replaced the peach fuzz of bygone years. He stood slightly taller than Dr. Suess and wore a windbreaker and worn-looking jeans.

"Remember me?" Dr. Suess was at his side in a trice. "Larry Drummond," he said, extending his hand. "How could I not remember?" Dr. Suess ushered him into the room and gestured to a front row seat. "If you're expecting a class," said the visitor, "I don't want to interfere." "Nonsense," said Dr. Suess. "Sit down." Dr. Suess took a seat beside him and studied him a moment.

"Been long time," he said at last. "You're a sight for sore eyes. Whatever brings you here, anyway?"

"You have my daughter?" "As a matter of fact, she's in the class that's coming in here in a minute or so."

"I've come to take her home for spring break," explained the visitor. He then eyed the charts covering the chalkboard. "Giving a test I see."

"Mid-term."

A pause. Dr. Suess studied him further.

He suddenly realized that his visitor had been a classmate of Ginger Wallace, whose murder remains unsolved even to this day.

He recalled with poignancy the petite, child-like sprite. How gifted; how talented, he reflected. She had majored in music—vocal. Her bel-canto soprano voice thrilled faculty, students, and townspeople alike in her performances in recital and stage production as well.

She had just one drawback.

She seemed attracted to people who were fringe-types, Bohemians, counterculture—bizarre of dress, countenance, and life style.

Dr. Suess' attempts to warn her that these people could be dangerous fell on deaf ears.

He tried to dismiss troubling thoughts with an exchange of small talk and pleasantries.

He briefly reminisced on the days when this father sat as a student in this very classroom. *Teaching and testing was so easy in those days*, he thought. *To coin a colloquialism, we never had it so good.*

"Tell you what," he said finally. "Just for kicks, why don't you take a seat in the back of the room and take the test with them? This could prove quite interesting."

The man hesitated. "It's been a long time," he said. "One forgets a lot of things."

"Come on," urged Dr. Suess. "Just for kicks. Like I say, this could prove interesting."

As his former student reluctantly moved to the back of the room, bluebook in hand, they heard a clamor in the doorway. Soon students began pouring into the room.

"That's not fair," lamented another student.

"I'm gonna complain to the dean," threatened another.

Amid the hubbub, Dr. Suess strode to the front of the room. From the bottom desk drawer, he seized a football referee's yellow flag. He held the flag aloft over the desktop.

"Quiet!" The word boomed out across the room like a cannon shot. However, instead of silence, the student noise reduced to a nervous chatter. As he continued holding it out over the desktop, he gave the following ultimatum: "Anybody whose mouth is still open when this flag hits the desk is out of here!"

He released the flag.

Silence quickly fell on the classroom.

While the students sat in a state of shock, he picked up a bundle of blue books and started toward the head of each row. "Take one and hand the rest to the person behind you," he whispered to the front person.

Once the students settled into their tests, he retreated to his desk atop the platform in the front of the room the better to observe the entire exam proceedings.

Fifty minutes later, he again broke the shocked silence. "Turn your blue books face down on top of your desks," he said in a tone barely audible. "Leave quietly and in single file. Last person in each row pick up the blue books and bring them up here."

Once the room had been cleared of students, the visitor left his rear seat and approached Dr. Suess, exam book in hand.

"Still haven't lost your touch I see," he said, laughing.

Dr. Suess shook his head. "When I graduated from college," he said, picking up the yellow flag, "my first job was with a junior high school. This was a technique I used back then. Now I have to use it in college."

As the visitor started to leave, Dr. Suess' parting words halted him one more time.

"First day after spring break," said Dr. Suess, "why don't you stop back again. I'll have the tests graded by then. This should prove interesting."

* * *

"I trust everyone had a pleasant spring break?"

Dr. Suess eyed his students as they settled in their chairs. "I have corrected your mid-terms," he said. "I have a few choice words to say about your performance."

THE TITANS

He began pacing the front of the room. "The day of the exam," he began, "some of you may have noticed a visitor in the back of the room. Not only is he the father of one your classmates, he is a former student of mine. Twenty-five years ago, he sat where you sit today, taking this exact same course. Just for fun, I suggested he take the test, even though after twenty-five years, he walked in cold."

He paused, slowly walked back to his desk. He picked up the stack of bluebooks, studied them a moment and then threw them down again.

He could feel tension in the room.

"Before I hand them back to you, like I say, I have a couple of choice comments."

Again, he paused. He thrust his hands into his pockets and began rocking back and forth on his heels. "Only one person in this class got an 'A.' Half of you flunked outright."

Another pause to let it sink in.

He continued. "Our visitor who took this course twenty-five years ago got the only 'A.'"

He then pulled out his chair from underneath the desk and sat down. He leaned on his elbows and looked at his class.

With a smile, he made the following remark. "I am so glad that I am retiring at the end of this term."

He called a couple of students to the front of the room. He handed each a stack of bluebooks.

"Give these out," he said tersely.

He again looked at the rest of the class. "As soon as you get your bluebook, your can leave. You are dismissed."

The students hesitantly rose to their feet. "How come we're leaving so early?" asked one.

"Aren't you supposed to keep us the whole period?" said another.

Dr. Suess stood up and started for the door. "I'm dismissing you early and you're complaining? You mean you want I should keep you?"

They replied with a unanimous, but anxious "no!"

After a mere five minutes, Dr. Suess and his former student remained its only occupants.

"I don't think my sanity could take another minute with those kids," he sighed. "When the dean gets word that I dismissed them early today, he is going to have a hissy-fit. But screw him. Here's your test."

As his visitor approached the door, Dr. Suess halted him with one last remark.

"By the way," he said, "your own daughter got the only 'B.'"

Chapter 13

The dean eyed the frenzy of activity taking place in the Student Union faculty cafeteria. Two student employees busied themselves spreading white paper over set-up folding tables. Two more stood on stepladders behind the speaker's table mounting a paper banner across a wall curtain. The banner read:

'Good Luck on Your Retirement'

Another student stood on a high ladder attaching balloons and streamers to the ceiling. Presently a student kitchen employee in a white smock, wheeled in coffee urns on a cart. Other smock-clad students began bringing in trays laden with hors d'ouvres. From a side entrance the Student Union manager, a portly middle-aged man in a beige double-breasted suit, sidled up to the dean.

"Dr. Jone," said the manager, eyes twitching nervously, "I think everything is about ready."

The dean looked narrowly through his rimless glasses. With folded arms, he drew himself up to full height. "Good." The word oozed from his lips. "The faculty members should be arriving momentarily."

The manager scurried around making spastic little hand gestures to the student employees who subsequently began making rapid exits. In quick, short steps the manager slipped over to the main entrance and propped open the doors.

During the next fifteen minutes faculty members—sometimes by two's, sometimes by three's—began filtering into the cafeteria. Dr. Zelda Hezron presided over the punch bowl.

The dean slipped furtively over to Dr. Sirotka. "Where is Dr. Suess?" he asked with an unaccustomed look of concern.

"Probably at some watering hole getting sloshed," muttered Dr. Hezron.

"He should be here shortly," said Dr. Sirotka with a shrug.

Another fifteen minutes went by, still no sign of Dr. Suess. The dean looked at his watch and then looked out through the main entrance. After more minutes of nervous pacing, the dean again tracked down Dr. Sirotka through the increasingly impatient crowd. "Are you sure you gave him an invitation?" he said. Worried lines etched about his patrician forehead.

"I not only gave him an invitation," replied Dr. Sirotka, "I also checked with him personally this morning."

"And did he say he was coming?"

"Come to think of it," said Dr. Sirotka, "he was kind of non-committal."

When the dean noticed that some of the faculty members were leaving, he hurried over behind the speaker's table. He began tapping the side of a water glass with a spoon. "Can we have everyone's attention?" he said in slight tone of urgency. "It appears that Dr. Suess has been unavoidably detained. I don't think he would object if we therefore made this presentation in his absence."

He held up a bronze plaque mounted on polished hardwood.

He cleared his throat.

"It gives me great pleasure," he began, "to present to an esteemed faculty member of long standing a humble token of our gratitude for his many years of dedication and service to this college and to its students. Let us show our appreciation to our friend and colleague, Dr. Suess."

Amid the feeble applause from a dwindling crowd, he laid the plaque back on the table and turned to Dr. Sirotka.

"This is most distressing," he sighed. He picked up the plaque and laid it in a nearby attaché case.

"When you find Dr. Suess, tell him I have his plaque in my office."

THE TITANS

* * *

An hour later Dr. Sirotka pushed through the entrance of Lena's Bar and Grill. Through the murky interior he spotted Dr. Suess sitting alone in a remote booth.

Dr. Suess turned a sidelong glance as Dr. Sirotka crawled into the seat opposite him. "So how was the party?"

"Howling success." said Dr. Sirotka with a smirk. "The dean says you can pick up the plaque at his office."

Dr. Suess held up his shot glass. "Tell him I'm comin' right over," he said.

Dr. Sirotka reached down into his brief case. "Got a new report from the cryptology lab," he said, as he flung a bound sheaf of printouts on the table.

First up on the sheaf of papers lay an editorial memo:

'An interesting side issue has made itself manifest in the course of these texts. What of the relationship of the sexes among this alleged super race? To 'be fruitful and multiply' did these beings in order to procreate, commit incest?

'In short, is this a form of the conundrum, "Where did Cain get his wife?"

'That incest is today one of the last of taboos in our enlightened day and age is so for good reason. Many mental and physical defects such as retardation, cleft palate, and club foot can be traced to incestuous relationships or intra-familial marriage.

'Do the messages from these signals suggest that these genetic problems began with R'ya's curse?"

Dr. Suess laid the memo back into the attaché case.

He shook his head. "Wow," he said, "is this dynamite or what?"

A pause.

"So," he said finally, "what else do you have?"

Dr. Sirtoka pushed over the rest of the papers. "Here."

Dr. Suess set down his drink, picked up the report and began reading:

'So lay desolate the splendid Orb;
The beautiful, marbled ball;
Most highly favoured in all the heavens.

'So (thus) lay her glory now desolate.
She herself now the habitation
Of the fallen ones:
Powerful, yet foul, unclean, and angry.
'Dear mother Gaia (Earth), how now
Lies your (experimental laboratory)?
That you worked so hard to perfect?
'Dear mother Gaia, where now
Is the glory of your great (continent),
Pan-Gaia?
It lies broken and drifting apart.
Where drifts the Southern Continent (Africanus?)
Where drifts the Great Continent (Eurasian land mass)?
Where drifts the Long Continent (Western Hemisphere
Whence come the great upheavals from
Below your placid (Devonian) sea
(Paleo-zoic undersea volcanos?)
What has become of the glorious green
Vegetation? (Paleo-lithic plant life,
Tree life, and ferns?)
Grown as it were from smallest and weakest
Rock covering (i.e. mosses, lichens
And other primitive plant life forms.)
Where gone now are the myriad of splendid
Walking, flying, and creeping thing
That peopled your habitation
In time of old?
'All this and more lies beneath
The blanket of burning ash.
All things living have now perished

THE TITANS

Beneath pumice, brimstone, and lava.
'Yp'llu's proud chariot (sun?)
Rides no longer joyfully
Across the heavens.
'In the firmament (sky?)
Lies only thick clouds boiling
In sulphurous fury
O'er an earth that lies cold and barren.
'How long
O, how long
Before new life, though dormant,
Among the ashes,
Will geminate and re-emerge;
Will take root,
Grow and mature,
And take possession anew,
And Earth again
Rejoices with abundance of life?'

Dr. Sirotka eyed Dr. Suess as he continued reading. "Sounds like some sort of ancient lament," he said. "The people at the lab say that the signal is getting markedly fainter," he said. "They don't know how much longer their instruments can pick it up."

Dr. Suess flung the report back toward his companion. "That they were able to decipher anything at all is nothing short of miraculous," He said as he drained his glass. "It looks like we timed this about right. Our work is pretty much done here."

Dr. Sirotka returned the report to the attache case. "Are you coming with me?" he said standing up.

Dr. Suess waved him off. "I think I'll stick around a bit."

Dr. Sirotka stood in the aisle a moment and eyed his colleague with concern. Then, with a sigh, he started for the front entrance.

As he passed through the doorway, Dr. Suess caught the waitress' eye and raised his glass. "I'll have another," he called out to her.

Ten minutes later, he continued sitting in his booth and stared down into his refill. "And now," he said to himself, "for some quality time with my old friend, Jack Daniels."

Another fifteen minutes found him staring at the bottom of his emptied glass. As the waitress passed by with another customer's order, he held it up to her. Very shortly he became oblivious as to the passage of time or of how many more drinks he consumed. His next realization was that of the waitress standing beside his booth.

"We're closing." Her words had a ring of unreality.

From Lena's he staggered on through the silent, darkened streets.

Even in the balmy late spring evening it loomed like a giant mass grave, silent and threatening.

He tried not to look at the off-limits mound…

…As the hot summer progressed the counter-culture denizens increased in number, noise, and rowdy behavior. Townspeople had long since abandoned the park. Grass had become well trampled and had all but disappeared. Summer rains reduced the park to a quagmire. The visitors, having trashed the restrooms, openly and wantonly relieved themselves anywhere. Mounds of soiled pizza cartons and empty beer cans lay strewn like a carpet. Amid the blare of loud music from portable radios, they shot themselves up with unknown substances and left dirty syringes lying everywhere.

Picnic tables were broken up for firewood. By summer's end the pavilion and restroom buildings had gradually been razed to the ground.

Also that summer, Ginger worked the concession stand—that is so long as it was left standing.

The stench of garbage and human waste burned the nostrils of passersby.

Sometime over Labor Day weekend, it happened.

Recently registered Stillwell senior, Ginger Wallace, was reported missing. Weeks that followed, a manhunt fanned out over a multi-county area. A Missing Persons bulletin broadcast her picture nationwide.

In the meantime, as the fall season progressed, attendance at the park by out-of-towners dropped off considerably. Sometime in late October, cleanup crews carefully waded though piles knee deep in garbage, rubble, human waste, and dirty needles.

In the middle of the park, amid a heap of this unsavory mix, they found the unclad, partially decomposed body of the missing girl.

The mayor finally had to call the governor who in turn had to call in the National Guard to clear the park of the last remaining die-hards.

However he acted a bit late. The townspeople had already mounted a hasty recall election and ousted him and the town council forthwith.

Meanwhile, the Environmental Protection Agency declared the park polluted beyond repair and ordered it closed to all trespassors.

Thus the status of the 'people's park' in the quarter century since...

...Must have found my way home by auto pilot, he managed to think to himself as he worked his way up his front steps.

Finding the key to the front door proved another matter. At last he heard a hollow slam of the door bolt. It reverberated in the vestibule behind the heavy oaken door. He turned the knob and stepped into the cavernous dark. Again from memory he found his way into the library. He knew the location of the light switch and soon a desk lamp gave the paneled library a feeble light. Across the ink blotter lay the sheet of Marie's personal stationery. He started reading:

'Dear Henry:

'Just to let you know I have again taken the children and have gone to a motel. Please don't misunderstand. I am not leaving you. As I said on a previous occasion at least I'm not leaving in the formal sense. I have tried to be understanding, but I just can't go on like this.

'I still love you and I still want our marriage to work, but I am going to insist on your getting help. I have taken the liberty of contacting the brothers and St. Dunstan's Priory. They tell me they have a vacancy in their detoxification program. Any contacts can be made through the priory. I will keep in touch with you there. Once you have demonstrated your ability to live sober for at least a year, we can talk reconciliation.

'In the meantime, please don't try to contact me direct.

'As I say, I still love you.

'You can call it 'tough love.'

Love,

'Marie.

Now she's gone and done it, he thought. *Should have paid attention to her first note.*

He laid it back on the desk and exited the library. After mounting the darkened stairs, he found his way to the master bedroom at the far end of narrow, musty hall. He flicked on small nightstand light and entered an adjacent walk-in closet. From an overhead shelf, he pulled down an empty knapsack. He re-entered the bedroom, moved to his dresser and began pulling outdoor clothes from one of the drawers.

Flicking off the light, he exited toward the stairway.

Fifteen minutes later he stalked the corridor of the science building toward the geology lab. He thought it fortuitous that he had not as yet turned in his keys. Upon entering the lab, he stood a moment in the doorway and surveyed the darkness. He again studied the soft, purple glow that emanated from the glass case against a far wall. Picking his way through the darkened lab, he unlocked the case cover. Tenderly he picked up the trident and wrapped it in the army blanket the lay on the case's bottom.

If the campus security catches me here I would have some explaining to do, he realized.

But screw them, he added.

* * *

Another hour saw him, despite alcohol-blurred vision, behind the wheel of his enclosed Jeep hurling it through the night toward the Badlands.

Twenty-four hours passed by.

Sometime in the darkness of early morning, headlights picked up the winding dirt road. For him, the abysmal wilderness needed no signs. He knew every square foot of the barren landscape in the dark as well as in the daylight. He smiled in irony as he contemplated the fate of anyone trying to follow him into this remote, primeval terrain. They would become hopelessly lost within minutes. Again he looked out toward the ground picked up by his headlights. They no longer followed a road.

Only untracked wasteland.

Even the short stubble of a prairie grass thinned out and disappeared altogether. Still he pushed his vehicle onward heedless of the hard jouncing. Only when his headlights stopped picking out terrain of any kind did he finally hit the brakes. After sliding over gravel murrain, the Jeep finally came to a stop. Within the headlights, not fifty yards ahead, loomed a void that seemed to swallow the night.

He climbed out the Jeep, grabbed his knapsack and the blanket-bound trident and headed toward the precipice. With the aid of a halogen flashlight, he found a trail that led downward into the canyon. For the next hour, he carefully picked his way over loose stones until he reached the canyon floor. With a sigh he set the knapsack and trident down beside a large rock. Then he sat down and pulled from his bush jacket a fifth of whiskey.

He held the flask out toward the darkness.

Somewhere in his befogged memory, a thought occurred to him. Tomorrow was Mother's Day Sunday.

No doubt all the churches in Stillwell would be holding special services in honor of all the mothers in each congregation; even St. Sebastian's where Dean Jone occasionally worshipped. There would doubtless be many sermons delivered that paid eloquent and well-deserved tribute to mothers.

There very likely also would be quite a few that were downright mawkish and maudlin.

He recalled an old barroom pun. "Here's to all you mothers out there," he mumbled.

For an indeterminate period of time, he continued sipping the contents of the flask. Amid a fuzzy state of consciousness, he raised it to his mouth for a final gulp. He held out the emptied vessel studied it. Then he stood up and gave it a heave out into the darkness.

Simultaneously with the sound of broken glass came the peal of thunder from a far horizon. A flash of light jumped from above a mountain range dead ahead.

Another rumble of thunder.

He felt the wind picking up. *Gonna be a hell of a storm,* he observed as he began feeling droplets splashing against his face. With an ear-splitting crash, a giant shaft of lightning slammed into the ledge a short distance above him that made him jump. Dazed with shock and alcohol, he picked up his knapsack and struggled to get it over his shoulders. Another lightning bolt hit with equal suddenness, this time followed hard by a deluge that suggested Mother Nature turning on a shower head. Rising winds blew sheets of water that shortly penetrated even his water-repellent clothing. He staggered among the loose rocks and noticed a rising torrent rushing by his feet.

Flash flood.

The realization sobered him to the extent that again he knew that he had to get out of there. He fumbled around the ground until he found the trident. He pulled off the blanket, and summoning all his strength, hurled the heavy object toward the ever-rising waters.

"Here," he shouted, trying to make himself heard above the howling wind. "You can have it back."

It hit a rock formation still protruding above the rising current. When it struck, it sent up a shower of sparks.

Just as quickly the sparks disappeared and darkness again enveloped the scene.

In the lightning flash that followed he saw it plunge beneath the darkened waters that swirled over it. As it lay on the stony bottom it disappeared beneath gray, murky foam that spumed high into the night landscape. The torrent swallowed it from sight beneath the frothing current with a suddenness that surprised him even in his drunken state.

Meanwhile the floodwaters swirled up about his feet and began rising above his ankles. Whiskey fumes, the darkness, the suddenness of the storm, and rising deluge all had a disorienting effect. He pushed his feet against mounting torrent in search of dry ground. As the current pressed against his calves, he grasped his knapsack before it, too, swept away. He continued struggling in the water, and dropped his flashlight. He stood helplessly watching the beam of light wildly playing about in the inky void. He continued to stagger through the rising waters as the beam of light bobbed and swirled further downstream. With the weight of his knapsack bearing down on him, he dropped on all fours and felt his way over the wet, slippery rocks.

After more desperate moments, he reached out in the darkness and finally found a gravely surface not under water.

In the continuing downpour, he finally found a large rock.

Perhaps in daylight and when I'm sober, he thought as he sat down, *I can find my way out.*

* * *

The long mid summer evening cheered his spirit as he drove to the farthest of Stillwell's newest suburban neighborhoods. *Interesting,* he thought, *how now even small towns like Stillwell have suburbs.* He drove past recently constructed commercial strip malls. He drove past a large dirt mound of a construction area.

'Site of a Future Wal-Mart,' the sign read.

In the distance he spotted a complex of row houses built in neo Tudor style.

This must be the place, he concluded. In all his Friday Night poker games, he had never been to this colleague's home before.

He took a closer look at the architecture of the complex. The Tudor style bore the appearance of an imitation upscale of the *nouveau riche.* Upon closer examination he noticed the shoddy workmanship. He also noticed many units had opened doors with no screen door; a dead giveaway: the stuff of public housing. A Stillwell faculty member lives here? Knowing Dr. Cassius Edding, he was not surprised. He had previously occupied a studied hippie crash pad in an older, shabbier section of the original town.

He spotted a unit with cars parked in front and pulled up to a grassy spot across the street.

Dr. Suess paused at the threshold of the condominium before ringing the doorbell. *Awful nice of the old gang to still include me in their little circle,* he reflected.

Is it because they like me all that much or is it something else? He wondered.
Interesting
He rang.
Shortly the door opened.
"So it's the old lizard himself."

Dr. Cassius Edding, a current issues studies professor, a disheveled, bearded man appeared in the doorway. "Come in," he said, flashing crooked, rotten teeth, "and join the merry throng."

Yeah, right, thought Dr. Suess. *Join the merry throng.*

Dr. Edding had the reputation of scorning all convention: political, cultural, religious, moral, and even sanitary. He had no compunctions about waxing flatulent in front of his classes.

The students, consequently, clandestinely dubbed him 'Gaseous Cassius.'

He didn't know the man all that well. So why was he being so chummy?

He followed this Dr. Edding into a living-dining area furnished with a battered sofa, coffee table, and a couple of recliners. He saw walls covered with posters of English rock stars. Underfoot the floor was paved with grimy carpet samples.

In the far corners of the room he saw Dr. Sirotka, Dr. Ferguson, head of the science department, and Dr. King, a white-haired, elfin like man from the electronics department.

Hope you guys are sufficiently bankrolled, he was about to say.

However, before the words left his mouth, he looked around.

He saw no platters of cold cuts, cheeses, or sandwich bread on the pass-through counter top that opened to the kitchen. His gaze swept the table in the dining area.

He saw no cards, no drinks, and no carrier of poker chips.

What's happening, he thought.

"Hey, are we going to play or what?" he finally asked.

The room seemed to fade into a surreal twilight. His erstwhile poker pals seemed to take on a single dimension.

"We'll get to it eventually," he heard a voice saying. "We—thought we might like to have a little chat first."

Have a little chat? Since when did these guys talk like that?

"Let's sit down," someone suggested.

All right, he thought as he seated himself on one of the recliners, *let's do that.*

He waited. Now what?

"How's the family?" he heard another someone ask in a strained tone of voice.

"What?" He looked around with increased puzzlement.

"The family," the same someone repeated. "You know—Marie and the children?"

"They're okay," he answered tentatively. "They're out of town for the moment."

I wish she'd just quit that damned job, he thought. Her class room had the reputation of being an island of silence surrounded by an ocean of chaos. How long she could hold out was anybody's guess. Every day that she walks into that zoo, she is forced to commit educational prostitution.

"We—heard about Marie's leaving you."

He felt irritation mounting within.

"My problem," he said tersely.

A pause.

"Henry, old friend," said someone else. "We need to talk."

Old friend? This scene was really getting weird.

"About what?" he said with an edge to his voice.

"Your condition."

"My condition? *What condition?*"

Another pause.

"Your drinking," said another voice from somewhere else in the room.

Dr. Suess stood to his feet. "Look—guys," he said, trying to force a little laugh. "It's personal. Something I got to deal with, okay?"

The others in the room likewise stood to their feet.

"We heard that Marie suggested that you go for therapy at St. Dunstan's."

Dr. Suess folded his arms. A smirk crossed his face. "Well, well, word sure do get around don't it?" he said in a mock folksy tone.

They began closing in around him until they all stood within an arm's reach.

He assumed a more belligerent stance. "You guys invited me over here ostensibly to play poker," he said in subdued anger. "You two-faced bastards tricked me."

He brushed his would-be inquisitors aside and headed for the front door.

"Nice try—*friends*" was followed by a bellowed *"Good bye!"*

The entire building reverberated with the sound of the door slam.

Chapter 14

Father Michael looked about the dimly lit enclosure. The worn, paneled walls hemmed him in a phone booth sized cubicle. From out in the chapel sanctuary he heard a footfall. He recognized the sound instantly. He heard more footsteps as the confessor came nearer. The door to the adjacent cubicle creaked open.

How long had it been now? How many months had this one supplicant been coming?

Interesting that we continue with this tradition, he thought as he slit open the narrow window beside his shoulder, *a tradition largely abandoned even by the Church of Rome.*

Invasion of privacy.

He smiled as the politically correct cliché crossed his mind. With the church no longer attempting to help her communicants with issues of good and evil that plague the innermost recesses of the soul, what good is she? Have we not become just another social welfare agency? Why are we any different than, say, the Lion's Club, or the Department of Social Services? In our quest to become relevant, in our secularization have we not lost something? Where is the mystery, the awe, the otherness, or beyondness, if you will?

Have we not, in short, compromised away our uniqueness, our very legitimacy? Have we not, like Esau of Genesis, sold our birthright for a mess of pottage, a bowl of chili?

Someone in the adjacent confessional cleared his throat.

"Is that you Henry?"

"Yes," came the answer from the cubicle.

A pause.

"Father," the voice continued. "Bless me, for I have sinned."

"Hold it," said Father Michael, cutting him off. "Maybe we can save ourselves a bit of time. Is this about your drinking?"

"As a matter of fact it is, father."

"Then I don't want to hear any more about it."

Silence.

"Henry," continued the priest, "I've heard that confession so many times before, I don't want to hear it again until you are really serious in doing something about it. Is there any real reason you cannot join our brothers in their detoxification program today?"

* * *

Dr. Suess struggled with his luggage through the narrow doorway, put down the worn suitcase and surveyed the tiny room.

They call it a cell. How appropriate, he thought.

Immediately in front of him set a single army surplus bunk. The only concession for creature comfort consisted of a frame of single springs. It reminded him of his own service days, now a distant youthful memory. At the foot, two folded sheets, a pillow and pillow case, and two gray blankets of a coarse woolen weave set atop a folded mattress.

Big improvement, he thought, *over the wooden boards they slept on in the old days.*

At eye level on the wall opposite, a small window opened to the mountainous landscape beyond. Two metal frames, opening sideways, hung on hinges activated by a small crank. Plain, muslin curtains hung at the sides. The cinder block walls and ceiling had been painted a buff, neutral color. A plaster-of-Paris crucifix hung large and imposing above a small writing desk. He saw no closet. Against the wall opposite the bed, he saw a wardrobe and a small, battered dresser. The floor beneath his feet lay in a pattern of small pieces of well-scrubbed hardwood that remained neither finished nor carpeted.

He spotted a single outlet on a narrow strip of baseboard by the floor.

He congratulated himself on his foresight to bring a small desk lamp and chord. It would be the room's only illumination.

From a bell tower just outside, the tolling announced the arrival of the dinner hour.

Ten minutes later, he moved among robed men in a dining room furnished with heavy-timbered picnic tables. He followed the others to a line forming in front of a window wall. As he reached the window, he took a tray. The fare for the evening consisted of a beef barley soup, a chunk of black bread, a small salad, a half pint carton of milk, and a Jell-O desert. He picked up his tray and sought a seat. He worked his way to one of the tables but joined the others in remaining standing.

The robed men broke their silence with the chant in unison: "In the name of the Father, the Son, and the Holy Ghost." Each robed figure followed by crossing himself.

"For what we are about to receive, may the Lord make us truly thankful," intoned the voice of the Prior from other the end of the room.

"Amen," said the rest in response. They again crossed themselves and sat down.

Like the others he ate in continued silence. He noticed two robed figures walking among the tables with empty trays. Periodically they would stop beside a brother and whisper briefly. The seated brother would then perhaps break off a piece of his bread and hand it to the mendicant, or perhaps spoon off some his Jell-o and drop it into the supplicant's Jell-o dish.

From an earlier orientation, he understood that each supplicant was being punished for some minor rule infraction. They would not be fed for the next three meals. If they wanted to eat, they would have to wander between the tables and beg for their food.

When mealtime concluded, everyone remained seated. The Prior stood to his feet and read from a Prayer Book. The rest of the men then joined him in standing for prayer. Immediately afterward the Prior dismissed the brothers for a brief recreational period.

Henry spent the hour wandering the main hall on the ground floor. In a day room he saw men seated in front of a TV. He saw others on couches reading. In a far corner he saw two men at a small table playing chess. He left and wandered into another room used for more active recreation. As he entered, he heard the clacking sound of a bouncing ping-pong ball. He saw two others engrossed in a game of table hockey. He spotted an empty pool table. No sooner had he started toward it to try a few practice shots, he heard the muffled tolling of the chapel bell.

Straightway, he joined the others in wandering off to their respective rooms. Even without the wristwatch that he was now forbidden to wear, he knew the hour to be seven P.M.

Time for the Grand Silence.

Grand Silence meant sitting in solitude in his room for two hours. No leaving the room. No talking. No radios. No singing. No whistling. No splashing of water in the showers. No noise of any kind.

Only silence.

He fidgeted in his chair for an indeterminate period of time and eventually dozed off.

At nine P.M. the bell woke him with a start; this time for prayers and evening vespers in the chapel. Dismissal came at nine forty-five and lights out was at ten.

So Henry spent his first night at the Priory.

The rising bell would ring at five A.M.

* * *

After a few weeks of adjusting, he found the discipline strangely soothing. Once getting past the monotony of a predictable routine, he began to sense an inner serenity. As subsequent days merged into more weeks, he found a certain rhythm and found himself going with the flow, as it were, with an increasing effortlessness.

The Grand Silence, however, continued to present a challenge.

How could he—a man accustomed to the busy life of an academe and scientist; a man of outdoors field research unearthing profound secrets of our planet's distant past, a man of action, of sports, and of hunting—now acclimate himself to the discipline of sitting in his room doing nothing?

Of course doing nothing was not the purpose of the exercise. One was supposed to think about God. He found himself unable to sit for two hours and focus on anything, much less God. How does one focus on God anyway? Upon what or whom does one focus?

For the first time ever, he faced an unsettling realization.

Despite having been a lifelong churchman, he knew he couldn't just sit and think about God five minutes let alone two hours. Is God, as was the contention of the counterculture of the '70's, a fire hydrant? How could he, as a life-long practicing churchman, admit to himself to be so ignorant of the subject?

Sit in his room and contemplate God?

Where would he start? *At the beginning I suppose*, he reckoned. He reached into his writing desk and took out a Bible furnished by the Priory. The flyleaf indicated King James Version. The publisher: Oxford University Press under the auspices of the British and Foreign Bible Society. He turned to Genesis 1:1:

'In the beginning, God created the heavens and the earth—'

Ah yes, he thought, *the Bible.*

Is really the Word of God?

It's all about God, he concluded, *from Genesis to Revelation.*

It's the same story, namely the relationship between Yahweh and the human race.

It's one of the most comprehensive pieces of literature from antiquity, enduring for centuries despite efforts to suppress it; a perennial best seller.

World wide.

Ironically it is also the least read.

And by many, the least understood.

And is it also the most frequently misquoted? He asked himself. 'Money is the root of all evil?'—*No, no, no, no, no,* he thought, *the love of money is the root of all evil!*

* * *

"Do you think you are making progress, my son?"

"Progress?"

Dr. Suess looked questioningly at the Prior. He saw a tall, spare man with scholarly looking features looking back at him through rimless spectacles. He sat at a desk clean of all clutter. Behind him, on a plain beige wall, hung a plaster-of-Paris crucifix. A small bookcase in one corner consisted of the only other furnishings of the small office. The Prior also dressed himself plainly enough in the usual brown hassock bound at the waist with a white rope chord.

The Prior said nothing. He seemed to wait for Henry to go on.

"I suppose," said Dr. Suess, "that I have made progress. I haven't had a drink since coming here."

"That's a start."

A start? *Good Lord*, he thought. *Is he for real? How can anyone help but live clean and sober in a place like this? What happens when I get back home and run into some of my buddies on the faculty?* "I see a problem."

"And what is that, my son?"

"What's going to happen when I partake of the wine during Holy Eucharist?"

"Not to worry, my son."

Dr. Suess sat silent and waited for the Prior to go on. *What kind of mind games is this? Not to worry? I see plenty to worry for cryin' out loud.*

"You see," said the Prior, "does it make sense to you that that which is given for forgiveness and healing also contribute to one's downfall?"

Dr. Suess heaved a sigh. "No, I guess not."

"And besides," continued the Prior, "the stuff we actually use is nothing more than watered down Mogen David. No alcoholic has ever suffered relapse over it yet."

Dr. Suess stirred restlessly in his chair. "I see another problem."

"Which is?"

"It's easy to stay sober in a place like this. You know—in a controlled environment? What's going to happen when I leave?"

"God performs miracles, my son."

Omigod, he thought. *Don't pull this miracle jazz with me. Can't you give me any better help than mumbo-jumbo?*

He studied the gray stone walls that surrounded him. He eyed the bare unvarnished floor beneath him. From outside, the slanted sun rays beamed in through the narrow window. The rays played on a picture of a pallid looking saint that hung from a far wall.

He took it to be St. Dunstan.

"As a scientist, I have been trained not to look for miracles."

"What does the churchman have to say to the scientist about that?"

"Good point." Dr. Suess shrugged. *He's got me where he wants me*, he thought. The old struggle: science vs. religion raged in his mind anew. "The fact remains, how am I to recognize a miracle when I see it?"

The Prior sat back in his chair and folded his hands. "When the time comes," he said, "you will recognize it readily enough."

Dr. Suess got up and left the Prior's small office in confusion and disgust. *A miracle? Good Lord, is that all he has to offer? What am I doing here anyway?*

Nevertheless, as he continued down the hall, he reflected on the Prior's last words: *When the time comes,* he recalled, shaking his head, *you will recognize it readily enough.*

* * *

It happened on a Sunday.

As Henry was leaving chapel, he waited at the end of his pew to let front row worshippers file past. He idly surveyed the half dozen men dressed in civilian attire. He knew them to be from hospice. As the last of the group slipped by, he recognized him

The spare, bony figure no way resembled the robust man Henry had known from former days. Waxy skin stretched over cheekbones etched in sharp relief. Listless eyes stared dully ahead. Once luxuriant locks now hung in sparse, wispy strands, exposing, in an unnatural pattern, patches of baldness.

He nevertheless knew the fellow worshipper to be Marie's ex-husband.

* * *

The image of the stricken ex-husband haunted Dr. Suess. What a contrast from the leonine party animal he had known from the old days.

He recalled the nattily dressed dandy with cocktail in hand. His face would be flushed with the excitement of the feverishly intellectual conversation of party goers. His eyes glistened with animation and he flashed a toothy smile at the revelry that swirled about him.

The man, darling of the smart set, seemed never at a loss for words. Granted, he was not Dr. Suess' kind of man's man. His foppish humor and effete giggle never found favor with the rugged outdoorsman. Yet Henry had to acknowledge that the man did in fact have his own circle of admirers. Marie's ex never failed to find his personal space surrounded by fawning sycophants.

As the days continued, Henry continued adapting to the Priory's narrowly restrictive routine. He found a sort of inner peace and a sense of disconnectedness to his old life on the outside. The Henry Seuss of old seemed like someone else. The one enigma that remained continued to be the two hours of Grand Silence. What sadistic, pharisaic mind thought up such an institution in the first place? What unctuous killjoy designed such an impossible discipline anyway?

Spend two hours in silence thinking about God. This was surely the stuff of theology.

Theology.

Interesting word. It's definition: science of God. Does it mean we put God under a microscope and dissect him to see what makes him tick? Do we poke him with a probe to see if he wiggles?

In his mind, he conjured up imagery of tenured, tweedy theologians sheltered behind their ivied, cloistered walls puffing complacently on their curved meerschaums as they pondered some metaphysical vagary.

Jesus had said to suffer the little children to come to him and forbid them not, for of such was the kingdom of heaven, not theologians.

When Jesus chose his disciples, he chose real men working at real jobs such as fishing. He even chose a despised IRS man. He did not choose intellectual dilettantes.

In his quest to more productively ponder God, he had tried reading such material as his breviary, prayer book, and even the scriptures themselves. He found other devotional literature to be maudlin pap. The scriptures, however, presented a far different story.

The grandeur of the King James language impressed him; some of the ideas lofty and inspiring. However, he found other parts of holy writ perplexing. The writings revealed a powerful, all-knowing, covenant-making God. Yet sacred pages told of a jealous God, a vengeful God. Despite a loving, forgiving God whose mercies are from everlasting to everlasting, he found a God who commanded 'thou shalt not kill,' yet ordered his covenant people to commit quintuple genocide.

He read of a God who put a mark of dishonor on Cain for murdering his brother, Abel. Yet the mark was intended for Cain's protection; a mark as a warning to any who would kill Cain that God repay them seven-fold if they did so. He found a God with whom Noah found favor. (Noah found favor in the eyes of the LORD.) Favor for what; not joining the rest of the human race in their violence? He eventually spared Noah and his family but wiped the entire ancient human race because of its violent and iniquitous behavior.

Myth some would say? Perhaps, but how then do we explain the origin of such peoples we call Semitic or Hamitic? He realized that that was as valid a proof as was the contention that the city of Rome was founded by twin orphan boys suckled by a she-wolf. Both pretty far-fetched, he concluded, yet he thought one could not totally disregard such events of antiquity either.

God was also a God who directed his faithful patriarch, Abraham, to offer up his son, Isaac, as a human sacrifice, only to tell him at the last moment not to do go through with it; that it was only a test of his obedience. Furthermore, why was there no such last minute intervention when God seemed to have stood by as his own son was crucified?

'*It pleased the Lord to put him to grief;*' so said the prophet Isaiah in the Song of the Suffering Servant discourse. What kind of father would be pleased at the prospect of seeing his son nailed to a cross?

* * *

He shuffled his way across the dining room in search of an empty spot at one of the wooden tables. He carefully tried to hold his breakfast tray level as he slid into an empty space next to a slightly built ascetic known as Brother Benedict.

"How they goin'?" he whispered despite the no-talking rule.

"I am well." The narrow features still looked straight ahead. He said nothing further.

The pause quickly became awkward. *I'm surprised the guy hasn't shaved his crown like the old days*, thought Dr. Suess. He spoke surreptitiously from the corner of his mouth. "You—slept well I hope?"

The other nodded. "Very well, thank you."

Again, nothing further.

Dr. Suess fidgeted on his wooden seat. "Uh—do you mind if I ask a question?"

Brother Benedict glanced at him curiously. "What kind of question?"

Dr. Suess took a deep breath. "Well," he sighed, "about the Grand Silence."

"What about it?"

Brother Benedict said nothing more.

Again Dr. Suess fidgeted. He looked around uncomfortably. "How do I put this?" he said, again in a whisper. "I mean, what do you guys think about? How exactly does one go about thinking about God? Maybe you could share some of your ideas with me."

Brother Benedict cast him another quick sidelong glance and then reverted to looking straight ahead. "Meditations during the Grand Silence are intensely personal," he said, pursing his lips. "It's something we don't discuss."...

* * *

...He recalled the Te Deum: 'When Thou tookest upon Thee to deliver man, Thou didst humble Thyself to be born of a virgin. When Thou hadst overcome the sharpness of death, Thou didst open the kingdom of heaven to all believers—'...

...And what of our response? At his own bidding, we now eat Jesus' flesh and drink his blood. Dr. Suess recalled the taunts of unbelieving colleagues when they accused him of cannibalism. He remembered his resentment.

But were they right? To even entertain that possibility filled him with such revulsion that he concluded that no, they were wrong. They betrayed their gross misunderstanding of the Great Mystery. He himself had challenged his own parish priest with this question: After all, he had said, I could chemically analyze the bread both before and after it had been blessed and it would still remain bread. I could do the same thing with the wine.

"Quite true," countered his parish priest. "But have you not read Dr. Luther's analogy of the poker. Before going into the forge it is cold, black iron. After it has been held in the forge it comes out still iron. Yet it is changed. It is now red and hot. So it is that the bread remains bread and the wine remains wine, but now it as been blessed and Our Lord is now present in these elements in a new and unique way. As you have said, it's a Great Mystery."

Was he a believer in something about which his skeptical colleagues were clueless? An inner consciousness concluded that yes, he was, in fact, a believer.

For a long time he had resolved never to debate the existence of God with an atheist unless they were both crew members aboard a sinking submarine.

In which case such a debate would be largely irrelevant.

This, the result of getting into a discussion in the teacher's lounge with a Dr. Tudor McManus…

…The small man was an English Lit professor recently from the University of Missouri. Dr. Suess hated the way he wore his iron gray hair neatly slicked back. He wore wire framed glasses and had always dressed himself immaculately in a gray pin-striped suit with crimson tie and boutonnière.

Single, he lived alone. Dr. Suess hated the way he rented a week's supply of dress shirts from a laundry labeled 'bachelor bundles.'

How pretentious can we get, thought Dr. Suess?

In his classes, he had not been shy in expressing his contempt for the spiritual. When, after a hearing of a withering interrogation wherein he sent a young girl student out of the class in tears, Dr. Suess wanted to punch him in the mouth.

"I know something God cain't do," the man laughed, flashing a gold tooth.

Dr. Suess knotted up his fist. *Nervy bastard!* "And what is that?"

Dr. McManus continued his toothy grin. Eyes behind the wire bound spectacles squinted into long, narrow slits.

"He cain't make a yardstick with only one end on it."

I would like to see him make a yardstick with one end, thought Dr. Suess, *and stick the other end someplace real dark.* "Really?" he said, "I know something that he can do."

"Oh?"

Dr. Suess gave him a patronizing smile. "He can create a jackass."

…But how strong a believer? He had to admit to himself, however, not a very strong one.

He would have to work on that.

Another colleague had once confided that he avoided church attendance because he was angry with his parents. During his childhood, they had dragged him off to church every Sunday.

So what are you going to do when you die, he had replied, get mad at God when he drags you kicking and screaming off to heaven?

He pondered the account of Adam and Eve and the Serpent. Was the issue really the tree? What was so wrong in merely eating the fruit? Was it just about eating the fruit of a single tree, or was a particular variety of fruit tree? Or was that one tree especially charmed supernaturally to function as a bridge or conduit to an alternate universe or source of forbidden knowledge (similar to Pandora's Box of secrets of Greek mythology?) Would the eating of this fruit lead to a consciousness raising experience similar the ingestion of LSD of modern times? Would it be akin to Aladdin's letting the Genie out of the bottle and once out can never be put back in again?

In the meantime, all that Bible stuff continued to perplex him. Why did they call it the Good Book? Was it not replete with violence, intrigue, deceit, and lust? Were one to argue that holy writ is merely a recording of people's behavior, not necessarily an endorsement of it, how then does one reconcile the passage in First Samuel where the Almighty himself sends the prophet Samuel on a mission during the reign of King Saul to anoint a new king? When Samuel expresses fear for his life should Saul learn of this, the Almighty puts the prophet up to a ruse. He tells him to bring a heifer ostensibly for the purpose of holding a sacrificial feast as a cover up for his real purpose.

Did not Rahab the harlot lie to protect the two Israeli spies from the Jericho police and was thus rewarded for her deceit by being the survivor of the holocaust that destroyed the city?

Did not Stephan, the first Christian martyr, attribute Moses' murder of the Egyptian taskmaster as he was beating a Hebrew slave, an act of valor that earned him a place in the Hebrew hall of fame?

Why also do people call it the holy land? Is not the whole history of the near east an endless litany of wars, bloodshed, and violence? Is it not even today an armed camp?

Why do people call God good and then go blissfully about their lives as though he barely mattered? Why do they insist that God is too good to send anyone to hell and then invoke his wrath on, say, the driver in front of them in rush hour traffic?

Is being good necessarily the same as being nice? Is declaring God good more than just a mawkish, Pollyanna sentiment? Must true divine goodness also have a holy severity as the reverse to the coin?

He spotted a spider crawling up his window. Was that spider meditating on him? If that spider was at all aware of his existence, how could it actually conceptualize what it means to be human?

In all our meditations, discussions, and preachments are we not even further away from properly comprehending God?

* * *

Damn this Grand Silence business anyway, he thought. Where were the group meetings, the group therapy, he thought. Where was professional counseling with a psychiatrist, a psychologist, or even a social worker?

Or anybody but this priest turned Prior?

I've just about had it with Father Michael and his little fiefdom. Why don't I just blow this sanctified pop stand?

Another realization brought him up short.

Leaving now would beg a multitude of questions. Where would he go? After all he had been coming here to worship for years. They knew him here. They knew him well. Going somewhere else would mean starting a whole new treatment, all over again with total strangers.

Furthermore it could mean approaching his problem from a whole new perspective. It would very likely be secular instead of spiritual. Instead of the therapy being all about God, God would be completely left out of it. As far as he was concerned, they were all a bunch of head shrinkers; little better than witch doctors.

Besides Marie's condition for reconciliation stipulated that therapy take place at St. Dunstan's.

Period.

He found himself sitting at his desk a week later still struggling over a spiritual exercise that wasn't getting any easier. He had just beaten another brother handily in a poker game down in the day room just before the bell had summoned them up to their respective cells. They had to use checkers as chips and of course, no money was involved. But a win was still a win and he had been on a roll.

Now he had to go directly from a poker game to two hours of thinking about God.

How does one switch from thinking about poker to thinking about God on a dime, so to speak? *What a damned ridiculous exercise in futility anyway.*

A thought occurred to him. Is not life like a poker game? Are we not playing poker with our Maker? If so, who holds the high hand? If we try to keep a poker face, non-committal, are we fooling the other party? To hold our cards close to the vest as it were with a mortal player is one thing, but is trying to shield our cards from one who knows all quite another? Can we change the hand we've been dealt with? Can we throw in part of our hand for a better draw? Or, unlike terrestrial poker, is the hand we've been dealt with the final draw?

Is there a devil?

If so, is he also at this cosmic poker table?

And if so, who is our partner?

Who is our opponent?

What are the stakes?

Is this the ultimate strip poker tournament with our immortal souls out on there in the pot?

In the final showdown, who wins?

He sighed.

This is supposed to help me get sober?

"Why don't I just leave?" he finally asked himself out loud.

As soon as he said it again he realized: *where would I go? To what, to where, and to whom?*

Was not his being here in the first place something he had brought on himself? Marie had stated her position clearly enough. Get sober, get help. Get therapy, or forget about seeing her again. He felt trapped. He felt his life on dead center and going nowhere.

No choice but to tough it out here at the monastery.

If not here, where?

A thought entered his mind. If what he drank caused his problem, would his redemption lie in the same direction…?

* * *

… "So that's about the sum and substance of it."

The dean continued to sit up close at his giant mahogany desk, elbows pressed on the broad desk blotter. He continued to hold his folded hands in front of him. He seemed content to just sit and study the young brunette seated across from him.

Delicate looking gray eyes returned the dean's gaze as Dr. Judith Kolnick adjusted her horn rimmed glasses. Her porcelain features remained neutral. She continued leaning forward with her folded hands lying in her lap. She had hoped that her navy blue slack suit sufficed as correct attire.

"It all sounds interesting," she sighed. "I want to thank you."

"You are interested in the position, then?"

She struggled to maintain composure. "Could we see the facilities?" The dean eyed the legal sized envelope that contained a transcript, a sheaf of credentials, and an application for teaching position at Stillwell College. He studied the wallet-sized photograph in the upper left corner. He had a definite idea as to the type of candidate he was looking for.

Was this slip of a young woman with the delicate facial lines the one?

Please, he thought. *No more trouble makers. No more agitators. Send me someone nice and pliable.*

"Of course." He searched the top of the papers for a proper name. "Uh—Dr. Kolnick. I can take you right down there."

They walked across the quad from Old Main to the science building. A slight breeze stirred the stillness of the late August morning. The air seemed to presage the wane of summer in the Rockies: cool, but not altogether unpleasant. Ahead lay an ancient building of yellow brick. As if to add a jarring note to the Victorian architecture, a contemporary wing arose behind it with clean, plain lines of glass and steel. The geology department remained in the old part.

Before starting up the front steps, the dean paused. "We're rather informal around here," he said. "Small. Sort of like a family. May I call you Judy?"

"I would prefer Judith."

The dean turned his head away. His shoulders sagged slightly.

Without replying, he gestured toward the building. They mounted the worn steps and entered a marbled corridor that resonated with every footfall. Upon reaching the second floor, he led her into the geology lecture hall. Rolled charts and movie screens hung from a wall behind a low platform bearing a battered desk. Tablet-arm chairs stretching out in tiered rows formed a kind of amphitheater.

The dean moved to a door off to the side of the platform. "I'll show you the lab," he said, unlocking the door.

He ushered her through the lab. She tried pretending to not notice his locking the door behind her as she surveyed the rows of marble topped worktables. Each table bore a small sink and Bunsen burner outlet. The wall opposite the windows glistened with glass covered shelves.

She felt a twinge of discomfort with the dean's closeness when he pointed out the rock and mineral displays behind the window glass. They spent the next fifteen minutes studying geological specimens in the various displays.

Eventually she realized that the dean really wasn't all that interested in geological specimens.

She kept trying to edge away from him

From the corner of her eye she saw him gesture grandly "We have one of the most extensive geological collections in the west."

She knew from Dr. Sirotka that Dr. Suess had collected most of the specimens.

The dean had failed to mention that.

"I think I get the picture," she said, trying to step around him.

"Good," he said, still not moving. "I'll show you the office. It's upstairs."

He finally started for the exit and led her to a third floor complex of ancient looking offices that lay tight against a gabled roof. He unlocked a door bearing a bronze plate that said simply: 'Geology.'

"We had Dr. Suess' name there until just last week," he said, pushing the door open. "That's where your name will be."

She recalled Dr. Sirotka telling her that, actually, the dean had Dr. Suess' name removed the day of the retirement party.

She stepped into the office with the dean immediately behind her.

She could see little in the cramped office but a wooden desk and a swivel chair. The slanted roof broke to a dormer that provided a floor-to-ceiling window showing a tiled roof just beyond it. Against the wall opposite the desk stood a bank of wooden filing cabinets and a small, empty bookshelf.

"I'll want to rearrange the desk so that I will be facing toward the door," she said without turning to the dean.

She could feel his breathing as he spoke. "I'll have the maintenance department change that today."

She glanced at her watch. "I have a luncheon appointment."

She tried to step around him to get to the front door. She stood beside it. Again, she tried to pretend not to notice as he unlocked it.

"I can have a contract drawn up and ready for signing at one," he said as they again entered the corridor. "Would that be all right?"

"Yes," she said as she stepped past him. "That will be fine."

Chapter 15

"So the dean finally stopped contemplating his navel long enough to hold an interview," said Dr. Sirotka, "How did it go?"

Dr. Judith Kolnick shrugged. At first she felt taken aback by Dr. Sirotka's mildly obscene remark. Why had his attitude and his remarks served only to reinforce her premonition that in coming on this campus she was stepping into a den of vipers, as it were?

"Pretty much the way you said it would," she said finally.

A pause

"I hate to admit it," she sighed, "but when I'm in his presence, I feel intimidated."

Dr. Sirotka sat back in his booth. "He's that way with everybody," he said. "Tell you what. Next time you're in his office and you feel intimidated, try this: look him straight in the eye and in your mind, fantasize him sitting on the john."

The hustle and bustle of the noon rush hour at the Old Heidelberg restaurant strangely enough gave their corner booth an illusion of privacy.

After another brief silence Dr. Kolnick again spoke. "I noticed the nameplate on his office door," she said. "It seems a bit odd."

"What's odd about it?"

"The name: 'Jaked Negley Jone?' It sounds like something's missing."

Dr. Sirotka gave a wry smile. "Something's missing all right."

The pause in the conversation lengthened.

The bespectacled young brunette that sat opposite Dr. Sirotka fixed serious looking gray eyes at him. "Mike," she said finally, "I don't have to tell you. I need this job."

Dr. Sirotka carefully crafted his reply. He continued studying her intense mien. "I'm not going to kid you, Judy," he said. "Working for this guy is like picking your way through a mine field. However, you have one thing going for you: you're a woman."

He held up his hand as she was about to give him a dirty look.

"No, I mean it," he insisted. "I'm not trying to be cute here."

He paused and surveyed the dining room's throbbing interior.

"Just take what I say at face value," he continued. "Henry got him with a couple of zingers. First, when the dean insisted he write an apology letter to the Student Government, he told him to shove it; he had just applied for retirement. Then he does a 'no show' at his own retirement party. A final touch came at commencement time. Just before the dean came out on the platform, some student had secretly stuck a streamer of toilet tissue to the heel of his shoe with a wad of gum. When the dean took center stage to give out the diplomas, that streamer waved out behind him like a banner. The tittering in the student audience created some quite unsettling moments, but the dean never caught on until later.

"The dean is not a particularly forgiving man. In fact, he's out for blood. If another man were to try what Henry got away with, he would be toast. However, with you he's going to have to come up with a different strategy and that could take a little time."

Dr. Kolnick took a sip of her tea. "But I hate having to play these kind of games," she said. "I just want to teach; just like I was hired to do."

"You're taking the position, then?"

She shrugged. "I suppose so."

He paused.

"Oh, well," he sighed, "at least you'll know that going in. That helps, believe me."

Dr. Sirotka eyed the now thinning crowd. Noon rush dissipates quickly on weekdays, he observed, especially early in the week. The momentum would pick up as one got closer to the weekend. He glanced at his watch.

"It's quarter to one," he said. "We'd best get back."

THE TITANS

For a moment she didn't move. "I guess," she said with a note of resignation, "one could look at it this way: he isn't going to be around forever."

Dr. Sirotka absent-mindedly surveyed the dining room crowd.

"Interesting you should say that," he said with a slight chuckle. "I think he may already be on his way out. For years the students have called him 'naked Jaked' behind his back. Lately they've taken to calling him that to his face."

She stood up. "I'll still be here long after he has gone."

* * *

"So how was your first week?"

Dr. Kolnick smiled thoughtfully. "As well as can be expected, I suppose."

Dr. Sirotka again sat opposite her in their booth at the Old Heidelberg. "Any interaction with the head poo-bah?"

"Haven't seen him all that much actually," she said as she studied the menu. "I suppose both of us are plenty busy just getting organized."

"How are your classes?"

"Okay, I guess," she said with a shrug. "So far I feel I'm doing well just keeping a chapter ahead of them."

A stoutly apportioned waitress appeared beside their booth. Dr. Sirotka looked at his young colleague from over the top of his menu.

"I recommend their braunschweiger with black bread with a side of German potato salad."

He studied Dr. Kolnick further. "Make it two," he said to the waitress. After she left, he continued with the conversation.

"Have you had a chance to really go through the filing cabinets?"...

* * *

...God.

Is he more than just a three-letter word?

How did the American Indians come by their concept of Manitou, the

Great Spirit? Why is it that the American Indians, the most intensely religious people ever to inhabit the hemisphere, have no word in any of their 400 languages for religion?

Why does the Spanish-speaking world of the Western Hemisphere—a scene of wars, bloodshed, revolution, poverty, political unrest and corruption—also be replete with such geographical place names as Trinidad, El Salvador, and the names of saints? Why does the statue of Christ stand atop Sugar Loaf Mountain overlooking Rio de Janeiro, Brazil: a veritable Gomorrah as sensuous and as any city on this planet?

After long moments of struggle during the Grand Silence, random thoughts about God began to have free flow. Dr. Suess studied the orange twilight afterglow just outside his window. The last remaining leaves of autumn hung miserably on otherwise naked tree branches in the sloping yard.

Did God originally create a universe luxuriant with biological life impervious to death as Genesis seemed to indicate? If there were no death before the fall, why was it necessary for Adam and Eve to eat? If they were free to eat from any tree in the Garden, did that not also mean the death of the fruit? How was it ever possible for any biological form to exist without the death of another, whether apple, plankton, or antelope? Why does the very soil contain herbaceous existence that draws its nutrients from other forms of dead and decaying plant life? From whence come ancient corals in the sea and limestone deposits in, say, the Carlsbad Caverns of New Mexico; from whence come the great deposits of coal and petroleum?

Was God's warning of death to the erring couple something more profound than mere physical demise?

'Life is real; life is earnest,' so says Longfellow's *Psalm of Life*, 'and the grave is not its goal. "Dust thou art and dust returneth" was not spoken to the soul.'

Was Longfellow on to something? *If I came from dust*, he thought, *will I not eventually return to dust?* Is it literally true as some astronomers and astrophysicists claim we are made of the stuff of stars? Were the atoms, electrons, and protons that now make up my body an infinitesimal part of gaseous clouds billowing out into the ethereal void untold eons in the past? Will these same atoms millennia in the future again constitute stardust expanding across to distant galaxies? *Will this be at a time when not only I as an individual, but my entire planet, have long since disintegrated into formless inter-stellar waste? Will I still be a self-conscious me? If spirit is a form of energy, whether electrical, chemical or a hitherto unknown form and if energy is indestructible, will I not as a self-conscious, thought inducing entity still exist?*

Is time merely measured eternity or does eternity differ from time not in only degree, but also in essence? Is time measured by change, transfer of energy, and molecular movement? What happens in eternity? Does eternity usher in a complete equilibrium of all energy and matter? When all molecular movement stops does the entire universe assume the theoretical ultimate cold of absolute zero? Is eternity a state wherein all movement stops and does it exist in a 'universe' that is completely static? Is this where God dwells? Is he outside and beyond any universe of movement and change?

Is this the Presence to which my spirit will return when I die? Will I be any different at that moment? Will I think and feel any different? Will I think or feel anything at all? Of course if spirit is energy, and since energy it is indestructible, won't I exist somewhere in some sort of state out there in that vast metaphysical ocean beyond all that is time and sense? Is that a future to look forward to or a future to dread? Or will it be neutral? Will the seat of my thoughts, emotions, volition, and memory be as intact as it is now?

Who was right? Plato or Aristotle? Does ultimate reality lie within the world of ideas or of matter? Will we ultimately know? If we do, what then?

Does the path to sainthood lie in giving a goody-two-shoes lip service to God or is it a life of unrelenting wrestling with God over life's thorniest issues? Do the plaster of Paris statues in the church narthex, the one-dimensional figures on stained glass windows, or the cloyingly sentimental figures on greeting cards portray accurately who saints really are? Or are they merely the figment of some unregenerate artist's imagination?

An artist who has as much a concept of what a saint really is as that of an ant crawling on my windowsill has a concept as to what I really am?

Dr. Suess got up out of his chair and began pacing his room.

From deep within the cloistered bowels of the compound he heard the tolling of a bell.

Time for evening vespers…

* * *

… "Thanks for meeting me here on such short notice."

Dr. Kolnick again settled in a corner booth at the Old Heidelberg. Dr. Sirotka sat opposite her, scanning a luncheon menu. "On the phone you said you had something to show me," he said.

"I do," she replied, "but before I get to that, I have another concern."

He waited for her to continue.

"For some time," she said finally, "I've been suspecting the dean of coming on to me."

She maintained that it was not just her imagination or paranoia. Whenever she had any business to conduct with him, he persistently invaded her personal space, as it were; that off-limits area surrounding one's person that sub-consciously is set up as a barrier to all but the most intimate of relationships. In short, he insisted on moving too close to her.

"Has he ever touched you?"

"Are you kidding?" she answered with a sardonic smile. "That guy is part octopus."

The touching, however, did not involve delicate parts of the anatomy—yet.

"He's been awfully subtle," she went on. "Persistent but subtle."

"Subtlety is his middle name," commented Dr. Sirotka. "Have you voiced any objections to his attention?"

Dr. Kolnick shrugged. "So far, I have tried to be diplomatic."

Dr. Sirtotka flipped a page on his menu. He shot her a quick glance. "Next time drop the diplomacy."

Easy for you to say, she thought. You're on tenure. Me, I'm on probation. He could fire me on the flimsiest pretext. And would I have enough money to take him to court? Could even the Stillwell Women's Caucus afford to take on not only him, but the whole administration, and

THE TITANS

Board of Regents? All this tough talk is easy, but when it comes time to putting it on the line. Well, that's another story.

As if to change the subject, Dr. Kolnick pulled her brief case up from her seat and laid it on the corner of the table. "You might be interested in this," she said. "Apparently this is what the dean was looking for."

She went on to relate anecdotal incidents of coming into her class room, lab area and even her office and finding evidence of things rearranged from the way she had originally left them. She had also encountered this kind of evidence while going through her filing cabinets, storage cabinets, and even her desk drawers.

"Tell you what," said Dr. Sirotka. "Dr. Koenig of the Electronics Engineering department and I are rather close. Maybe we can set up a surveillance system in your area. Now let's see what you have."

Dr. Kolnick reached into her brief case and with sweaty hands pulled out a file folder stuffed with computer printout.

"When I first looked this stuff over," she said, "I couldn't believe what I was getting into. No wonder he's having such a hairy."

She opened the page and Dr. Sirotka scanned the following:

'A vision.
So say the multitudes:
Give us a vision.
But how can I give
Unless I be given?

'How can I see through time
When years, millenia, and eons
Pass with such blurred swiftness
They make even the speed of light
Seem all but glacial?

'Light as energy
Speedier than anything
In all creation
Save time itself.

Behold.
The dizzying, spinning vision
Slows.
A landscape takes shape
As in a cauldron,
A cooking pot that
That begins to coagulate
Or thicken. Jell-like
With a firmness.

The scenery waxes discernable.
It appears a landscape
Like no other
Since life on this bejeweled ball
First began.

Dr. Sirotka eyed the document. He fought to conceal a feeling of excitement. "Where's the rest of it?" he said, reaching across the table for another page. Dr. Kolnick shook her head. "It just ends here," she said with a puzzled look.

Dr. Sirotka sat back in his seat. "Damn," he said softly.

* * *

Dr. Kolnick entered the door of Dr. Sirotka's third floor office. It had the same cramped features with its floor level window looking out of a dormer and onto the roof. He sat waiting for her behind his desk as she settled in the battered wooden chair opposite. From a side drawer he produced a video.

"I think you'll find this interesting," he said as he rose and headed for a video-TV monitor against an opposite wall. After inserting the cassette and pushing the 'on' button, he resumed his place behind the desk. The familiar furnishings of Dr. Kolnick's office jumped to the screen. As they watched, they saw the door open and the trouser legs of a tall male came into view. Presently they saw the figure of the dean rummaging through her office. Dr. Sirotka again got up out of his chair. This time he shut off the video and started the rewind. After again returning to his desk

He leaned toward Dr. Kolnick.

"What do you think?"

Maybe word will finally get to 'Babs,' he thought. *This could be fun.*

She gestured to a phone that lay on a far corner of his desk. "Could I use your phone a moment?"

She dialed and waited. "Is this Schelwe, Waite, and Seigh?" she said finally. "Oh, Gina. Yes. This is Dr. Kolnick. I'd like to speak with my attorney."

Chapter 16

"Hi."

He gestured tentatively toward the figure in the recliner. The figure appeared wan to the point of near transparency. Hollow eyes looked up at the source of the greeting and blinked in the unaccustomed glare as he tried to focus on the image of Dr. Suess in the doorway. A pale blue denim shirt hung loosely about his skeletal frame. The pant legs of his faded jeans flapped as he crossed legs thin as broomsticks. Long, slender feet were shod in worn sandals. Claw-like hands lay discolored in his lap in a folded position.

"You're looking for something?" He spoke with difficulty. The cadaverous face continued a hard stare at Dr. Suess.

"May I come in?"

The wraith like figure gave a disgusted sigh and gestured toward the room's interior.

Dr. Suess surveyed the narrow chamber. Immediately to the front of him stood a hospital bed high and imposing and filling the center of the room. Beneath the mattress and innerspring was attached a bewildering array of cranks, levers and other adjustment machinery. Heavy chromium bars along the sides were designed to keep the patient from falling out.

Like a baby crib, thought Dr. Suess.

Behind the headboard hung the ever present Plaster-of-Paris crucifix. The room appeared similarly furnished as was that of Dr. Suess with a nightstand, small dresser, and wardrobe. Near the window set the writing desk and chair.

The one exception: it had its own bathroom.

Dr. Suess stepped tentatively toward the writing desk and pulled out the chair. He knew the man's reputation of possessing a tongue that cut like razor wire. Should he—no matter how inadvertently—curry this person's disfavor, he could in a trice be slashed and skewered by the man's verbal arsenal.

How ironic, he thought. He, who faced down wounded big game with only a couple of rounds in his rifle, he who felled taproom adversaries with a solid right hook to the jaw, he who made a career of riding herd over classes of young people, now sat cowed and intimidated before this wasted invalid.

"I take it you want something." The figure in the chair still made no move as Dr. Suess sat down.

He cleared his throat. He wondered if he had already blown it by taking the liberty of seating himself.

"I was just wondering if there was something *you* wanted," he said with deference.

"Oh, really?" The voice had a hollow hoarseness. "Why?"

Dr. Suess sighed. His suspicion that this wasn't going to be easy increased by the minute. The silence quickly became uncomfortable.

Almost as uncomfortable as the Grand Silence.

He recalled the Sunday evening after he first spotted Marie's ex-husband at chapel…

…Two hours of thinking about God. Never gets easier, he reflected.

He recalled the many times he had argued vehemently with atheist colleagues back on campus regarding the existence of God. Now, during the daily two-hour exercise given to meditating about God, he regularly found himself up against a mental brick wall.

The debate, he concluded, makes as much sense as two dog fleas debating the existence of me They no doubt gratefully acknowledge the existence of the dog. That's their meal ticket. But to debate the existence of me? Totally irrelevant to the fleas. Or so they think, if they possess any thought process at all. Yet who owns the dog? In this instance, the flea's perception is that I am irrelevant.

But is perception reality?

I could stand on a Kansas Prairie, he thought. *If I saw a tornado on the horizon with the twister appearing not to move, is the funnel in fact, standing still, or is it headed straight toward me?*

Recollection of the previous day's interview in the priory office broke that chain of thought.

During a therapy session, the Prior suggested that Dr. Suess do some volunteer work about the compound.

What did the good father suggest, Dr. Suess wanted to know.

We need helpers to work in the hospice, the Prior had replied.

Dr. Suess immediately went into deep introspection.

He recalled how long Marie had harbored deep suspicions that something in her first marriage was terribly wrong…

…First of all, there was a Gilbert Wilkins, a classmate at dental school. He was, as it had turned out, the same Gilbert Wilkins that Dr. Suess' own son years before had rescued from high school bullies.

Her first husband and Dr. Wilkins set up a joint practice after graduation. At first she harbored no real suspicion.

However, after she had married Dr. Suess, she showed him the letter she had intercepted between her first husband and his partner:

'Dear Puss:

'I think that a good definition for 'art' is as follows: "Art is the emotional, aesthetic, and tangentially intellectual expression of its creator's world and life view through any one of several media e.g. sound, print, flat surface, or a multi-dimensional solid."

'Poetry differs from prose in that it is in some way metrical and its subjective nature emphasizes the emotional rather than the objective and logical. Prose, on the other hand is just the reverse. Prose conversely is non-metrical, objective and deals primarily with facts and logic.

'This is not to say that the two literary forms cannot overlap, nor does it say that either literary form cannot nevertheless still have an emotional impact.

'Anyway, my dear fellow, I hope that this should give you food for thought.

'Sincerely,

'Hosky'

For some moments Dr. Suess stared at the letter.
"Good Lord," he said finally. "What the hell is so incriminating about that? It's just an artsy-fartsy discourse. What's so salacious about that?"
Marie's mouth took disgusted downturn.
"Just don't get it, do you?" she snorted.
She searched his face. It still registered blank.
"These two shared nicknames between the two of them," she said finally. "'Hosky' was my husband and 'Puss' was this Gilbert Wilkins person. If you've ever read a biography of Oscar Wilde, you would have known that he and a Lord Alfred Douglas carried on the most notorious liaison of Victorian England. 'Hosky' was the nickname of Oscar Wilde and 'Puss' was the nickname of Lord Alfred Douglas."...

He had wrestled long with his feelings on homosexuality. He had nursed a lifelong hatred and disgust of queers, as he had called them. Their predilections and practices were unnatural, simple as that. After all, never could their particular intimacies ever result in biological reproduction. Back in ancient times were not a fruitful womb and many children necessary for survival? Did not the strength of every tribe, clan and city state lie in numbers? Was it not logical then, to proscribe erotic behavior that would contribute nothing to the propagation of the race? Also, did these very acts themselves necessitate one of the partners to role play a member of the opposite sex? In other words—pretend to be something that they were not?
Was not the confrontation in Genesis chapter 19 between Lot and the men of Sodom and their insistence on the right have mass sex with his two

angelic guests the first gay rights demonstration in recorded human history?

And yet? *And yet?*—did not the prophet Ezekiel of holy writ catalogue the real reasons for Sodom's downfall?

'Behold, this was the iniquity of thy sister, Sodom:
Pride, fullness of bread, and
Abundance of idleness were in her
And in her daughters,
Neither did she strengthen the hand

Of the poor and needy.

'They were haughty,
And committed abomination before me.'

Committed abomination before me!
Mentioned dead last?
These guys are human after all, he concluded. *They're dying. They need our condemnation like they need another hole in the head. What greater act of penance could I now show than to try to minister to these guys?*

He continued in his introspection. Wasn't the guy's greatest sin in particular lover for whom he left them really all that relevant?

Besides, as it turned out, didn't that free up Marie and me to get together?
So wasn't it a case of all's well ends well?

With that conclusion he had told the Prior he might consider trying to minister to their needs.

The Prior appeared pleased and gave his approval.

"We have a new patient who needs a helper," he said. "He calls himself Sebastian Melmoth. However, I suspect that that is a pseudonym. Interested?"

Dr. Suess squirmed uneasily in his chair. "What do I do?"

This could get messy, he thought. *These guys have a literal witch's brew of medications to take. How could I ever stay on top of their schedule to make sure they took which pill at which time? Also, these guys are accident prone—hygiene wise.*

The mere thought of cleaning up a patient's bed clothes, pajamas, and worst of all, their person freaked him out.

"You just check in on them regarding personal needs such as toilet articles, stationery and reading material. We have professionals to handle the rest of their care."

He paused and studied Dr. Suess for possible reaction. Finally he again spoke.

"As I said: interested?"

"I guess."...

* * *

...Subsequent contacts with Marie's ex did little to affect a thaw in their relationship.

First of all, he couldn't understand why the man had admitted himself to the hospice under the assumed name of Sebastian Melmoth.

Only when discussing it with another brother did he learn that Sebastian Melmoth was Oscar Wilde's pseudonym during the last two years of his life in Paris; where he died poverty stricken, friendless, and in exile.

Dr. Suess had again settled into the writing desk chair. "How are you fixed for toothpaste?"

Eyes set in darkened sockets again fixed a hard gaze at him.

"What's your real reason for coming here?"

Dr. Suess tried to avoid the man's stare as he searched for an appropriate answer.

Lips thin to the point of near non existence formed a wry smile. "Is it to satisfy curiosity?"

"I don't follow you."

"Are you waiting to see the outcome of my bout with the Marquis of Queensbury?"

Marquis of Queensbury? What the hell is this guy talkin' about?

Marie's ex explained. "Is it to see what it looks like to see someone die in slow motion?"

Dr. Seuss struggled for an answer. "No of course not," he said, finding nothing else to say.

A pause.

"Well," said 'Sebastian' at length. "At least Bunky hasn't called me to the big one yet."

Bunky? What Bunky? Who Bunky? The guy is full of riddles, thought Dr. Suess.

"You're probably wondering who I'm referring to," said 'Sebastian.'

Dr. Suess shrugged. "I guess you'll tell me when you're good and

"Bunky and I have an interesting relationship," said Marie's ex.

Rays of sunlight filtered in between the plain window curtains. They cast a shaft of light on the wall crucifix. As Dr. Suess' eyes followed him, Marie's ex gestured to the figure

Oh, my God, thought Dr. Suess. "You mean—?" he said also nodding to the wall relic.

"Yes."

Bunky? "For Chri'sakes," he said indignantly. "How sacrilegious can we get?"

"Indeed!" said 'Sebastian' with raised eyebrows, "and when was the last time you heard anybody take a name like 'Bunky' in vain?"

Silence.

Dr. Suess swallowed hard. "Good point," he said. It was his turn for his voice to go hoarse.

'Sebastian' continued to study him with quiet amusement.

His eyes finally narrowed to mere slits.

"By the way," he said. "How is Marie?"

"She's fine."

Marie's ex lowered his voice. "No, I mean, how *is* she?"

What the man was driving at finally dawned on him.

Dirty bastard, thought Dr. Suess. That's it! "If you want me to leave," he said, standing up. "Just say so—'*Sebastian.*'"

"Before you leave," said Marie's ex, with a lordly wave of the hand, "don't forget the toothpaste."

The recent mention of Marie triggered within him a train of thought. *I suppose my leaving her and the children makes me the villain. How could I explain to her or anyone else that in marrying her and giving her two children marked my attempt to try the straight life.*

Am I culpable?
Conventional idiots like this clown will never understand.
So forget them.
Dr. Suess was about to tell 'Sebastian' to go to hell.
No, no, he thought, *I mustn't lose it. That would be too easy. I can always give up.*
"I'll be back tomorrow," he sighed.
He paused in the doorway and gave the room a backward glance. "*With the toothpaste.*"
As he left the sickroom and stepped into the hallway, he stopped briefly. *I almost told him to go to hell,* he again realized.
That's not funny.
After Dr. Suess left, 'Sebastian' with great effort rose and shuffled across the room to a small dresser. From a top drawer he found a package of generic label cigarettes. With his new-found treasure he laboriously made his way back to his armchair. He placed a tea saucer-turned-ashtray on one of the arms.
Thus ensconced, he proceeded to light up.
Smoking is a no-no, he reflected as he blew billows of second hand smoke out into the room. *It can shorten your life. It can cause lung cancer or emphysema.*
He took another puff.
It can also stunt your growth.
So said a scoutmaster from his youth.
Let's see, he asked himself, *what else did that scoutmaster say?*
He recalled the scoutmaster and other well-meaning youth leaders, such as a Sunday school teacher, YMCA worker, and a school hygiene teacher warn against the dire consequences of masturbation. It would weaken you, they had said. It would make your muscles flabby they had said. It would cause insanity, they had said
'*Better to leave your seed in the belly of a whore than to spill it on the ground.*' So says the Bible.
Allegedly.
As a joke, guys at school also had said that it would cause hair to grow on the palm of your hands.

One also got venereal disease off from toilet seats.

Even in his youthful naiveté he knew he was being fed a bunch of malarkey. He decided very early on to follow every impulse of his id and libido and to deny himself no fleshly pleasure.

He pondered his wasted skeletal frame. A sardonic grin crossed his skull-like features.

As he was wont to conclude: b*een quite a ride.*

He sat back contentedly and blew more puffs into the air and pondered his new-found friend; his would-be benefactor; a rugged, outdoors, macho, knowing nothing of the exquisitely decadent life of the dilettante. *Despite his scientific expertise, what did he know of the subtleties of we who are the erudite?* How crude and uncouth; how prosaic and boring those like him. How pedestrian and lacking in excitement their humdrum existence.

That man is a fool, he concluded.

He tilted his head back further. *Ah, yes,* he thought, again with the same sardonic grin. *I must be careful about my health. I should give up this filthy habit.*

His face sobered. He again studied his wasted body, wracked by a malady that rivaled the Black Death of the middle Ages, or the leprosy of biblical times.

Or take diabetes. Before the invention of insulin in the 1920's it was considered as sure a death sentence as was his affliction today.

Despite his difficulty with breathing, he still managed to inhale deeply the numbing and soothing source of nicotine.

How long did he still have? He knew he no longer could reckon it in months. It now had to have been a matter of weeks.

Or even days.

He pondered the bleak, late autumn scene outside his window. He realized he would never see another spring time. He would never again see the crocuses break the green earth so recently freed from winter's frozen snows. He would never again hear the singing of the newly-arrived song birds. He would never again feel the gentle warmth of a sun gradually moving northward in the blue sky.

He knew he would miss those simple earthly delights.

Ah yes, he mused, *simple pleasures.*

The poignancy of having to say farewell to these delights sharpened within him. The sunrise. The sunset. The changing of the seasons. Summer zephyrs blowing through the lush green of the trees. The sight of wild geese flying southward in V-formation against a bright October sky as he walked ankle deep among dead leaves beneath trees gilded with foliate colors of red, yellow, and orange.

He knew would he would miss the white fairyland of winter with its bare trees laced with hoarfrost. He knew he would miss the gently falling snowflakes in the early evening darkness as mentioned in Robert Frost's beloved poem.

He would miss savoring the summer sunrise from his patio lounge chair over a leisurely mug of coffee.

He found himself trying to bargain with the Almighty—an Almighty that he had been not all that sure that he believed in. *Just give me more time*, he thought. *Never mind letting me live to a ripe old age*, he pleaded. *Just give me another year or two in reasonably good health and I'll die a happy human being. Just give me a few days to the savor blessings of the simple life that had been there for me all along while I stupidly wasted my life and strength in foolish pursuits.*

As soon as these ran through his mind, he realized that he was in no position to ask God for anything; not so much because he lived in the flesh pots of kinky sensual pleasure, but because he had all but ignored God for most of his life.

As soon as he realized this an overwhelming conviction came rushing into his psyche.

Such a grant was not to be.

So be it, he thought with resignation.

Why dread the inevitable?

What goes around comes around as they say.

Why should he be any different?

He determined not to indulge in self-pity or ask why him?

He knew why.

In the deadness and despondency of his spirit he would set his face as flint as he moved irresistibly to the darkened unknown void.

As he continued consuming his cigarette, his mind went in retrospect to his childhood.

He recalled being sent to summer camp. Again, he visualized his counselor, a tall, spindly gentleman with a scholarly mien named 'Fergie.' Rimless spectacles framed the features of 'Fergie's' face. Dark, graying hair tousled about in a disarray of gently unkempt waves topped the narrow head held high in a parsimonious hauteur. His thin face bore a perpetual five o'clock shadow.

"Fellows," (or sometimes 'boys' but never 'fellas,' or 'guys,' or 'gang.') he would address the campers.

The counselor would speak in precise, almost prissy accents: "It's time to get ready to go to the dining hall (never 'mess hall.')"

He recalled while on a hike, the slim figure in khaki shorts walking past him in a mincing gait on the wooded trail. "Fergie" would pass him by until he walked alongside an older camper just ahead. As he walked beside the older boy he would hold hands with him. In fact, he couldn't resist getting handsy with any male within reach.

'Sebastian's' own first encounter occurred while attending Breathewaite Academy, an exclusive boys' boarding school. At age twelve he found himself in a milieu of boys and men that made the school a notorious hotbed for that culture. His first experience occurred when pressed by a male student two years his senior. Was he coerced, or did he submit willingly?

Hard to tell.

The only question he now asked is why? Why him? Why was he singled out by this older boy? What did this older boy see in 'Sebastian' that he found so attractive? Why did 'Sebastian' not resist or call for help? What sort of vibes passed between the two of them that made the encounter inevitable?

Again he reasoned within himself. Was he pre-ordained to live this way? Or was it of his own volition?

Anyway, did it matter any more?

Had he subconsciously known that this was to be his final destiny?

He sighed and took another puff on his cigarette. •

Just outside his window, howling winds shook the corner of the building.

So a thought, reap a deed.

So it is, he mused, *the most highly erogenous zone of the human organism is not the lips, not the legs, not the eyes, but the mind.*

Was it genetic or was it strictly a conscious decision that gave the go-ahead?

Anyway, why worry about it now? What's done is done.

The finality of it all hit his psyche with renewed force. Where could he turn? Could psychological counseling really prepare one for the inevitable? Could such counseling ever cushion against the ultimate?

Words, words, words, he thought. *That's all they have to offer. What a cruel joke.*

He recalled the framed motto that Marie once told him graced the front chalkboard in Dr. Suess' classroom.

'*Sow a deed; reap a habit.*

Try it, you'll like it, he realized, was the original message blandishment with which the Serpent appealed to our first mother.

'*Sow a habit; reap a character.*

'The devil made me do it.' So said the popular bromide. However, are we not what we do?

'*Sow a character, reap a destiny.*'

His thoughts took an abrupt about-face.

How damnably boring these who are so bound by convention.

Damned prudish sonofabitch anyway, he fumed inwardly.

He paused, snuffed out his cigarette and lit another. As he again began inhaling, he studied the far wall wherein hung the ubiquitous plaster-of-Paris crucifix.

There you have it, he mused, *talk about in-your-face.*

The itching sensation began again to assail his forearms. He knew that to scratch would only aggravate but he couldn't help. The rash, the itching he knew to be a side effect of one of his medications.

He had, at times, difficulty in trying to decide which was worse: the disease or the treatment.

Laying aside his cigarette, he began vigorously scratching the affected area.

Again, he studied the Crucifix on the opposite wall.

He died for our sins, or so they say, he thought, giving a sardonic nod. *I never asked him to die for mine. Were I alive then, I would have told him 'don't bother I'll die for my own sins, thank you very much.'*

He contemplated his physical strength, waning noticeably by the day, his decreasing breathing capacity, his burning temperature, his lingering nausea, his watery bowels, his increasing frequency of leg cramps; in short, his own frail mortality.

Guess I'm doing just that, he concluded.

He slumped down lower in his chair. He already felt a sense of detachment from this world and everything and everybody in it. He felt no longer to be any part of anything.

He recalled days gone by when despite the reality of the deadly virus that lurked silent, dark and lying in wait within, to make manifest its symptoms, he still felt good. He still enjoyed his status as social lion. He recalled days when he pranced about in a party scene face flushed, smiling a toothy smile and cocktail in hand; he entertained his tight little group of admirers with an endless glitter of repartee.

As he studied the rain beating against the window pane he marveled.

How different now, he thought.

He felt alone.

All alone.

We enter this world alone; we leave it alone, he reflected.

That being the case, how could he now attach any meaning of love, bonding, or comradeship with other human being on this planet? He realized himself to be rapidly descending a psychic slope that no healthy, living human being could ever relate to, or empathize with him.

Only those who have already gone on before.

And they weren't telling.

What thoughts could he grasp and meditate on that give him even a modicum of comfort?

Could it come from William Cullen Bryant's Thanatopsis?

'...So live that when thy summons comes to join that
Mysterious caravan that moves on to the silent halls of death,
Thou go not like the quarry slave
Condemned and scourged to his dungeon,
But sustained and soothed by an unfaltering trust,
Rather as one who wraps the garment of his couch about him,
And lies down to pleasant dreams.'

He picked up his cigarette resumed puffing and inhaling. He had actually quit many years before. Only recently, after his illness had robbed him of all other pleasures he had once held dear did he take it up again.

Ah yes, he mused, *pleasure.*

He had lived his whole life in one mad pursuit of fleshly pleasure.

What else was there?

He recalled asking himself this many times.

In his long, mad pursuit he made a rather disconcerting discovery. The more he indulged himself, the more he found his neurons reluctant to respond. He found them becoming increasingly callused to external titillation.

He recalled the intensity of his early youthful incidents. How fierce were the sensations then. How in contrast had this same sport now grown stale?

Yet he found the desire burning within with ever increasing ferocity.

He also recalled reading certain mortality rates. Heavy use of alcohol shortens life expectancy by about seven years. Ditto heavy use of tobacco.

Expectancy for those in the life style, so said the tables, would be shortened by about thirty years.

As the drunks would say, he thought, *a short life but a merry one.*

Not.

It wasn't the plague as many think that threatens. It is hepatitis.

For the time being anyway, nicotine seemed the only pleasure left for him.

"How quickly one forgets," he said to himself, "just how good these babies really are."

He again brooded over how he had noticeably been deteriorating with a rapidity that convinced him that it was all now just a matter of days; the increased gasping for air and shortness of breath, the burning temperature, his increased rash and itching, his lingering nausea, his watery bowels, and the increasing muscle cramps. It all added up to the overwhelming reality that he was gradually and inevitability checking out.

When that happens, what then?

Brave words, these, he thought. *Brave words in face of life's most frightening reality.*

Which is worse? Total annihilation, cessation of all thought and memory? Will it be as thought never existed—having once tasted the human experience with all its joys, its sorrows—will it all become completely erased and a self-conscious entity such as 'Sebastian Melmoth' be forever eradicated from all records mortal and divine?

In a way is not that prospect more frightening than an eternity in a cosmic active volcano of molten lava?

At least there one still retains his self-conscious awareness.

When one is still sound of body and mind, such a concept may seem ridiculous and far-fetched, but when one is thrust full press against the ultimate reality?

Well, that's quite another matter.

The howling wind outside continued unabated.

The rain hardened into a fine sleet. That tapping on the window provided the only sound in the room.

As he mused on the dark, dismal night swirling in the cold, rainy lashing outside, he recalled the bright, balmy days of summer only a few weeks ago. How in contrast the sweet, gentle breezes, the clear blue skies, and the luxuriant green foliage.

He felt emotionally dead to an inescapable reality.

He had seen his last summer.

He laid his cigarette on the edge of his saucer-turned-ash tray and glanced toward the window. Again, with agonizing effort, he pushed his hands against the arms of his chair until he stood to his feet. With the help of a walker, he slowly worked his way toward the window.

He looked upon the cold, autumnal afternoon that rapidly enveloped itself in twilight. A stiff wind began blowing billowy, leaden clouds across the darkening sky. The few dull orange leaves clinging to the stark branches fluttered fitfully as if in defiance to the gusts that would dislodge them.

Perhaps other literary gems better expressed his mood.

He recalled lines from Henley's *Invictus*

'...It matters not how straight the gate
How charged with punishment the scroll;
I am the master of my fate,
I am the captain of my soul.'

As the raw blasts assailed the corner of the building, they emitted whistling sounds mingled with a low moan.

Like spirits from another world, he thought.

In a matter of days, would he be among them?

What message were they, even then, trying to convey to him?

'*Abandon hope, all ye who enter here.*'

He contemplated the moisture forming on the cold window pane.

As he stood, a lonely figure in an increasingly existential world, he suddenly felt tired. Despite the support of his walker, he felt that he had all he could do to keep from collapsing to the floor.

Yet he felt loathe to break the spell of the brooding landscape. Such a dark and gloomy scene served as the only comfort to his already tormented soul.

Away with your Pollyanna notions of happiness and cheer, he mused.

Spirits, you say? He thought, *praying to the mere wind? God, I'd better get back to my chair before I go completely bonkers.*

He painfully worked his walker and himself around to wend his way back to his chair. More moments went by. The rapidly fading sunset outside, partially covered over with the cloud cover, eventually sank below the distant mountains, leaving only a pale afterglow. Soon it too faded, leaving the scene outside enshrouded in an abysmal void.

In all this time, 'Sebastian' did not turn on any lights, contenting himself to sit in darkness. The kinship to his inner mood bore with it a strange kind of soothing sensation.

He recalled the flyleaf of Frank Harris' *Oscar Wilde, his Life and Confessions*: *'Crucifixion of the guilty is more awe-inspiring the crucifixion of the innocent.'*

He realized that he sought no comfort.

He again laid his cigarette aside, pulled himself to his feet.

He was about to start for the TV set on his desk when it happened.

A crash shattered the silence of the darkened room. He had accidentally knocked his ashtray onto the floor. Without the aid of a light, he could feel the sensation of cigarette butts under his feet.

That and the ashes.

With the help of his walker, he worked his way to his desk whereon sat the small table model TV. When the image flashed on the screen, he heard the bell tolling in the distance from the brothers' dormitory.

Time for their Grand Silence, he realized. *I'll spend mine watching reality shows.*

After he labored his way back to his chair he settled in and resumed his smoking. As he watched the action on the TV screen, he contemplated his benefactor wannabe, Dr. Suess.

How like the Edenic serpent, he mused. *At least I'll go out knowing both good and evil. This poor schlep will exit without ever having really lived.*

That man is a fool, he repeated to himself, *a bloody, well-meaning fool.*

* * *

"How are you and your patient getting on?"

Father Michael sat at his desk and fixed a benign gaze at Dr. Suess.

"Just fine," he said in a flat tone of voice.

"Oh, really?" Father Michael's face took on a look of skepticism.

A pause.

Golden rays of a late afternoon sun gave a soft, slanted light into the narrow rectory. The crucifix on the wall opposite and the painting of St. Dunstan behind the Prior remained as passive as ever.

"All right," admitted Dr. Suess. "It's not going well."

Father Michael waited. He folded long, aged looking hands atop his desk. "And what were you expecting?" he said. "Do you think a terminally ill patient is always going to be the epitome of congeniality?"

Dr. Suess shrugged. "Guess I was a little naïve," he admitted.

"The test of true sainthood," said Father Michael, "is not always ministering to the grateful. More often it means serving the unloved and unlovely as they say."

But I'm not a saint, dammit, he almost said. "I see what you mean," he did manage to say.

He rose to his feet. "I'll keep trying." he said as he replaced his chair under the desk.

Father Michael likewise stood up. "I know you will." He said. "I believe in you."

Dr. Suess genuflected toward the crucifix and then turned to grasp the doorknob.

"Don't let me down, my son," said Father Michael as Dr. Suess made his exit.

* * *

More days passed. Dr. Suess continued to drop in on Marie's ex, offering to do small chores or run errands for him.

In all his visits, a nagging question remained: had he risked a faux pas by being too presumptuous?

"Since you admitted yourself under an assumed name, I take it that it's O.K. to call you 'Sebastian?'"

Marie's ex gave an indifferent wave of the hand. "You already have, remember?"

Dr. Suess stood dumbfounded a moment. Finally he shrugged. "I guess."

As he stepped to the door, a faint voice arrested his exit. "Wait."

Dr. Suess cast him a look of curiosity.

"I do need some reading material."

Dr. Suess was about to suggest his going the Priory library when he realized that it lay at the far side of the property. *The poor guy probably hasn't the energy to walk that far anymore*, he concluded.

"No problem," he said with a shrug.

'Sebastian' held out a list. "See if they have any of these writers," he said. "Anything by any of them would be fine."

Dr. Suess studied the list. It contained names such as Andre Gide, Jean Genet, and Marcel Proust. "I'll see what I can do."

Later that afternoon, Dr. Suess stood before the librarian's desk in the small library. Bookshelves bearing worn volumes lined the walls. Above the shelves the walls were painted with the same dull beige that colored the rooms throughout the compound.

He showed 'Sebastian's' list to the brother behind the desk.

The brother shook his head and sighed. "I'm afraid we can't accommodate," he said.

He reached into a side drawer and pulled out another list. "Maybe your patient would enjoy reading these."

The next day, Dr. Suess again stepped into 'Sebastian's' room.

"Well?" Marie's ex looked up at him expectantly.

"They didn't have the books you were looking for," said Dr. Suess. "However, the librarian suggested something from this list."

'Sebastian' studied the list a moment. It contained such writers as St. Augustine, Dante, Pascal, Newton, and G. K. Chesterton. He wheezed a sigh of disgust. "What the hell is this?" he demanded.

He wadded the paper and threw it to the floor.

Dr. Seuss remained on his feet, nervously shifting his weight.

'Sebastian' summoned an unexpected bolt of energy as he sat upright and glared at Dr. Suess. "Get out!" he ordered.

Dr. Suess started for the door.

"Wait!" Again the patient's voice took on new strength that riveted Dr. Suess to his spot.

Silence. Dr. Seuss wondered what would come next.

'Sebastian' sat silent a moment as if trying to summon strength to again speak. "I haven't been to a McDonald's in ages." He said finally. "Could you get me a Big Mac and order of fries?"

Dr. Suess' spirits picked up a little. *Maybe the guy's appetite is coming back,* He thought.

He paused.

How do I get out of here? He asked himself. He knew he was free to leave, but—?

"What do I do for money?"

'Sebastion' gave a feeble gesture toward his desk. "I have a five in the desk drawer."

"But how do I get there? We're way out in the country."

"I drove here in my car. It's still in the parking lot. There's a set of keys also in the drawer."

As Dr. Suess stepped toward the door, 'Sebastian' added: "While you're out, check the town library."

Dr. Suess' spirits picked up a little. *Maybe I can still get back in this guy's good graces.*

Another thought occurred to him. *My clothes,* he realized. *I still have my jeans in my ward robe.*

Three hours later Dr. Suess was back. He placed a stack of library books on the writing desk. Beside them an order of hamburger and fries lay untouched.

"Aren't you going to eat?" he asked.

"Later." The tired look returned.

When Dr. Suess started to leave, the voice again halted his steps.

The voice grew weaker. Marie's ex gestured toward the food still in its wrapper.

"Take that down to the kitchen and put it in the fridge," he whispered.

* * *

"You again."

Again the hoarse, raspy voice lashed out a challenge.

Marie's ex cast a jaundiced eye at Dr. Suess just as he crossed the threshold. *Oh, no,* he thought. *Just when it looked like I was making some progress.*

The man's face metamorphosed into a look of undisguised mockery. "If you're looking for a little action," he said. "You're a little late."

God, you're vicious, thought Dr. Suess as he sat in the writing desk chair, *even when you're terminally ill.*

"You never really did take a walk on the wild side," Marie's ex said still taunting him. "I can see that."

And where did it get you thought Dr. Suess? *The guy's mood swings are wild. Was he always this way, or is it aggravated by his medication, or is it his anger—as he calls it, with his 'Marquis of Queensbury.?'*

The face of Marie's ex still bore the smirk. "You're way too up tight," he said.

Dr. Suess studied the face that had frozen into a prolonged expression of total scorn.

No, I mustn't go there. I've just got to let this guy get it out.

The features of Marie's ex changed to an expression of thoughtfulness. He disclosed how that he had some thousand different partners during the past decade. That's partners—not incidents.

Dr. Suess eyed him with curiosity. "How did your 'significant other' take all this?"

Again the smirk crossed his would-be beneficiary's face. "We split years ago," he said with a cough. "We fought constantly anyway. He always wanted to watch cooking shows on television when I wanted to watch sit-coms. When we got bored with each other, where else could we go?

"I gave up my 'significant other' as you put it, for a whole lot of insignificant others."

'Sebastian' seemed momentarily lost in thought. *Ah, yes,* he reflected, *dear Gilbert was useful for a while.* Better a long term relationship than the furtive clandestine contacts in seedy points of rendezvous such as freeway rest areas, public men's rooms, or bars. There were, of course, all kinds of signals unique to the sub culture: the eyes, the look, the hand gestures, the words, and the double entendres.

However, one had to be careful.

The signals could be mixed or misunderstood. One could also encounter a straight bully with whom one always risked getting beat up, or robbed.

Or worse.

'Sebastian' again picked up the thread of conversation. "Anyway, six months after we split, he committed suicide."

Suicide? The word shot through Dr. Suess like an electric shock. In retrospect he lived again the days of his own son's fight to protect the pathetically delicate youth from adolescent bullies.

Poor Gilbert Wilkins, he thought; *persecuted by the straight world; used and eventually discarded and thrown away by the other world.*

A sense of curiosity flooded over him. "How did you feel when you learned this?" he asked. "Didn't it affect you?"

"Oh, I suppose."

"You suppose?"

A hardened expression set in 'Sebastian's' features. "My dear fellow, I'm going to level with you," he said "I'm afraid that dear, dear Gilbert took our relationship far more seriously than was warranted."

Dr. Seuss seethed inwardly. *I can't believe this.*

"Ah, yes," Marie's ex continued, pensively. "I'm afraid he didn't realize that the whole thing was just a fling."

Another pause. Time seemed to press in on the room's occupants with depressing heaviness.

"However," he added with a shrug, "after a while I simply found it not fun anymore."

Dr. Suess stared dumbfounded with disbelief. *How do I read this guy?* He thought. *Is he a bona fide, genetically programmed perv, or is he just a jaded, dissolute libertine?*

Dr. Suess knotted his fists deep into the palms of his hands. "But weren't you two more or less committed to each other?"

'Sebastian' examined his fingernails. "He may have been looking for a commitment," he said, "but I'm afraid he misunderstood. To me he was just a toy."

Eventually the one night stands with total strangers with all their attendant risks only heightened the excitement. Steady relationships just got too prosaic. The risky stuff provided the only thrills.

The impulse to leave surged strong through Dr. Suess' inner being. *Damned amoral bastard! What kind of psychopath am I dealing with?*

Here's a guy who admittedly set out early in life to live a strictly hedonistic life style, he reflected. *And the result? His second partner committed suicide and his first wife and her children were still in therapy when I first met them.*

Dr. Suess continued inwardly with the pitched battle.

I believe in you. Don't let me down, my son. The words of Father Michael came rushing back into his memory.

A thought occurred to him.

"And of all your other partners," he said, choosing his words carefully. "Were there any that brought you satisfaction of fulfillment?"

Marie's ex coughed. "Are you kidding?"

Dr. Suess realized a similarity with alcoholism. *When the stuff all tastes like water,* he recalled those further advanced in the disease than he had told him, *you know you got a problem.*

He searched for a way to craft his next remark. "This was actually Don Juan's plight."

Marie's ex nodded. His face sobered. Eyes set deep in his head, instead of their dull, listless stare now fixed fiercely on Dr. Suess.

"I'm going to share with you something I very seldom discuss with anyone. I determined early in life to 'go for the gusto' as they say. At risk of repeating myself, I decided to wring every last ounce of pleasure from every nerve fiber of my gorgeous little body. I purposed to deny myself nothing. Existence for me became a frenzied toboggan slide down life's steepest and most treacherous slopes in pursuit of ever more outrageous titillation.

"However, along the way I made an interesting but disconcerting discovery.

"Our nerve endings are capable of registering only a certain amount of sensuous pleasure. Eventually we no longer respond to external stimuli. To coin the vernacular: the kick is gone.

"We are then left with two choices: Give it up, or go further out in search for more extreme sensations.

"Eventually all ability to derive even a semblance of physical pleasure is gone and we become a complete burn-out."

Dr. Suess shook his head.

He heard a hoarse laugh. "To coin a cliché: left wing love, don't knock it you haven't tried it. It's like pedophilia, or crack, or ice. Experiment with it once or twice and you're hooked.

"I've known this ever since my first contact at thirteen."

"I thought it was genetic."

A half cough and half laugh rose from the chair. "You'll never hear this from anywhere else but in a place like this," he said flatly. "The truth is, that the jury's still out. Don't let the experts shit you. We're no surer of this than which came first: the chicken or the egg?"

What is this, Dr. Suess asked himself, a deathbed confession? He hesitated. *No, I mustn't. Oh, well, what the hell.* "No regrets then?"

"Only this." Marie's ex gestured to himself. "It looks like it's a matter of time before the Marquis of Queensbury gets his last laugh."

Dr. Suess couldn't resist asking the next question. "You keep mentioning the Marquis of Queensbury. Who is this Marquis of Queensbury? I mean originally?"

"Ever hear of Oscar Wilde?"

Dr. Suess thought. He remembered attending a performance of *The Importance of Being Ernest*. "Vaguely."

"Then you are no doubt aware of the scandal and trial that rocked Victorian England during the 1890's. It made the Alfred Dreyfus trial in France like a mere ripple in pond water."

'Sebastian' sat thoughtful a moment. "Lord Alfred Douglas, son of the Marquis of Queensbury and Wilde were lovers," he continued. "The Marquis intercepted incriminating correspondence between the two and decided to haul Wilde into court. The trial was a bitter and vicious affair. Wilde, in his own defense fought back tooth and nail. He gave as good as he got."

He paused.

"You see," he went on, "the life style actually ran rampant in upper class Victorian society. Why Wilde was singled out when so many others were allowed to go Scot free was the most outrageous part of the whole sordid mess."

With a pensive expression he momentarily looked off into space. "Ah yes," he sighed. "Old Oscar and I had much in common. He too had a wife and family before he took off for a walk on the wild side."

Another pause.

"It was actually class thing," he continued. "Oscar was born middle class—bourgeois, as the intelligentsia called it. All the others were born into the aristocracy. They were envious of Wilde because he was the literary darling of the upper class. When they saw an opportunity to crucify him, they took advantage of it.

"However, Wilde eventually turned tables on the whole legal system and made them the defendant before the whole thing was over."

Again he paused. All this talk he apparently found tiring.

Then: "However, since the system held all the high cards as it were, Mr. Wilde eventually was sent to prison for two years. The unkindest cut of all came when Lord Alfred Douglas turned star witness."

Dr. Suess sat motionless in his chair and stared at the floor as he let the epiphany sink in. The Marquis of Queensbury personified the man's own death struggle.

The sallow features turned sober. "I'll let you in on another secret," he said, his voice getting faint. "I've been celibate for the last three years."

He broke off into a cough.

When he finally recovered, he continued. "That is the longest I've lived that way," he said, "since junior high school."

An idea occurred to him. Dr. Suess fidgeted in his chair. "Look," he said, eyeing the door, "aren't you going to want to go to confessional?"

Marie's ex sat back in his chair. "Don't even suggest it," he said with a contemptuous toss of his head. "Anyway, a month or so at the outside, it won't matter."

"I saw you in chapel a couple weeks back," said Dr. Suess. "Don't you at least want to celebrate the Eucharist?"

The frail face glared at him. "You're talking to someone who is facing the big one and all you have to offer is a tasteless wafer?"

"Just a thought," said Dr. Suess as he stood to his feet. "Sunday is the feast of St. Dismus."

Thin, brown lips twisted downward. "Who the hell's St. Dismus?"

"The penitent thief on the cross," replied Dr. Suess. "He's the patron saint of the down-and-out."

Marie's ex gave a dismissive wave of the hand.

"Whatever," he sighed.

Dr. Suess stood silent a moment. Had his little attempt as a 'missionary' come to an impasse?

The sudden change of 'Sebastian's' countenance alarmed him. In a flash his expression went from contemptuous complacency to one of alarm.

He sat up in his chair. "Oh, God," he pleaded helplessly.

As he made a feeble gesture to Dr. Suess, the sound of a loud juicy fart filled the room.

"Help me, quick!" Panic edged an ever weakening voice.

Dr. Suess moved quickly to help him to his feet. Another flatulent blast reverberated in the room. Dr. Suess could read blind horror in his eyes. He could see streaks of brown liquid running down under his jeans. While Dr. Suess held his hand in a firm grip, another blast of fluid shot up from behind his patient. This time the brown liquid spread upward under his shirt until it spilled out over his collar.

More nasty brown stuff oozed out over his slippers and onto the floor.

"Get me to the bathroom. Please get me to the bathroom." He pled in a voice close to tears.

"I'll have to summon a nurse," said Dr. Suess. He released his grip on 'Sebastian' leaving him standing a trembling and helpless statue He reached for the buzzer alarm that lay pinned beside 'Sebastian's' pillow.

He resumed his place beside 'Sebastian.' "A nursing brother should be along shortly," he said in an attempt to reassure him.

Just as the brother came into the room, 'Sebastian' emitted a groan that barely sounded human. He doubled over and grasped at his mid-section. From deep within him rolled up a gurgling sound. His mouth shot open as he spewed out an unholy concoction of brown and yellowish.

The stench became so penetrating, Dr. Suess feared for his stomach.

A second nursing brother entered the room. "We can take it from here," he said, moving alongside Dr. Suess. However Dr. Suess resisted his impulse to flee as he watched the aides ease 'Sebastian' into the bathroom. They stripped off his clothes and left them in a soiled, stinking heap on the tiled floor.

He marveled at their words of encouragement. "Now don't worry about a thing, Mr. Melmoth, everything is going to be all right. We'll get you cleaned up in no time."

This in spite of what had to be their own sense of revulsion.

They gently helped him onto a bathtub seat under the shower.

As Dr. Seuss studied the naked body of 'Sebastian' the emaciated condition shocked him. The shit begrimed skeleton could very well have been a survivor of Dachau. Every rib and every spinal joint stood out under a sallow skin in bold relief. His shoulder blades protruded like chicken wings. The round fleshly cheeks of his buttocks had shrunk to the 'W' shaped contour of his hip bone. He could also see, under the film of refuse, an abundance of sores and ulcers.

A nursing brother turned to him. "See if there's a change of clothes in the wardrobe."

Dr. Suess opened the wardrobe and pulled out a clean T-shirt, shorts, sport shirt, and a pair of jeans. From an upper shelf he pulled a clean pair hospital socks. These he lay on the toilet seat lid. He looked through the doorway that opened to the major sanitary overhaul in the shower room. The brothers had him seated on the bathtub stool. Water—cleansing, redemptive water—began cascading in a rejuvenating torrent from the shower head.

In the midst of their sacrificial work of mercy, one the bothers turned to him.

"It's okay, Brother Henry, we got it."

Chapter 17

"Can you use a fourth hand?"

Dr. Suess pulled a chair out from under the folding card table. The other three brothers already engrossed in a poker game gave him a nod. "Can you wait till we finish this hand?" asked Brother Boniface, a portly comfortable looking man, fortyish with rimless spectacles.

Dr. Suess pulled his chair up to the table and waited.

Several hours had now passed since the emergency in 'Sebastian's' room and the brothers had finished their evening meal and now had one hour to pack in their recreation before the Grand Silence. Dr. Suess looked around at the interior of the day room reserved for quieter activities. Four card tables set strategically about for parlor and table games.

There was action at three of them.

Other brothers sat on couches or easy chairs reading newspapers and magazines, or sat at writing desks busying themselves with correspondence.

Over in a far corner one brother sat at a massive mahogany upright softly improvising jazz.

"Here we come, ready or not." Brother Praisegod's voice from across the table broke the inner silence. Pasteboards came sliding at him with a quickness that caused them to pile five high before he could pick them up.

Brother Ambrose, at his left, looked up from arranging his cards. "Nice work this afternoon."

Dr. Suess shook his head. *Just one nasty afternoon*, he thought, *and they make me a hero. These guys devote their lives to this.*

And I'm the one supposed to be doing penance.

He cast an anxious glance from Brother Ambrose to Brother Boniface. They had come to the rescue when 'Sebastian' was having his difficulty.

Brother Boniface noticed his discomfiture. "It's okay. Brother Praisegod is also from hospice. He's familiar with the Melmoth case. We can talk freely here."

Dr. Suess studied Brother Praisegod more closely. His closely cropped sandy hair and square, granite looking face set on a neck more nearly resembling a tree trunk. His brown hassock spread broadly across the massive chest underneath. A broad, strong looking mouth set off the chiseled cheek bones, the long patrician looking nose and fierce looking blue eyes that looked out at the world from behind wire rim glasses.

Could have been a line backer from the Pittsburgh Steelers, thought Dr. Suess. *Probably gets called on to handle unruly psych patients.*

Brother Boniface turned to Brother Praisegod. "The guy vomited up liver bile and feces," he said, his face turning serious.

Brother Praisegod held his cards up close to his chest. He eyed Brother Boniface and furrowed his forehead in a worried look.

Dr. Seuss looked from one brother to other in puzzlement. "*What?*" he said finally.

The ensuing silence became prolonged and uncomfortable.

Brother Ambrose heaved a sigh. "It's usually a sign of the beginning of the end," he said slowly.

Dr. Seuss tried to lick away the dryness in his mouth. "How much time?" he said with huskiness in his voice.

Brother Ambrose stared expressionlessly at his hand. "A week, maybe ten days."

He put down his discard. "Or—it could come in a matter of hours."

"We've seen a lot of patients die," said Brother Boniface. "You name it, we've seen it: cancer, emphysema, heart trouble, whatever. Some patients die hard. Others die quite peacefully."

He paused. Dr. Seuss again eyed him. *Was there something else he was trying to say?*

What? He again asked himself.

"With these cases," Brother Boniface said finally. "It's never pretty."

Again a heavy silence descended on the table.

"We've had to keep him under rather heavy sedation," said Brother Boniface, again picking up the conversation.

Dr. Suess continued looking puzzled.

"We've given him just enough dosage to take the edge off the pain."

Why? Dr. Suess wondered. "But why not give him dosage sufficient kill the pain completely?"

"We don't want him to become addicted."

Don't want him to become addicted?

Dr. Suess' features tensed. *Not become addicted?* His mind screamed out in disbelief. *For crying out loud, the man is dying! So what if he's addicted? He's only got days left. Why not make his last moments as comfortable as possible?*

Dr. Seuss threw his cards.

All interest in the game had left him.

Off somewhere in the grim stucco building with the tile roof, the leaden sounds of a chapel bell began tolling.

Time for the Grand Silence.

* * *

The final reverberation of the chapel bell finally faded off into nothingness.

Outside the scene lay in the early darkness of November.

Dark.

Dark outside.

Dark inside.

The glowing tip of 'Sebastian's' cigarette provided the only illumination of the sick room.

Beyond the immediate glow one saw only shades of grey and black. The rancid smell of the unholy mix of effluence that spilled forth from his body earlier that day still carried a faintly foul scent.

That and an equally omnipresent smell of disinfectant.

Oscar Wilde who believed in art for art's sake, held a lifelong philosophy of aestheticism, he recalled. *How ironic.*

How aesthetic is this?

His wasted form slumped back in his bedside chair. His broomstick like legs sprawled spread-eagled out in front of him. Scarecrow like arms draped over the flat wooden arms of the chair. The hand that held the cigarette shook with an uncontrollable tremor.

However he studiously managed to avoid spilling his saucer ash tray a second time.

Now it bore a mound of squashed butts which prompted him to be extra careful.

He inhaled deeply as he stared at the grey-dark night just outside his window. As he blew smoky billows out into the room, he groped for his pack.

It felt nearly empty.

Once he ran out of his cigarettes, then what?

They provided him his one remaining source of pleasure.

Then what would he do to shield himself from the pain, the misery, the difficulty of breathing, and the rapidly waning physical powers?

When would it all end?

Next week?

Two days?

Tomorrow?

Or would it be tonight?

Again he reflected on the vices that shortened longevity. Heavy smokers and heavy drinkers shorten their longevity by about seven years respectively. Those in the life style shorten theirs by thirty.

Oscar Wilde died at age 46; Robert Mapplethorpe died at 42.

I guess I've already beaten the odds, he mused. *So why complain?*

He felt the psychic wall, the void, his Marquis of Queensbury closing in on him.

He felt alone.

Even his would-be benefactor, this erstwhile scientist, the casual churchman in his struggling attempts at piety and penances would likely be also alone.

Thinking about God.

What an exercise in futility, he thought. Yet in a short while—perhaps a very short while he would not have to sit and wonder. He would know for sure the answer to the Ultimate Riddle.

In the meantime where could he turn? St. Dismus just moments away from eternity finally turned from mocking the one on the center cross and pled to him for mercy.

It was not too late for that first century terrorist; was there still time for him?

His next thoughts were the most serious of his lifetime.

Chapel tomorrow.

All they have to offer are pious words, a tasteless wafer, and a sip from a chalice.

And yet?

Oscar Wilde, the life long atheist, the once witty, brilliant, and proud literary darling of Victorian aristocracy, in his final days—sick, friendless, and alone—sought out a Parisian priest and embraced Catholicism.

Ironic, he thought, *he embraced Catholicism late in life; I abandoned it early in life.*

He recalled his fifth grade class in parochial school. He recalled the sister requiring them to memorize the Shepherd's Psalm:

'Yaweh, is my shepherd; no want shall I know…

…Yea, though I walk through death's dark valley,

I will fear no evil, for thou art with me…'

* * *

Dr. Suess paced the floor of his cell. Periodically he would stop and stare out his window into the blackened void outside.

Grand Silence again.

Spend two hours thinking about God. Were that not enough, he faced an even more daunting ordeal.

Tomorrow the brotherhood had scheduled a mission-wide day of prayer.

And fasting.

Twenty-fours of total kitchen shut-down...

Dr. Suess recalled conversation during dinner hour...

...Again he sat beside the ascetic Brother Benedict. Again, he tried to ask some questions about how to meditate during the Grand Silence. Again to no avail.

As the hushed pall resettled in over the dining room, he could overhear a conversation from the kitchen, subdued though its tones.

Apparently they were cleaning out the refrigerator.

"Here's some stuff in a McDonald's wrapper." The voice sounded like that of the kitchen assistant. "What shall I do with it?"

A pause.

"I don't know where it came from," said the head kitchen steward. "Why don't you just throw it out?"

Dr. Suess almost pitched himself to the floor jumping over his bench. To the startled looks of his fellow diners, he rushed to the kitchen.

"Hey, hey, hey, hey!" he shouted.

Facing disapproving frowns of both dining room and kitchen personnel, he added: "Leave that stuff alone!"

The head kitchen steward held the food package in his hand. "What is the meaning of this?" he demanded.

"That belongs to somebody," Dr. Suess said.

"So?"

"It belongs to a hospice patient," he added breathlessly.

The head kitchen steward cast a glance at the package he still held in his hand. "A hospice patient?" he laughed. "He'll never eat it."

Dr. Suess snatched the package from the steward's hand. "Never mind," he said flinging it back into the refrigerator. "It's only important that he knows that it's there."...

...There had been periods of fasting before; however, the normal work schedule went on as usual.

Tomorrow would be different.

He would spend the day not only going without food, but he would spend it on a kneeling bench in chapel in prayer.

Prayer? For what? For Whom?

He continued pacing the floor. He was about to conclude that he had had it. He could suffer the austere living, the simple food, and the tedious work schedule.

However, the contemplative stuff was beginning to get to him. He had been an outdoorsman all his life, a man of action. He simply was not cut out for all this prayer and meditation stuff. He could leave at anytime, he realized, but that's not as easy as it sounds. He would have to go to the Prior for the key to the warder where his valuables and personal effects were kept. He knew that there would be no overt pressure to dissuade him from leaving. However, he knew that the covert, subtle pressure would be enormous. The brothers were masters at that kind of psychology, knowing with uncanny accuracy just what mental buttons to push.

* * *

In the grey, numbing cold of a November morning, Henry joined the procession of robed mendicants along the stone path to the small, gothic building that housed the chapel. Just ahead the sexton pushed open the stained, oaken door and Henry passed through the arched entryway into the foyer. In the dim candlelight he spotted rows of straight-backed pews with hard, wooden seats. He followed the line of worshippers in front of him. When he reached his spot, he pulled out the low kneeling bench and crouched down to it. He crossed himself and then looked down at it his folded hands. He could see the vapor of his breath form around him.

Pray? His only thought was to get warm.

The shivering spread in uncontrollable spasms. *If this is heaven*, he thought, *give me hell.*

At least hell was warm.

Or so say the theologians.

He blew on his hands and rubbed them to re-invigorate the circulation. Why they must be so damned serious about all this masochism escaped him. Pray? Even if he knew what to pray for how could he shiver and pray at the same time?

A thought occurred to him.

If we have to get comfortable before we can pray, is the Almighty impressed? He reminded himself as to why he was here in the first place. Was it not because of problems of his making? Were not the cold, somber surroundings his private purgatory?

Yet had not the Church of England abolished purgatory back in the sixteenth century? Had not broad churchmen abolished hell back in the nineteenth century? And now had not the so-called radical theologians even abolished heaven in the twentieth century?

Ours is a marvelous faith, he recalled the dean saying. *All the pageantry of Rome with none of the guilt.* Was the church notoriously loathe to make substantive demands of any kind on its adherents? But are not the guys who run this Priory also of the Church of England? What about them? Who are the nutty ones here?

Clearly they were against the mainstream. Clearly they were a throwback to the days when faith was made of sterner stuff.

God, he thought, *break me of this addiction. Whatever it takes. Bring me a miracle, and reconciliation with Marie.*

He recalled asking the Prior how he would know if God had in fact miraculously restored him to sobriety. After all, staying sober in a monastery is one thing. Staying sober once back on the outside would be something else. How could he be sure?

It will take a miracle, my son, the Prior had said.

"How will I know the miracle?" he asked.

When the time comes, the Prior had replied, you will know.

Chapter 18

...Dr. Suess sat at the battered writing desk and gazed thoughtfully out the window of the furnished studio apartment he currently called home. A small gooseneck lamp cast a circle of illumination over the desktop. He studied the worn, dated furnishings with which the apartment was appointed.

He re-read the article in the *Denver Post*. Two years previous, a cold cases team of the Colorado State Police reopened the investigation of the murder. After an intensive nation wide sweep involving hundreds of police from state trooper forces from a half dozen states, they began to fit the pieces together like a puzzle. They were finally able to subpoena a dozen witnesses and extradite five actual suspects; they began holding hearings in the Mariposa County seat. *At last*, he thought, *after 29 years, we get closure to that ugliness.*

Rest in peace, Ginger.

Despite his prayer for the soul of Miss Wallace, he felt despondency pressing down on him like a gray, wet blanket. *I guess she doesn't really need my prayers at this juncture*, he concluded. *Maybe she's praying for me.*

The view beyond the windowpane opened out to an aging near-downtown neighborhood and the somber November sky.

Almost as somber as that day of prayer and fasting at St. Dunstan's.

He opened a file folder that lay on his desk and pulled out the final installment of the cryptologist's report. While up at Stillwell the week before, he had gotten together with Dr. Sirotka at the Old Heidelberg.

There had been the business of reconciliation. They had not seen each other since that intervention attempt at Dr. Edding's.
Dr. Sirotka also had yet another cryptology report.
I thought we had gotten the last of these Dr. Suess had said.
Miraculously, they still keep coming, Dr. Sirotka had replied.
Dr. Suess began reading the following:

'Behold, a grassland
Grown sparse.
Amid a wide rolling savannah.
Lying burnt and brown
Sits a hollow.

'It holds a cup like bottom;
A brackish mud hole;
The remains of a once sparkling pool.

'Amid the thick ooze
Bubbles up a strange liquid.
Its viscosity clings
To the mud and rocks
And surfaces with a sheen on the last
Vestigial water.

'A hairy upright
Appears over a knoll,
And eyes the thick, cloying liquid.
He sniffs the sulfurous smell.

'The creature studies
Its dark heaviness.
Eyes set forward in the head
Register obvious curiosity.

THE TITANS

'In his hand,
The creature carries a staff.
He dips it into the thick liquid
And puts it to his mouth
To taste the mysterious elixir.

'His countenance grimaces
As he turns to climb
Back up the hillock.

'Just over the rise
He makes camp with others of his kind.
They show that they have discovered
The secret use
Of that sacred flower:
Fire.

'Around it they sit
As night descends.

'The upright plucks a brand
From the glowing coals
And returns to the slime pit.

'He carries his feebly glowing brand
In the darkness.
He dips it down into the greasy mud.
The staff flares up
And burns brightly.
In the night.'

    Dr. Suess studied the report. Below the last line, Dr. Sirotka had added a footnote:

'The people at the cryptology lab told me that deciphering this last raw signal was very difficult. The signal itself was almost too weak to register on their most sensitive instruments. Also, in terms of time line, this signal was, of course, much more recent that the first ones. If our reckoning is correct, the first signal must have been a good 65 to 70 million years old while this last one a mere 50,000 to 100,000 years old. Later signals came through so garbled they were all but unintelligible.

'Could it be that the trident's exposure to the atmosphere hastened the rapid deterioration of its radioactivity?'

He laid the report back on his desk. Would the trident have provided once and for all incontrovertible proof that we were are not alone? It demonstrated being bombarded with intelligent messages not only from outer space, but from the terrestrial past as well. If we could only have developed technology to crack other codes latent in say, cosmic rays, radiation from the Van Allen Belt, and radiation from earth elements such as uranium, what revelations might they not give?

Also, why did some signals appear to originate from earth while others seemed to come from outer space? Could application of Einstein's deceptively simple equation, $E=mc2$ eventually lead to the invention of something akin to H.G. Well's time machine? Is it possible that audio and visual signals radiating from earth's spoken words and earth events could some day be retrieved and the past be brought back? If enough interest and money could be devoted to this kind of research, who knows what surprises may be in store for humankind?

Were the dean's suspicions that something earth shaking was afoot when two of his faculty engaged in secret, extra-curricular research well founded?

I'll bet that sonofabitch would have killed to have gotten his hands some of these reports, thought Dr. Suess.

He regretted having flung that trident into the flash floodwaters while in a drunken rage. Had that alcoholic, has-been scientist thrown away a possible source of mankind's many unanswered questions?

At the time, however, he didn't much give a damn.

He inserted the report back into the folder and slipped it into his desk drawer. Again he gazed pensively out his window.

THE TITANS

Atop the desk sat a second manila folder bearing a later post date than the first.

Accompanying the report was the following letter:

'Michael J. Sirotka, Ph. D.
Professor of Physics
Stillwell College
Stillwell, CO

'Dear Hank:

'A strange thing happened since I sent you that last report. The cryptology lab told me that they were about to shut down the project when a sudden burst of energy blasted into their dials. From it they deciphered the following:

Y'rranhu's Solliloquoy

'So see we now a final turn of things.
'So find I myself caught
In a never-ending downward spiral
Into everlasting darkness.

'Darkness
Even light cannot penetrate.

'G'ya,
My wife, my beloved,
I ask not your forgiveness,
Only understanding.
I once was a lord with great power,
A being bigger than life,
A man of heroic passions.
I was one who could never
Be expected

To confine my affections
To just one partner.

'Never, my dear, underestimate
The perverse pleasure that awaits
Those who explore dalliance
With young females.

Once experienced it becomes
An obsession.
One becomes driven with such mad desire that it
Leaves one unfulfilled until one drinks
Again at that well.

'It is akin to ingesting the lotus flower
Or hashish;
A fleshly lust that causes one to lose all desire
For old crones very quickly.

'When ones tastes of hatchlings,
Of what care has one for an adult hen?

Dr. Suess laid aside the report. *How like Dean Jone,* he thought.
He recalled the quatrain learnt during his own school days:
'Sow a thought, reap a deed.
Sow a deed, reap a habit...'
He continued with the report:

'To,
My child, my delight,
You gave me much pleasure.
You bore me a magnificent child;
P'ssudohn the illustrious.
Was it not worth it
To bear such an excellent son?

THE TITANS

'I regret not the pain
I may have caused you,
But that I cannot be with you
In the land of the Blessed Spirits.

'R'ya,
In your rage over a harmless dalliance
By your spouse, Oss'yanhu,
Was it necessary
To curse me as well?
And that with such a draconian curse?
Really, my dear,
Did you not over react
And thus cause such far-reaching disaster?

'Favor'd, treasured one of the Great Abv's bosom
once was I.
No blessing nor honor was denied me.
Power and pleasure only did I know.
I who was given all but total rule
Over the vast celestial realms
Burned with discontent; I sought usurpation of even that.

'So was my undoing.

'So be it, then.
Let us play this little drama out
To its final summation.

'I who was once called
Lord Light-Bearer
Am now knighted
Prince of Darkness.

BENN K. LEAVENWORTH

'Yet
I am not alone.

'Fully one-third
Of Heaven's citizens followed me.
I will entice still others
To join me, ere this plot
Plays out.

'Abandon Hope
All who enter here.
Forget joy,
Embrace sorrow
Forget singing,
Lend your voices
To wailing, lamentation,
And gnashing of teeth
With equal gusto.

'Abandon Hope.
Embrace despair.
Learn to love it.
Make it your daily sustenance.

'Learn to hold with relish
That you are permanently severed
From All-That-Is-Good.

'Here is only darkness
So dark
That even perdition's fires
Cannot illuminate.

THE TITANS

'Here is darkness
So dark
That it feels solid.

'Yet
It is oblivion,
Void,
Abyss,
A bottomless Pit
With no boundaries.

'Always burning
But never quenched.
Always falling
But never landing.

'Bodies that stink of death,
Eaten of worms that never die.

'All pain and aguish
You may have suffered on earth,
Will seem as pleasure
When you see
What awaits you here.

'The gravity that pulls you down,
Ever down
With increasing force,
Never ceases.

'So I bid you welcome
To my dark Universe.'

'I realize that the cryptology lab said that the signal had become so weak they could no longer pick it up,' the letter continued; 'but then all of a sudden, like a power burst this thing flashed on their dials. After that everything went blank.

'Anyway, they said funds for the research have also dried up. They are closing the project down.

'Officially, there will be no record of this anywhere in Washington.

'Sincerely,

'Mike.'

Dr. Suess studied the page for still longer moments. *Probably just as well*, he thought. It was beginning to look like something he'd just as soon not mess with.

He tried to shake a feeling of dread and depression. Why had this last message affected him this way? Why had he begun harboring a wish he had never opened this last message?

What demons were now plaguing his psyche?

Demons?

He recalled the gospel accounts of Jesus on the eastern shores of the Galilean lake exorcising the unfortunate wretch of a legion of demons.

Demons.

Just exactly what are they?

Figments of benighted imagination? Pre-Freudian names for psychological hang-ups or mental illnesses? Spirit warriors of the devil?

Or are they spirits of a fallen pre-Adamic race; disembodied intelligent malevolent entities?

Do the spirits of the once great races of T'tanyu and Y'pullu still inhabit this planet?

Neon and automobile lights began lighting up the darkening city streets below him. In the far distance mountain peaks still etched against a cold, leaden sky. He took out other stationery and began writing:

THE TITANS

'Dearest Marie…

…He paused.
Again, worried thoughts not only for her mental and emotional well-being, but for her physical safety as well tore at him inwardly.
Wish she's just get out of there, he thought…

… 'The day I came home and found you gone, you assured me in your letter that this was not a formal separation. You stated that the condition of your coming back to me was my seeking help.

'I have done that. I have spent several months at St. Dunstan's Priory like you wanted.

'To coin a cliché, a funny thing happened to me while I was there.

'As Father Michael had predicted, it was a miracle.'

Dr. Suess' thoughts went in retrospect to that other November day; the day of the chapel service…

…Sunlight filtered through the stained glass windows, shedding the interior with a diffuse, multi-colored softness. As Dr. Suess slipped down to the wooden kneeling bench, he studied the worshippers across the aisle. He could tell by their casual lay attire that they were from hospice. Later in the service, he watched them file out toward the altar. As the ushering brother gestured for him to rise, he got a closer look at the last communicant.

He found himself following the wasted figure hobbling behind a walker.

Marie's ex husband.

After that emergency accident in the man's room two days before, he marveled that 'Sebastian' was still living.

Upon reaching the communion rail, he found no way to rearrange the order without creating a ruckus. As he knelt, he found Marie's ex kneeling on his right with his walker beside him. The cadaverous wretch would receive the wafer and chalice ahead of him. He sighted a robed figure moving from that direction passing out the wafer.

As he cupped his hand, he heard the words: "This is my body, given for you."

He pressed the wafer to his lips.

No problem here.

But what about the chalice?

Why couldn't these guys use individual cups like a lot of the so-called non-conformist churches? Why do they have to be so damned traditional and have everybody drink out of the same cup? Don't they have any respect for modern standards of sanitation?

Beyond Marie's ex he saw three other hospice residents lined up at the rail. On his left four robed fellow initiates took their place across the aisle. *Why don't these guys get wise as to what's going on,* he asked himself. Why don't they rise up and raise hell about being set up like this? Don't they realize the mortal danger they're in? Good Lord, are they so dense that they don't realize that they are about to be exposed some of the deadliest germs on this planet?

"This is the true blood, shed for you."

The celebrant had just handed the cup to the farthest hospice resident on the right.

Beads of perspiration formed on his forehead. *Just like lambs led to the slaughter*, he thought. *If I die because of this I hope Marie sues these holy-Joes for a bundle; maybe they'd even have to close this place down.*

"'Do this in remembrance of me.'"

The celebrant had just served the second man in line.

'Do this in remembrance of me,' reflected Dr. Suess.

He saw the celebrant hand the chalice to the man on other side of Marie's ex.

A miracle, the Prior said. He looked around but saw nothing that seemed miraculous. *Here I am, ready to obey my Lord in the drinking of the wine. Is he going to mock my faith and my obedience by allowing me to contract a terminal illness simply because I drank out of the same cup with a bunch of wasted sickos?*

'Thou shalt not be afraid for the...pestilence that walketh in darkness'. Where did that thought come from? Must have been from one of the Psalms. Where had he learned that passage? How long ago? The stream of words went on:*'...a thousand shall fall at thy right hand but it shall not come nigh thee...*

Hindu fakirs able to walk barefooted over a bed of live coals?

Is it really mind over matter, he wondered? Something that is the butt of ridicule to the scientific world trained in accepting as truth only that which can be empirically discerned through the physical senses?

Is not the bench on which he kneels and the communion rail against which he leans, according to all perception, solid wood? Yet is not that wood, in reality, made up of sub-microscopic particles called molecules that are surrounded by ninety-nine times as much empty space?

He saw the celebrant approaching Marie's ex with the silver cup in hand. *God*, he thought, *I'm next. Help me.* "'*This cup is the communion of the blood of Christ.*'" Did it or did it not strike him as particularly miraculous? Or was it all to be scorned as too quaint for this modern day and age?

According to the Torah, the three young exiles by order of a pagan king were thrown into a blast furnace for refusing to bow down to a heathen idol. Not only did they come out unharmed, so said holy writ but the smell of fire wasn't even on their clothing.

When he saw his Rabbi walking on the water, was not Peter able to do the same thing and then sink only when he fixed his eyes on the storm instead of on his Master? Even outside the Christian frame of reference how are

As the priest got nearer, he again heard the liturgical words: "The blood of Christ which was shed for you."

That faggot doesn't even believe in this stuff, thought Dr. Suess in increasing turmoil. *What's he doing here, anyway? Why do they have to serve these diseased perverts first and contaminate the cup for the rest of us for Chri'sake? Why can't we just serve them in their rooms?*

He had actually brought up this suggestion to the Prior.

Father Michael's response: We actually serve those too sick or too weak to get out of bed in their rooms. However, we feel it's best for the morale of the ambulatory patients to join us in chapel. It helps make them feel that they are still connected with the rest of society.

Nice!

Anthropologists tell us that we are five people removed from every person on this planet. They contend that when we consider the network built by five friends or relatives, couple them with everyone they ever knew or were acquainted with, and then extend that on out to a larger network of people we have never met yet with whom we have a connection, no matter how remote, we eventually reach every inhabitant on this globe.

And this with just people with whom we have had social contact.

What happens with those of us who are promiscuous, or to put it in more modern parlance, sexually active?

That damn' dirtbag admitted to me, reflected Dr. Suess further, *that he must have had a good thousand partners over a ten-year period. How could anyone have such an intimate exchange of body fluids with that many people and not expect to pick up something? That must make him surrogate sex partner with half the gay population of the Western Hemisphere. This also from a guy who expressed reluctance to drink from a public drinking fountain. Now he's going slop his germs all over that cup for me to drink.*

He looked up at the rose window immediately above him. Soft light filtered through a longhaired, robed figure. The gentle face appeared cloyingly sentimental. In one soft looking hand the figure held a shepherd's crook and in the other he held a tiny lamb. Larger sheep pressed in about his feet looking up at him with adoring eyes. A halo of sheen radiated from the figure's head. An idyllic landscape of bucolic paradise filled out the rest of the window.

Dr. Suess knew that the actual holy land lay as arid and dry as the bleak deserts of his own western United States. *That portrayal is a crock of shit,* he thought.

A damned lie.

Despite the numbing cold of the unheated, stone chapel, he felt the palms of his hands getting sweaty. A realization came to him. Like many of his fellow churchmen, the burden of religion rested on his shoulders entirely too easy: Occasionally attend divine services and enjoy the pomp and pageantry. Join in singing the staid old hymns. Let the rhythmic cadences of the spoken liturgy fall as soothing balm to the soul. Sit comfortably in a cushioned pew. Bask in the soft glow of stained glass windows. Listen to a brief homily of predictable platitudes. Leave a stipend in the offering plate, and then go home.

In the doing of all this he had contented himself that he was doing the Almighty a great favor.

Where was there any challenge, any testing, any crisis, any sacrifice?

No religion, ideology, or prophetic system makes so little demand of its followers as does contemporary American Christendom. So said one acerbic critic whose name had somehow escaped him.

He looked up again at the figure in the rose window.

He swallowed and fought to frame the words in his mind: *Lord, help me. Show me what I should do?*

Again he looked up. The figure hadn't moved. The same languid facial expression hadn't changed. The sheep around him continued to look up at him with the same cloying adoration.

Sheepherders! The ones he met in real life were the scum of the earth. Their flocks were the dumbest of creatures that snipped the grass right at the roots, spoiling the rangeland for cattle and horses. He had always sympathized with the ranchers who hated their guts. And now he's praying to one of them?

Was this whole thing a farce? Was Henry Suess the churchman making an ass out of Henry Suess, the scientist? Were he to chemically analyze that wine before it was blessed and then reexamine the residue after the service, would not the analysis be the same? What's with all this mumbo-jumbo, anyway?

He recalled the words of the Prior. *It's a mystery, my son; don't try to analyze it. Just accept it. After all, can you explain why untold trillions of snowflakes have fallen to the earth since the beginning of time, and despite their all having the same basic hexagonal pattern, no two of them are alike? Can you explain why lake water freezes from the top down and not from the bottom up?*

What good is a mystery, father, he had said. *I need help.*

Look for a miracle, my son.

A miracle? *What miracle?* The picture on the rose window still hadn't changed. The cold closing in on him from the walls of stone still chilled him until his hands turned blue and stiff. His legs began to cramp from the prolonged kneeling.

He had a mind to pass it up.

As he searched about for a way to make a graceful exit, a thought occurred to him.

He recalled mentally taking the Lord's name in vain just now while kneeling at the communion rail. ('Whoso drinketh of the cup in an unworthy manner, drinketh damnation to himself.') How many times had he read ('Let each one examine himself and so let him eat.')

('Judge not that ye be not judged.') A realization came to him. Both he and Marie's ex had one thing in common: they were here because of what they had brought on themselves. Do we have tendency to blame the Almighty for difficulties of our own making? Is the biblical teaching 'whatsoever you sew, that shall you also reap' about judgment, or about retribution? Is not the current buzzword 'what goes around, comes around' saying essentially the same thing? He again recalled the motto from childhood that hung in the front of his schoolmaster's classroom:

'Sew a thought; reap a deed.
Sew a deed; reap a habit;
Sew a habit; reap a character;
Sew a character; reap a destiny.'

He had placed a similar motto at the front of his classroom. Some students complained to the dean that it made them feel guilty. The dean had tried to persuade him to remove it but he repeatedly had refused.

Hope standing up to that rotten sonofabitch will win me points with the Almighty he thought.

He glanced briefly to the skeletal figure on his right. The head was bowed toward folded hands as the robed figure approached him.

Was Brother Praisegod right the other night in the day room about 'Sebastatian' having so little time left? *How much of this is 'Sebastian' aware?* Dr. Suess wondered.

Is he actually more penitent than I, he asked himself?

Would he, the devout high churchman, be so base as to deny this dying wretch his last moment of absolution? Did Our Lord come into this world to shed his blood only for good people? For nice people?

Did he not assure the penitent thief that that very day the thief would accompany him in paradise? Did he not allow Mary Magdelene, that demon-possessed slut, to touch him when she washed feet with her tears? Did not the parabolic father run halfway down the road to meet his erring son and then fall on his neck and kiss him?

Would Henry want to deny the man next to him what could very well be his last chance for Grace? Did not the high churchman himself suggest that Marie's ex attend the service?

If he really believed that the contents of that cup had in some way been miraculously transformed into, or perhaps had been infused with some mystical power emanating from, the blood of Jesus Christ, how is it possible that that which was shed for healing and cleansing now also become a source of contamination?

He realized that he had just been doing more hard thinking about God in the past few seconds than all the hours of the Grand Silence put together.

Put up or shut up time, he thought as he saw the vestment-robed figure moving in close.

"The blood of Jesus Christ, shed for you." No sooner had he heard the voice say this, when he saw the chalice being pushed toward him.

('To the pure, all things are pure.') Was this his moment of truth?

The choice: refuse or participate.

As sweat trickled down his back under his 'T' shirt, he felt a surrealism to the situation. *Where is the miracle*, he thought?

Again, a realization: If miracles occur at all, they obviously occur only in times deepest extremity, in the most desperate circumstances when, humanly speaking, all is lost. They certainly don't happen just to satisfy idle curiosity.

He stared trance-like at the chalice.

As if it had a will of its own, he saw his hand reach out for the cup...

Epilogue

...Dr. Suess inserted the letter into an envelope, sealed it, and slid it into his shirt pocket. He stood up from the writing desk and before turning away from the window he took another look at the article in the *Denver Post*.

As he re-read the details of the account, he shook his head.

By late summer Ginger still managed the small concession stand, by then the only structure still standing. It still served a menu of hot dogs, pop, coffee, and potato chips.

This despite the fact that more often than not, she was 'stiffed' by the customers.

She had hired one of the park patrons to help her: a plump, unibrow clad in dirty jeans named Bea. The girl had claimed to be a biker's 'old lady' although not one of the hirsute denizens of the park would claim her.

Consensus among the guys was that she was 'butt ugly.'

However during their many drug busts, the males would throw money into a 'pig pot' and cast lots to see which lucky fellow would be chosen to bang her to the cheering audience of the other revelers.

Ginger thought it desperation on her part that she attached herself to Ginger with a fierceness that made Ginger's heart burn in sympathy for her.

It was only on a Labor Day week-end when Bea made lesbian advances on her that she understood the girl's real intentions.

Eventually Ginger spurned Bea's advances once too often.

THE TITANS

Love turned to hate.

Bea then began a whisper campaign against her among the park patrons.

The word was that Ginger was stuck up, conceited; that she considered herself too good for everybody else. She needed to be taught a lesson.

During a Saturday night in late September, the venomous gossip had evolved into a plot that involved mass rape, sadism, and murder.

He recalled nights when searchlights played among the park trees and the PA system blared music from live rock bands performing at all hours of the day and night. That noise must have covered any of the screams.

The following Sunday morning the denizens of 'people's park' held religious services. Again, the blare of loudspeakers blared the ritual chanting:

"Henikee, blenikee, hail Satan!"

Can you say 'wolf pack mentality, boys and girls?' reflected Dr. Suess as he read the account.

Shortly thereafter, all but a few die-hards had left town, leaving behind a toxic dump of debris, trash, and waste.

And a park floor carpeted with dirty needles.

Around Halloween, when the trees finally stood bare and their leaves carpeted the sordid mess, city crews set themselves to the monumental task of clean-up.

As the raw winds of late fall moaned through the naked tree branches they discovered Ginger's unclad and battered body buried in a pile of rubble.

Poor Ginger, he thought. *What must her last moments have been like?*

She couldn't have picked worse company to run with, he reflected further. Was she a classic Dr. Jekyll and Mr. Hyde case? Much as she tried to fit in with that crowd, unbeknownst to her, they never really accepted her. Despite her attempts to emulate their wild ways they knew that she was not one of them.

And in the end they turned on her.

How now, my poor, sweet Ginger? He wondered.

What does she feel regarding her last moments now that she is safe on that peaceful shore as it were? Do those final horrendous moments still haunt her memory, her psyche, her emotions, as they most likely would were she still with us?

Concern for her mental well-being even in heaven prompted him to discuss this issue with Father Michael during one of their therapy sessions.

If God wills to forget our iniquities, he had told him, surely he can cause the redeemed to forget traumas of earth. After all, does not the Apocalypse state that he will wipe away all tears from their eyes?

Dr. Suess questioned Father Michael further. "One thing that puzzles me, your grace" he said, "is that how a loving God would allow one of his lambs to suffer such a horrible fate?"

Fr. Michael leaned forward over his desk. "When a child runs away from home," he said, eyeing Dr. Seuss, "and assuming that it is a good home, does she fare better in the outside world or worse?"

"I would say worse."

"Does it not stand to reason then, that when a child of God wanders from the path of righteousness, do they not enter the devil's domain?"

"Assuming that there a devil, yes I suppose they do."

Father Michael eyed him incredulously. "You question the very reality of evil itself? You question what is obvious to any sane and honest observer of our life and world today? Look to your own cryptology research."

He paused.

"Again, 'assuming that there is a devil' as you put it," he continued. "Does it stand to reason that they will fare any better at Satan's hands than in the hands of a loving heavenly Father?"

"No, I guess not."

"There you have it."

...And the earth was filled with violence. The words from holy writ came flooding back into his memory of lectern lessons of days long since.

Violence.

Ah yes, he thought. *Violence. Naked, gratuitous violence.*

Violence for its own sake.

Today we're awash in it. TV, movies, newspapers, pop music, you name it.

That and sex.

Freely wheeling, promiscuous, gratuitous sex. No love, just lust; an erotic sneeze.

Wham-bam, thank y'ma'am.

Bang-bang, you're dead.

No thought given to what led up to it or why, nor any thought given to after effects. Each act is an isolated incident with no preliminary causes or repercussions afterward.

In reality, there are no isolated incidents. Each act is like a pebble dropped in the middle of a pond that sends ripples out to every shore.

Ripple effect is never shown.

Each sexual or violent act is shown as though there were no consequences; no tomorrow.

It's a lie.

A damned lie.

He stared into the darkened interior of his efficiency apartment for a moment and then began pacing the floor. He glanced at the luminous dial of his watch and then reached for the door handle of his clothes closet. Grabbing a windbreaker from a hook, he started for the door.

After having transferred the envelope to his jacket, he strode briskly along a broken, uneven sidewalk. He bent forward against the raw wind.

Be a hoot if I spotted Dean Jone down here soliciting a hooker, he thought.

The lighted window of a chili house about a block away beckoned him. Upon reaching the entrance he swung open the door and stepped inside.

He paused a moment to savor the moist warmth of the interior. Finally he ambled to a booth well away from the front door. As he slid into the seat, he picked up the menu and studied it...

...In the weeks that followed the chapel service, he continued doing volunteer work at the priory. Marie's ex died a scant three days after that chapel service. Dr. Seuss had visited his bedside briefly only twice during that period. Most of the time Marie's ex lay in either in a deep sleep or comatose, Dr. Suess couldn't always be sure.

'Sow a thought, reap a deed...'

...However, Dr. Suess was at the bedside when the Prior administered the last rites and the attending physician pronounced him clinically dead, Dr. Suess caught one noteworthy feature.

Despite the waxy, mummified appearance of the man's face, he bore an expression of complete serenity.

From the priory library, he had subsequently taken out a biography of Oscar Wilde. In it he again read how that during the last two years when Wilde, alias Sebastian Melmoth lived penniless, alone and sick in Paris, he called a local priest. After being a life long atheist, he had converted to Catholicism...

... "Have you ordered yet?"

Her words broke his reverie. He sensed a slender female figure standing closely by his elbow. He became aware of the loud, juicy chomping on a wad of chewing gum. He looked up to see a twenty-something blonde in a canary and white waitress' uniform. The young face bore a bland, empty expression.

He held up the menu. "How can I have ordered when I still have this?"

As he studied the menu, he looked at their variety of hamburger servings. A realization came to him.

Just before he left the priory, he found the head cook again cleaning out the refrigerator. The head cook found stale food wrapped in a McDonald's wrapper.

This time however, without a word of objection from Dr. Seuss, he threw it out.

He flipped the menu back on the tabletop. "I'll have a bowl of your four-alarm chili and a black coffee."...

...Was Marie's ex's demise an example of God's judgment? Or was it merely God's retribution, sort of like putting one's hand on a hot stove and getting burnt? Or was it an example of God's mercy?

After all, we all have to go sometime. When one is terminally ill, one has a more definite idea as to the time and place and therefore such a one has ample to time to make any preparations one is inclined to make to get ready for the Big Event.

Marie's ex in any event has departed this life. Where is he now? Buried in the ground mentally, emotionally, and spiritually annihilated with no further self consciousness or memory? Or does the soul once known as 'Sebastian Melmoth' still exist as a non-corporeal thought-entity? If this self-consciousness still exists, in what state is it? Is there a heaven and hell?

Do gays go to hell? (Do alcoholics go to hell?) Do adulterers, murderers, whoremongers, liars, cheaters (as on exams?), users of drugs (or users of people, like a certain college administrator?) go to hell?

If these kinds of people go to hell, what kinds of people go to heaven? Good people? Again, he recalled that parable of the prodigal, of that corrupt but penitent tax collector, and of that harlot, Mary Magdalene?

No.

Heaven, he was convinced, was just as populated with thieves, drunkards, and terrorists (St. Dismus, the penitent thief, for example.)

Hell, if it exists, is not for gays, harlots, and thieves. According to holy writ it was originally prepared for the devil and his angels.

Is it also the final abode of impenitent mortals?

Is there a final judgment? Is Marie's ex even now standing before his maker having his life's final evaluation report as it were or his life's final exam just as Dr. Suess once graded the exams of his students?

Is there a purgatory?

Dr. Suess thought about the young men who inhabited the rooms about him when he lived at the Y. Most were wards of the state still serving prison sentences in less restricted circumstances than in a regular cell block. This was society's way of easing them from the confining life of an institution (as was his monastic life at the priory) into the full freedom of life on the outside. They prepared for that final freedom by living in a kind of halfway house.

Is purgatory like that? Is it a process whereby we, once having been released from the restricting and binding existence of terrestrial life, go through a decompression chamber as it were in preparation for the vast, limitless expanse of life in eternity?

Are we, in fact like the moth? Or the butterfly? Are we like the pupa when in the womb? Our earthly sojourn our larva stage? Is purgatory like being in a cocoon? Are we like the larva in this nascent state wherein it undergoes its wondrous metamorphosis unseen by all living beings and becomes what it eventually becomes? Is our final release into God's limitless expanse of Heaven like being in the butterfly stage in all its beauty?

Also, then, is purgatory our cosmic halfway house?

His own halfway house like existence seemed indeed a purgatory. The loneliness pressed in on him like a vise. He missed Marie and the children. He missed his friends back at Stillwell...

...After the waitress had left, he studied the diner's garish interior. The bright lights contrasted with windows blackened by the numbing cold night outside. At the tinkling sound of the front door a grizzled citizen of the neighborhood shuffled in. Legs sheathed in worn, soiled suntans swung over a stool as the little man edged up to the lunch counter.

Shortly after a couple of equally unkempt youths also entered. Students, thought Dr. Suess, from a nearby community college.

Speaking of which, Traci is now in her sophomore year. How time flies.

He reflected on the situation with that counselor during her junior year in high school. He wondered if they had creeps like that in the administration at Black Canyon. Given the way things go today, who knows? He still nursed indignation over that pervert's attempt to put the move on her. He still wanted to go back and punch the guy's lights out.

Community college, he pondered further. *Best idea for democratizing higher education yet. Anything that gives those damned elites a nervous rash, I'm all for it.*

The waitress had just brought his order...

...As per an agreement between Father Michael and himself, he had agreed to take directorship of a newly opened counseling center sponsored by the priory in downtown Denver. Later, he took a small, furnished apartment. He found that his pension kept him in room, board, and a little spending money. He occupied much of his time in the downtown public library. Since business at the center had been initially quite slow, he had also obtained a part time teaching position with the Denver Unified School District Community Ed program.

In spite of efforts to fill the void of restless days browsing in the library and teaching night school he could not crowd out the loneliness…

… "Are you done?"

Again, he looked up. Again, the slender figure stood at his elbow, chewing her stick of gum; again twirling her pencil eraser around a lock of hair.

Again the vacuous expression.

Dr. Suess looked down at his chili bowl. He then shot her a hard glance.

"Young lady," he said, pushing it away. "A cake gets done. If you mean 'have I finished?' yes, I have finished."

Five minutes later, he stepped back out to the sidewalk. Raw winds pushed at him as thin raindrops stung his face. His features felt like cold, chiseled granite. He glanced at the dark, hulking mound that was the corner mailbox.

He pressed his hand against the letter lodged in his jacket pocket.

He reflected on his past life and the emotional hits that came along the way. First there came the death of his first wife; then there was his marriage to Marie. Together they saw her two children through their stormy adolescence.

Speaking of which, he recalled an incident that Marie related to him in her most recent letter. It seemed that her son, Tim, had recently enrolled as a freshman at Stillwell College. Shortly after he had been enrolled, he had gotten himself expelled…

…He had been assigned to one of Dr. Tudor McManus' English classes. Also in that class was a blond, bespectacled innocent, a Miss Kathy Hammel. She had just transferred from a small Bible college up in Nebraska. Without even looking up her transcript, he could tell from her quiet demeanor and appearance that she would be an easy target. While most women students wore jeans or slacks, Miss Hammel always wore dresses that came down half way between her knees and her ankles.

Despite a campus code of conduct that forbade teachers from verbally assaulting students because of their sex, race, color, sexual preference, or religion, he seemed to take delight in needling her with barbed questions.

'Where did Cain get his wife?'

'Can God create a rock so heavy that he can't lift it?'

'Do you really believe Eve talked to a snake?'

'When you hear God speak, shouldn't you seek counseling?'

Things finally came to a head when, unable to take any more, like a female student of a previous decade, she fled the classroom in tears.

Unbeknownst to him, Tim had recently begun dating her.

After her tearful exit, Dr. McManus flashed his gold inlay to the class and his eyes slanted in triumphant humor. He chuckled through his teeth with a hissing sound.

"What she needs," he said in obvious self pleasure, "is to go out and sin a little bit."

Tim's ears pricked up on that one. "Do you recommend that for all of us, sir?" he said, "that we all should go out and sin a little bit?"

For a moment, Dr. McManus seemed taken aback.

"Why yes," he said finally. "I—I do. It would make us all more genuinely human."

"So—you really mean that?"

Again, Dr. McManus briefly appeared flustered. But, he soon recovered. "Yes, I do. But why are you pushing the point?"

A pause.

Then:

"Why you no-good sonofabitch. You dirty bastard." Tim's voice took on a hard edge as he leveled a steady gaze at his instructor. "You slime ball, you stink horn, you moldy piece of shit."

The class sat back in stunned silence. Dr. McManus face colored a sweaty crimson before he found his next words. "I say," he said, struggling to clear his throat. "What is the meaning of this outrage?"

Tension crackled in the air like electricity.

"This—this is completely uncalled for," said Dr. McManus when he again found words. "I demand an explanation."

"Just following your suggestion."

"Suggestion—?" his voice turned rasping, "what suggestion?"

Tim sat back complacently. "You suggested that we all be better off if we went out and sinned a little bit."

Another pause.

"So I thought I'd start out by insulting you."...

...Dr. Suess smiled. *I couldn't be prouder of that kid*, he thought, *than if he was my own flesh and blood.*

In the meantime he saw his own two children grow to adulthood and move away, having little contact with him in recent years.

Questions regarding his first family began assailing his conscience. During those earlier years, had he been too busy with his teaching and his research to spend adequate time with Sheila and the older children? Is it now retribution that they are too busy with their own lives for him? Is it true that 'what goes around comes around?'

Did his attempts to rectifying the situation with Marie and her children by going to their basketball games and picking them up after basketball and cheerleading practice elicit further resentment and jealousy from his older children? Had he been remiss as a father in not keeping in closer touch with them?

Was it too late to mend fences as it were or was there still time to make things right?

Also in the meantime the epochal discoveries in the Badlands took much of his interest. Then not the least of stresses was the running battle with the dean and the administration.

He should have known better than to let his drinking get out of control. He could have put Marie's two children through college with what he spent on booze. He had to admit that that was his fault.

A major change came with his retirement. But did this have to be followed so closely by Marie's leaving him?

Another major adjustment came with the therapy at the priory. It took a bit of doing to finally feel acclimated to the austere routine followed by the brothers. And now he lived alone in a dingy, downtown apartment. He could come and go as he pleased. His friends and cronies these days consisted of ne'er-do-wells, transients, and down-and-out-winos that he would meet in the city library, on downtown park benches, and in cheap restaurants...

...He habitually would sit on a park bench during the bleak autumn months with only his thoughts for company. It would be but a matter of time before some denizen of the streets with a week's growth of beard would approach him for a handout.

Don't give them anything! The words of common wisdom shouted in his ear. *They won't spend it for food. They'll only spend it for booze or drugs. Send them off to a homeless shelter or a rescue mission. That's why we have them.*

He recalled one of Ebenezer Scrooge's lines from Dickens' *A Christmas Carol*. ('Are there no prisons? Are there no workhouses?')

He turned to the mendicant.

"Tell you what," he would say. "Come to think of it, I'm kind of hungry myself." He would gesture to a nearby McDonald's. He would then usher the man into the entrance.

"What'll I get?" mumbled his new friend.

"Just order," said Dr. Suess, "whatever you think you can eat."

The stranger would usually order modestly: a hamburger with fries.

"What do you want to drink?" Dr. Suess would ask. "Coffee okay? Two small coffees," Dr. Suess would announce to the youth behind the counter. The recipient would usually decline Dr. Suess' offer to sit down with him at table but instead would thank him and then exit eating the hamburger while washing it down with the coffee.

Dr. Suess remembered from chapel back at St. Dunstan's, a homily based on an epistle lesson from Hebrews: 'Do not forget to entertain strangers, for by so doing some people have entertained angels unawares.'

Could this bum actually be an angel? Dr. Seuss would ask himself as they parted.

Before taking his leave, the beneficiary would often make one last request. "Excuse me, buddy," the phlegmatic voice would arrest Dr. Suess' footsteps. "But my pal across the street is hungry too, Could you loan me a five for him?" (Or, the man also needed money for bus fare to get to that rehab place downtown.)

The question would disabuse Dr. Suess of any notions of angelic origin.

"Can't do it, friend," he would reply, turning away quickly...

...As bleak as was his current existence, had he somehow fallen into its pattern to the point of comfort?

What if he went back to her and she agreed to take him, and he fell again, then what?

He felt gratitude that Marie and the children had now moved back into the house. Would it have still been standing had they not? In the meantime, as per their agreement, he had to stay away. *Oh well*, he thought, *in the meantime, I got stuff to do right here.*

The wind grew more boisterous. Clouds thickened in already darkened skies. The night grew black as the Pit itself

Despite the cold he felt perspiration trickle down the back of his shirt.

He shivered as he stood against the raw, autumnal bluster. Immediately in front of him loomed hard and menacing, the black metal case on four spindly legs: the mailbox. Cold and inanimate it stood. Yet it filled him with misgivings.

What was his problem anyway? Was he actually so accustomed to his current loneliness that the prospect of returning to life with Marie; and the love, the warmth that that life afforded was actually frightening?

Another thought came to him. He had only recently heard from his old buddy, Dr. Sirotka, of an incident involving Marie. She had been the victim of an assault by a student up at the high school.

It seemed that she had attempted to stop an eleventh grader from running in the hall. The student responded by striking her in the face, blackening her eye and breaking her glasses. She had to stay out of school three days recuperating from her wound. When she complained to the principal she got a strange response.

What did you do to provoke him? The principal wanted to know. Was it something in your approach, your demeanor, your tone of voice? Perhaps the student was hurting from lack of love or understanding from home.

Perhaps—who knows?

Anyway, the principal had then concluded, we have no disciplinary problems at this school; only teacher-pupil personality conflicts.

Perhaps the both of you need counseling—like crisis management; or anger management.

Or some such thing.

Things just didn't happen in vacuum, Dr. Suess realized. This incident had to have been the end result of a multitude of unrecorded offences—major as well as minor—that previously had been allowed to go unaddressed. Had the school been run like his kind of tight ship, as it were, something like this would never have happened.

He wondered how this squared with the school's newly announced policy toward student misconduct of zero tolerance.

Zero tolerance, he thought, *is this a euphemism for draconian measures intended to paper over a previously permissive situation allowed to get out of hand?*

Useless.

The only word that Dr. Suess could think of when thinking of Marie's building principal.

Useless. Like a boar's teats useless.

He was convinced that the gentleman made his own Dean Jone look like Richard the Lionhearted.

That does it, he resolved. *I've to get back there and handle this myself.*

He determined to press criminal charges against the student, press civil charges against the school, and possibly the same against the student's parents.

Failing that he would personally deck the student himself.

Meanwhile the time had come.

Mail that letter now or forget about it.

That chapel service had now been over a year ago.

He had been sober ever since.